16.44

MAR   2021

MARRIAGE AND MURDER

SOLVING FOR PIE: CLETUS AND JENN MYSTERIES
SERIES BOOK #2

PENNY REID

WWW.PENNYREID.NINJA/NEWSLETTER/

COPYRIGHT

DEDICATION

For my son, who knows everything.

CHAPTER ONE
CLETUS

"I don't know half of you half as well as I should like; and I like less than half of you half as well as you deserve."

— J.R.R. TOLKIEN, *THE FELLOWSHIP OF THE RING*

"This is all very . . . fancy."

"How do you mean?"

My eldest brother glanced around us, at the long tables covered in shining silk tablecloths, white porcelain dishes, sterling (I checked the back) silver flatware, ornate centerpieces nickel-and-rust-colored metalwork hearts, and up at the pearlescent handblown glass chandeliers strung above.

I followed his eyes to their last destination and mumbled, "I reckon it's a little fancy."

"Where'd Jenn's momma get all this stuff? Last time Sienna and I had dinner here, it looked totally different."

Here being the Donner Lodge dining barn—and I meant *barn* in the loosest sense of the word. The building had never been used as an actual barn, nor had it been built with the intention to house live animals. Just dead ones. For consumption.

Jethro scratched the back of his neck, looking down at his clothes. "Should I go home and change?"

"You should always strive for change, Jethro. But your garments are perfectly adequate." Plus, we were more or less wearing the same thing: black pants, button-down suit shirt—his gray, mine red because I'd been explicitly instructed to wear a red shirt—no tie.

If he went home and changed, then he'd pressure me to as well, and I didn't want to change. I'd already changed three times today, which was one more than my absolute maximum: from my PJ's to my work clothes, from my work clothes to clean jeans and flannel to help set up, and from that perfectly acceptable outfit to my present stuffier attire. Of note, changing back into pajamas at the end of the day didn't count, especially if I opted to sleep in the buff.

Jethro's pained eyebrow pinch told me I'd failed to persuade him. "What about that guy?" He lowered his voice, gesturing to a fella across the room in possession of a silver tray. "He's in a tuxedo. Should we be wearing suits?"

"That man is a waiter, Jet. You want to dress like a waiter, go for it."

"Point is, the waiter is in a tux. I don't think Sienna knows it's formal dress, but I could be wrong. Whatever. You didn't tell anyone this would be so fancy, Cletus."

More than just the waitstaff were beginning to materialize in the fancy barn. As such, I lowered my voice, "I didn't know it would be so fancy, Jethro."

He crossed his arms, disbelief persisting. "How is that possible? You know everything about everybody, and you're telling me you didn't know your own engagement party was going to be—"

"A stuffy shindig? A bourgeois bash? A hoity-toity hellscape? No. I did not."

Jet seemed to be bracing himself for an outburst of nerves or anger. He knew surprises tended to muddle and aggravate me.

I'd arrived here at 3:10 PM after a full nine-hour shift at the auto shop, fatigued and looking for a beer just to discover Jenn's momma's event planning had ventured beyond the pale. Far, far beyond the pale, to the land of excessive extravagance and profligacy.

The decorations, the sit-down, seven-course meal, the string quartet. Okay, fine. I could've shouldered the burden of such trappings. But who in their right mind wants to sit down for five hours and eat portions the size of dimes and quarters when hunger could be satiated by a plump sausage in five bites and three minutes?

I don't know. I've never met the person. What a monumental waste of time.

My main issue had been the guest list, which I hadn't been privy to— nor had I requested access to—until fourteen minutes ago. Good Lord, the woman had invited everyone in East Tennessee and all their neighbors but none of their children. An intimate engagement party is what she and Jenn had promised me last year when the wedding planning had begun. This evening would be as intimate as an orgy in Times Square and would likely be better attended.

Jethro exhaled loudly. "Well, we need to do something, and quick." He examined his clothes. Again.

"I agree." Meanwhile, I eyeballed the chandeliers. "You still got that baseball bat in your car?"

After a moment's pause, he hit my arm. "No, Cletus! I didn't mean wreck the place."

"That was said in jest, brother. Obviously, I'm not taking a bat to the chandeliers. Besides, what did you mean?" I finally allowed some of the exasperation I'd been sitting on this afternoon to manifest.

"I meant we need to do something about what we're wearing."

"You're starting to sound like Roscoe. Clothes shouldn't make the man, ain't nobody care if your shirt has a designer label or a generic one."

"But Diane will care if your family are the only ones present not in suits and formal dress."

I waved him off, grumbling, "Do what you want, but I'm not changing." Besides, what could I do? The time for the doing of something had passed. "Serves me right, I reckon," I mumbled.

"Serves you right? For what?"

I shrugged, pressing my lips together to seal them. I didn't want to admit the truth; I'd been ignoring the wedding and all the planning asso-

3

ciated with it, including tonight's ostentatious affair, because doing so had served both altruistic and selfish interests (but mostly selfish). And now I'd been slapped in the face with a brouhaha bombshell, paying the price for my lack of attention.

"You look unhappy." He eyed me anew.

"So what if I am? If it makes the woman happy, then . . ." I narrowed my eyes on the heart centerpieces, wondering if the welding had been Shelly's handiwork. They were quite impressive, to say the least, and looked like they belonged in an art gallery or a museum, not on tables in a faux-barn.

"Which woman are we talking about?" Jethro questioned. "The future wife or the future mother-in-law?"

I glanced at the gaggle of folks filtering in through the wide barn doors. Thus far, I recognized 90 percent of those present. But I wouldn't say I was exactly friends with these people. In short, I wouldn't invite a single one of them—except Jethro, of course, maybe the sheriff and Janet James, perhaps the tuxedoed waiter—to my birthday. Nor would I attend any of theirs if invited.

Thus, Jethro's question had been exceptionally pertinent. This party wasn't what I wanted, and I felt certain it wasn't what Jenn really wanted either. But the planning of it sure had made Ms. Donner happy. The woman had been positively glowing since Christmas in particular, her happiness leaked out of her like spring showers on fertile soil, and the entire Donner Lodge was feeling the impact of her incandescent bliss. Business was booming, her staff blooming, and I was happy Jenn's momma was happy.

But more importantly, I was *ecstatic* Jenn's momma was distracted.

Diane had stopped crying over her failed marriage and she'd ceased plotting the demise of her ex-husband ever since we'd handed over the reins for the wedding, exponentially more so since the holidays. The divorce papers had finally been signed and her ex had all but disappeared from our lives—though I made it my business to keep tabs on the man—Jenn's momma had buried herself in party planning, seemed to find joy in being exhausted by details.

In turn, Diane Donner's distraction had made me very, *very* happy.

'Til right now.

Jethro placed a hand on my shoulder, redirecting my attention to his. "I've never known you to be unhappy and do nothing about it."

"Well, you've never known me to be on the precipice of marriage either. In marriage, sacrifices must be made. Compromises."

Jet's eyebrows ticked up as his hand fell away. "You? Compromise?" He looked truly flabbergasted.

"I am capable of compromise." I sniffed, checking to see if the bar had opened for customers. It hadn't.

"When have you ever compromised?"

"Just wait and see."

I'd—somewhat cheerfully at the time—resigned myself last year to the fact that the entire wedding would be a compromise, back when Jennifer and her momma had suggested Diane take over. Looking around at the opulence now, I suspected the next few months leading to the actual wedding would be more akin to complete surrender than a compromise.

This chafed like wet pants on a ten-mile hike.

"All right then, start compromising with what you're wearing. Diane Donner sees us dressed like this, she'll have a conniption. We got to go home and change." This last part he said on an urgent whisper.

I made a noncommittal sound. There must've been over fifty guests here already, and this thing didn't technically start for another ten minutes. Soon we'd be surrounded with hangers-on and the grating sounds of snobby southern small talk, which is like Yankee small talk except there's significantly more "Bless their little hearts" and sharing of recipes.

"Cletus. For the last time, we can't wear what we have on. Look at them—not the waitstaff, Sheriff James and Jackson. They're in suits, they got jackets. The only jacket I have in my car is a leather one."

"What? You don't want to look like Indiana Jones during my engagement party?" I didn't look at the sheriff or his son, not wanting to inadvertently make eye contact with the Deputy Jackson James, an action that might be misconstrued as an implied invitation to join us. I wasn't in the frame of mind to interact with acquaintances at present.

"Listen, this is what I'll do." Jethro put his hand on my shoulder again. "I'll send a text message to everybody on my way out, let them know this thing is fancy dress, and pick up our suits from the homestead. Then I'll come right back, and you can change."

"I don't want to change, Jethro," I said stubbornly. "I've already changed too many times today. I'm not changing again."

"Come on, Cletus. Be reasonable."

"Hey guys." Jackson James's approaching voice had me lifting my eyes to the ceiling after Jethro mouthed the words, *Be nice.*

I didn't get a chance to mouth back, *Or what?* before Jackson drew even with us, asking, "Where are your jackets? Folks are arriving."

For the love of all tarnation—

"I'm on my way to go grab them," Jethro cut in, locking my eyes in a death stare. "We just finished helping with the setup. And so now I'm driving back to the homestead to go get our suits. Goodbye."

With that, the eldest of my brothers turned on his heel and marched out of the faux-barn toward the parking lot, leaving me with Jackson and his skinny tie.

I looked him down and up, not hiding my perturbed hostility. "Where and when did y'all get the suit memo?"

"Pardon?"

"How did you know to wear a suit?" I spoke slowly, carefully. If I had to repeat myself a third time, I was liable to grab his head and shout in his ear.

"Oh, well, I just assumed." One side of his mouth smiled, the other side communicated wariness, like my question might be a riddle. "I've never known Mrs. Sylvester—I mean, sorry, Ms. Donner—to throw a shindig that wasn't suit and tie required."

I nodded faintly, considering his words and all the information he'd just disclosed, likely without meaning to do so.

Fact: Jackson had attended one or more Diane Donner "shindigs" prior to now.

Fact: I had never attended a Diane Donner shindig prior to now.

Fact: I had never been invited to a Diane Donner shindig prior to now. But Jackson had.

Fact: The Jameses and the Donner-Sylvesters were friendly previous to the divorce in the sense that they attended parties together, which—I supposed—made sense. Being a shrewd person of business, Jenn's momma would want to court the sheriff's good favor as often as possible. Whereas my momma and our family hadn't any favors to offer someone like Diane Donner. *Until recently.*

"Plus, you know, Ms. Donner tries to one-up herself. Momma always has to buy a new dress each time. It's expected. Since this is the first Donner Lodge party in years, I figured it'd be something intense." He glanced around, taking his time to register all the splendor. "I was not wrong."

I didn't like the idea of Jackson knowing more than me about anything, let alone Jenn's family's customs. Therefore, I offered a terse grunt and looked at the bar again. *Finally! Open for business.*

"Excuse me," I said, stepping around the blond officer and making a straight line for the promise of whiskey.

"I saw Jenn yesterday at the station." Jackson's voice followed me. I didn't need to look over my shoulder to know he followed me as well.

"Was she under arrest?"

"What? No." Jackson laughed between saying hi to the folks I brushed past. "She was bringing bakery stuff to the deputies and staff who couldn't make it tonight 'cause they're on duty."

Upon reaching the bar, I held my thumb and index finger about two inches apart and said, "Whiskey. Neat. And a lot."

Patty Lee, who sometimes filled in at the Donner Lodge but mostly tended bar at Genie's, her momma's place up the road, gave me an apologetic smile. "We're only serving beer and wine tonight. Ms. Donner's orders."

No . . . whiskey?

Beer and wine *only*?

I made a mental list of whiskey brands I enjoyed in order to calm myself and did my utmost to keep the pitch of my voice steady as I said, "Patty. I can see the whiskey. It's right behind you."

She grimaced, looking undecided.

"Put it in a mug and I'll say it's tea. No one has to know."

After another moment's hesitation, and before I had to threaten her with blackmail, she nodded. "Fine. But don't tell anyone else. Got it?"

"It shall remain our secret until the day I die."

Her lips tilted to the side like the solemn vow amused her, but she nodded and turned.

Jackson stepped up next to me, chuckling. "Nervous?"

"No."

"Okay. If you say so. But for the record, I'd be nervous."

If Jackson hoped I'd ask follow-up questions, he'd be sorely disappointed. My plan—now that my drink was en route and I'd begun to overcome my initial shock at the grandeur of the evening—was to find an inconspicuous locale, then hover and blend until duty called. I would use the time to drink whiskey and ruminate. A solid plan.

But before I could grab my drink and dash, my brother Billy's unmistakable tenor reached me just as he did. "There you are." Billy placed a hand on my shoulder after giving Jackson a quick nod of greeting. He then lowered his voice. "Where's your jacket? Do you need a jacket? I have an extra in the car, and a tie." Of course Billy wore a suit. He always wore a suit these days.

I wasn't usually one to make faces, preferring to keep my thoughts to myself unless situationally necessary to achieve specific aims. But right now? After arguing the point with Jethro for ten minutes and being surrounded by a sudden swell of strangers?

I made a face. "I don't want one of your suit jackets. Thank you."

"You don't even need to change," he said, calibrating his voice to entirely reasonable, earning him a glare.

"Here's your tea, Cletus." Patti set a teacup and saucer on the bar top and turned to Jackson and Billy. "Can I get y'all any beer or wine?"

I picked up only the teacup, having no use for the saucer.

"I think I'll take some of that tea. My throat's a little scratchy," Jackson teased.

Patti looked unimpressed. "We're all out of tea, deputy. How about a beer?"

Billy used their exchange and his hand on my shoulder to steer us away. "Roscoe can bring one of your jackets, he was just getting out of the shower when I left."

"For the last time, I am content with my present attire. Cease and desist, s'il vous plaît." I didn't have to lower my voice as the cacophony of chatter had mushroomed, the faux-barn filling with people and their inconsequential discussions.

"Cletus—"

"Jethro already harassed me about it. My mind is made up. I am not in the mood for more brotherly pestering."

I should've known this would be an ostentatious affair as soon as Diane and Jenn turned down my donation of homemade moonshine and superior boar sausage last month. But, again, I hadn't been paying attention to anything much these days other than Jenn's magnificence.

Within my woman exists such a vast quantity of magnificence, I shouldn't be chastising myself for being blinded by it.

Billy sighed, shoving his hands into his pockets, looking me over as though assessing my state of mind. "Are you nervous?"

That earned him another glare, but I was saved from answering by a ruckus followed by a whispering hush rippling over the crowd. Something by the faux-barn's main entrance had seized everyone's attention, even Billy's.

My brother's concerned expression cleared almost at once and a soft, appreciative-looking smile took its place. "Well, look at her."

"Who?" I snuck another deep gulp of my whiskey.

"Jenn."

"What?" I craned my neck to peer over those gathered, and I spotted her instantly, breath catching in my lungs, the sight similar to the effect of sunlight on snow.

Jenn.

She stood at the big doors next to her momma, smiling graciously at people as she greeted them, welcomed them, and the knot in my stomach eased, my troubles and muddles and irritation forgotten. She looked genuinely relaxed, happy. Seeing Jenn happy always improved my mood.

But her being relaxed and happy was likely not the source of Billy's soft appreciation nor the crowd's gentle hush. Her exterior, her hair, the dress she wore and how it fit, the artful makeup were likely culprits.

Jenn's long brown hair had grown even longer this past year. She'd said she wanted to grow it long for the wedding and planned to cut it after. Presently, she wore it loose and wavy around her shoulders, which were bare. A single strap on each side held up the fire-engine red fabric that wrapped around her body like a second skin.

The dress—which, as a point of note, I heartily approved of—was basically a cloth tube starting under her arms and ending at her mid-calf. She looked sophisticated and classy as hell. The neckline was a straight line mostly above her breasts, the top curve of them just visible. So add sexy to sophisticated and classy and you'd have it right.

Also, her breasts looked *fantastic*, which I had no choice but to notice. *A pleasant topic for my planned rumination.*

"I swear, she gets more beautiful every day," Jackson said, suddenly next to me again and sounding a little winded. "You're a lucky, lucky man, Cletus."

"Beautiful is not the correct word," I mumbled on autopilot, but not because I disagreed with him per se.

Objectively, Jennifer was stunning, and sexy, and beautiful. Absolutely.

Now imagine if you will being in love with someone who is objectively stunning, and all the sorrow and joy that accompanies true, deep, abiding love. In her I saw flaws and strengths others would never see, secret parts of her known only to me, and my private knowledge of this stunning woman elevated her from the one-dimensional being implied by the pithy descriptor *beautiful* to someone quantum, cosmic in nature.

To Jackson, she may have been merely beautiful. To me, she existed as a multi-dimensional angel and devil, owner of my heart, my joy and my pain, light-years beyond beautiful, or celestial, or exquisite. Because when I saw Jenn, I saw all of her, all versions of her, and all our history, and all the wonderous and frightening possibilities of our future.

So, no.

Beautiful was not the correct word.

Especially not in that particular dress.

"Yes! She wore it." Sienna appeared out of thin air and inserted herself next to me. She then placed a big old kiss on my cheek and wrapped her arm around mine, squealing a little. "Doesn't she look amazing? I told her it was perfect. And here you are, in your red shirt. Good on you, Cletus."

Tearing my eyes from Jenn, though it physically hurt, I inspected my sister-in-law. She wore a fancy dress too. Despite Jethro's fretting, Sienna must've received the memo. "You're responsible for that dress?"

"I wouldn't say *responsible*." She seemed to debate how best to answer. "Unless you consider 'responsible' being the one who commissioned the designer to make it and being the one to pay for it? Then, yes. I am responsible."

Sienna, who I already adored, was now my second favorite person in the world. "I'll be sending your thank-you gift post haste."

"As you should." She winked. "Now shouldn't you be over there? Go get her!"

I returned my attention to where Jenn and her momma—who I realized was also in a red dress, just a tamer, more matronly one—stood greeting folks, making their way through the crowd like royalty at a coronation, and I rocked back on my heels. A renewed string of disquiet wrapped around my chest and squeezed.

"Nah."

"Nah?"

"They got it covered."

Sienna barked a laugh. "Cletus. You're the groom. You have to."

Was she out of her mind? If I went over there, I'd have no choice but to do one of two things:

A) Sweep Jenn off her feet. Leave. Maybe we'd go to my car—I'd brought one of the Buicks—or perhaps we'd abscond to one of the lodge's swanky cottages overlooking the mountains. Then I'd make love to her. Then we'd make love to each other. Then, perhaps if she wasn't too tired, I'd make love to her again. A solid plan, but perhaps not what she'd hoped for this evening.

Or—

B) Talk to people I barely knew about subjects other than cars, sausage, or my superior banjo playing and pretend to care about their inanity.

Of the two scenarios, the latter was the most likely. Therefore—

"Pass." I'd rather sit through a lecture on climate change delivered by flat-earthers than be forced to chitchat with no ulterior gain.

"Don't look like that." Sienna's face fought a grin at something she saw on mine. "This is your night—yours and Jenn's. People want to wish you well and tell you how excited they are for you." She looked to Billy as though to seek his help.

He gave Sienna a stare which was likely inscrutable to her, but which I read as, *Don't look at me. Cletus does what he wants.*

About that, he was right. I didn't want this, I didn't sign up for it, I didn't subscribe to it. I wasn't angry at being caught unawares and unprepared, not anymore, not now that I'd seen Jenn and how happy this spectacle seemed to make her. But acceptance didn't mean I felt moved to participate.

I took another gulp of my whiskey, finishing it.

"Is that—is that whiskey?" Sienna made a frustrated sound, pulling her purse up and digging around in it. "Ugh. You boys. You're lucky you're so cute. Here—" she held out two breath mints and took the empty teacup "—if you're nervous, just say so."

I accepted her mints and wrinkled my nose at the bitter cooling effect on my tongue against the lingering heat of the liquor. "I'm not nervous."

I wasn't nervous. I was avoidant. There's a difference.

And, honestly, I was still of half a mind to scoop Jenn up in my arms and just flat-out leave. I appreciated the dress, I absolutely did. It was splendid, and Jenn was magnificent in it. But the dress being what it was, and Jenn being who she was to me, should I venture within its gravitational field, I wouldn't be responsible for my actions. Best I didn't venture too close, else the urge would become overwhelming.

"Uh oh." Jackson stood straighter, his eyes sharpening. "Farmer Miller is here."

I followed the deputy's line of sight and, sure enough, Farmer Miller —or I guess just Mr. Miller given the current state of his non-farm—was threading through the crush of people, on a collision course with Jenn's momma.

"I'll get Boone, and we'll stop him without causing a scene. Maybe Evans is here?" Jackson said, sounding resigned to his fate, and set off through the crowd.

"What's going on? What's wrong with Farmer Miller?" Sienna placed the empty teacup on a tray set up behind us to receive used dishes.

It was Billy who explained, likely because I was too absorbed by the alluring picture sublime happiness painted on Jenn's features. "Well, you know that trouble last year? Where Kip Sylvester—you know, Jenn's daddy—bought all those farms and promised to lease them back to the former owners? Kip was going to open a farm stay business. He promised the farmers they could stay on their property and host guests. Experience minded tourists, like spend a week on a working farm sort of thing."

"Ah, yes. I met Jenn's father once. He made a lasting impression, like those tuna eyeballs I ate in Japan that one time, or the smell of an LA dumpster on fire. And I've also heard of this farm stay tourism phenomena. Interesting idea," she said, sounding like she didn't actually find it interesting. Sienna loved living at the homestead with Jethro and their progeny, but I knew she had no interest in keeping animals other than as pets.

They had a dog. He was cute. His name was Morty. We'd bonded. But I digress.

"Except the farms are no longer actual working farms. The farmers sold off most of their livestock, keeping just a few animals to make the experience feel authentic." Billy gestured to where Diane and Jenn stood talking to Scotia Simmons and her husband. I kept my attention trained on Jenn to ensure Scotia didn't say anything untoward that might dampen my lady's happiness.

Billy continued, "Which is why Diane had the opportunity to buy all of Miller's cows at auction last year. He sold off almost everything, keeping just a few goats for the tourist experience."

"Didn't she buy the cows for a ridiculous amount of money? That was—when? Over a year ago, right?"

"Yes. I believe she purchased them in the month of January last year. We've had those Guernseys for going on fifteen months." Mention of the cows had me reluctantly looking away from Jenn so I could elucidate for my sister-in-law. "Once upon a time, they may have belonged to Farmer Miller, but now the lodge has the Donner Dairy." I couldn't help the pride in my voice. The Donner Dairy had been my brainchild and—like my brain—it was a beautiful thing.

"I know all about the dairy, the milk is outstanding. But did the other thing ever happen?" Sienna plucked two glasses of red wine off a tray as a server walked by, handing one to Billy. "The farm stay business?"

"Thank you." Billy accepted the wine she offered. "No, Kip turned all the farmers out of their houses—Danvish, Miller, and a few others had already signed and sold—and hasn't done a thing with the farm stay business."

"Kips has been a little busy," I muttered.

"The farmers are—excuse my language—pissed," Billy said. "As are Kip Sylvester's investors. He basically took their money and did nothing with it."

I didn't volunteer that Kip had done quite a few somethings with the money. For one, he'd paid his legal bills. For another, he'd bought himself and his girlfriend a big house in Maryville.

But I did say, "And Miller wants his cows back. He's been trying to get Diane to sell them back since last spring, even offering the colossal two hundred thousand purchase price Diane paid. But she won't budge and has sought a restraining order against Miller."

I'd counseled Diane at the time not to seek the restraining order and instead to try to forge a partnership of some sort with Miller.

With regards to Jenn's father, the court had granted a restraining order for both Diane and Jenn, which was good indeed. However, he and his lady friend—Elena— had been given just probation for their assault of Jenn last year. The prosecution had negotiated a guilty plea in return for a sweetheart deal of time served, no additional jail sentence. Much to my chagrin.

Then again, the deal had saved Jenn from having to testify in court. His admission of guilt had also greatly favored Diane in the divorce settlement, with Kip getting exactly zero of the Donner Lodge or Diane's substantial portfolio. Just half the value of their house, the small vacation house and big boat in Key West, and that's it.

He'd disappeared for a time after, only to reemerge in downtown Green Valley the day after Jenn and Diane's restraining orders expired. The degenerate was planning something, and I felt certain it had to do with the farms he'd hoodwinked away from their rightful owners.

Don't get me wrong, Nancy Danvish in particular held a good measure of my ire due to her—albeit ignorant—part in what happened last year. Nevertheless, she and Miller, the other farmers who'd been duped, and Kip Sylvester's ring of investors had all been sorely cheated by Jennifer's father. They were still angry, incensed even. I didn't care about their woes, but I did care about justice. If Diane had sought to use their collective wrath against Kip, the common enemy, she could've destroyed him once and for all.

Sadly, Jenn's momma was and would always be a reactionary, acting before thinking, where Kip Sylvester was concerned. Diane fundamentally lacked the foresight, patience, and sinister strategic acumen required to bring her ex down. At some point, I'd have to step in, organize folks, and just make it happen.

After the wedding.

"Oh! So Diane Donner has a restraining order against the farmer whose cows she bought? And that farmer is here tonight?" Sienna looked at me with wide eyes, engrossed.

"No. The restraining order against Miller wasn't granted," I clarified, sneaking another peek at Jenn. She still looked happy. *Good.* "Miller hasn't made any threats against Diane, so the court ruled against her. I think he just really wants those cows back. But Miller has made threats against Kip."

"Kip Sylvester." Billy supplied the cretin's full name once more.

"Kip Sylvester, Jenn's father," Sienna said, like she was trying to untangle all the ways folks in our small town intersected. "Kip was also the principal of the high school, right? Before running off with the school secretary, Elena Wilkerson—"

"Wilkinson," Billy gently corrected. "And Elena's sister is the one in jail for hitting Diane over the head and leaving her for dead last year by Old Man Blount's bee boxes." Billy sent me a quick glance, not voicing that Elena's sister had also been the one who held Jenn and I up at gunpoint in Jenn's house. The woman's fifteen-year prison sentence included her attempt on our lives.

"So Miller doesn't like Kip Sylvester." Sienna took a sip of her wine, looking around at the crowd thoughtfully.

"No one likes Kip Sylvester," I said. "Miller, Danvish, the Hills, Leffersbees, Badcock, Gangersworth, Lees, Lamont, Paytons—the list goes on and on." It really did go on and on. I couldn't think of a single person in Green Valley or the surrounding areas who didn't wish ill on the man.

"He's got a lot of enemies in these parts. If he knows what's good for him, he'll stay far away." Billy glanced down at his glass, studying it, and I knew he had his own private thoughts on the matter.

We stood in contemplative wordlessness for a brief moment, and I again took the opportunity to seek out the sight of Jenn. She was now engaged in discourse with my big dumb brother, Beau. For the record, I meant *dumb* in the best sense of the word, sweet and loyal, like a dog. He and his lady friend, Shelly Sullivan, held her attention, and Shelly must've said something funny because Jenn—

"Oh my God." I heard Sienna suck in a surprised-sounding breath a split second before she gripped my arm, clearly startled.

I covered her hand with mine. "Are you okay?"

"Cletus!" She stepped in front of me, blocking my view of the rest of the room. "If Kip Sylvester has so many enemies"—her unmistakably alarmed gaze arrested mine, and then jumped to Billy's—"then why is he here?"

CHAPTER TWO

JENN

"Rejection steals the best of who I am by reinforcing the worst of what's been said to me."

— LYSA TERKEURST, *UNINVITED: LIVING LOVED
WHEN YOU FEEL LESS THAN, LEFT OUT, AND
LONELY*

Gasps from behind me distracted me and my momma from the joke Shelly had just told. She and Beau also seemed to find the sound distracting as her smile faltered at the swell of exclamations fluttering around us.

Laughter forgotten, both Shelly and Beau leaned to the side and peered around us. My friend's reaction—flinching back, the way her smile immediately fell and her gaze hardened—was the second sign something was amiss.

"Oh good Lord!" my mother—who'd already rubbernecked to assess the issue—hissed at my side and gripped my arm. I started to glance over my shoulder too, but my momma's hand tightened. "Do not turn around. Don't give him the satisfaction." She straightened her back, lifting her chin, her lips pinched. "I will deal with this."

Despite my mother's instruction, I turned and watched her walk toward the barn doors and to the couple who'd just entered. Now I gasped, the hairs on the back of my neck stood up painfully, and a shiver chased uncomfortable goose bumps over my skin as my stomach fell right to the floor.

Oh no.

"Diane." The distinct disdain of my daddy's voice rose above the remnants of conversation his presence hadn't yet quieted. Just the sound of him . . . *Oh no!*

He wasn't looking at me. Even so, my heart took off at a gallop, my throat suddenly dry, and a tremor of either fear or rage—or maybe both —made me feel unsteady on my feet.

"Jenn, I'm here." Cletus, abruptly at my side, slid his arm around my waist like he knew how much I needed his support, his strong hands and assurances, his solid warmth, his strength; like he knew how much I needed *him*.

A relieved rush of air left my lungs, and I leaned into him, grateful beyond words for his timely appearance. "Cletus."

"I've been here the whole time," he whispered against my ear in a tone meant to soothe. "I've got you."

I nodded, able to swallow around the rocks rising in my throat. Of course I'd known Cletus was here. I'd spotted him hiding (or trying to hide) along the far wall as I'd entered. Even though I'd felt his eyes follow as I greeted our guests, it had been obvious to me he had no desire to budge from the safety circle of his family.

And that was fine.

We would sit next to each other at dinner. I'd made certain our table's seat assignments were occupied by his family, despite my momma's protests such an arrangement would be gauche. Cletus didn't have to venture into the crowd and chitchat if he didn't want to.

But the sudden appearance of my deranged father and his equally deranged mistress had been enough to spur him into the crowd and to my side. I wasn't surprised. When I needed Cletus, he was always, always there.

"This is awful. Why is he here?" I moaned, searching his handsome face. Both compassion and frustration were etched into the lines around his mouth and on his forehead.

"We'll get rid of him." Cletus smoothed his big, warm hand up and down my back while shifting his eyes to Beau. The brothers then stared at each other, as though communicating silently.

After a protracted moment, Beau leaned toward his older brother, his whisper urgent, "I'm sorry, Cletus. You're not Duane. What do you want me to do?"

"He wants us to stand between the clusterfuck over there and Jennifer, blocking her from view so her father can't see her," Shelly answered, already pulling Beau by the wrist to position them both.

"Well, isn't this nice. I guess the invitation to my own daughter's engagement party got lost in the mail?" My father's voice boomed over the continued murmurs and gasps of those assembled, like he wanted to make sure he was heard by all.

I couldn't see much, not with Beau and Shelly now forming a wall between me and the unfolding ugliness, but I could make out the line of my mother's stiff back, confronting my father all on her own. My heart lurched, hating she was over there all by herself, dealing with those people. *I should be with her, helping!*

I was just about to say as much when—just as abruptly as Cletus had appeared next to me—Billy Winston and Hank Weller came out of nowhere and flanked my mother, causing my lurching heart to soar. *Thank goodness.*

Yes. Thank goodness. Because, truth be told, I did not wish to face off with my father or Elena ever again. I still had nightmares and scars from the first time.

Momma said something like, "You need to go." But she wasn't talking to be heard by anyone other than my father, so I couldn't be sure of her words.

Tearing my eyes away, I craned my neck, searching the stunned faces for folks from the sheriff's office. "Where are the sheriff and Jackson?"

"They were dealing with Farmer Miller." Cletus's hand smoothed down my back again, his attention on me. "What do you want to do? Should we go help your momma?"

I couldn't answer his question as I was still stuck on his earlier statement. "What? Miller is here too?"

What a disaster!

"I thought Miller was invited," Cletus said as he, Shelly, and Beau moved as a unit, ushering me further into the crowd and behind Reverend and Mrs. Seymore. They paid us no mind, busy as they were gaping at the drama in progress.

"Miller was invited?" I found that impossible to believe. Farmer Miller had been badgering my momma about his—or, what used to be his—dairy cows for over a year. I couldn't imagine my mother had invited him.

This was all happening so fast, I needed to think.

"I didn't see him on the guest list but it seems like everyone else was invited—except your father. He was—most definitely—not." Cletus's words were hushed, presumably because he wanted to hear what was being said between my mother and my father.

Even if he hadn't wanted to know, there was no escape from their rapidly rising voices.

"—will not tell you again, you and your paramour are not welcome here or within a hundred miles of me or Jennifer. Leave. Now."

My momma turned like she was going to walk away, but something held her in place—or someone. Suddenly both my father and Billy were talking at once.

"No, no—you don't walk away from me. We're going to talk about thisss right here right now—"

"Get your hand off the lady." Even from where I stood, I saw Billy's broad shoulders move forward and in front of my mother.

Elena, clearly still miles off her rocker, spoke over Billy, "Don't you threaten him!"

"You'll know when I make a threat." Billy's tranquil baritone sent another shiver down my spine, but I didn't mind. As usual, Billy Winston's calm and understated demonstration of strength often gave me comfort.

Cletus and Beau shared a look, and I suspected they successfully read the other's thoughts loud and clear this time.

But in the next moment my mother said, "It's fine, Congressman Winston. *These people* desire a stage, and you can't expect them to be decent about anything."

"You sure are one to talk about decency, *Diane.*" Elena's typical quiet timidity seemed to be absent tonight. "Everyone knows you've been cavorting with that biker trash—"

"Nor will he be satisfied until they're given a stage, even if it means ruining his own daughter's engagement party and everyone's evening." My mother carried on like Elena hadn't just interrupted. "I know how his selfish, weaselly little mind works. So go ahead, Kip. What is it you're so desperate for all these fine people to hear?"

My father didn't respond right away. Rather, he allowed for the crowd to digest my mother's words. Or maybe he wasn't expecting her to acquiesce so quickly. Whatever the reason, he paused long enough for a murmur to rise among the partygoers before lifting his voice.

"As I was saying, I didn't receive an invitation to this here party. I guess being a father isn't much valued by the world anymore, nor does it mean much these days to people who defy God's commandments." My father paused here as though he expected my mother to respond, maybe defending her position on the subject. But when she said nothing, he continued, this time addressing our guests, "This woman—this fallen woman of ill repute—is allowing our beautiful, innocent daughter to marry the town s-simpleton, y'all know I'm right. And sseeing as how my ex-wife has always been a sshrieking banshee, an ungodly, unclean soul, we can't be too surprised by the rudenesss."

I sought out Cletus's gaze and saw his focus had turned inward, his eyebrows pinched above his nose like his mind was working through a problem.

"Does he sound drunk?" I asked, wondering if I was the only one who heard the slur in my father's voice.

"He sounds . . . something. Maybe drunk." Beau nodded, his eyes wide. "You reckon that's why he's here? He's drunk and thought it would be a good idea?"

"Billy should antagonize him," Cletus muttered, like he was speaking to himself.

"Antagonize him? What are you on about?" Beau whispered harshly, echoing my thoughts while my father continued to rant more of the same nonsense about my momma.

Stealthily, I glanced around us to make certain no one had overheard. My skills from a lifetime spent quietly observing resurfaced. No one in our vicinity seemed to be paying us any mind. From the looks of things, they were fully distracted by the unpleasant scene.

However, I noted some people were more absorbed than others. Or rather, absorbed in a different way. Whereas folks like Reverend Seymore, Mrs. Seymore, Genie Lee, and Vanessa Romero were gawking, other folks—like Posey Lamont, Roger Gangersworth, Nancy Danvish, and Nikki Becker—weren't gawking.

Yes, they were absorbed, but their expressions betrayed more than just simple curiosity or nosiness. Their features and their postures were *intent*, like they had a horse in this race and wanted to make sure their bets were going to pay off. Perhaps I noticed these individuals in particular because I didn't trust them, not after their failed partnership with my father and their attempt to gang up on me and my momma last year.

Whatever the reason, and even though I was flustered, I took note.

"—you don't tell me what to do, woman! 'Wives, submit to your husbands.' That's what the Bible says! But you were willful, you're to blame, for everything!"

"Now he's quoting Bible verses?" Shelly seemed to be particularly perturbed by this. "I don't care if he's drunk, Cletus is right."

"How will Billy antagonizing Kip help anything?" Beau looked just as confused as me.

"Billy gets Kip to punch him, then anything else Billy does is self-defense. One punch from Billy could put anyone in the hospital for a while." Cletus replied. His frown held a distinctly scheming edge.

Though I shouldn't have been shocked by the direction of Cletus's thoughts—not after knowing him my whole life and knowing him intimately for over a year—I was.

"Cletus!" I shook my head vehemently. "Violence is never the answer."

"Never say never." With that dark proclamation, he pushed me—

albeit gently—into Beau's arms and, before I could comprehend his intentions, he left.

Now *I* gawked. I reached for him mindlessly, but it was too late. He'd always been surprisingly quick and agile for a man so broad and muscular.

"Do you want me to stop him?" Shelly asked, looking and sounding serious.

My tongue tied, I couldn't answer. I wasn't sure what I wanted. Everything was happening way too fast.

Cletus stepped between Billy and Diane. "As the aforementioned town simpleton and the fiancé of Ms. Donner's lovely daughter, may I just say—"

"No, you may not!" Elena snarled, stunning not just me back into silence. The crowd, which had started to talk among themselves and shift toward the exits, abruptly held still and quiet. They seemed to strain, every person's focus on the tiny blonde woman next to my father, seemingly a shadow who'd always been so quiet and meek.

Like me. No. Not like me.

Like old me.

But I knew better. I knew for a fact that Elena Wilkinson was just as dangerous as my father.

"Now, ma'am, really. Please use your inside voice," Cletus chided, sounding entirely affable, like he was reprimanding a child. He then addressed my father. "Kip—in the spirit of mending fences, I'll call you Kip and you have my permission to call me son—now, Kip, we all know why you're here. You feel slighted, like you haven't been given the proper respect due the father of the bride. And I think that's something everyone here would be able to understand."

A few flutters of surprised and uncomfortable laughter tittered around us, like folks couldn't believe Cletus's words, and I didn't blame them. My father was universally despised in this town and any attempts by Cletus to mend fences would be met with cold shoulders from everyone gathered. I suspected the only reason people hadn't left yet was because they *wanted* to see Kip Sylvester humiliated, and now Cletus was going to offer an olive branch?

But that wasn't what Cletus was doing, not at all. Knowing him, I knew full well what he was about to do. I gripped Beau's hand harder, which I didn't realize I'd been holding until just this moment. Cletus did this so well, lulling folks into a false sense of security before he made them lose their minds with rage, befuddlement, or embarrassment, and then rage again.

"Oh no," Beau said under his breath. "Here we go."

"Cletus Winston, you shut your mouth."

Elena's vitriol had my father cutting in, "Elena, the men are talking. Let me handle this." His tone remained superior despite his slurred words.

"Are *we*, though? Men?" Cletus paused here, and I knew it was for effect, before adding thoughtfully, "I mean, you're not really a man, are you?"

"Now you listen to me—"

Cletus didn't listen, he didn't even pause. "You weren't man enough to take care of your family or keep them together. You weren't man enough to step up and cherish a wife as exceptional as Diane, a pillar of Christian charity and goodness in this community. Unlike *this*—what did you say?—woman of ill repute?"

I expected my father to lose it at this point, but Elena was the one to step forward. "You hillbilly, club-trash bastard. I'll make you pay for what you did to my sister."

Cletus continued like she hadn't spoken, "And you're obviously not man enough to keep your mistress from making you—a fallen man, a person of ill repute—look like a fool. Now an even bigger fool than you already were, which I didn't think was possible. You two deserve each other."

My father lifted his voice, spewing slurred insults that ran together and made no sense. But it was no use. Cletus's voice was bigger, more commanding. Plus, Cletus wasn't drunk.

"And in front of—I mean—the whole town is here. Literally every-body you know." Cletus chuckled like he couldn't believe it, like our guests had suddenly materialized. "How mortifying for you, but I reckon you're used to that by now. So, on second thought, don't call me son. I think I speak for everyone here when I say associating with you would be an embarrassment. Embarrassing even for the town simpleton."

My father must've done something then, maybe tried to throw a punch, because a scuffle ensued and exclamations of surprise and distress from onlookers followed. I covered my mouth, trying to see past the heads and shoulders of those blocking my line of sight, but it was to no avail. Even in these shoes I was too short!

Without thinking, I left Beau and Shelly and pushed to the front, needing to see what was going on and that Cletus and my momma were okay. My father and Elena were psychotic, I knew this. I should've made them leave, I should've stepped in already, and now fear had completely gripped me. What if they wanted to hurt Cletus? What if all their failed business dealings and drained bank accounts meant they had nothing left to lose?

I was assaulted by the delayed suspicion, maybe they'd wanted this to happen? Maybe one of them had brought a weapon? *What if they'd planned this?*

Billy, bless him, held Cletus back, and my father was fighting off Hank's attempts to do the same to him. Meanwhile, Elena was scratching at Billy and Cletus, and my heart seized for a split second as I braced myself for whatever was coming next, too paralyzed by the train wreck to think past my own bystander status.

Out of nowhere, like a miracle, Sheriff James's voice boomed from somewhere, "Y'all cut this out, right now. Right. Now. Shame on you."

Like a knight of goodness and righteousness, the sheriff was there. And even though he wore an *I'm getting too old for this shit* expression, he'd inserted himself between the parties, holding his hands up.

Elena screeched, "This piece of trash tried to—"

"You hush." Sheriff James pointed a finger at her face. "Unless you'd like to be arrested, and don't think I won't."

"They should be the ones arrested, this club garbage and *her!*" Elena smacked away the sheriff's hand and charged at my mother.

My father was raving again. "Soon everyone will know what you did, the two of you. You'll rot in jail! Jennifer will see then, she'll come back to me then, begging for forgiveness!"

Mid-rant, the sheriff began forcibly pushing my father toward the door.

"All right, all right. We're taking this outside. Jackson, Evans, Boone —" he lifted his hand toward the entrance of the barn, motioning to his deputies who'd just arrived "—take Mr. Sylvester and Ms. Wilkinson out. Ms. Donner, Billy, you're with me."

I'd almost caught up to Cletus, but then he moved like he was going to follow the deputies outside. Before he could, the sheriff turned and put a hand on Cletus's chest, unveiled disappointment in his eyes.

Because I was close enough, I heard the sheriff's whispered, "Stay here and apologize to Jennifer. She deserves better from you. Your momma would be ashamed, she raised you better. And, for the record, I expected better."

With one more lingering hard look for Cletus, Sheriff James lifted his eyes and addressed the crowd, "I know I speak for Janet when I say we've been looking forward to celebrating Jennifer's happiness and this engagement for many months. Let's not let temporary unpleasantness cast a shadow over what is supposed to be a joyful event. Those cooks are working hard, and the tables are set. This is a party. You'll never hear your sheriff say this again, but I'm insisting y'all go grab a drink. Or two. Possibly three."

The sheriff's attempt at humor was met with laughter that sounded less strained than relieved, like folks were happy to see a levelheaded adult step up and take over. The big man's gaze gentled considerably as it settled on me, and he gave me a small, rueful-looking nod. Then with a visible rising and falling of his chest, he left, presumably to catch up with his deputies.

Cletus shoved his hands in his pockets, making no move to follow this time. My heart in my throat and needing to see for myself he was okay, I stepped next to him and slid my fingers around his wrist, drawing his attention to me as I pulled his hand free. I wanted to hold it. I might be mad later, but for now I just *needed* the reassurance of his touch.

His glare, icy and agitated, melted almost at once as it met mine, a flare of worry and pain turning his eyes a vivid blue. Someone—likely Elena—had scratched his face. Red, angry nail tracks stood in stark relief starting at his hairline, over his forehead, and down his cheek. He was bleeding.

I sucked in a breath. "Oh, Cletus."

"Don't."

"Don't what?"

"Don't feel sorry for me." He brought my hand to his mouth and kissed my palm, his voice monotone. "I deserved what I got, probably more."

Now I breathed out, feeling suddenly tired and relieved it was over, but—strangely—still not angry. "Cletus, can we . . ." I pointed over my shoulder with my thumb. After what had just occurred, I needed a minute with him, just the two of us.

He seemed to need it too. Wordlessly, he led us to the fringes of the crowd, out one of the side doors, and into the night. I let him guide me, wishing I were angrier, knowing I should be. He was so infuriating sometimes.

But Cletus was mine. And I was his. And I wouldn't change that fact for anything in the world.

CHAPTER THREE

JENN

"Question everything. Your love, your religion, your passion. If you don't have questions, you'll never find answers."

— COLLEEN HOOVER, *SLAMMED*

"What are you thinking about?" I dabbed gently at the cuts on his face with a ball of cotton soaked in hydrogen peroxide and blew on the wound. The scratches already looked a little better, but he also had a wee little bruise under his left eye where my father had punched him. Apparently, Cletus's plan had almost worked and would've been fully realized if Billy hadn't held Cletus back.

After Cletus and I left the party, he'd taken us as far as the parking lot by the bakery. There, he'd seemed to hesitate. The Buick was just a few feet away. Eventually, as though finished with a wieldy internal debate, he'd grumbled and turned from the car. He took me to the Donner Bakery building instead. He'd unlocked it and opened the door for me, the bell jingling as we entered.

I'd walked past the storefront, the bakery case, and back to the kitchen where I'd grabbed the first aid kit while he'd flipped on the set of lights over the sink.

28

Presently, he lowered himself to the edge of the kitchen counter, and I stood between his legs. We were more or less at eye level, which made it easier to tend to his face.

Cletus hadn't yet answered my question. I ceased dabbing at the wounds and leaned back a bit, catching his eyes. "Cletus Byron, what are you thinking about?"

The set of his mouth was distinctly grim, so I didn't expect him to say, "I really love this dress."

Something about the way he said it struck me as immensely charming, like he loved the dress, but he also hated the dress because he loved it so much. This dichotomous delivery of a sweet statement had me fighting a smile.

"Oh? You do?" I backed up a bit more and felt the reluctant slide of his hands release me from where they'd been resting on my waist. I turned to the side, modeling it for him. "Did you see the back?"

"I don't need to see the back." His eyes closed, like the sight of me overwhelmed him a little, and he moved to rub his forehead, wincing when his fingers made contact with the scratches. "Dammit."

Crossing my arms, I watched as frustration played over his features. Confound it, but I wasn't mad at Cletus. Yet I didn't feel sorry for him either. Well, I didn't feel sorry for him *much*. Cletus knew what he'd been doing.

"Actually—" he placed his hands on the counter at either side of his waist, his gaze on the floor "—what I was really thinking was I wished we were alone."

"We are alone, silly. I don't see anybody else here." I laughed, coming back to stand between his legs and finish what I'd started. The scratch extended into his beard, and I swallowed around a thick knot of anger. As much as I wasn't angry at Cletus, I was furious at my father and Elena.

The last time I'd seen my father was at his court sentencing last spring, where he and Elena had been given probation for what they'd done to us last year. I'd been . . . well, I'd been angered by the outcome. The court considered what they'd done "assault," which was a Class A

29

misdemeanor, punishable by up to 11 months and 29 days in jail, a fine up to $2500, or both.

Up to 11 months and 29 days in jail and $2500 for ruining my peace of mind. Good to know what the court thought it was worth.

They'd put their hands on me, harmed me, invaded my sleep and robbed me of my tranquility, and ultimately got off with a fine and probation. The injustice of it had left me feeling pretty bitter about the state of the legal system. I hadn't admitted as much to Cletus, nor had I discussed it with anyone else, but a darkness had followed me ever since that day. Truth be told, I was coming around to Cletus's way of thinking.

Perhaps it was necessary to take matters into your own hands if you wanted to see *real* justice served.

Maybe that's why you're not angry with Cletus now, even though you should be . . .

"I meant tonight. I wish we were alone tonight."

"We'll be alone later."

"All of tonight."

I lifted an eyebrow. "You're being greedy."

"With you? Always."

I rolled my eyes so he couldn't see how I loved his answer. "It's only one night. Don't you think the barn looks pretty?"

"It does . . . look . . . pretty," he conceded, haltingly.

I ceased dabbing again, again catching his eyes. They looked as cagey as his words had been. "What's wrong?"

"I'm not in a suit."

"So what?" I glanced at the fit of his red shirt and black pants, admiring the shape of him and taking a moment to thrill in what I knew his clothes concealed. "You look perfect just as you are." I meant it, scratches and all, he was perfect.

"Your momma expected menfolk to wear suits, and Jackson James knew to wear a suit," he grumped, his hands coming back to me. But this time they settled on my hips, holding me a little tighter, his grip feeling somehow more possessive.

"So?"

"So, aren't you concerned we're nearing the end of days?"

I looked at him blankly. "End of days?"

"Jackson James knowing something I don't."

I laughed again, lowering my eyes to his beard and the hidden scratch left by that—that—that *harpy*. The next time I saw her, I'd scratch her eyes out. *So much for violence not being an answer. . .*

"I don't care whether you're in a suit or not. It's no big deal." I shrugged away the dark turn of my thoughts and his concerns about wearing a suit.

"Jethro left some time ago to pick something up for me, so I'll be *suitably* attired." His tone was both officious and droll, a cute combo.

"That's very funny." I smiled appreciatively at his pun.

"Yes, I know. But Jenn, all this—" He reached for my wrist and lowered my hand; this time he was the one to catch my eyes. "Why are we doing this?"

"What?"

"The fussy tableware, the suits, the guest list filled with acquaintances. We don't need all that. We could've just had a small engagement party at the Winston house. Then your father—"

"I know we didn't—don't *need* it. But my momma, the staff here at the lodge, your family, they love us, and they want to show it. I was excited about tonight."

He looked confused by my statement. "You were?"

"Yes, I was. I mean, not all the people I barely know. But what they did with the barn, everyone at the lodge pitched in to decorate, staying late and helping. They are *excited*. And your family helped too."

"My family?"

"Shelly and her sculptures? Did you see the hearts? They're beautiful. And Jess and Duane sending those fancy place settings over from England, brand-new for the lodge, and we'll use them for the first time tonight. Sienna having a dress designed for me by one of her famous friends—*and* she designed my wedding dress. Billy arranging for us to use the governor's silverware. It's real old, special. Drew and Ashley arranging for those glass chandeliers to be flown in from a glass blower in Texas. Actually, Ashley did a lot. She's responsible for the planning just as much as my momma, they did it together. Heck,

Roscoe worked with Claire McClure to arrange the string quartet. Did you know that?"

"I—I did not know that," he sputtered.

"He did. They did! Roscoe went to her with the idea and she made it happen, musicians she knows in Nashville. They drove all the way out here and my momma is putting them up at the lodge. Everyone is being so sweet, coming together to celebrate us and—so—I know we don't *need* any of it, but it sure made me feel good, feel grateful that your family wanted to welcome me like this."

Cletus's confused frown persisted, and he stood from the counter, setting me to the side. Pacing away, he pushed his hands through his hair roughly. "Jethro didn't seem to know."

"Jethro has been pretty busy with Benjamin. I think he can be forgiven for not pitching in. I think Sienna said he's getting about three hours of sleep these days. You know he doesn't want a night nurse, and I guess I understand that, but—"

"I didn't know either."

"But isn't it great?" I tracked him, bothered by his reaction.

"It is . . . great."

I tossed the used cotton ball to the counter, irritated with Cletus's continued agitation. "Then why do you sound so unhappy about it?"

"Because I had no idea it was happening!" In a rare demonstration of temper, Cletus's voice rose.

He didn't shout, didn't yell, but it was an unmodulated, unintended display of feeling, something he never, ever did. Especially not with me. Even after being together for over a year. He was, for better or for worse, always controlled in my presence, his tone perpetually thoughtful and measured. Unless we were . . . well, having sex.

Intimacy, sex, making love seemed to be the only time Cletus allowed himself to let loose the reins he otherwise held with a white-knuckled grip, and not every time. Just sometimes. It drove me a little crazy.

I watched him now as he breathed out, seeming to shake himself. I remained silent because the thoughts running through my mind would likely sound absurd to anyone else. To me, Cletus was sexy as hell when his control slipped, when that edge entered his voice and the rough, sharp pieces of him were revealed. His eyes would narrow, flash, spark, and a gravel entered his voice, one that made my mouth dry and my tummy flip, made me chase my breath and my lungs squeeze.

I couldn't explain it. It's not that I wanted him yelling at me, or that I wanted him mad or frustrated. But I wanted uncontrolled . . . Passion? Desperation? Intensity? All three?

When I needed to rant and rave, I did with him. When I was angry or feeling desperate for his touch or frenzied because I missed him so badly, I showed it. But he rarely did. He stuffed it down, buried it, and that left me feeling oddly neglected.

I loved all of Cletus, was greedy for every part of who he was. This was a side he'd continued to keep hidden, only to ration out in bite-sized portions, and only in the bedroom, and only for a few minutes at a time. After, he'd put it away, high on a shelf out of my reach.

Requiring only a second to regain his slipped control, Cletus lifted his eyes, dimmed by forced calm and restraint, and spoke as though he measured each word with a mental ruler, "I'm sorry. It's just that I have trouble with surprises, with feeling unprepared, and with crowds. Especially when I'm expected to—uh—perform in some way in front of people."

I knew this, but it hadn't been my intention to surprise him. "I don't know what to say, Cletus. It's not like we hid anything from you. You never asked about it, about the plans or how things were going. I honestly thought you knew." He seemed to always know everything about everyone, sometimes before they did.

"I've been a little distracted," he admitted, glancing to the side, an exceedingly small, wry smile tugging at the side of his mouth.

That made me blush, a hot surge of knowledge, a certainty as to what and who had distracted him, made my tummy flip.

He heaved out a breath, again shaking himself. "But, Jenn, as much as I appreciate what everyone did, if we'd kept tonight small and private, your father wouldn't have had a chance to make a spectacle. Whatever the plans are for the wedding as of right now, we should rethink them in light of tonight's events."

That all sounded very reasonable, except—

"Nope. I'm not going to let my father's behavior—what he does, or what he might do—dictate how I live my life. You helped me learn that." Nor was I going to allow myself to mire in unhappiness now. Tonight was our night, dammit. My father was not going to ruin it and I refused to waste another moment thinking about him or Elena.

There. All done. Moving on.

Cletus grimaced, looking grumpy. "I suppose I did help you learn that."

"And I was having a good time tonight. Sometimes it's nice to get all dressed up. How many times do people get engaged? I only ever plan on getting engaged once."

"That's the right answer." He looked considerably less grumpy until, abruptly, he frowned again. "Wait, Ash helped plan tonight?"

"Yes. Like I said, she and my mother basically planned it together. And they're planning the wedding together."

"What? How is this possible?"

"They actually get along just fine."

"No, I mean, Ashley planning a wedding, *any* wedding. Drew has asked her to marry him several times, and I know for a fact she wants to say yes. She won't commit to her own wedding, but she'll gladly plan ours? And you know their babies are going to be incredibly cute."

It was obvious thought of Ashley's involvement in planning our nuptials renewed his agitation. "Cletus, it's fine. If it makes Ashley happy, let her be happy. We've been through so much. It's been a crazy year. Let's enjoy this big fancy party we had nothing to do with organizing—tonight and the wedding. This is something my mother excels at and enjoys doing, so we didn't have to do a thing."

"That's not the point—"

"And at no trouble to you or me. It's not something that we need to worry about or fret over. You can just sit back and enjoy yourself."

"Sit back and enjoy myself?"

"That's right. Just relax. Everything has been done. You don't need to do a single thing but show up and smile."

34

"I am not accustomed to sitting back and enjoying myself. Nor smiling."

"I beg to differ. You've done quite a bit of both with me."

Another wry smile tugged at his mouth, but I could see he planned to keep arguing the point.

Obviously, he needed me to spell out the actual point. "The point is, let's celebrate!" I crossed to my big, sweet man, slid my arms around his waist and tilted my head back to peer up at him. "Despite my father and that woman trying to ruin our fun, I want to celebrate with you. I want to celebrate us. I want to show you off, my brilliant, handsome fiancé. I want to show the world how much I adore you."

Everything about him seemed to soften at my words, and I felt the moment he became putty, witnessed the precise second I'd won him over.

His arms came around me, his hands sliding from my back to my bottom. "You want to show me off?"

"Of course." I brushed my lips against his, just a light touch. "Don't you want to show me off?"

"Honestly?" He continued stroking me—back, hip, bottom—as he seemed to debate his answer. "I don't know. Sometimes I do. Only if you're keen on it, only if it's something you want," he added solemnly, knowing better than anyone how my parents had trotted me out as a kid and teenager when the attention used to terrify me. I loved him for wanting to take my past and my present feelings into consideration.

"But mostly—" his hands paused on my backside, his fingers gripping and pressing me to him possessively, his voice adopting just a faint hint of that gravelly tone I adored—"I want you all to myself."

"Okay." I grinned up at him. "Then if I don't get my party, you have to attend to my every whim."

"When?"

"Forever."

His eyelids drooped, his eyes darkening to indigo, and a true smile laden with sinister thoughts—such a sexy smile—curved his mouth. "I'm fine with the party, and we should go back soon. But I'd also enjoy attending to your whims. Likewise, the thought of forever suits me just fine. Perhaps you could give me a task list of said whims, to get me started."

"I know how you like your lists," I whispered, my toes curling in my high heels as his mouth lowered to mine and I lost myself in it, in him, in the hot slide and press of his generous lips, the slick, knowing heat of his tongue.

He stroked the inside of my mouth reminiscent of how he'd feasted on my body last night before we'd gone to bed. My knees wobbled. *Maybe we don't have to go back to the party at all?*

"Cletus," I gasped, lifting my chin, untucking and undoing the buttons of his suit shirt because I needed the hot and hard feel of his skin and body *right now*. I was delighted to find he wore nothing beneath it. "You can't kiss me like that if you expect me to think straight."

"Who says I expect you to think straight? Let's think crooked." He toyed with the thin strap on my shoulder, pulling it down, placing a wet kiss where it had been, and sliding his fingers into the neckline of my dress, his knuckles grazing my breasts. "I thought I wanted you out of this dress, but now I think I'd like you to keep it on . . ." The words he'd left unspoken swirled around my head, making me dizzy.

Keep it on *while we fuck.*

He didn't usually speak while we were intimate, and I'd started to suspect it was because he didn't trust himself. We'd only had phone sex the one time last year and that was the most he'd talked—ever—during the deed. But just last month, after coming back from a boxing gym with Drew, sweaty and sporting a few bruises, he'd backed me into the door of my bedroom and growled in my ear, "I'm going to fuck you against the wall."

It was like he'd flipped a switch in my brain. I'd gone from bemused to hot and ready in zero point three seconds. He hadn't used the word since. Instead, he'd been *not* saying it, leaving the insinuation in the air between us, and it was driving me wild.

I couldn't recall ever saying the word out loud. It felt so off-limits to me, so ripe with prohibition. It wasn't proper, and maybe that's why I loved the idea of *doing* it with Cletus. Like I was awakening to a new, primitive part of myself, essential yet forbidden, engaging in a naughty activity that—if caught—meant I would be punished, perhaps even shunned. And yet it felt crucial, necessary to use him, his glorious body. And to be used in the same way.

Not making love. Not cherishing each other's hearts, minds, and bodies.

Fucking.

"Lift up your dress."

I breathed out on a rush, my heart taking off, and immediately began to comply. "You're not going to help?"

"I don't know how it works, and I don't want to break it." Cletus had released me and worked on the complicated mechanism he called a belt, his movements unhurried as he stepped back to watch me gather the material of the skirt.

Are we doing this? Now?

"But where—?" I whispered the question, my thighs flexing as cool air met the newly exposed skin. In fact, my entire body felt taut, tight, tense.

"Lean back," he ordered, already guiding me up to the countertop, catching on the front of my dress to yank it down as I finished pulling the skirt up.

Leaning over me, Cletus roughly palmed my breasts as they were exposed, twisting and pinching my nipple, making me whimper. A dark, appreciative grunt rumbled out of him as he gazed upon my bared torso and his hands where they touched me. He lowered and his mouth closed over the center of my breast, hot and wet. His tongue swirled, sucking almost to the point of painful, making my back arch off the table. My fumbling fingers sifted through the hair at the back of his head and pressed him closer. *God.*

It felt so good. Always so good, and I felt so lost. My upbringing had not prepared me, I'd not been raised in what folks now called a sex-positive household. And perhaps that was why every time we were together I always experienced nagging shame and worry, like it shouldn't feel good and I shouldn't enjoy it and I was a bad girl because I did.

"Open up." Cletus moved a hand between my knees, pushing them apart, sliding fingertips up my inner thigh and cupping me over the lace of my underwear, massaging with a firm hand.

A clumsy moan slipped past my lips as I glanced down the topography of my body, watched him touch me. I trembled and he slipped a long finger into my panties and inside me, then drawing it out and painting a circle around the sensitized flesh at my center.

I closed my eyes against the sight of myself like this—my breasts out, my legs open and bare, the dress hiked up and pushed down—the sensations too much. "Oh God, I'm going to—I'm going to—"

He withdrew his finger immediately and pulled my underwear off, halting the coming crisis. I was so close, and we'd just started, but this is what he did to me. I was always so ready. All he had to do was look at me and I wanted it, him.

I heard him release his zipper and my sex clenched, aching, needful. The rustle of fabric preceded the sound of his pants falling to the floor. Then a pause. I didn't open my eyes, but I knew he was rolling on a condom. A second later, he pressed his erection against me and stroked, making me pant and gasp, my fingers flex for purchase, my toes curl again. I couldn't breathe, I wanted him so badly. But he didn't enter me.

"You're too close," he mumbled as though this information were a problem to solve.

Another pause.

I opened my eyes and found him standing between my spread legs, his eyes on my breasts trailing to where the dress was bunched around my middle and lower to where he held himself just above where I needed him.

His shirt was open, showing off the gorgeous hard planes of his chest and stomach and lower. My mouth watered at the sight. If he didn't take me soon . . . I opened my legs wider, an invitation. I *needed* him.

"Cletus. Please." I was on fire.

He licked his lips. "Turn."

"Turn?" I swallowed, my voice cracking, not sure I'd heard him right.

He was already moving me, hooking a hand behind my knee and tugging me down the countertop so I was on my feet again. He then turned me such that I was facing the counter instead of him. His knee spread my legs and he guided me forward before I could catch my breath. I lowered myself to my elbows, feeling thrilled and uncertain as a new ache pooled between my legs.

We'd never done it this way, him taking me from behind. We'd always faced each other. And, for some reason, not being able to see him or touch him—only feeling how he chose to touch me—ramped up my nerves anew and wound me tight.

I felt him shove my skirt higher, the cold air against my completely bared bottom and lower back just as I felt the thick, hard length of him push inside, opening me. I sucked in another gulp of air at the intrusion and closed my eyes, trying to hold myself away from the counter as he withdrew and then entered me again with a second quick thrust, again and again, his thighs making a slapping sound against the back of mine each time.

We groaned in chorus, and I could not believe what I was feeling. He was so *deep* and so *everywhere* and I was so *full*. The forcefulness of his movements rocked me forward and backward, making my breasts sway against the friction of the wooden countertop.

Instinctively, I tilted my bottom up, and the harsh sound he made followed by the raspy words "Good girl" sent a shiver of goose bumps racing over my exposed back and arms, pinpricks of delicious agony. In this position, my clitoris neglected, I felt like I'd always be just a hair's breadth from unraveling, and it was the most exquisitely painful, tortuous feeling, all anticipation and longing and wanting. I hurt and I suffered, and I could not get enough of it.

"Are you okay?" he growled, sounding like he spoke between clenched teeth.

I immediately and enthusiastically nodded, a breathless and sobbing "Yes" spilling out of my parched mouth. "It feels so . . ." I didn't know the word. I couldn't think.

Why the hell hadn't we done this before?

Why would he keep such a thing from me? After we were done, I was going to demand answers! I was going to—

"Oh my God!"

I think that was me who'd cried out because Cletus had reached around and slid a finger between my legs, circling then pushing that glorious little button and I was sent spiraling, falling as his movements grew harsher, lacking in rhythm or finesse, avaricious and wholly without his precious control.

He leaned forward, his other hand gripping my hip and pressing me down fully, the hard muscles of his stomach flexing against my bottom, his hips and thighs pushing and retreating inelegantly as I reflexively arched my back. My seemingly endless orgasm originated from some-where deep within my body, this new place he'd invaded and touched with each animalistic stroke. And it just went on and on.

He'd finished, I knew he had, but my body still shook, and I cried out. He seemed to understand what was happening because he brought me to a standing position and sucked my ear into his mouth, one hand rolling and tugging at my nipple while the other petted and stroked between my legs, prolonging each of the cresting waves.

I was out of breath like I'd run a marathon, my chest heaving, my legs—all my muscles, in fact—unsteady. And when the last of the tremors abated, Cletus seemed to understand this too. He lifted me into his arms, holding me tight, close. My cheek pressed to the space over his thundering heart, I felt the rapid rise and fall of his chest as he also fought for air.

"I . . ." I started, but would never finish the thought because I had none. I had no thoughts. My brain had been wiped completely clean. I wasn't even sure who I was anymore.

"Shh." He kissed my forehead, leaned his hip against the counter and held me tighter. "Just . . . take a minute."

So I did, and in that minute I had my first thought, *This is what people mean by "mind-blowing sex."*

I thought we'd had mind-blowing sex before, but I'd been mistaken. This was *it.* Don't get me wrong, we'd had some amazing sex, lots of sweet, wonderful, lovely sex. I'd loved everything we'd ever done, obvi-ously. If I hadn't loved it so much, then why else would I always be ready for my next dose? My next hit of Cletus?

But this? *Chef's kiss.* This was the Michelin-four-star rating of making love.

Then I had a second thought, *That wasn't making love.*

Then I had a third thought, *If my appetite has been insatiable up to now, what's it going to be after this? Am I doomed to be a Cletus sex addict?*

. . . I could think of worse things.

"Jenn." Cletus whispered my name against my hair. "As much as it pains me to say it, we need to get back to the party."

As though fate wished to punctuate this, the lights over the sink turned off. After closing, they were set on a timer, partially to save on electricity and partially to discourage baking after hours, like I used to do all the time. We both chuckled at the kitchen-light fairies basically kicking us out, and I nodded, still winded.

My words sounded breathless. "You're right, let's clean up."

I wiggled, and he set me down on the countertop. Cletus, kissing my lips and cheek, inspected me for a moment as though ensuring I was steady enough to hold myself upright. Apparently convinced, he pulled up his pants and turned, walking in the direction of the bathroom at the back. He completely disappeared for a moment, and I gingerly hopped off the counter, easing my weight to my feet still encased in high heels, and I winced—but just a little bit.

I was sore. Between my legs. That hadn't happened since the first time we'd been together. Righting the straps of the dress first while I searched the darkness for my underwear, I couldn't help but replay our encounter, not knowing how to feel.

Did we really just do that? Had I just pulled up my dress, bent over, and spread my legs in the place where I work?

"Here." Cletus suddenly appeared, looking devilishly handsome in the dim light and seemingly all put back together—like we'd been in here holding hands instead of. . . *ANYWAY.*

He held out my underwear. His eyes were bright even in shadow, and I could see they were half-lidded as they lazily trailed over me. He looked at me like he was hungry, and I was dinner. Despite all the encore orgasms I'd just had, the effect hit me right between my legs.

I wondered what he was thinking, watching as he licked his bottom lip and drew it into his mouth. Was he just as insatiable for me? And if so, was he okay with that?

Tearing my eyes away, I pulled on the lace and fixed my skirt, telling my body to settle down. We were getting married for hootenanny's sake!

Cletus cocked his head to the side while I smoothed my hands down the red fabric, working to get a hold of all this raging *want* always coursing through my veins whenever he was near. Maybe it was because he was my first, and I guess, my only. Was that why I felt so crazed for him all the time?

"Miraculous," he said.

I surmised he meant the dress. "Right? The wrinkles are hidden, if there are any. It's 'cause they ruched the outer fabric at the seams, see?" I turned to the side to show him the seam, and he stepped forward as though he were going to investigate.

Instead, his hands cupped my face and tilted my chin back. He stared at me with a vibrant intensity I felt all the way to my fingertips. "No, Jenn. Not the dress. You." Cletus gave me a soft kiss, ending it by gently nipping my bottom lip. "You are my miracle."

I sighed. And I smiled. And I felt like I was walking on a cloud instead of in four-inch heels, which was also probably something of a miracle. "You say the sweetest things."

"I think you mean, I say the truest things."

I laughed, and he kissed my forehead. He held me there, in the dark with his lips pressed to my forehead. "I love you so completely, with every cell in my body. I wonder sometimes if I'd cease to exist—just evaporate or disappear—if anything ever happened to you."

"No." I anchored my hands to his wrists and squeezed. "Don't think like that. We've got our whole lives in front of us. There's nothing anyone can—"

Three bangs in quick succession pierced the quiet moment, and not a second later Cletus had me on the ground beneath him, covering my back with his body.

"Gunshots," he whispered in my ear. "From the parking lot. Don't move."

CHAPTER FOUR

JENN

"Violence is the last refuge of the incompetent."

— ISAAC ASIMOV, *FOUNDATION*

I didn't move.

The spike of adrenaline fierce and sudden sent blood whooshing between my ears as they strained, listening, waiting. I could barely see a thing, and perhaps that only served to heighten my other senses, because I did hear shouts and screams coming from the direction of the barn.

Oh no!

God, please. Let everyone be okay.

I felt Cletus's muscles beneath my hands start to relax and he leaned to my ear, whispering, "We shouldn't leave yet. I'll text Ashley, make sure everyone is—"

Another shot, two, three, four, and I bit my lip to keep from screaming because these came in through the back kitchen window, glass raining down around the kitchen island. More screams from the barn, still far away from where we were, trapped.

"Shit." Cletus squeezed me tighter. As soon as the gunfire stopped, he grabbed my hand and let the rest of me go. "Stay low," he ordered, pulling me after him to the big pantry.

We'd had a break-in over the summer, and they'd cleaned out our truffle oils, saffron, salts, freeze-dried strawberries, and anything else gourmet or hard to find. Therefore, the pantry now had a steel door which we kept locked during non-baking hours where all the nonperishable expensive food items were kept, along with the flours and sugars and such.

With steady hands, Cletus unlocked the door and pulled it open, pushing me inside. A second later, he followed. Instead of shutting the door like I assumed he would, he left it ajar just a few inches. I moved to stand, and he grabbed my wrist, pulling me back down.

"No, don't stand. But take off your shoes, in case we have to run."

Dumbly, I nodded and crouched again, then tried to do as he instructed but my hands were shaking too much. The only light coming in was from the crack in the door, and Cletus's body blotted most of it out. I couldn't see in the dark to untie the fastener. I was about to admit as much when the audible and recognizable sound of the bakery shop bell, jingling as someone entered, strangled the words in my throat.

Cletus held perfectly still and was so quiet, I couldn't hear him breathe. But I did hear footsteps—multiple people's footsteps—the squeak of soles against the floor. Forcing my breath to slow, I closed my eyes, listened, and prayed.

God, save us. God, protect us. And God, if one of those people out there is my father intending to do us harm, please strike him dead.

I wished Billy hadn't held Cletus back from my father at the party. Assuming this person creeping out there now was my father and he'd been the one who'd shot into the bakery, if Cletus had been allowed to punch him in the face and send him to the hospital, we wouldn't be hiding in the pantry right now.

I've learned my lesson, Lord. Even the Bible has smiting in the Old Testament. Violence might not be "the" answer. But clearly, it's "an" answer from time to time.

The sound of cabinets opening and closing made me jump. Someone cursed, a distinctly male voice. One of the intruders turned on a faucet, at the main sink from the sound of how far away it was. The water ran and my heart—which had already been put through its paces for the night—sped as another set of footsteps came closer to the pantry.

Forcing my eyes open, I peered at the outline of Cletus crouched in front of the cracked door, sparse light coming in through the opening. I couldn't really see anything else, but I wondered what or who Cletus could see. I swallowed the urge to ask, or to reach for him, or to do anything other than hold perfectly still and be frustrated.

Then someone banged on the back kitchen door, and I just about jumped out of my skin. Cletus reached for me and held one of my hands while I covered my mouth with the other.

"Who's in there? Open up! It's the police!" Jackson's voice boomed from the outside and that sent the kitchen invaders running, heavy footfalls and then the jingle of the bell over the front door marking their exit.

"Who's at the front?" we heard Jackson ask and another voice yelled something I didn't understand. Then Jackson ordered, "Well go around then, go get him. I'll go this way."

In the next moment, Cletus turned and wrapped me in a hug, pulling my body flush against his and stroking my hair as he kissed my shoulder, neck, and face. "Are you okay?"

I nodded because I couldn't speak.

"You did great. You did so great."

He kept kissing me while I held him and gulped for air, not caring if my nails dug into or even tore his shirt. One of his arms held on as he shifted and pulled something from his back pocket. The phone screen woke, and I could see right away he had a ton of missed calls and unread messages, a fact confirmed when he navigated to his texts. Most were from within the last five minutes.

Billy: We heard gunshots. Is Jenn with you? Where are you?

Ashley: Please tell me y'all are okay. We just heard gunshots and the sheriff, Jackson, Boone, and Dale left to go check it out. Chris is still here keeping everyone calm.

Beau: If Shelly calls will you actually answer your phone?

Shelly: Pick up your phone if you're not dead or having sex.

But there were also two older texts, one from Jethro and another from my mother, both sent about twenty minutes ago,

Jethro: Roscoe and I are about to leave with two of your suits. He likes the gray, but I think you want to wear the black, so we're bringing both. Do you need anything else from the house?

Diane: I'm assuming you and Jenn are off somewhere together. Would you please ask my daughter to return to her party? Folks are starting to ask where she is and tonight has been embarrassing enough without covering for y'all. I'm pretty sure she doesn't have her phone, which is why I'm texting you.

I'd left my phone in the lodge's honeymoon cabin where my mother and I had changed out of our work clothes and got ready for the party. This dress, though I loved it, had no pockets, and I didn't want to carry a purse.

The messages disappeared as an incoming call from Billy changed the screen to mostly black. I stared at his phone just before he brought it to his ear, realizing it hadn't made a single sound or seemed to vibrate. Cletus must've set his notifications to silent.

"Cletus. Is Jenn with you?" Billy sounded very concerned.

"Yes," I said, no longer needing to whisper.

"Thank God. Are y'all all right? Did you hear the shots? Where are you?"

"I'm going to answer in reverse. We're in the bakery kitchen pantry, we heard the shots, we're all right. Are y'all okay? We heard screams coming from the barn."

"Yes. Everyone here is fine for the most part, just a little shaken up. The screams were in response to the sound of gunshots. Some folks took off, running out the doors, but almost everyone stayed."

"Did they find the shooter?"

"Not to my knowledge, and I'm standing next to the sheriff right now."

"Billy, listen for a sec. I need you to tell the sheriff where Jenn and I are."

"Okay."

"Furthermore, I want you to tell him we've been inside the kitchen the whole time and saw the—the guys who came in and left."

My eyes widened with surprise. It hadn't been pitch-black, but it had been dark in the main kitchen after the timer flipped the sink lights off. Then again, Cletus always had been able to see fairly well in the dark.

"What? What are you talking about? Who came into the bakery?"

From the other side of the line we heard the sheriff bark, "Bakery? Where is Cletus?"

"Just tell the sheriff to meet us here—specifically in the pantry—but don't tell anyone else. Just him. We'll wait."

"You're going to wait inside the pantry?" Billy asked.

"He's in the pantry?" The sheriff's voice emerged muffled.

"Yep," Cletus answered. "We'll wait here."

"Roger that. Talk soon."

As soon as Cletus hung up, I grabbed his forearm. "Who was it? Who came into the kitchen?"

I felt his stare on me for a long moment before he finally said, "It was two people, but the only one I saw best looked like it might be, uh, Roger Gangersworth."

I reared back and almost fell on my backside. Roger? Gosh, that . . . well, that made no sense. Sure, he hadn't been pleased when I won the state fair again this year—and he ended up with pie in the face, although it had been an accident—but I'd won every year and he'd never shot up the bakery during a party before.

Cletus reached for me and helped me find my balance. "Are you still in those shoes?"

"I'm sorry, I can't see." As gracefully as possible, I leaned back to sit on the floor. "And these straps are tied with a double knot."

"Here—" Cletus remained crouching and reached for my ankle, guiding it to his knee "—I'll do it, I can see well enough."

"But do I need to take them off still? There's glass on the floor out there."

I felt his fingers already working on my leg. "Yes. The shooter is still out there."

"You mean Roger is still out there?"

PENNY REID

Cletus released a restless-sounding breath, like my question flustered him. "I doubt Roger was the shooter."

I agreed, but I pressed, "Then why was he in here? And what was he looking for in the cabinets? And why did he use the sink? And why did he run when Jackson came to the back door?"

"I don't know. Yet. But I'll carry you over the glass when we have to leave, one way or the other. And if you have the shoes off, you can run easier once we're outside." He finished with one shoe and gently set my newly bared foot down, reaching for the other.

Cletus worked for a bit in silence, and in the silence I allowed my mind to drift, which was a mistake. The scary reality of what had just happened, what was still happening until the shooter—and Roger—were caught, attacked my conscious, gathered and built like a swarming ant hill, and I inhaled an unsteady breath. Even though it was still quite dark and I could barely see, I closed my eyes so I could concentrate on pushing the overwhelming thoughts and feelings away.

I couldn't think about it, not yet. It wasn't over. We were still hiding. No one was safe. I had to focus and stay calm. So I did my best to shut the door in my mind on fear. Growing up like I did, I'd learned how to shut doors in my mind on all sorts of things: unpleasantness, hurt feelings, expectations, wants, desires, hopes, dreams. I'd grown up sheltered, but at compartmentalizing emotions in the moment, I was an old pro.

However, once the evening was over and Cletus and I were home, safe, and in each other's arms with the alarm on and the safety of our panic room just steps away, I was going to open the door and cry my eyes out.

To distract myself from the wave of doom that continued to press against the door in my mind, I broke the silence to ask, "Did you set your phone to silent?"

Cletus must've really been concentrating on my shoe because he flinched a little when I spoke, like the sound of my hushed voice startled him. Or maybe he was still on high alert. "Pardon?"

"Your phone, you set it to silent. All those messages and calls, and it didn't even vibrate while we were hiding in the pantry."

I felt the lace loosen but Cletus didn't give me my foot back,

48

instead he kept it on his lap and held my calf, rubbing circles on my skin with his thumb. "Oh. That's right. I set it to silent when I'm with you."

"What? Why?"

"Well, I don't want to indulge my family by being reachable all the time, they might start taking me for granted."

I breathed out a little laugh tinged with the nerves I was trying to suppress. "When did that start? Your phone used to vibrate when we were together."

"I reckon . . ." He paused, and the thumbs on my calf halted their circles. "Do you hear that?"

My heart jumped to my throat and Cletus gave my leg back, pivoting toward the crack in the pantry door. Not a second later, the bell to the bakery jingled and I resumed my crouching stance, pushing the shoes to the side so I wouldn't trip over them if I had to run out of here. But also positioning them next to me in case I had to use the spiked heel as a weapon.

Cletus's hand connected with my knee and he squeezed. "Don't make a sound." The words barely audible as the unmistakable sound of footsteps—multiple people's footsteps—marched from the front bakery to the back kitchen. Déjà vu.

Someone flipped on a light. "Cletus, it's us. Come out."

I heaved out a breath at the sound of Jackson's voice, relief flooding through me.

But Cletus pressed me further back and against the shelves. "Who is *us*? 'Cause I only see you."

"Me and Boone." Jackson's voice was still some distance away, like he stood by the doorframe from the bakery shop leading into the kitchen.

I felt Cletus hesitate, I felt it in the tensing, relaxing, and tensing of his muscles. "I told the sheriff just him."

"Yes, we know. But on the way here we stumbled across Elena Wilkinson's body, and he's dealing with . . . that."

"Elena?" I squeaked and was speaking before I could catch the question, "Is she okay? Was she shot?"

"We can't say." This statement came from Boone and was firm.

"Now y'all need to come out and keep your hands where we can see them."

"Oh good Lord," Cletus mumbled, and from the way he said the words I knew he'd paired them with an eye roll. "Fine. I'm coming out. But until y'all put those guns away, Jenn is staying inside the pantry."

"No, you're both coming out," Boone ordered.

"No. *I'm* coming out." Cletus pushed the pantry door open and lifted up his arms, and for some reason I felt like someone was both strangling me and sitting on my chest.

Clearly, Boone didn't trust us. *Boone!* If Boone didn't trust us, then could we trust him? What the hell was going on?

"Wait—" I whispered, trying to catch Cletus's shirt before he left. Just like earlier in the barn, it was too late.

I watched with a strange mounting terror as he stepped further into the room and out of my sight. "Now y'all want to tell me what—other than some crazy person shooting into the bakery—has you on edge?" Cletus demanded, sounding like he was near a fit.

"How long have y'all been in here?" Jackson asked, his tone appearing to be much calmer than Boone's, and I resisted the urge to peek out the door so I could see if they'd lowered their weapons.

"After the sheriff escorted Kip, Elena, and Diane out of the barn, Jenn and I took a moment."

"A moment? You've been gone for over an hour." Boone's statement was accusatory. "What were y'all doing?"

I covered my face, bracing myself for Cletus's answer, and he certainly seemed to be debating it.

"Well?" Boone demanded.

More silence from Cletus.

I heard the distinct sound of clicking metal. "Cletus, if you don't answer the question, I'm going to have to arrest you."

"We were having sex!" I shouted, coming out of the pantry with my hands up and finding both officers with their guns pointed at Cletus. A pair of handcuffs swung from Boone's other hand.

They gaped at me and, as absurd as it was, I felt my cheeks heat with embarrassment. But it was too late for modesty now.

"Okay? We were having sex. Right there, on the counter. If you need evidence, Cletus left the condom in the bathroom," I said tartly, letting my hands drop and gestured to the kitchen island. "We came in here, I cleaned up the scratches on Cletus's face, we talked, we had sex, we talked some more, and we were on our way back to the party when we heard the first set of shots. Cletus pushed me to the ground. Are you happy now?"

Both Jackson and Boone had lowered their guns as I spoke, and when I finished, Jackson's stare shifted to Cletus as he mumbled something like, "Not as happy as y'all, clearly."

Cletus had lowered his hands and now held one of mine. While I related events, he simply stood silent. I snuck a quick look at him and found his eyes apologetic, his jaw in a dour line.

Rolling my eyes—at myself, because I was still blushing—I squeezed Cletus's hand to communicate that I was okay and addressed Boone and Jackson. "Now it's your turn. Why would y'all come in here with your guns drawn? What the heck is going on, Boone? We were hiding in that pantry, scared out of our wits after someone shot the windows out, and you're treating us like criminals."

Boone frowned, clearly remorseful, but there was still something about the set of his mouth and how he hadn't stopped inspecting us since I emerged from the pantry, like he was looking for a lie.

"Jenn, you may want to—uh—sit down." Jackson holstered his weapon, his tone bracing and gentle.

I stepped closer to Cletus. "What? Why?" I searched their faces. "What happened? Is—is my momma okay? What happened to Elena? Was that—"

"It's your father." Boone re-hooked his handcuffs to someplace hidden, but he didn't put away his gun.

"What? Did he hurt someone? Was he the shooter?"

Boone seemed to be readying himself for something, watching me with a scrutinizing intensity, and said, "He's dead."

CHAPTER FIVE
CLETUS

"Police work wouldn't be possible without coffee," Wallander said.

"No work would be possible without coffee."

They pondered the importance of coffee in silence.

— HENNING MANKELL, *ONE STEP BEHIND*

I hadn't thought about killing Kip Sylvester as often as I thought about murdering my own father. However, over the past year, the man had taken Razor Denning's place as a close second on my *To Murder* list. Discovering that someone else had beat me to the deed filled me with a strange, chaotic assortment of feelings.

Also inspiring chaos? The lie I'd told Jenn back in the pantry. The person I saw in the kitchen had not been Roger Gangersworth.

After the debacle in the bakery with Boone and Jackson, I'd carried Jenn out of the building, and she'd carried her shoes. She didn't say much. Her eyes had gone cloudy, distant. Jenn was in shock, and I was not surprised. I mired and marinated in a fair bit of shock myself. Everyone present in the fancy faux-barn for the evening's events seemed to suffer from various levels of shock as well. Except, unlike everyone else, Jenn had just lost her father and her mother was nowhere in sight.

Presently, we were in the fancy faux-barn, but before we'd left the kitchen, I'd snuck a peek at the sink. Traces of red liquid pooled around the drain.

Hmm. . . That wasn't good.

Boone and Jackson had asked for our consent to swab our hands and the front of our clothes—I assumed for gunpowder residue—and "requested" we return to the barn on the sheriff's orders. Everyone was to stay on site at the lodge—specifically here, in the barn—until questioned and whereabouts during the murder were accounted for. Meaning, they wanted everyone's alibi.

Jenn and I had been swarmed upon our return. Shelly, Beau, Billy, Sienna, Jethro, Drew, and Roscoe encircled us, creating a barrier between Jenn and the rest of the guests. They'd obviously heard about Kip's death. To my family's credit, they didn't ask her a single question.

Sienna had pulled Jenn into an embrace and held her. She and Jethro had then distracted Jenn with light and silly banter, observations about wood floors, condiments, and ordering coffee in different countries. Shelly and Drew stood guard, keeping other folks at bay. Beau and Roscoe put their lethal levels of charm to work, intercepting anyone who approached and redirecting attention elsewhere.

Ashley, it had been explained to me, was off with Elena Wilkinson, tending to the woman's injuries, whatever they were. We'd heard an ambulance pull up just after leaving the bakery, I'd assumed it was for Elena.

During all this, I endeavored to contemplate the present fiasco and what I knew about it as well as the facts I hadn't shared with anyone.

I knew: Kip was dead. Elena was incapacitated at least. Jackson and Boone had suspected me and Jenn for one or both of the crimes.

Facts I hadn't shared: The first in the pair of people I'd seen in the kitchen had been a motorcycle brother of my father's who went by the name of Repo. The other, the woman with him, had been none other than Jenn's mother. Neither Repo nor Diane were presently in the barn. I felt certain this was the case since I'd been scanning the space for their faces since we'd entered.

And, last but not least, Diane had been cleaning either red food dye, cherry pie filling, or blood off her hands in the bakery kitchen sink.

"Hey. I need to talk to you." Jackson James materialized before me, redirecting my attention outward. He lifted his chin toward Billy. "You too. Both of you, come with me."

I glanced behind me at Jenn. Her eyes were cloudy, her expression detached, and I swallowed around a discomfiting tightness at the base of my throat. But I also saw that Sienna and Jethro seemed to be doing a good job of keeping her distracted.

As such, I followed Billy and Jackson out of the barn. The blond deputy led us along the outside wall and around the corner. He then turned, his hands on his hips, his expression stern under the cloudless night of a waxing moon and bright stars.

"Let me fill y'all in, then we need to compare notes," he said, in a very uncharacteristic display of getting right to the point. "Elena was knocked out, but she seems to be okay. We don't know what or who knocked her out, and she's not speaking to us. She said she wants her lawyer present. So we don't know if Kip was with her when she was knocked out or why they were back here after being escorted to their car earlier and told to leave."

"Y'all escorted Kip and Elena to their car?" I asked. Since Jenn and I left for the bakery, I didn't know what the resolution had been with the Kip and Elena showing up uninvited situation.

"Yes," Billy answered hurriedly. "The sheriff pulled us out of the barn, gave Kip and Elena a talking to, then had Evans and Jackson escort them to their car."

"And I watched them drive away," Jackson added. "So I know they left."

"What about you Billy? What about Boone, the sheriff, and Ms. Donner? Diane? Did she go back to the barn?" I successfully modulated my voice to the frequency of mildly curious.

"We all went back to the barn."

I nodded, absorbing Billy's information. "And all y'all stayed put?" I'd been holding out hope that the blonde woman wearing a red dress in the kitchen with Repo hadn't been Diane. Based on Billy's statement, maybe my eyes had been playing tricks? . . . *Unlikely.*

Jackson and Billy swapped a look before turning narrowed eyes on me. "I remained in the barn until the shots were fired." Jackson looked to Billy.

"So did I." Billy's hands came to his hips, mimicking Jackson's posture. "So did the sheriff. He was there issuing orders right after the first few shots then took off."

Jackson blinked, glancing over my head. "I don't know if Ms. Donner was still there, though."

Time to change the subject. "Okay, so shots fired. What happened after that? Other than mass hysteria at the barn."

"Evans stayed and kept folks calm while my dad, Boone, and I ran toward the parking lot by the bakery—'cause that's where the shots sounded like they were coming from. Then we heard another round and stopped, ducking behind those big azalea bushes halfway between the barn and the bakery. When nothing else happened, we ran to the parking lot and checked the cars." Jackson paused here, his jaw ticking, his eyes narrowing. "That's when I spotted Mr. Sylvester's car in the lot."

"So Kip and Elena left and came back," I said, voicing the obvious.

"Yep. And this time they parked at the bakery, not the main lot. And when I got to the car—" Jackson drew in a shaky breath "—there was a lot of blood. He was sitting in the driver's seat and the window looked like it had been shot out. I checked for a pulse. There was none."

"And Elena?"

"She wasn't there. Boone said he heard something, a bell from some-where. My dad told us to go check it out while he phoned in to the station. Boone and I went to the back of the bakery first, and I thought I saw someone moving around inside in the kitchen, so I banged on the door."

"We heard you banging. We were in the pantry, though. I couldn't get to the back door without alerting the—uh—prowler in the kitchen."

"Did you see them? Who was inside with y'all?" Jackson shifted on his feet, restless.

I frowned, breathing out, and working through how to answer

without lying. "It was dark. The lights were off and, like I said, we were already in the pantry, visibility reduced."

Jackson nodded grimly. "I figured as much."

"What did you see?" I asked Jackson, readying myself for the very real possibility that Jackson and Boone had seen Diane.

Maybe she was their number one suspect. Maybe this was the real reason Jackson had pulled me and Billy outside. If this was the case, I needed to come up with a plan to protect Jenn from the fallout ASAP.

I knew my shock would be shorter lived than hers, it might not even last a full day. I knew this for a fact. For one thing, I had a vengeful heart. She did not. For example, as mentioned previously, I often thought about the death of my own father, and how I would exact that revenge.

Not many people were aware that I had the means and opportunity to end his life any time I wanted, whenever the mood struck, even now that he'd been paroled. Furthermore, no one but me knew I'd toyed with making it happen on the anniversary of my mother's death. But then a short woman baker blackmailed me, distracted me, and changed my life and my heart forever with a dark chocolate confection she'd called *compassion cake*.

I never made the call that day. Darrell continued to breathe because last year, under Jenn's continued influence, I'd decided to hold off indefinitely, an active decision based on something she'd once said about my past being in the past, that I got to choose the road I was on in the future as well as who I shared that road with.

But I digress.

Another difference between the two of us contributing to the likelihood of her experiencing prolonged shock: I'd been witness to violence on many occasions during my formative years. She had not. At least, not the severity of violence I'd experienced. Her parents had been wicked to her growing up, using hurtful words, and that was definitely a type of violence. But what I'd seen . . .

Again, I digress.

Presently, Jackson hemmed and hawed, heaved a giant sigh, and finally answered my question. "I didn't see much. We heard them coming out of the bakery's front door when that bell jingled again.

Boone was around the side of the building from where I was, but he wasn't near the entrance. We took off, running like hell for the front door, but it was too late. We saw two figures enter the north forest line and we gave chase. But that's when we found Elena."

"Elena was—"

"Wait—" I lifted my hand to interrupt Billy. "Wait, before we get to Elena, are you sure you saw two people?"

"There were definitely two of them, Boone will back me up on that. A woman and a man."

"Is that why you and Boone were on high alert when you came into the kitchen?"

Jackson gave me a tight-lipped—some might even call it apologetic —smile. "Yeah, sorry about that. You kinda fit the description of what we could see. A woman and a man, about y'all's height and build."

I lifted my chin, both acknowledging and absorbing this information. *Damn.*

"May I ask about Elena now?" Billy looked to me. I shrugged, having no idea of Elena's whereabouts when she was found. "So Elena was the body in the woods?"

"Yep. She was unconscious. I tripped over her, went flying, tore my suit." Jackson laughed lightly. "Anyway, important part is, whoever ran out of the bakery, they got away from us. Boone didn't know what had happened when I tripped, thought I'd done myself harm, so he came back, and they were long gone. I then called my dad, let him know about Elena."

"I think I was with your dad then, in the parking lot." Billy pointed at me with his thumb. "Right after you hung up with me, delaying the sheriff from meeting Jackson and Boone in the woods. He heard my call with Cletus. After that, he left me with—uh—with Kip's car and went to find you in the forest."

Good thing Billy hadn't been asked to accompany the sheriff into the forest, he'd likely still be in there wandering around, seeing as how he could get lost in a rose garden with three bushes.

"Yes, but my dad called me after he left you in the parking lot, on his way to meet us. He told Boone and I to go back to the bakery. He was the

PENNY REID

one who stayed with Elena while we went—going in through the front door this time—for Cletus and Jenn."

"Why didn't he just go to the bakery himself? I'd asked for him to come meet us, not y'all." I crossed my arms, not understanding the sheriff's motives.

Jackson gave me a very small smile without humor. "Do I know? My father does what he thinks makes sense."

"My guess is that he wanted to be with Elena when she woke up." Billy scratched his cheek through his beard. "If she woke up, he wanted to be the one with her, to get answers, while she was still disoriented and would answer honestly. That'd be my guess."

"Seems like a sneaky thing to do." I stroked my beard, nodding my appreciation for the sheriff's tactics, if that had indeed been his aim.

"More like shrewd, Cletus," Billy corrected. "The sheriff isn't sneaky, and he isn't a fool."

"No. He is not a fool. . ." I agreed, hiding a spike of alarm. If Jenn's momma had been involved in her ex's death, Sheriff James would find out.

"But listen." Jackson glanced over his shoulder and lowered his voice, pulling me out of my maudlin thoughts. "That's the timeline, yes. But what folks don't know yet is that when I found Kip in the car, he had a thick wire or a kind of metal rope around his neck. I had to nudge it out of the way to check for a pulse."

"Like a chain?" I asked.

"No. No, it was a heavy rope. Hard to explain without showing you."

"So . . ." Billy's confused stare swung from Jackson, to me, and then back to the deputy. "He wasn't shot?"

"No. He was definitely shot. Like I said, there was *a lot* of blood. But it looks like he was also strangled in his seat."

"Before or after he was shot?" Billy asked inanely. He was having trouble keeping up, and so was I, not because we were dumb, but because none of this made a lick of sense.

The man had been strangled and shot? Which had Diane done? Not the shooting, I was sure of that. Plus, shooting someone usually didn't require a rinse off in the kitchen sink. *Strangling someone didn't require a wash off in the kitchen sink either.*

I was all muddled. What had Repo and Diane been doing in the kitchen? Why did she have blood on her hands?

"Someone strangled him first . . ." I spoke stream of consciousness, working through how it must've happened. "Whoever it was, they left the rope."

"Why would they leave the rope?" Jackson asked the question like this detail bothered him. "Rope is evidence. Why leave evidence?"

"Maybe whoever strangled him was in a hurry?" Billy proposed.

"Or the shooter came up to the car and the person who was doing the strangling hid in the back seat, caught unawares mid-strangle? Before they could remove the rope. The shooter blasts out the window, puts two bullets in Kip, and then leaves. Meanwhile, the strangler—as I said, caught unawares—gets the hell out of there, forgetting to take the rope," I postulated.

"Unless the strangler and shooter were working together?" Jackson made a face like he found all this thinking too strenuous for his meager brain.

I made a face. "Then they would've taken the rope, right? And why strangle *and* shoot someone? One or the other is plenty."

"Okay, yeah. That's what I was thinking too." Jackson nodded with vigor. "And there's more."

"More?" Billy and I asked in unison.

"Yep. I just left the parking lot to come find y'all. My father called in a team from Knoxville to handle the crime scene. Sorry for keeping everyone so long, but the Knoxville crew took forever to get here. We're not prepared for this kind of mess, don't have that kind of expertise or all the right equipment. The only dead bodies we find up here are motorcycle gang casualties, not former high school principals."

"What'd they find?" Billy leaned in.

"They don't know which killed him yet, the rope or the gun. But they did find handprints—bloody ones—on his cheek, chest, and the outside of the car."

"What does that mean?" I asked, because I had no theories.

"The investigator thinks someone, for whatever reason, opened the door after Mr. Sylvester was shot. They touched him where he was bleeding, touched his face. But the car door was closed when we showed up, so they must've closed the door after."

I shook my head. "Why would someone . . ." *Oh!*

Diane.

Damnation and all the demons in hell! She'd touched him. I dropped my chin to my chest as though tired, but in reality I needed to hide my face so I could think.

Diane touched Kip. That's why she'd been in the bakery kitchen. That's why she'd washed her hands in the sink while Repo was searching the cabinets. *Maybe he was looking for a towel to dry off her hands?*

I pushed the irrelevant suspicion away. It didn't matter if he was looking for a towel or dinosaur bones. What mattered was that Diane had touched Kip after he died.

"I need y'alls help." Now Jackson leaned in, his brow wrinkled in consternation. "I need you and your brothers to look at everyone's hands. Search the tables for a missing napkin, something someone could use to wipe their hands clean."

"Hoping to catch someone red-handed?" Billy asked in a very un-Billy-like attempt at pun humor, earning him a squinty look from both Jackson and me.

"Really, Billy?" I shook my head. My steady and cool older brother had a history of being awkward or downright stupid at the weirdest of times, usually during a crisis or when he felt uncertain. I supposed I couldn't fault him too much. Stress and anxiety were like the stormwater runoff of mental health issues. If ignored over time, they carved away at even the sturdiest and strongest.

I turned to Jackson, stroking my beard again. "Why us? Why do you want our help?"

"Because I know where all of you were before, during, and after the shooting. And I trust your family. And I already checked all y'all's hands."

"Fine. We'll help." Billy adjusted the cuffs of his suit, a nervous gesture. I wanted to give him the side-eye, but I refrained since Jackson was still with us and watching.

"Okay, let's go," Jackson said, walking around us to head back to the barn.

My brother and I followed, shoulder to shoulder, and I tried not to dwell too much on what Billy would have to be nervous about. It wasn't hard to redirect my thoughts since I already knew—or strongly suspected —who had touched Kip after he'd been shot.

Given what I knew as of now, Diane must've washed her hands and ran off with Repo into the woods.

She'd been there.

And that meant she probably knew who'd done it.

CHAPTER SIX

CLETUS

"The most difficult kind of strength -- restraint."

— RICK RIORDAN, *THE BLOOD OF OLYMPUS*

I'd resisted the urge to ask Jenn if she was okay last night. Initially, I'd refrained while in the bakery kitchen after Boone broke the news about her father. Then I'd continued resisting the urge at the barn while half-heartedly pretending to inspect folks' hands for blood I knew I wouldn't find. Furthermore, I'd persisted in my resistance on the drive home, after everyone had been released by the police around 2:00 AM.

Ignoring this urge felt akin to ignoring a pant leg full of spiders, or a plate of my sausage left uneaten at a family picnic, or a special on blueberries down at the Piggly Wiggly.

I hadn't been able to sleep. Too much to process, too many unknowns and details that didn't fit together shoved my eyes open every time they'd drifted shut.

The first rays of sunlight peeked through the blinds in Jenn's bedroom. Sneaking another peek at her profile as she lay curled against my side, finally sleeping after tossing and turning for hours, I bit the inside of my lip and wrestled with the big question: When should I tell Jenn about seeing her momma in the bakery kitchen?

Jenn looked relaxed, peaceful. I knew her present slumber was neither. Last night, watching her when Boone had relayed the truth of her father's fate, she'd appeared to be genuinely grief-stricken. Watching her reaction, I suffered an uncanny glimmer of relief that I hadn't yet pulled the final lever to end my own father's existence.

I'd thought a lot about the moments leading up to Darrell's eventual demise. I'd assumed I would feel nothing but satisfaction after the fact, having rid the world of his evil influence; justice for all the wrongs he'd committed; the righteous gratification of recompense for all the ways he'd hurt my mother, my siblings, even my dog.

However, at no point had I considered the possibility that I would mourn him . . . *would I mourn him?* I didn't think so. But how could I know for sure? The last thing I wanted was the unintended residue left by emotional upheaval after Darrell's postmortem.

And yet I might feel something unexpected, something akin to what Jenn was feeling now.

Pushing the notion aside (for now) as likely irrelevant, I gently extracted myself from the bed, replacing my body with my pillow. Urgent matters required my full attention.

First thing I did was walk to the panic room just off the hallway and check the camera facing the driveway. Boone was still out there, sitting in his car, probably cramped, cold, cranky, and hungry. The sheriff had sent him home with us last night with orders to watch the road leading to Jenn's house. Sheriff James had said it was to keep an eye on Jenn, but I suspected the real reason was to keep an eye out for Diane.

Jenn's momma had been missing since the gunshots. Some folks claimed Diane had been present when they heard the shots, some folks said she'd slipped out just moments prior. Regardless, last I heard, no one had seen her since. Obviously, I hadn't shared what I knew with anyone. I needed answers first.

Pulling out one of the burner phones I kept stashed in the hidden safe within the panic room, I powered it on and moseyed to the kitchen. It was a Saturday. I didn't have work until Monday. Although there were leftover giant cranberry bran muffins on the counter, my mood dictated waffles. Blueberry waffles. *Let there be waffles!*

Breakfast decided, I texted my contact at the Dragon the following message:

Cletus: Owl to Burro. Call when time permits, this number. Need info on Repo's current time commitments. Urgent.

I then set about making coffee while contemplating the most pressing of this morning's questions. Namely, what in hellfire had Diane been doing last night with Repo—the Iron Wraiths' main money man and career criminal—of all people?

Washing blood off her hands? Okay. Sure. Perhaps she'd decided mid-party to butcher a side of beef. So be it.

Running from the police? Yeah. I could see that. Jackson could be irritating and perhaps the thought of his company struck her as odious. I'd about-faced and power walked in the opposite direction from the deputy more times than I could count.

But . . . Repo?

I couldn't fathom a scenario where Diane and Repo in each other's company wasn't a parallel universe kind of situation.

Coffee made and mixed, I filled a second cup for Boone—but without molasses and apple cider vinegar, 'cause most people just aren't as enlightened as me about their coffee—and pulled on a pair of pants. Grabbing his cup and one of the leftover muffins, I turned off the alarm and strolled out the front door.

Even though it had been mild last night, some folks might've found the spring morning cold, too cold for just a pair of pants and slippers. I was one of those people. It was damn cold, too cold for just a pair of pants and slippers. But my choice of attire had been purposeful. I didn't want Boone thinking I was available to loiter. Deliver coffee, a muffin, ask a few questions, and then I'd be on my way.

No mentally healthy person would be able to chitchat with a pair of cold, hard man nipples at their eye level.

Boone had already started rolling down his window before I reached the car. "Is that coffee?"

"Yes, sir. Also, this is a muffin, cran and bran."

"Did Jennifer make it?"

"Yep, yesterday morning."

He held his hands out to receive the goods, snatching them into the car and immediately taking a drink of coffee. "God bless you, Cletus Winston."

"Don't get carried away. How'd you fare?"

"It's cold out here," he said around a bite of muffin. "Sorry if I woke y'all up, turning the car on and off for the heater."

"You didn't. Jenn couldn't sleep, but it didn't have anything to do with you or your car." *Speaking of . . .* I lifted my chin toward the car. "How long you gonna be out here? Do you need to use the bathroom?"

"Uh, no. I'll be leaving soon. Williams is coming to relieve me. But thanks for the offer."

I scratched my cheek, nodding. He'd given me the information I'd been after; the sheriff wanted Jenn's house watched. They'd come and go in shifts until Diane was found, or until some undefined future event, or until the sheriff couldn't spare the deputies for the assignment.

"Well, all right then." I made a show of shivering. "I'm getting my ass back inside. It is cold."

"Tell Jenn I said thanks for the muffin."

"I will." I turned and lifted my hand, giving him a little wave.

I hadn't taken three steps before I heard Boone's radio click on and Flo McClure's voice say, "They found her, boys. Time to head home."

I stopped in my tracks.

"Roger that," Boone said, followed by a chorus of other voices acknowledging the order.

It only took me a split second to decide what to do. Glancing over my shoulder, I watched Boone set aside the coffee and the muffin. Then he turned the engine. I cleared my throat, making my way back to him and raising my voice over the hum of the car.

"I thought you said you were here 'til Williams arrived?"

"Oh, no. That was Flo with dispatch. We're all done." He gave me a tired and mostly flat smile. "But I guess you probably knew that?"

"How'd you mean?"

"Diane Donner."

"Yeah? What about her?"

Boone's eyebrows pulled together, and his eyes flicked over me in an inspection. "They found her. I thought you would know."

I allowed my actual and genuine surprise to show. "I did not. No one called us."

"Jenn's momma didn't call her? Last night or this morning?"

"Well, no. Jenn's phone is missing. And Diane didn't call me."

"Jenn's phone is missing? Since when?" Even in his exhausted state, this news seemed to perk him up.

I wrapped my arms around myself, shivering again to stall answering the question. The truth was the phone had been missing since last night. Apparently, Jenn had left it in the honeymoon cabin during the party. Since everyone she knew was going to be in the fancy faux-barn, she had no reason to bring it. Plus, it's not like her delightful red dress had a phone pocket.

But when the police had released everyone at 2:00 AM and we went to retrieve her things before driving home, her phone wasn't where she'd left it in the cabin. Her bag, wallet, clothes, and even her earrings were present and accounted for. But no phone.

"You know, I can't rightly say when she misplaced it." I shivered harder, backing away, and raising my voice. If he asked me something else, I would pretend I couldn't hear him, what with his car engine, the distance, and my slow brain. "Sorry. I didn't sleep much either, and it is damn cold out here. Maybe when I warm up my brain will work better." I said this last bit from the front porch, waving again as I backed into the house. "Well, see you later!"

With that I shut the door, and just in time too. The burner phone in my pocket buzzed.

Burro.

Jogging on the balls of my feet, I silently vamoosed to the kitchen and shivered for real. Once there, I skadoodled to the pantry, closed the pantry door—*Hmm. Hiding in pantries. Seems to be becoming a habit*—and answered the phone.

"What I really want to know is, does he have an old lady?" I launched right into it. Burro and I didn't exchange pleasantries. Ever.

"I wondered when you were going to find out." He chuckled, sounding pleased as a pig in pie. Or more precisely, like a donkey. He had this crazy laugh, like a *hee-haw*, even when he chuckled.

"You knew?"

"Of course."

I made a sound of disbelief, not catching it in time. "You knew and you didn't tell me?"

"That's not our arrangement. I answer all the questions you ask and none of the ones you don't."

That was our arrangement, mostly because Burro liked to talk, and I didn't always have time for his stories.

"Fine." I narrowed my eyes, frowning. No use schooling an expression he couldn't see. "Just to be sure we're both referring to the same person, who is Repo's woman?"

"Diane Donner."

"Fuck." I stopped myself just before hitting a bag of flour with my palm. How was this possible? How had I not known? How . . . many bags of flour did Jenn have in here?

Focus!

"How long?"

"Well, that's complicated." Burro still sounded gleeful. "The first time I saw them together was Christmas, over a year ago now. Believe it or not, she just showed up here, la-di-da. And in a miniskirt."

"Well, God bless her."

"Repo saw to that." He was chuckling again.

"Moving on. They've been together for over a year?" That didn't seem right. What else had I not noticed while I'd been pleasantly ensconced in *amor facit* with my fiancée?

If Diane and Repo had been together for over a year and I'd failed to notice? Then this was the intervention I required, the wake-up call. Mind you, I didn't plan to do a single thing about it. I would not change my current course of pleasurable actions for anything in the world, but at least I'd be prepared for the fact that I was no longer omniscient.

"No, they have not been together for over a year. And I kept an eye out, 'cause that was something worth knowing. I'd started to think it was a one-time thing, a fluke. No contact for a year, at least none that made it into my net. And then all of a sudden, as of the week after this past Christmas, they've been fucking around a lot."

I grimaced at his choice of words but remained on task. "Where do they meet?"

"One of the safe houses known only to the top brass, barely used."

"I can't see that going over well," I mumbled. Dammit. There I went, volunteering my thoughts again. What was wrong with me?

You haven't slept and you haven't had your coffee yet. You left it on the counter.

Oh. Well. That explained it.

"Repo has been diverting funds for upkeep recently. Had the interior painted two months ago I think, outside still looks like shit, though."

I opened the pantry door and peeked around the corner. Coast clear, I stepped out just long enough to grab my coffee. "Send me the address. And where is Repo now?"

"He's here. Walked in about an hour ago looking like the sole of my boot. I reckon he's sleeping now."

I swallowed a gulp of my now disappointingly tepid coffee. "I need to know where he was for the last—uh—twelve—no—fourteen hours. Where he was, how long he was there, in each place. Send everything to this phone. And I want to know when he leaves again and where he goes."

"Yes, sir."

"Thank you," I said. Burro may have been helping only because he owed me—big time—but I had no reason to take the man for granted. "I'll be in touch, different number next time, same area code."

"Wait, one more thing. Isaac Sylvester—Twilight—I think he found out last night, about his father."

I took another gulp of my coffee and swallowed before asking, "Why're you telling me? I didn't ask."

Isaac Sylvester could go die in a fire for all I cared. Jenn would be broken up about the death of her brother, but the guy was a piece of work. In my book, he was just as bad as his father.

"Well, I thought you should know, you being so close to the family. He's not a bad kid."

I grunted. Burro and I had two very different definitions for the word *bad*.

"Listen, Cletus. He was gone all night, and no one knows where he went."

"But you do."

"Of course I do. I checked when the news came over the scanner. He was at the lodge, or the vicinity. You know that slope on the north side through the forest? The dirt road through the trees? That's where he went. After a while, he left and went to y'all's place."

"Jenn's house?"

"No. The Winston homestead. Or, you know, around there. He parked at the abandoned convenience store, and so I figured he went on foot to your place, at least that's what his phone's locator says."

"Hmm." *Why would he be there?* "Where is he now?"

"Last I checked, still there."

I pondered that. Billy, Roscoe, Jethro, Sienna and baby Ben were all at the homestead. Isaac would have to be an idiot to attempt anything with three of my brothers there. Especially Billy. He'd beat the tar out of any Iron Wraith he found on the property.

Nevertheless, better to be safe than sorry. "But where specifically? How close to the house?"

"You know I can't be certain, but it looks like he's still in the forest, to the west."

"Okay. Thanks for the heads-up." I'd call Jethro and let him know. *Jethro is tired. Leave Jethro alone.*

Right. I'd call Beau and Shelly, let them know to head over and keep an eye out. Shelly was due for some baby-holding time in any case. I knew how much she loved holding babies (almost as much as me).

"Sucks, though. His dad dies and he can't, you know, be there for his sister, his momma." Burro, who wasn't prone to sympathy for anyone for any reason, surprised me.

Unsure what he expected me to say, I settled on, "That's the life you live. He chose it."

"Yeah, but . . . it's his dad."

"His dad was seagull guano left on a plastic trash island in the middle of the Pacific Ocean. No, actually, Kip was the plastic trash island. Guano has purpose."

Burro chuckled. "Sure. But the kid is gonna grieve."

"He shouldn't."

"Name a person alive who doesn't have a lot of feelings about their father."

Hmm. "Good point."

To my knowledge, there existed no handbook regarding suitable actions when one's fiancée has learned of their father's untimely demise on the evening of her engagement party. Nor, I suspected, did a resource exist that summarized appropriate methods for offering comfort when said fiancée's mother is hauled into the police station the morning after afore-mentioned father's untimely demise, to be questioned and without the ability to receive visitors.

This is all to say, Kip was exceedingly dead. Diane was somewhere in the police station being questioned. Jenn wasn't allowed to see her momma, and that seemed to make her sad.

And I didn't know what to do, so I made lists. I'd already made several mental lists to pass the time, one of which centered around things that needed to be done straightaway at the lodge. Someone needed to see about the logistics of continuing bakery operations with reduced capacity —Jenn wasn't going back to work anytime soon—and, given what I knew of Diane's whereabouts last night, I'd assumed she wouldn't be going back to work anytime soon either.

Out of the corner of my eye, I saw Jenn's chin wobble and she glanced down at her lap. A new tear fell, trailing down her cheek and upending the mental list I'd been working on. She dabbed at it with a tissue. I shifted in my seat to lean closer but was careful to ensure our hands stayed linked. Sensing someone watching me, I glanced up to the where Flo McClure sat behind her desk at the far side of the police station's waiting room and met the woman's dark brown gaze.

She gave me a tight-lipped smile. It did not reach her eyes.

"I don't even know what I'm thinking," Jenn whispered, drawing my attention back to her.

She hadn't said much this morning. I'd woken her up after alerting Beau and Shelly about a potential Iron Wraith camping out in the woods behind the house. I told them my sources said the Wraith was Isaac Sylvester but asked them to keep his identity from the folks at the homestead.

When I roused Jenn to tell her Diane had been found and was safe, I'd hoped Jenn would go back to sleep. Instead, she'd insisted on going down to the police station and seeing her mother for herself.

That had been hours ago. There'd been no Saturday waffles. We hadn't eaten breakfast. I was starting to worry about her blood sugar levels. If Diane didn't materialize from wherever they held her soon, I was going to call in an order at Daisy's and bribe Roscoe to pick it up and deliver it.

"I don't know or understand what I'm feeling." Her stare remained unfocused, forward and down.

I leaned in close, squeezing her hand. "If you need to talk about it, about anything, I hope you know you can talk to me. But I'm not going to push you to talk if you don't want to."

"I know." She nodded, wiping her nose with a tissue. Then, after inhaling a tremendous breath, she turned her head and faced me. "Cletus, I have to tell you something."

"Anything. Tell me anything." I cupped her jaw, not caring that Flo McClure might as well have been eating popcorn as she enjoyed the show. I swear, that woman.

"Last night, when we were in the pantry, hiding after the gunshots?" Her voice was so quiet, and I knew she didn't want anyone to overhear. Posey Lamont, Vanessa Romero, Jedediah Hill, Nikki Becker, and a few others from the party last night were scattered around the waiting room. They'd given us soft looks as we entered but hadn't approached.

I bent forward so she could talk directly into my ear. "Yes? What about it?"

"And Roger came in?" Her voice was more breath than sound. "I thought maybe my father had shot into the bakery and he was the intruder and I—I—"

"What? What is it?" I leaned away so I could see her face. My brow furrowed because she looked so darn sad. And guilty.

"I said a prayer." Her face crumpled, more tears leaking out of her eyes.

"That's okay. Saying prayers isn't—"

"No. I prayed that God would strike my father dead, and now he is!"

"Oh." *Oh no.*

Jenn nodded, clearly beside herself, and she sorta leaned, but mostly fell into me, pressing her face against my shoulder as her arms came around my neck. She sobbed.

I held her tightly, knowing that a single *Oh* wasn't going to suffice as a response to her confession. "There, there," I added, the words *clumsy* and *unhelpful.*

But, Lord help me, I had no idea how to respond. I thought about admitting that I'd also prayed for Kip Sylvester to be on the receiving end of a biblical smiting—more than once—but dismissed that idea right out of the gate.

"You know . . ." I paused, cleared my throat, thought for a bit, and tried yet again, "You know you're a good person, right?"

She cried harder.

Dammit.

I felt certain the internet was full of all sorts of information related to guilt, grief, and end of life issues. Yet I seriously doubted it contained anything remotely related to our present predicament. What I needed was something entitled, *How to support your fiancée as she tries to process the death of her evil bastard of a father who was found in the parking lot of her mother's hotel and realize she's not to blame for his being strangled then shot on the evening of her engagement party when he wasn't even invited.*

That's what I needed.

Maybe I'll write it.

"Uh, Cletus?" In an uncharacteristic display of tact, Flo McClure had approached us and gentled her voice to say my name.

I looked up without pulling out of Jenn's embrace. "Yes?"

"Diane is almost done. She'll be out in a sec."

"Thanks, Flo."

Jenn sniffled and pulled away, wiping at her eyes again. The tissue she used was more crumbles of lint than solid form. "Thanks, Flo," Jenn echoed.

"Oh, Jennifer. I'm so sorry," Flo said, surprising me. The woman was not usually one to offer comfort. At her most agreeable, she was saltier than a sardine.

"Thanks." Jenn grabbed her purse and pulled the strap to her shoulder as she stood.

"That must've been a real blow, having all your careful planning ruined like that," Flo continued, earning her a confused look from both Jenn and me.

"What?" Jenn's voice was nasally, rough with lack of sleep and tears.

"The party, hun. That was a real shame." The older woman shook her head sadly. "Nancy and I were so looking forward to it. And to have it ruined like that, by those people." She clicked her tongue. "Any chance your momma will try for a round two? I heard scallops were on the menu."

Jenn glanced at me, I glanced at Jenn, and I believe we had the same thought at precisely the same time.

I opened my mouth. Closed it. Raised a finger. Dropped it.

It was Posey Lamont who eventually spoke up. "Florence McClure. You know that girl just lost her daddy, and you're asking her to reschedule a party so you can try scallops?"

Flo cast Posey—who was dressed in an ill-advised chartreuse ensemble with fringe at the cuffs and shoulder pads—a withering stare. "Of course I know Kip is dead, Posey. We were all there. But I also know that asshole got what was coming to him. I bet the girl is crying over her good fortune, sure. That man was a menace."

Ah. There she is. Salty as a sea shanty.

Posey and Vanessa, who'd been sitting next to each other, reared back in perfect synchronization.

Vanessa's mouth dropped and she pressed her hand to her chest. "Don't presume to know Jennifer Sylvester's feelings about anything, Florence. Just because Nancy Danvish told you some story about—"

"He stole her farm! Stole it right out from under her, her life's work. Turned her out of her own house, kicked her off her own land. So don't *you* presume to tell me what Nancy did or did not say. I know the truth, and the truth is whoever killed Kip Sylvester did us all a favor."

With that, Florence lifted her chin, turned on her heel, and marched back to her desk.

"Well!" Posey Lamont and Vanessa Romero exchanged wide-eyed stares, huffing in unison.

"Good grief!" This came from Jedidiah Hill, flinging his own wide-eyed stare around the room.

"I should say so." Nikki Becker pursed her lips together, flicking a disapproving glance to Flo and then turning her body as though to give the woman her back.

This was how southern folks shunned each other. Pretty soon everyone in town would know that Flo McClure had been rude to sweet, simple Jennifer Sylvester about the death of her father. Not the worst thing Flo had done, but definitely one of the most bizarre. However, the town never shunned Flo for long. As the main dispatch, she was the center of all the county's legal rumor mill.

If she didn't like you, she didn't share her information.

The sound of ruffled feathers abruptly ceased as the door leading back to the main station swung open. Now everyone, even salty Flo McClure, stopped doing whatever they were doing and stopped thinking whatever they were thinking as all eyes, attention, and curiosity rested on the woman revealed.

There she stood, Diane Donner.

CHAPTER SEVEN
CLETUS

"Accept who you are. Unless you're a serial killer."

— ELLEN DEGENERES, *SERIOUSLY... I'M KIDDING*

I didn't know I'd been holding out hope until right this minute, that I'd mis-seen or misinterpreted Diane's presence in the bakery last night, but I guess I had. Hope I was now forced to emancipate from false incarceration and release into the ether.

Looking at her now—her hair, her height, her build and frame—the woman washing blood off her hands had definitely been Diane. I'd studied and memorized the woman at the sink in a way I'd never taken the time to study Diane before. I'd never wanted or needed to. I can't memorize everyone! That's a waste of valuable memory nodes.

But now I did, and now I knew for sure.

The sheriff stood on one side and a tall, imposing woman in a suit stood on the other. She looked like a lawyer. You know, learned and poised to argue. Since I'd likely have very few interactions with this woman, I went ahead and looked at her, sizing her up from afar, not caring if I made assumptions about who she was based on her exterior instead of—as was my habit—taking the time to listen, learn, and ask questions first, and then judge.

Of note, and of particular interest to me, Diane no longer wore the red dress she'd donned last night. She wore a pantsuit of navy blue and a white shirt beneath, as close to casual attire as she ever came. At some point she'd changed. Did her red dress have Kip's blood on it? Or had she simply changed because it was a new day?

Jennifer immediately crossed to her mother. I held back, watching. The sheriff looked unhappy, troubled, and exhausted. The lawyer looked . . . poised to argue. The sheriff and the lawyer shook hands, but Diane did not shake Sheriff James's hand when offered. She didn't even look at him. This wasn't a snub or a rudeness, she simply seemed overwhelmed, in a daze.

When Jenn pulled her into a hug, Diane likewise appeared to be surprised by Jenn's presence. After a moment's hesitation, her arms came around her daughter. The lawyer placed a hand on Diane's back and whispered something into her ear which had her pulling back from Jenn, turning to the sheriff, and shaking his hand.

Then the lawyer and Diane moved toward the exit. Jennifer took a moment to give Sheriff James a hug. He accepted it readily, but his stare remained troubled as it followed Diane's progress out the door. After a few words were exchanged, Jennifer turned to catch up with her mother, which was my cue to leave.

Catching his eye, I nodded to the sheriff. He nodded in return, his stare inscrutable but sharp. The man then turned and retreated into the station. He'd been right last night to reprimand me for riling up Kip, and I didn't fault him for it. But I didn't regret it either. I had my reasons.

Nevertheless, the sheriff was a good man. A conscientious, smart man. Him being good, conscientious, and smart was liable to be a problem. Point was, I had nothing with which to blackmail Sheriff James, and that was an inconvenience.

What about Jessica James's true paternity? Hmm. *There's a thought.* I didn't like it, but it was a thought, one I'd have to contemplate later.

Tangentially, pushing out the door to follow Jenn, I wondered what it would've been like—how different all our lives would've been—if my mother had settled down with a man like Jeffrey James, if she'd chosen different, better than Darrell. Someone who couldn't easily be manipulated or blackmailed because he had nothing to hide.

You wouldn't be here, for a start.

I placed a hand on Jenn's back as I drew even with her and caught the tail end of the lawyer's spiel, " . . . under no circumstances, you understand?"

Diane nodded, her gaze downcast. "I promise, I will not speak to anyone about last night. And I will not speak to law enforcement—friend or otherwise—at all unless you or one of your associates are present."

I lifted an eyebrow at this version of Diane Donner. I'd never seen her meek before, not even when she'd been married to Kip. She'd always been in possession of grit, even when Kip had patronized her in public.

The lawyer turned to me and Jenn. "Ms. Sylvester, Mr. Winston, that goes for you too. None of you are to speak to law enforcement, the press, no one. If any of you are brought in for questioning, you call our office immediately. *Immediately.* Do you understand?"

I endeavored not to take it personally that her voice reminded me of Charlotte Henderson's when she spoke to her children about not asking for candy at the Piggly Wiggly checkout line. I reckoned, this woman being a lawyer, the tone was an occupational hazard.

Jenn and I nodded dutifully.

"Good. We'll get time on my calendar this week for us to meet. If at all possible, please don't discuss the events even with each other. I'd like for each of you to meet with me first before comparing notes. Got it?"

The lawyer, apparently satisfied, retrieved her cell, said her goodbyes while tapping out something on her phone, and dashed to her Audi like she had a hot tip on an underground debate meetup—like a fight club, except all they did was argue.

"Here, Momma. Cletus brought one of the Buicks. Do you want to sit in the front?" Jenn escorted her mother toward my car, and I followed a bit behind, ready to open whichever door Diane picked—except the driver's side. I wasn't going to let her drive, not in her state.

"The back, if you don't mind."

I moved around the women to make this happen and that's when, upon opening the back door and moving out of the way so Diane could slide in, I spotted a familiar face watching us, peeking around the corner of the station, still straddling his motorcycle. Though his helmet was on his head and the visor covered his face, I knew he had blond hair and eyes that were just like Jennifer's.

Isaac Sylvester.

Well, at least he wasn't skulking around the homestead anymore.

I let my gaze linger, hoping he saw me, and narrowed my eyes in warning. The last thing Jenn or her mother needed right now was Motorcycle Club Ken Doll and his misogynistic hypocrisy using the death of Kip to exhort holier-than-thou bullshit while they tried to grieve . . . assuming *grieving* was the right word for what Jenn and Diane were trying to do.

Anyway. He must've seen me looking and read the threat. In the very next moment, he brought his motorcycle to life and took off. Neither Diane nor Jennifer had seemed to notice his presence. *Good.*

Diane settled, I opened the passenger door for Jenn and scanned the road, parking lot, and tree line for additional assholes. I found none. That done, we were on our way.

"I know what your lawyer said, but do you want to talk about it? About last night?" It was Jenn who broke the silence, turning around in the front bench seat to face her momma. "Do you, um, want to tell us where you were?"

"No, baby."

"Are you sure?"

"It's just anything I say right now would come out as complete nonsense."

I glanced at Diane's reflection in the rearview mirror and tried not to be bothered by how colorless and drawn she looked. "Please let me know if there's anything I can do."

"Be a good man, Cletus." Diane leaned her elbow along the windowsill, her voice unsteady. "But you're already a good man. So just keeping being you."

I fought a grimace. I was not acquainted with this version of Diane Donner. She was—to use a technical term—acting super weird. On the one hand, I understood why. But on the other hand, her level and severity of weirdness alarmed me. Was she acting weird simply because Kip was dead and she'd found him and ran from the law? Or was she acting super weird because she'd been the one to kill him?

Hmm. What to do, what to do . . .

If anything would serve as a catalyst for knocking Diane Donner out of her stupor, it was me being high-handed and bossy.

I cleared my throat. "Okay. Well. In that case, let me tell you what I have planned."

"What you have planned?" Jenn faced me.

"Yes," I confirmed for Jenn, but then addressed Diane, "We're driving you home. Then I'll be making you some tea, and I'm going to put alcohol in it. Not a medicinal amount, just enough to help your muscles ease and help you sleep."

Diane nodded.

I continued, "I will also be calling your assistant to ensure he has things handled at the lodge and ask him to see about the window repair at the bakery." I then rattled off various tasks, concerns, suggestions, and opinions, as though using the opportunity of having Ms. Donner trapped in the back seat to bend her ear and explain her own business to her.

Jenn must've known or realized what I was doing because she sat quietly, glancing between me and her momma at intervals. As well, throughout my spiel, I examined Diane's reflection in the rearview mirror, looking for some sign of a spark.

Diane only nodded quietly, her eyes closed.

When I finished, pulling into her driveway, Diane said, "That all sounds fine, Cletus. Thank you," her subdued tone ringing hollow in the car as I brought us to a stop.

I squirmed in my seat. *This is not good.*

Jenn glanced at me and I glanced at Jenn and, just like before in the station after Flo McClure's uncouth comments, I got the sense we were both having the same thought at precisely the same time.

"Cletus, we need to talk."

I put down the invoices I'd been reconciling and slowly rotated in the office chair to face Drew. He stood in the doorway, attired in his game warden regalia, hat in his hand, and a concerned expression on his face.

I gestured to the chair he often occupied when he visited our small office above the auto shop. Drew dropped by unannounced every so often, usually to meld minds regarding our family's interests. On rare occasions, he came—and always at my behest—for business purposes, and only when I insisted he bear witness and behold the grandeur of my investment stewardship.

Drew, our initial financial backer for the Winston Brothers Auto Shop, took the "silent" in silent partner to an extreme level. Which is all to say, I hadn't "behested" him today. Therefore, financials and invest-ment returns were not the purpose of his visit.

"Why are you here?"

His sandy eyebrows ticked up at the question, and he tossed his hat to the top of a filing cabinet. As was his habit, he picked up the chair, turned it, and sat straddling the back of the seat. This was how he always situated himself. He was too big, too tall, too solid to sit in the small folding chair any other way.

"Something is wrong. I'm here to help."

I steepled my fingers, peering at him over the tips. "I admit nothing, but what is the origin of your supposition?"

"When I show up here unexpected, you always say something like, 'To what do I owe this great and profound honor?'"

"I'm switching things up. You know I don't like being predictable."

"You're unhappy."

I breathed in through my nose, considering my future brother-in-law (should he and Ashley ever get off their asses and walk down the damn aisle), and announced my conclusion aloud, "You were sent."

A small smile, a very small smile, curved his lips, shone from his eyes. "Your family, we're worried about you. We're worried about Jenn. We haven't seen much of y'all, not really, not since . . ."

The engagement party of calamity.

I sighed, rubbing a hand over my face. My family was smart to send

Drew, and that was a fact. Drew never had ulterior motives that weren't based in kindness, and my siblings knew that I knew that they knew that.

"It's not my family's fault, they did nothing wrong, if that's what they're thinking." Neither Jenn's, nor Diane's, nor my mood had improved over the last several weeks. In fact, Diane's continued detachment seemed to fuel Jenn's discontent. Jenn's discontent fueled my disgruntlement. My disgruntlement fueled absolutely nothing but frustration at Kip Sylvester.

Speaking of the extremely dead Kip, my personal investigation had hit a dead end. No one on the police force was talking to me. Not Jackson, not Boone, not even Evans or Williams. Everyone and everything had been locked up tight. Even Flo McClure's geyser of gossip had been sealed shut.

And yet gossip abounded in town. It was all rumor and conjecture. Most of what I heard I knew to be false. Karen Smith reportedly had told Bobby Jo Boone that Kip had killed himself in the parking lot of the bakery, having no reason to live if he couldn't walk Jennifer down the aisle. Another crazy claim had been that Isaac had done his father in as a way to prove allegiance to the Iron Wraiths.

Presently, Drew settled his forearms on the back of the chair, inspecting his hands. "We want to help, if you'll let us."

I sighed again, tired enough to admit the truth without preamble, "Drew, if I knew what to do, if I could think of something that would help, I promise, you'd be the first to know."

"That bad, huh?" Drew appeared to be genuinely alarmed by my admission, as he should be. This was one of maybe three times in my adult life when I hadn't been able to coerce or extort answers. If anything, his reaction felt understated. He should've been panicking.

"Worse," I grumbled, my unfocused attention moving over his shoulder.

Though I'd tried on several occasions, I couldn't get Diane to talk. *At all.* Jenn had been bringing dinner to her mother almost every night, and I attended as often as possible. The shrewd business owner never seemed to be hungry let alone chatty. She'd lost weight. She never smiled. A stark contrast to the vitality she'd freely displayed prior to the party.

Furthermore, Diane had not gone back to work yet. I knew her assistant, a French fella with a penchant for baseball, kept her informed of the day-to-day via email and often drove to her house to obtain signatures on documents. According to the efficient Monsieur Auclair, Diane never answered her phone, never took his calls, but she did respond to email.

I hypothesized this was because the police were watching her and she didn't want them in Lodge business. They had her under constant surveillance, and this alone caused me no end of consternation. Firstly, townie murders were never given—and I mean *never*—this kind of attention from law enforcement. I couldn't think of a single murder in Tennessee or North Carolina where a suspect had been under a similar amount of scrutiny unless it was a federal matter being handled by the FBI.

To what extent the law was watching, I wasn't yet fully apprised. Recording devices probable due to the van parked on the street; but maybe also cameras pointed at the house? The surveillance agitated Jenn to no end, especially the nondescript van parked on the street and how the stakeout team would wave to her as she drove past.

"Why are they doing this? They can't think she's a suspect, can they?" Jenn had asked me after two weeks of passing the van daily. I'd told her the truth in as few words as possible. Yes. Diane was a suspect and left it at that.

What I didn't say out loud was that, by most accounts, she'd been missing from the barn during the shooting and she'd refused to talk to the police about anything, lawyering up the moment they'd pulled her in that first morning and every time since. It didn't help that, upon the advice of Diane's legal team, Jenn and I had also lawyered up and we weren't answering any questions either.

Jenn had shut down and anger-baked for three hours after our brief conversation that day.

But back to Diane and her odd behavior. In addition to not returning to work, she ventured out rarely, and I do mean *rarely*: twice to go grocery shopping, another time to meet with her lawyer, the three times she'd been called in by the police. Then nothing. One week, two weeks, three weeks, she never left the house.

I'd asked her lawyer—during my interview with her firm—whether she'd advised Jenn's momma to become a shut-in and she'd not answered, instead chuckling like the question had been a joke. She'd met with all of us, one at a time. She took notes but didn't share any details from other interviews. Obviously, I didn't tell the lawyer I'd seen Diane and Repo. I gave her the same story I gave Jackson.

But Jenn must've told her what I'd said that night about seeing Roger Gangersworth because she asked me about it. I told the lawyer I was no longer sure, and this seemed to ease her mind a great deal. She did not ask me if I saw Diane in the kitchen.

"Jenn's bridal shower is coming up," Drew said, pulling me out of my reflections. "Ashley can't reach Diane. Ash isn't complaining, and she's happy to finish the planning on her own, but she doesn't want to overstep."

I narrowed my eyes into slits. "Now that you bring it up, why is Ashley involved in planning events for my wedding when she can't be bothered to plan her own?" I wanted to change the subject, and this particular subject rankled.

Drew's attention drifted to his hands again, his small smile a little bigger. "Cletus, you'll have to ask Ashley that. But she has her reasons."

"Reasons is another word for excuses."

"Actually, you *should* ask her. I know she misses you and she'd welcome any contact, even if it's you giving her a hard time."

Ugh. *Well, that statement makes me feel like a floating trash island.*

I sighed for a third time, leaning forward in my seat to set my elbows on my knees. "Drew, I don't want to give y'all a hard time. Just answer me this, because I have to know for my own sanity, and I need a dose of sanity right now: Do you want to marry my sister?"

"More than anything."

"Does she want to marry you?"

"Absolutely. Yes." No hesitation.

"Are you engaged?"

"No."

"Why the hell not?" I resisted the urge to throw my hands up. These days, I'd been resisting so many urges, my resistance could be measured in ohms.

He shrugged, not looking bothered by my interrogation. "Tell you what, I'll do my best to answer your question if you answer one of mine."

"Deal." I skootched to the edge of my seat.

"Tell me, honestly, how can I help—how can your family help—you and Jennifer, and even Ms. Donner, through this dark time?"

Once more I glanced over his shoulder, searching for something, anything that might help but that also didn't require the divulging of secrets.

"You can . . ." I leaned back in the chair again, shaking my head. "You can tell me who killed Kip Sylvester."

All the humor drained from Drew's features, leaving his silvery eyes stark. "The police investigation isn't going well?"

"I have no idea. No one will talk to me about it. I don't even know if they found the gun." There. That was the truth. I'd never been stonewalled so completely by the sheriff's office, and stonewalling plus the surveillance of Diane told me everything I needed to know. Jenn's mother was obviously their number one suspect, for some reason someone had decided to dedicate a ridiculous amount of resources to the investigation, and I needed to intervene as soon as possible. I needed to direct the law's attention elsewhere. But I had no leads.

"What about Jackson?" Drew's forehead wrinkled with what looked like disbelief.

"No. Not even Jackson will talk to me."

"Really? I'm sure he'd talk to one of us."

"You think so? You think you can get Ashley to make him talk?" I chuckled tiredly at the sarcastic suggestion, expecting Drew to do so as well. Jackson's adoration for my sister was no secret, though she did nothing to encourage him.

To my surprise, Drew shrugged. "Sure. Why not? If you think it'll help."

That had me leaning forward in my seat again. "Would she? Would she do it?"

"If you asked, she'd do anything. You know that."

I stroked my beard, considering the idea for real. *It might work.*

I didn't need her to do anything untoward, just invite the man out to lunch, get him talking. Ash could do it, I knew she could, and she'd make it all seem like his idea.

At this point, my options were drying up.

Not all options . . .

Repo was a thread I hadn't been able to nail down. Three days after the engagement party, Repo stopped using his Wraiths-issued phone and borrowed other Iron Wraiths' bikes at random rather than using his own. Burro couldn't track him reliably anymore. I hated that Repo was so smart. It was almost as inconvenient as Sheriff James's incorruptibility.

Complicating matters, I surmised Jennifer and I were also under some sort of surveillance as of last week when I caught a man in a white Ford four-door watching me load groceries into my Geo at the Piggly Wiggly. *Ridiculous!* Sheriff James's office did not have the resources to conduct this level of reconnaissance, but obviously someone within the legal system had made tracking Diane and her family a priority.

Which was one of the reasons I'd delayed my plans to approach Elena Wilkinson. Under normal, non-murder investigation circumstances, I knew she'd likely hesitate before speaking with me, seeing as how my testimony was a big reason her sister rotted in jail.

So under these tense murder investigation circumstances, I felt certain Elena wouldn't so much as give me the time of day. I'd have to intimidate her into talking. Side note, I despised how police surveillance made extorting and threatening people difficult. *So frustrating.*

But I did keep tabs on the woman.

After being released from the hospital, she'd arranged Kip's funeral. My spies on the ground told me the event had been sparsely attended, but that Isaac had made an appearance, sitting in the back and speaking to no one. Jenn hadn't been there. She'd considered it, but finally made up her mind that very morning not to go. Instead, she'd returned to work and baked for fourteen hours straight.

I did have one chance to question Elena coming up, however. The reading of Kip's will, scheduled for this coming week, would be a golden opportunity and one I didn't plan to squander. Now, I know what you're thinking; there's no such thing as a "will reading," it's just something movies, TV shows, and mainstream fiction have propagated and harvested for dramatic effect.

Nevertheless, according to the dead man's lawyer, Mr. Leeward Esquire, who was also the executor of the will, Kip Sylvester had wished there to be one of these propagated will readings before the document was sent to probate. He'd specifically asked for it and had named the people he wanted in attendance: Diane, Elena, Isaac, Jennifer, and—randomly—my brother Billy.

Diane had decided not to go.

I had no idea what Isaac or Elena planned.

Billy had asked Jenn first thing if she wanted him there, she'd said she did. He was going.

Jenn planned to attend. She'd asked me to come and support her, and of course I absolutely wanted to do so. Jenn may have been discontent over the last several weeks, and she may have been working through unwieldy thoughts and feelings without sharing them all, but she relied on me. She trusted me.

Which brings me to the lie.

"What's wrong?" Drew, again interrupting my thoughts, tilted his head to the side. "I'm telling you, if you ask Ashley to help, she'll do it."

"Yes. I know that. Thank you," I said, distracted by the albatross of guilt hanging around my neck. Guilt wasn't a state I succumbed to often, but when I did, it suffocated like drowning in sand.

"So, you'll call Ash?"

"I will ask for her assistance with Jackson."

"Good." Drew's stare sharpened. "So why do you look troubled?"

The lie. I hadn't yet told Jenn the truth.

I'd wanted to, but she'd been so withdrawn, worried, sad, and unusually uncommunicative. She jumped at small sounds but didn't seem to hear big ones. It's not that she avoided me—she didn't, not at all, we spent every night together and each of our days off, just like before—but she never seemed to have words to share. I wasn't going to push her.

I'd threaten and coerce anyone else who required threatening and coercing in order to keep Jenn and her kin safe, but I'd never do so with her. Ever.

No. You'll just omit the truth to keep her safe.

"Cletus?" Drew prompted, his eyebrows ticking up again. "What's on your mind?"

"Well now, I believe you owe me an answer first." I wiped my features of inner turmoil and mimicked his eyebrow tick. "Why aren't you and Ash engaged? Why is she planning my wedding and not hers?"

He openly considered me with his kind eyes, his lips twisting to the side. "Like I said, you should ask Ashley."

I threw my hands up. "Drew—"

"But—" he lifted up a finger "—I will tell you this." His eyes dropped to his knuckles again and he frowned, like maybe now he was troubled, or he had troubling thoughts. "Losing Bethany hit Ashley hard, as I'm sure it did with all you boys. But think about Ashley's perspective in particular."

"What does my mother have to do with whether or when y'all get married?" I asked, not following.

"A daughter planning a wedding without her mother," he said slowly, carefully, his voice low and sad. "Trying on wedding dresses, for example. That's not something Ash is ready to do, ready to face."

My eyes stung. I blinked them.

"I hadn't—" I had to clear my throat again "—I guess I hadn't considered that."

"I know Jethro got married last year, but Sienna's momma was there to mother them both, both Jet and Sienna. I don't have anyone. Ash and I don't have anyone, between the two of us, to fill that role. Bethany's absence, my mother's absence, will be felt acutely during the planning, and we have to plan a wedding before we can have one."

"I guess . . ." *Dammit.* "I shouldn't have been pushing y'all."

He lifted his eyes again, this time they were appraising. "You know, Cletus. You and Jenn, you're lucky to have Ms. Donner. Diane, I mean.

She's a force, and I realize the waters haven't always been smooth for Jenn and her momma, but she loves you both something fierce."

I gave Drew a tight smile and a somber nod to disguise the unpleasant and growing sensation in the pit of my stomach. At his well-intentioned words, the albatross around my neck nearly tripled in size.

CHAPTER EIGHT

CLETUS

"Facts do not cease to exist because they are ignored."

— ALDOUS HUXLEY, COMPLETE ESSAYS, VOL. II:

1926-1929

The time had come to tell Jenn the truth.

After talking matters over with Drew, and with the reading of Kip's will looming on the horizon, I accepted there'd never be a right time to break the news to Jenn about her mother. A reason would always exist to not tell her. Like I'd said to Drew, *reasons* was just another word for excuses.

Today. I'd tell her today.

I wasn't certain how closely the police were tracking us, how much they were listening, but I needed to find out. As such, I'd sent a distress call to my friend in Chicago asking for help and relied on Drew to communicate my immediate needs to Ashley. *I hope they didn't bug the office . . .*

No biggie. It's not like we'd said anything incriminating.

In the meantime, in an abundance of caution, I decided to escort Jenn someplace private but loud in order to break the news.

"We're going to a nightclub in Knoxville. I brought clothes for you. This is what I'm wearing. You can change when we get there, if you want." We were sitting in one of my Buicks. I'd just picked her up from work. It was presently 11:07 PM on a Friday.

Jenn looked at me. Her work clothes—jeans and a plain white T-shirt—were sprinkled with a mixture of flour, cinnamon, nutmeg, and cardamon which I collectively referred to as *bakery dust*. She nodded, her eyes wide as they held mine. She wanted to ask questions. I could see them pressing plain as day behind her stiffly accepting façade. Yet she remained quiet.

I turned the engine, staring at her schooled features, and my heart quickened. Something was wrong.

How much did she know about the level of police surveillance we were under? Did she know more than me? Had that been why she'd been stingy with her words? Was that . . . *wait a minute.*

Is that why sex over the last several weeks has been silent and in the dark? I'd assumed our subdued intimacies were related to Jenn's inner turmoil, not due to suspicions of exterior voyeurism.

My mind an obstacle course of suspicion, I sifted through our interactions over the past several weeks as I pulled out of the bakery and took the road to Knoxville. Her mostly single-word answers; her (albeit sad) acquiescence to Diane's lack of conversation over dinners; her rebuffing my overtures during daylight hours only to wake me in the dark with quiet kisses and searching hands. Middle of the night was now the only time we made love, but we made love in the middle of the night all the time.

I glanced at Jenn out of the corner of my eye. She sat stiff and straight in her seat, her features free of any telling emotion. *She knows something.*

Well. Thank God I'd taken action today!

How long had she been planning to keep information from me? I tried not to twist myself into a tizzy, but as soon as we were in that club, she was going to give me answers. I wasn't even going to wait until we were on the dance floor, the upstairs office would have to suffice. My attention flicked to the rearview mirror, force of habit, and I was not surprised to find what looked like the white Ford four-door some distance behind us. I could tell by the headlights.

Our drive was over in thirty minutes. She let herself out of the car as I grabbed our things from the back, and then steered her toward the side door. I gave the bulky bouncer my information when he answered my knock. Giving us a once-over, he pulled out a phone and tapped out a message. The owner and I were friendly and, though I hadn't informed her of my intentions, I knew she'd be fine with it. A short moment later, he nodded and stepped to the side, allowing us access up a set of stairs, the music thumping, chasing our heels as we climbed the two flights.

"You can change in here." I opened the door to the office and followed her in. The space appeared unused. An empty desk shoved against a wall and nothing else, not even a chair.

As soon as the door closed, I faced her. "Your phone, did you leave it in the car?" The phone she'd lost the night of the engagement party was still missing. We'd had to replace it with a new one.

She nodded eagerly, "Yes. It's in the car."

"Good. Mine too. We can talk in here freely then." I dropped the bag full of clothes and accoutrements to the floor and stepped into her space, gathering her hands in mine. "What is going on with you?"

She exhaled a tremendous breath, her expression pained. "So many things. First, thank you." She released my hands and threw her arms around me. "Thank you for arranging tonight. I don't know what all they're watching. I assume our phones, right? I thought about writing you a note, and then I thought maybe they'd get a hold of that. I thought I could burn it? Only, it'd be weird for me to burn a piece of paper. I mean, I don't know how this works!"

"How what works?" I held her tighter. Despite her distress and tension, I enjoyed the feel of her soft, luscious body pressed against mine. We hadn't been hugging as much as before, I guess now I knew why.

"You know what! I've never been under surveillance by the police before." She leaned away, her voice strained. "I know I'm not acting normal, but it's hard to act normal when you're being watched."

"Jenn, what—specifically—do you know?"

Her head reared back on her neck and she blinked at me. "What do you mean? What do *you* know?"

"Do you know for a fact we're being watched?"

"Uh, yes. They've bugged, or tapped or whatever, my house."

Really? Just how much money and man power were the police dedicating to this? "How do you know this?"

"Because I found a bug—or whatever. It's called a bug, right?"

What? "Where?"

"In the kitchen. And a camera in the hall. Lord, it's hard not to look at it now that I know it's there."

Ice entered my veins followed by white-hot rage. Stepping away from Jenn, I took a breath. Then another.

"What? What's wrong?"

"Jenn." I had to clear my throat of gravel before I could continue. "Jenn, did you let anyone inside the house recently?"

"What? No. No one."

"Not a—a repair person? Anyone?"

"No. Of course not. Why?"

I endeavored to keep my voice steady, but what THE FUCK good was a state-of-the-art security system if folks could just willy-nilly enter and exit as they saw fit.

Alex and Quinn. That's who's going to redo the system. And I'm adding a moat. With alligators.

"Fourth Amendment laws are tricky. But the law can't place video cameras in your house unless you invite them inside. They can be under cover at the time, pretending to be a repairman or something, but you have to invite them in."

"Uh . . ."

"So, without a warrant, which are usually rare for video surveillance inside people's houses, the police are not allowed to put cameras on private property. They might point a camera at a house from the street, like what they're doing with your momma's place. But, honey, that's not a police camera inside your house."

"What?"

I shook my head, covering my mouth with my hand, working to get a handle on my temper.

"Not the police? Then who?"

"Someone else." And when I found that person—

"Oh no! So—so the police aren't—"

"At this point, I honestly don't know anymore." I thought about the man in the white Ford. He was probably parked outside. I crossed to the window and peeked out the blinds. I didn't see him, so I paced away. "I think they're watching as much as possible, maybe even listening, following. The bug you found might've been theirs, but I doubt it. Local police usually don't dedicate resources like this to a townie murder. This whole thing doesn't add up."

Jenn collapsed in the chair, her eyes wide, her lips parted, all the color draining from her face. She stared forward, and I was grateful for the minute her internal deliberations afforded me. I didn't want to tip off the voyeur, yet there was no way I'd continue to let someone invade Jenn's—our—privacy. I was so disappointed in myself. How long had it been going on? Hopefully, Quinn and Alex in Chicago could tell me.

"You know, I was trying to be strong. I was trying to follow your lead and pretend like everything was fine." She huffed a laugh. "And you didn't even know."

Her words weren't an accusation against me, she was upset with herself, and that only made it worse. Protecting Jenn, keeping Jenn safe, that was *my* job.

Dead ends and missed details. *What has happened to me?* I used to be sharper than this. I used to be a katana and now I'd become a butter knife. Maybe even a spoon.

Her chin wobbled and she sighed again, this time it sounded watery. "I missed you so much."

In an instant, I was kneeling in front of her, my hands on her face. "Oh, Jenn. This is my fault." It was my fault. I wasn't sure yet how thoroughly I'd failed, and that was also a problem. "I will find out who did this, and I will devise a punishment to suit the crime."

Maybe a spoon would be involved.

"I don't want to talk about the—the stupid camera." She leaned forward, slipping off the chair until we were both kneeling, her hands now on my shoulders. "I was trying to be strong when all I really wanted to do was talk to you. I should've found a way, and I'm sure there were so many ways, but I didn't want to—to—"

"What?"

"Be the weak link."

"The what?"

"You're so good at being sneaky. I figured, this whole time, you needed me to sit tight and follow your lead." I felt her stiffen abruptly, lean back. "Wait a minute. You are trying to figure out who murdered my father, right?"

"Yes. Of course."

"Oh. Good." She breathed a sigh that sounded relieved. "I assumed you were. I also assumed other things, obviously wrongly, so . . ."

Assuming. That was the problem. We'd both been assuming. I'd assumed she wanted space to work through grief, she'd assumed I had some masterplan. I did have a masterplan of course, but not inclusive of all the details she'd been privy to and I had not. If we'd talked prior to now, then maybe Kip's murder would be solved, Diane would be back at work—assuming she wasn't the murderer... another assumption—and we'd be having sex with the lights on.

"I need to be honest with you, Jenn." I sat back on the floor and encouraged her to straddle me. As she settled, I continued, "I *assumed* you were going through a tough time and needed space."

The side of her mouth quirked up. "I am going through a tough time, but I don't need space. Not from you."

"Then I shall give you no space." I kissed her nose, allayed. "Tell me what's been on your mind. Tell me everything."

"I guess . . ." Her smile soft, her gaze lost focus and drifted downward. "I've been really confused about everything. I meant what I said at the police station, I don't know what I'm feeling. I love my parents. I still love my father. Isn't that awful? Florence McClure is right. He was a bad man."

"I don't think it's awful that you love your dad."

She continued as though I hadn't spoken. "I mean, he treated everyone so terribly. He treated Isaac terribly, my momma terribly, me terribly."

Or maybe she hadn't heard me, and that was fine. I took it as a sign to simply listen. I missed her voice, so I was happy to oblige.

"I have good memories of him and the pictures to prove it," she said, sounding defensive. Jenn bit her thumbnail, her brow stern. A second later, her forehead smoothed, and she said sadly, "Actually, no I don't. I have a few pictures of us together when I was real little and we're both smiling. But I was always on my momma's lap. That's what I have."

I rubbed her back, my hands moving under the fabric of her T-shirt.

"But I have to believe, in his own way, in the way he was capable of, he loved me too. Right?" Her eyes came back to mine, searching. When I said nothing, she seemed to deflate. "I know what you're going to say. Not all love is created equal. And my definition of love never matched his, and vice versa."

I swallowed the impulse to point out that Kip's definition of love didn't even resemble apathy.

"So"—she lifted her chin stubbornly even as it wavered—"I'm not sad that he's dead. I guess." Her voice cracked and she swiped at new tears. "But I am sad. And I feel guilty about how little sadness I feel. But I am sad. I'm sad because a person lost their life before they chose the righteous path, before they chose the path of love over selfishness. And that makes me really sad. Because I do believe in heaven and hell, and given the way he behaved even to the end—" Jennifer covered her face and cried softly.

I pulled her into a hug, my mouth sour.

The underlying difference between us could be summed up by her reaction to her father's death. Here she was, sad because she believed her father was in hell, and she didn't want *anyone* to go to hell. Now, here I was, also believing in a heaven and hell, and content in the knowledge that folks like Kip went to the latter.

See the difference?

She wanted everybody to reform and do better, make better choices, make reparations, and make amends. She found peace in the idea of redemption. Whereas I found peace in the idea of someone like Kip

Sylvester suffering through the perpetual anguish of a fiery eternity. Basically, she was New Testament, I was Old Testament, and we cohabitated in the biblical sense—figuratively and literally.

I wondered if, fundamentally, the world was made up of people who either sought justice at the expense of redemption, or those who sought redemption at the expense of justice. To be honest, I was always a little bit disappointed when people reformed. Watching a bad person choose the straight and narrow path was the *deus ex machina* of real life.

. . . Except Jethro, of course. But Jet wasn't ever really all that bad.

No. He was bad. He hurt people.

I frowned, severely, not liking that my empirical experience—how my brother had reformed, and we were all happier and better for it—undercut my thirst for justice being served in the general population. Well, I supposed that made me ordinary. Folks like it when justice applies to other people, but always think it's unfair when applied to them.

Moving on.

I continued rubbing her back, hoping she drew comfort from my hands on her skin like I drew comfort from the feel of her in my arms. I should've made her talk to me before now, and not just for us to compare notes about police surveillance. She needed to talk about what she'd been going through. I didn't completely understand her perspective, but she needed me. I knew she wasn't okay, asking her if she was okay would be a banal waste of words, which was why I'd resisted.

But she obviously needed to talk. *No more giving her space.*

Instead, inspired by Drew's forthrightness earlier, I asked, "What can I do?"

The sudden sound of my voice seemed to draw her out of whatever dark thoughts she'd ensconced herself within and pulled back, blinking several times, her tears dry. "Pardon?"

I studied her gorgeous eyes. "What can I do? How can I help you?"

"I . . ." She gave her head a subtle shake, like she had difficulty processing my question.

Hmm.

Anxious for action, I decided to make a list of obvious tasks that would or might help, starting with us sleeping at the homestead instead of her place. Then I'd hold her to ensure she continued to feel safe by getting rid of those cameras. And then—then—

Damn.

Beyond that, I needed instructions. If I were expected to be adequately prepared to see to Jenn's needs over the next several days, weeks, years, and the rest of our shared life, I required feedback. This was the main issue with loving someone *and* respecting their wishes.

I loved my family plenty, but I didn't always respect their wishes, seeing as how they were prone to having dumb, self-destructive wishes. Take Billy, for instance. He wanted me to let his tragic-as-of-now past with Scarlet (Claire) St. Claire (McClure) go. That's what he said he wished.

I would let their past go the same day he did, which meant never.

"I want us to talk. I need to talk to you. If they're bugging the house, fine, whatever. But we need to find a way to communicate."

"Already on it. Next."

"I want you to help me find the killer."

"As I've said, I've started looking. I'm not happy about that camera being in the house, but it might give me a new lead. I want to be certain the police catch the real killer, not that I don't have faith in the sheriff, but sometimes the police only go where evidence leads."

"And you don't go where evidence leads?" She shifted on my lap, like she was getting more comfortable.

"Evidence is important, but evidence can be placed in an attempt at misdirection." I'd done a fair share of planting evidence, I knew what to look for when determining whether evidence had been planted purposefully or left by mistake. "It's not just the evidence itself that's important, it's the very existence of the evidence that must be questioned."

"Give me an example."

"All murderers seek to conceal vital evidence when planning a murder unless it's a crime of passion, done without any planning or forethought. We're going to assume that your father's death was not a crime of passion."

"Okay, yes. Makes sense. I feel like this is obvious."

"It should be. But in a planned murder, like your father's, when critical evidence is found easily and has fingerprints that implicate a suspect —like the murder weapon—you have to ask yourself two questions: First, is the suspect implicated a moron? If not, then you can assume that evidence was planted with their fingerprints."

"Right. Of course. Again, I feel like this is obvious."

"It is, but the police have to follow the evidence. A murder weapon with fingerprints is easily found and points to a suspect, that suspect is now the primary suspect—call that person suspect A—for the police. Because they have to *prove* a person is guilty to a jury."

"Are juries that stupid?" She made a face. It was cute and made me smile.

"No, that's not what I'm saying." Unable and unwilling to stop myself, I brushed my lips against hers before leaning back. "It's about the trial, getting a guilty verdict, not always about convicting the guilty. If suspect B really committed the murder and the police put suspect B on trial, but the murder weapon has suspect A's fingerprints, then how's that gonna look to a jury? It's going to give them reasonable doubt to acquit suspect B. Even if the police have additional evidence suggesting that suspect B planted the murder weapon with suspect A's fingerprints, the doubt will linger."

Jenn trailed her nails down the front of my shirt. "Okay, I see what you mean."

"However, we're not the legal system. You and I, we don't need to care about the burden of reasonable doubt."

She marinated in that statement for a bit before saying, "At the same time, I don't want to become one of those obsessed zealots who *decide* a person is guilty, looking for evidence after the fact. I get what you're saying, but we need to follow the evidence too. We need to keep an open mind and not jump to conclusions based on who we'd like to be guilty."

I gripped her hips tighter as her fingers slipped under the hem of my shirt, her knuckles brushing against my stomach. But I couldn't be distracted by her touch. The time had come.

Carefully schooling my expression and my tone, I said, "Or who we'd like to be innocent."

"What do you mean?" She lifted my shirt higher, taking a greedy eyeful of my stomach and chest, and I felt myself lengthen, harden beneath where she sat. It'd been so long since I'd seen her body. I missed —no, I *needed*.

Nope! Do not veer off course. Do not be distracted by her sexy shenanigans.

"Just that—" I caught her hands before she could wreak any more havoc "—part of keeping an open mind is being open to all possibilities, even ones that are inconvenient. Or painful."

Her gaze lifted, scrutinizing, suspicious. "Cletus."

"Jenn." *Okay, well, here we go.*

"What are you not telling me?"

CHAPTER NINE

CLETUS

"The truth will set you free, but first it will piss you off."

— JOE KLAAS, *TWELVE STEPS TO HAPPINESS*

"No. No, no, no. No."

I'd told her almost everything, and she'd handled it remarkably well until—

"You've got to be pulling my leg. Repo? The one who kidnapped Jess and Claire?"

"He didn't. That was—"

"The one who tried to get Duane and Beau to run their chop shop?"

I lifted an eyebrow. "How'd you know about that?"

"No way." She scrambled off my lap, standing, pacing back and forth in the office like it was a cage.

As soon as I'd mentioned that Repo had been the one with her momma in the kitchen, she'd—excuse the technical term—lost her shit. She was no longer handling it well.

"I'm telling you what I know to be true."

"No!" She stopped at the bag I'd brought, picked it up, set it on the desk and unzipped it. Her movements were angry and perfunctory.

"There's no way my mother did this and there is no way my mother would be with that man. No."

"I'm not saying she killed your father." I stood and crossed to stand behind her. "I'm relating what I saw, what Jackson told me that night, and—"

"Did you tell Jackson?" She spun, shoving the black dress I'd packed for her at my chest. "About my momma being in the kitchen with Repo?"

"No. I didn't lie. I said it was dark."

"Ah ha! It was dark! So maybe you mis-saw? Maybe it wasn't her?"

I scratched the back of my neck. "It actually wasn't that dark."

"Cletus!"

"I'm not going to apologize for telling you the truth, but I am sorry this is the truth."

She frowned. It was a big one.

I sallied forth, determined to settle this. "And I apologize for keeping it a secret for so long."

She waved this apology away like it was a gnat, with a distracted flick of her wrist. "No. Don't apologize for that. I'm glad you did, seeing as how some weirdo is recording everything we do at the house. I felt better thinking it was the police, to be honest." She shivered, like the thought of a stranger watching and listening to us gave her the heebie-jeebies.

Honestly, it gave me the heebie-jeebies too. The *second* we were back in the car, I'd message Alex using our secure mechanism and ask him for help resolving the issue, starting tonight, if possible.

"You're sure it was her? Absolutely sure?" Her voice sounded plead-ing, like maybe by asking nicely I'd give her a different answer.

"Yes. Your mother and Repo came into the kitchen. He turned on the sink faucet for her and went through cabinets while she washed her hands. Jackson banged on the back door, they left through the front. That's what I saw."

"I just . . . she wouldn't." Jenn lowered her hand holding the dress, her attention now on the article of clothing. She shook it out. "She wouldn't."

"For what it's worth, I don't think she killed your father. Who shoots someone through a window, opens the car door, puts their hand in the victim's blood, touches their victim's face, and smears blood on the car after? No. Your momma isn't that dumb."

Jenn nodded, her gaze still affixed to the dress. "We have to ask her."

"I . . . agree."

"What?" She peered at me, another inspection. She must've heard the hesitancy in my voice. "Is there something else?"

"Did you know your mother has been seeing Repo since Christmas?"

"What?!"

"I confirmed it the morning after the murder, with one of my contacts at the Dragon."

Jenn took a step back, staring at nothing. I pushed my hands into my pockets and waited.

"How long have you known?"

"The morning after the murder. Before that, I had no idea. After I saw them together in the kitchen, I . . . well, it was a surprise. I couldn't figure out what they'd be doing together, so I called my contact and he told me."

"Oh my God." Jenn pressed her fingertips to her forehead and stared at the carpet. "That must be the guy."

"What guy?"

"Not last Christmas, but the one before—" she shook her head quickly, grimacing "—I found my momma the day after Christmas at her house, hungover and crying. She told me she'd had a one-night stand with someone at the Dragon, a biker. But she never told me who. And now they're together? She made it sound like a one-time thing."

"Looks like that first time was a one-time thing, until a few months ago."

Her hand fell to her thigh with a smack. "So the whole Iron Wraiths motorcycle club knows my mother has been—is involved with this Mr. Repo and she didn't say anything to me?"

"No. Not at all. My contact is in a delicate position, one that sees folks come and go and has the opportunity to track them unobserved. He thinks—believes—no one is aware of their relationship but him. They meet at a safe house only top members of the club know about."

"She's sneaking around? With a—an Iron Wraith? With this *reprobate*?"

I rolled my lips between my teeth to keep from smiling. She sounded just like her mother. I would not respond as I hypothesized Jennifer did not need, nor would she appreciate, my feedback at present.

"I can't believe her. I cannot believe her!" Jenn threw the black fabric to the desk and whipped off her shirt. She then reached for the dress again. "What is she thinking? Why would she do this?"

"Maybe he makes her happy." I let my attention linger on the bare skin of her back, the dip of her waist, the flare of her hips. The dress I'd packed wasn't worn with a bra, and that had been a purposeful choice. "Maybe she loves him—"

"What?" Her eyes cut to mine, hot, sharp as a knife. "You expect me to believe that my mother is in love with a criminal?"

I braced my feet apart and met her glare steadily, uncertain whether it was worthwhile to have this conversation at all. Jenn could have her feelings about her mother's love life, and I didn't have anything to gain by encouraging Jenn to see things from Diane's point of view. Why cause strife with my beloved when I truly did not care one way or the other who Diane chose to spend her evenings with?

But a man had been murdered, Jennifer's father. Diane was definitely the prime suspect. I surmised whoever (or whomever) watched Jenn and I were not the police, but I felt certain the police were the ones watching Diane *all the time*. Repo was a criminal, no denying that. As the money man for the club, he was a money launderer and a thief. Indirectly, he was also complicit in any number of crimes—drug dealing, smuggling, destruction of property, assault, murder, prostitution—you name it, his hands were covered in it.

And yet I was no angel. I was a criminal who'd never been caught, and Jenn loved me. Was I more worthy of love than Repo because I'd been smart enough to evade the law—thus far—and he hadn't? Or was it the nature and number of our crimes that separated us?

That seemed like a slippery slope, a maple syrup hill with a slathering of lube.

"Cletus."

"Jennifer." I sidled up to her.

She tracked me with her eyes. "She doesn't love him. And there's no way someone like that could ever make her happy. He's a terrible man."

"He's pretty terrible." He was also pretty smart, clever, and based on other facts I knew about him, surprisingly unselfish at times. I wasn't sure what the man's hard lines were, what moral code he subscribed to, but I knew he had hard lines and a moral code. That was more—much more—than could be said for my father. Or Jenn's.

But enough about Repo. Jenn and I were alone with a light on. I'd told her the truth and she wasn't angry at me. The bass from the club below thrummed in the background, just enough to provide a soundtrack for . . . activities.

Reaching around, I slid my fingertips down her spine. Her lashes fluttered, a new kind of heat kindling behind her gaze.

"I didn't bring you here for this." I bent, then brushed a kiss against her lips, nuzzling her nose with mine. "But since we are here."

"Cletus," she said my name, the word breathless, and I reveled in the sudden change.

One of the sexiest things about my woman was how very ready she was for me, each and every time. One moment we'd be discussing tulips, and she'd be lamenting that they only bloomed once a year, and then I'd look at her or I'd touch her and this—this look right here, this dreamy, hopeful look—lit behind her eyes.

She'd said once that she didn't think she was made for love. I'd told her, *It's exactly what you're made for,* and I'd been right. I should've known something was amiss when she'd rebuffed me weeks ago only to reach for me at night.

"I miss looking at you," I said, hooking my fingers into the strap of her bra. I slid it down her shoulder. "I miss doing things to you with the lights on. I miss watching . . ."

Her body trembled and she swayed, pulling air into her lungs as though the oxygen was in short supply. Reaching down, I unbuttoned her jeans, and she moved the black dress out of the way, setting it on the desk behind her. Her bra sagged without the support of its straps and I bent, swirling my tongue around the center of her breast.

Jenn's nails were in my hair and she shimmied her hips, helping me remove her pants and underwear. "What are—what are you gonna do?"

"What do you want me to do?" I asked. I was open for anything, always. But what I really wanted was her sitting on the desk naked, legs open for my mouth. There were very few things I loved more than watching Jennifer Sylvester, short woman baker, lose her mind while I ate out her pussy. Prior to the solidifying of our relationship, it had been my most frequent—and at the time, most inconvenient—daydream. And night dream. And wet dream.

"Can we—" her breath hitched, and I moved to the other breast, encouraging her to lean back on the desk and sit on her dress "—try something new?"

Something new? Getting naked in a strange office above a club we'd never patronized wasn't new? Images of her and me together, things we hadn't done yet, possibilities flitted through my head. *Both heads.*

"What did you have in mind?" I asked. Though I had *many* ideas, *many, many, many* ideas, I wanted to know what she fantasized about. Then I wanted to do that. Jennifer successfully freed herself from her shoes and pants using her feet while I lavished her breasts with wet kisses, keeping my eyes open the whole time. I didn't want to miss a moment.

"A shower."

I paused, frowning. "A shower."

She squirmed, pushing her chest toward my mouth, and smoothing her palms down my body. Fitting her hands inside my jacket, she shoved it off, and then grabbed the hem of my shirt, lifting, pushing it up.

"I guess not here, but later?"

"Taking showers together has been on your mind?" I smiled, liking that she'd been thinking sexy thoughts.

Her fingers reached inside my boxers, encircled me, tugged. "*Yessss . . .*"

I grunted, the muscles in my stomach, back, bottom, and legs tensing, and my palms came to the table on either side of her for balance because she'd started stroking me with one hand while shoving at my pants with the other.

"I need you," she moaned, opening her legs wider, pulling me forward by my dick. "I need you, I need—"

"Shh." I covered her hand with mine, slowing her movements and staring into her eyes. She looked desperate.

Jenn was already on the cusp, and I'd barely touched her. If I took her like this, in this position, she'd come in ten seconds.

"Lie back." I fit my hand in the crook of her back and encouraged her to recline on the desk.

Once in position, her legs dangling over the edge, I stepped between her thighs, entering her slowly. Panting, her body bowed, her hands grabbing at nothing, her eyebrows lifting, her lips parting.

I swallowed a rush of saliva, my heart hammering in my chest as I greedily devoured the sight of her, prone, naked. I thought about withdrawing and kneeling, taking her with my mouth first, like I'd wanted. Our eyes locked, and she must've read the temptation in my eyes because she moaned again, her head rolling back, exposing her neck. She tilted her hips, her body instinctively seeking friction for that sweet spot at the juncture of her thighs. *Not yet.*

Canvasing her body, every delectable dip and soft curve, I lowered my eyes to watch as my cock stretched her opening. Hot and tight and slick. A shock of electricity climbed up my spine, the feel of her was too good, perfect, I couldn't think. She felt—

"Fuck." I began to withdraw, my stomach muscles tensing. Some base instinct had me pushing deeper inside, lulled by the feel of her walls against my bare skin. No wonder she felt so good. I wasn't wearing a condom!

"Wha-what's wrong?"

"I didn't put one on." I managed the words between clenched teeth while the thought tethering them slipped away, some primitive part of my mind urging me to just fucking forget about the stupid fucking condom. Jenn was on birth control.

Enjoy. Yourself.

"Put . . . what . . . on?"

God, watching her body move in response to mine, how she shifted, her lips parted, her breasts jostled with each rhythmic roll of my hips.

Hypnotizing. Skin against skin felt amazing, so amazing, so perfect and hot and tight and yielding.

"Cletus?"

I loved every part of her, I wanted to worship her. She would be worshiped, it's what she deserved. Peeled grapes and handcuffs. And an ice cube. And a feather. Maybe a blindfold. Definitely a spreader bar. When we got home, I was going to tie her up and kiss every inch of her body. I was going to use my fingers and tongue and the ice cube to make her squirm and beg.

Start now.

"Put what—ah!" She moaned again because I'd brushed the back of my fingers through the hair between her legs, teasing, giving her just a little friction but not enough.

"Please," she cried, angling her hips for more.

I bent to trail kisses between her breasts, nipping at her shoulders and neck, parting her folds with my fingers but not touching her where she needed.

I growled against her neck. "You want it? Touch yourself."

A shocked-sounding breath was quickly replaced by a hitching one as I laved my tongue into her ear, biting the lobe as I retreated.

Nonsensical words, part prayer, part praise, tumbled out of her, a litany of promises and pleases. Sliding a hand down her torso, to her hip, along her thigh, I hooked it behind her knee and brought it up, pushing deeper inside, harder. She whimpered, her reluctant fingers inching toward the inside of her leg.

I bowed my back, my attention on her hand hovering above her body. I needed a full view, so I straightened, bringing her other knee up and spreading her legs wider. The pretty pink nub revealed itself, wet, swollen, neglected. I bet it ached. My tongue darted out to moisten my lips. I wanted to lick it.

"Cletus?"

She'd asked for something new?

Threading our hands together, I brought her middle finger to where she needed, just a light tap, and instantly her body clamped around me, spasming. A cry building on a low moan became uncontrolled. She was gone, lost to her own bliss, and I was right behind her. Watching her fingers take over, touching and rubbing with no skill, clumsy, needful strokes. She squeezed around me, over and over. It was too much. Fire erupted at the base of my spine. I fell as I pushed and pushed until spent, my heart beating out of my chest, seeking hers.

God, she was lovely. Sexy. Spread out before me, all soft skin and sweetness, breathtaking, vulnerable and strong.

I still wanted to worship her. I wanted to get down on my knees and pledge troths and undying devotion and unending worship. Every time it was the same, the overwhelming sense that it could never get better than this.

But then, somehow, it always did.

CHAPTER TEN
JENN

"Paranoid? Probably. But just because you're paranoid doesn't mean there isn't an invisible demon about to eat your face."

— JIM BUTCHER, *STORM FRONT*

C letus and I spent the night at the Winston place.

More specifically, we slept in the carriage house's second bedroom, typically reserved for Roscoe on the weekends Jethro, Sienna, and Benjamin were in Green Valley. When Jethro and family were away, Billy stayed in the big house, keeping an eye on things. Otherwise, Billy opted for the master suite in the carriage house, a two-bedroom Victorian structure Jethro had remodeled a while back.

Originally, Jethro, Sienna, and their cute-as-pie baby had used the carriage house when they were in town. But with Duane and Jessica James off traveling the world, Roscoe in school, and everyone else—Beau, Ash, and Cletus—mostly cohabitating with their significant others, the Winston siblings only occupied their original rooms on the rare night here or there.

As much as Sienna encouraged Billy to stay in the main house all the time, it was clear that the second oldest Winston brother wanted to give the growing family their space and privacy. Plus, Benjamin hadn't been a good sleeper, keeping anyone within a hallway's distance up most of the night.

I suspected Billy enjoyed watching the aftereffects of Jethro's sleepless nights from afar, but still be close enough to witness his brother's suffering firsthand. Their relationship had been an interesting one to observe and gave me hope that, one day, Isaac and I might reconcile, settle into something similar despite the years and hurt feelings between us.

Point was, if Jethro Winston could repent and embrace a better life, anyone could.

Cletus and I did stop back by my place to grab a few items before heading over for the night, making a big show of talking about how much fun we'd had at the club, how it was just what we'd needed after the last few weeks. Of course Cletus used the opportunity to drop some innuendos—

"You should lie back and relax more often."

"We should get a desk in here, they're so useful."

"Trying new things should always be a priority."

"Do you think it's too late for a shower before bed?"

And the worst, "It was a pleasure to see you get in touch with yourself."

By the time we'd packed up and skedaddled for the homestead, my face was on fire. But we didn't talk at all during the drive. I didn't feel like we could speak freely, not yet, not until we knew for sure who'd put that camera in my house and the extent to which we'd been bugged.

Following Cletus's lead, we both left our phones off and in the car. He'd sent a group message to Billy, Sienna, and Jet from the club's office to expect us after midnight. Billy had texted back: 1) that the second bedroom in the carriage house was free since Roscoe hadn't come home for the weekend, and 2) to please be quiet when we arrived as he had a big meeting in the morning.

Sure enough, all was quiet and dark when we arrived. Despite Cletus's earlier innuendo, he passed out within minutes. Whereas I took a shower. A sleepy, lonely shower.

I slept better than I had in weeks. I figured this was because Cletus and I had finally talked freely. Perhaps I was paranoid, but I wondered if the carriage house had also been bugged. Maybe even the big house too. I worried we'd have to drive out of town to different clubs each time we wanted to talk.

I was awoken by my big man feathering my face with kisses and copping a feel over my pajamas. "Are you awake? Alex sent a drone," he whispered.

I opened one eye. "A drone?"

"Yep." He leaned away so his eyes could meet mine, no longer whispering. "Your house has cameras and listening devices and—get this—they're DEA."

"DEA?"

"Drug Enforcement Agency."

I shook my head, uncertain I'd heard him right. Or maybe this was a dream. *Am I asleep?* "Why would the DEA want to bug my house? And how can Alex tell the difference between FBI and DEA surveillance equipment?"

"I don't know the particulars, only that he does something with high frequency sound waves and can, uh, tap into government inventory systems undetected. The man is magical. And, furthermore, I have no idea why they're interested in us, but we'll find out. And your momma's place has no cameras, but it does have bugs—not the cockroach kind—all FBI."

"FBI?!" I opened the other eye. "Why would the FBI be interested in my mother? What is going on?"

"I have thoughts about that, but let's save them for later. The best news is that the homestead has nothing."

"Nothing?"

"Nope. Nothing. The big house and the carriage house are clean. I guess no one wants to bug the house of a congressman." The side of Cletus's mouth quirked up. "Finally, something good comes out of Billy winning the state seat."

"So we can do whatever we want here? Say whatever we want?" What a relief!

"Looks like. But to be sure, let's leave our phones off and in the car until Alex takes a look." Then he wagged his eyebrows. "We don't have time for a shared shower, but we do have time for a quickie."

I sighed happily, flinging my arms wide and lying back. "Please. Be my guest. Do whatever you want."

"Whatever I want?" I'd closed my eyes again, but I could *hear* the challenge and eyebrow raise in his tone.

"Whatever you—Oh!"

One hand was already in my underwear giving me light, skillful strokes, and another had clamped over my mouth. "Shh. Billy's definition of early is different than ours. He's still here, getting ready. Can you be quiet?"

I nodded, spreading my legs wider and tilting my hips, seeking more of his touch.

Uncovering my mouth, he pressed a quick kiss to my lips, tasting of mint toothpaste but mostly mouthwash, the strong kind that keeps your tongue tingling after use. In the next moment, he'd whipped off my pajama bottoms and shoved my shirt up, yanking me to the foot of the bed and kneeling on the floor between my knees.

Now I was fully awake.

"Cletus!"

"Shh. This will feel new." His breath fell against my inner thigh and he sounded almost gleeful. Placing a kiss right at my very center, he then suckled me into his mouth, his tongue sliding back and forth with lazy sweeps, and a lightning bolt of peculiar sensation sent a shock up my spine.

The mouthwash.

When I would've jolted off the bed, he pressed me down, one hand on my belly, the other gripping my hip. I had to cover my mouth with my own hands to keep from crying out. It certainly felt new and my mind raced, wondering if the tingle would lead to a burning? But . . . no. It felt amazing. New and amazing seemed to be Cletus's specialty.

I didn't last long, maybe two minutes, so his promise of a quickie had been accurate. Stars burst behind my eyes and I pressed my head back against the mattress. Perhaps not satisfied with the expediency of my completion, Cletus pushed a finger—maybe two—inside and I was coming all over again.

Once I'd finished writhing and the aftershocks were at an end, he placed wet kisses on my thighs, stomach, ribs, pausing at my breasts and whispered a deep, "Hello, girls."

I covered my face because it made me laugh, like he was picking my boobs up in a bar or something. He was so funny and wonderful. Cletus spent a few long moments loving them, kissing, massaging, eventually coming to my side and propping his head up on one hand, his elbow braced on the mattress.

"Good morning, Jenn." His eyes twinkled down at me, his free hand moving over my body, just touching for the sake of touching.

"Good morning, Cletus." I turned toward him and reached for his waist expecting to find pajama pants. Instead, I encountered a belt. "What is this?!"

"We have things that need seeing to. I've been informed through the Winston family grapevine that Ashley is on her way over and Sienna is expecting us for breakfast. We got to go."

"Let me do something to you first." It was silly, but I still had trouble saying the words *blow job.*

"Uh, no." He rolled off the bed, fast as a sailfish, before I could get a good hold on his clothes.

Sitting up, I righted my shirt and scowled. "What? Why not?"

"I'll meet you at the big house."

"Cletus!"

I jumped off the bed and, miraculously, made it to the bedroom door before he did. Perhaps I was more motivated.

"Jenn—"

"Why won't you ever let me do that? I know you like it."

Cletus shoved his hands in his pockets, holding himself away, and my eyes moved over him. The man was entirely too sexy, especially today for some reason. He wore jeans that fit him well and a black long-sleeve T-shirt that did such wonderful things for the muscles in his shoulders and arms. But beneath the untucked shirt, he also wore one of his complicated belts. Cletus had begun special ordering these contraptions from some gadget guru on the internet, and I always had trouble taking them off. They might as well have been of the chastity variety. *I really need to practice undoing his belts.*

"I do like it, and I think we both know that's an understatement." Cletus was looking everywhere but at me. "And yet Sienna has made that fine breakfast. Plus, let's not forget Ashley coming over. She's working today, so we only get a sliver of her time before she needs to leave."

"I'll make it quick."

"I don't like it quick." An edge entered his voice and brilliant eyes.

I crossed my arms, inspecting him, feeling a tad put off.

He must've sensed my discontent because his gaze softened and he came closer, into my space, and pulled my arms from my chest so he could thread our fingers together. "I love how you love me. I love it a little too much. You know me. I don't like most desserts, fast food, music on a sound system instead of live, cars that are more flash than class."

This last one pulled a smile from me, and I tilted my head to the side. "You like quality."

"I'm particular."

"Are you saying my blow jobs aren't quality?"

"Oh good Lord, no." He appeared offended by the question, as though I'd questioned his love for blueberries. "No, no. Jenn. Often, after you do *that* to me and—you may have noticed—sometimes, immediately after we make love, I require recovery. I require time with you, and only you. Time we do not have at present, not if we want to have enough time with Ash to get things moving with Jackson."

I thought back over our months together, sharing a life. There had been times after we'd been intimate when Cletus hadn't seemed quite himself, when he'd seemed raw, when that infamous control of his had disintegrated. He'd get real quiet, but it was like he *needed* me in his arms, needed my body close, and if anything interrupted this time, he'd be grumpy for days.

"Okay," I conceded, withdrawing one of my hands from his so I could point a finger at him. "But we're doing it. And soon."

He grinned, it looked saucy, and I swear his handsomeness made me dizzy. "Yes, ma'am."

"This coffee is too hot." Cletus frowned at his mug first before turning the frown to the coffee machine. "And this machine is new."

"I got it for Jethro." Sienna pointed with a butter knife toward the machine. "He always pours himself a cup and forgets about it. I figured, if it's super hot to begin with, then it'll be at least warm when he gets back to it."

Cletus inspected Sienna for a moment as she resumed buttering toast. "Those for Jethro?"

She nodded. "Yes."

"And the eggs?" He lifted his mug toward the two eggs she had frying in the pan. Sienna, Cletus, and I had finished our breakfast earlier.

"Mm-hmm." Sienna moved to the pan and used a spatula to place them on the newly buttered toast.

"I'm really happy y'all got married."

The dark-haired beauty smiled but it held a question. "Why? Because you always wanted someone to make Jethro eggs on toast?"

"Something like that." Cletus crossed to the kitchen table, a pleased look on his face, and brought the mug to his lips before remembering the coffee was too hot. Frowning anew, he set the mug down.

"You should let me blow on it," I said, low so that only he could hear, and his gaze cut to mine, held. I smiled.

He did not. But his eyes sure did get real hot.

"I'm here." Ashley, announcing her arrival with a soft voice, stepped through the back door. She glanced at Sienna. "How'd he sleep?"

"I don't know." Sienna shrugged. "You know nothing wakes me up. But I'm about to wake up Jet. Shelly is coming over to watch Ben, and we need to leave in a half hour, so I'm making him breakfast. Do you want anything?"

"God, no," Ashley blurted, holding up her hand as though to stave off a carnival clown, earning her a questioning look from all three of us. "I mean, I—uh—already ate." She swallowed. The action seemed to take some effort.

I glanced at Cletus and found him inspecting his sister closely. "Ash, are you feeling okay?"

"Yeah. I'm fine. Just—" the Winston sister pasted a forced, closed-mouthed smile on her face "—tummy trouble."

"Are you sure? You seem to be on the precipice of a severe gastrointestinal . . . voiding."

"No. I already barfed." Ash chuckled and winced. "I should be fine for the rest of the day, I just need a lemon drop or something."

Cletus scratched his jaw through his beard, inspecting his sister as she walked stiffly to the table. "You want me to mix you a cocktail?"

"No, Cletus. The candy, not the cocktail. I have some in my bag. Just, hold on a second. Janie sent some . . . ugh, never mind. Just give me a minute."

Feeling the press of attention on me, I glanced at Sienna and found her watching me with an *intent* and *knowing* look, her eyes big as quarters, her full lips smashed together as though working real hard not to spill some beans. "Maybe Jenn could make you some lemon custard tarts . . ."

My mouth dropped, my eyes widening with the realization, *Ash is pregnant!* OH MY GOD! When Sienna was pregnant with Benjamin, the only thing that helped with her nausea—or so she said—were my lemon custard tarts.

This was so exciting. So exciting. BABIES! *YAY!*

Cletus looked to me and did a double take. "What? Why do you look like that?"

"Like what?" I squeaked, picking up my English breakfast tea and taking a sip.

"Like you gotta pee and you're real happy about it. What happened?"

I shook my head quickly. "Nothing."

"That's an untruth." He pointed an accusing finger at me, his back straightening as his eyes ping-ponged between his sister, Sienna, and me. "Someone is telling me what's going on, right now."

"Slow your gourd, Cletus." Ashley huffed, pulling a bag of yellow hard candies from her purse. "I'm pregnant, okay? Just give me a minute to get one of these suckers in my mouth."

Cletus flinched back. His jaw dropped and he blinked like crazy. "You're *what?*"

"With child."

I jumped from my seat and jogged to her. "Can I hug you? This is so exciting!"

"Of course. All hugs are welcome from you, anytime." She opened her arms and I immediately stepped into the embrace, careful not to squeeze too hard.

"I'll make you those custard tarts today," I promised. I no longer worked at the bakery on the weekends, but for Ashley, I'd make an exception.

"They really helped me," Sienna said as she grabbed the plate of eggs on toast and darted out of the kitchen. "See you later. Love, love, love all of you."

Waving to Sienna's departing form, I turned to Cletus, expecting him to be next in line for a hug. Instead, he stood by the table, staring at Ash like he needed a moment to process.

"Are you okay, Cletus?" Ashley gave me a quick look. "Do you need a lie down and a valium?"

"When were you going to tell me?"

"I just told you, right now."

He still looked confused, befuddled, caught off guard. "What about an event? Shouldn't you be telling folks this news at an event? This deserves fanfare and fireworks."

"Cletus. You spent half your engagement party complaining about having to be there and the other half being questioned by the police, and you want me to throw an event to announce the fact that Drew and I had sex that resulted in the begetting of offspring? All while I try to keep from breathing in through my nose?"

"When you put it like that, no." Cletus, a smile finally claiming his features, exhaled an enormous breath and positively beamed at his sister. "Wow, Ash. Congratulations," he said softly, sincerely, gazing at her like she was the most precious thing in the world.

My heart warmed as I looked between the two siblings.

"Thank you, Cletus—"

"I was talking to myself." His smile became a sinister grin, and he rubbed his hands together, shooting me an excited look. "This is going to be so good. I'll be the godfather, of course."

"Of course." Ashley, voice flat, popped a lemon candy in her mouth and spoke around it, shaking her head at her brother. "Let me just sit down and we can pick out colleges."

I walked back to the table and sat, picking up my tea and feeling buoyed by this wonderful news. Selfishly, I hoped Ash and Drew would make Cletus the godfather, then maybe I'd be the godmother. I'd always wanted to be one. Regardless, a new baby! To cuddle and kiss. I couldn't wait.

"Yes. Colleges. Good idea. And it'd be great if she were a girl. Just throwing that request out there." Cletus gave Ashley his signature somber nod.

"I'll see what I can do," she drawled, trying to look irritated. Mostly, she looked amused.

"And, obviously, your mission with Jackson is canceled."

"What? Why?" Ashley pulled off her jacket.

"I don't want him sniffing around you while you're in such a delicate condition. One look at his face and you'd barf for sure." Cletus turned back to the table, sitting down in front of his hot coffee. "We'll find another way."

"You are a loon." She set her jacket and her purse on the kitchen counter. "Besides, I already did it."

"What?" He glanced over his shoulder at her, frowning.

"That's right." Ash pulled her long sleeves up to her elbows. "Drew sent me a message after he met with you, to give me a heads-up, so I texted Jackson and we had dinner last night."

I hid my smile behind another sip of tea.

"Jenn, take note. Never underestimate the effect my sister has on blond law enforcement."

She rolled her eyes. "And I think I got you some good stuff, so listen up, I have to leave here in an hour for work." Ash pulled out the chair next to mine, her movements still a little stiff, her nose slightly wrinkled like the kitchen stank.

I took a quiet testing sniff and found nothing offensive. Just the lingering smell of toast and eggs maybe?

"What do you want to know first?" The candy in Ash's mouth seemed to be helping, she looked less green.

"Well, fine. Since you already suffered through a meal with Jackson. Have they found the gun used to shoot Kip?" Cletus folded his arms on the tabletop, leaning forward.

"No. They haven't found any gun. But there was a rope around Kip's neck when he was found in the car, which meant he was strangled and shot. Oh, Cletus, go look in my bag. Jackson gave me some pictures of the rope."

"He gave you pictures of the rope?" Cletus asked as he stood, looking confused.

"He sure did, and a list of folks who were at the party but left before the shots were fired. They either have no alibi or their alibi isn't rock solid."

I squirmed in my seat, an uncomfortable, heavy sensation settling on my chest. I thought about excusing myself. Hearing about my father, how he'd died, that there was a list of suspects, was much harder than I'd thought it would be. I wasn't prepared.

But, at the same time, I needed to know. I wanted to clear my momma's name.

Digging through Ashley's bag, Cletus pulled out two photoprints and a piece of scrap paper. He stared at the photos for a long time, giving none of his thoughts away. Then he flipped the pictures around to show us both. "What kind of knot is that?"

"Looks like a farmer's knot to me." Ashley crossed her arms.

I shrugged because I had no idea. I wasn't a knot expert.

Cletus frowned at the picture of the rope and knot again. "And what kind of rope is that?"

"Jackson said it was something called Leaded Polysteel rope."

Cletus's eyes moved up and to the left. "A farmer's knot in crabbing rope. How'd they do that?"

Sitting up straighter in my chair, I asked, "What's crabbing rope?"

He didn't seem to hear my question because, staring at nothing, he muttered, "It sinks . . ."

"Pardon?" Ashley tilted her head. "It stinks?"

"Sorry. Nothing." Cletus turned his attention to the scrap paper and scanned it quickly. "How many times was he shot?" He sounded so detached, like was asking about laundry soap instead of someone's death.

"Twice at point blank, both in the chest. He died almost instantly," came Ashley's equally detached reply.

"Do they know if the gun used to fire into the bakery was the same as the one used on Kip?" He came back to the table, placing the pictures of the rope flat in front of him and sliding the scrap of paper to me.

"Yes, and it was. Same gun."

I took a deep, steadying breath, and then read the list.

Diane Donner ✘
Nancy Danvish ✓
Florence McClure ✓
Nikki Becker ✘
Kenneth Miller –✘
Posey Lamont ✘
Jedidiah Hill ✓
Vanessa Romero ✘
Roger Gangersworth ✘
Elena Wilkinson ✓
Jennifer Sylvester ✘
Cletus Winston ✘

Wait. . . *WHAT?*

"Wait a minute." I picked up the paper and waved it. "Are these the suspects? Why are Cletus and I on this list?"

CHAPTER ELEVEN

JENN

"It is the mark of an educated mind to be able to entertain a thought without accepting it."

— ARISTOTLE, *METAPHYSICS*

I glanced between Ashley and Cletus, my heart in my throat. "Are we —are we suspects?"

Ashley gave me an unconcerned smile. "Y'all are each other's alibis. Nancy and Flo have each other as alibis too. Anyone who might've had a motive and who has no alibi or a questionable one is on that list. But don't worry, Jenn. Jackson didn't seem concerned about you. Boone spoke up for y'all, so did Jackson, even though you're using Diane's lawyer."

Cletus blew a puff of steam from his coffee cup, not seeming a lick concerned. "Ashley, did Kip die from the bullet wounds or from being strangled?"

"Technically, the gunshots killed him. But if he hadn't been shot, there's a case to be made that he would've died from strangulation. Basically, it's six of one, half a dozen of the other. He was dead either way."

I dropped my eyes to my teacup, inspecting it as I breathed in through my nose slowly, my momentary spike of alarm about possibly being a suspect replaced with a dark, painful wave of grief. Blinking my eyes against sudden moisture, I forced myself to suppress the distracting emotions.

I could do this. These details were important to helping my momma. *Pretend we're talking about someone else.*

"Jackson thinks there were two people, a shooter and a strangler. But, despite what Jackson thinks is true," Ashley added, "the official story coming out of the department is that the same person who strangled him also shot him."

"That's crazy," I said, looking to Cletus. "Why would they think that?"

"I have no idea." Ashley shrugged tiredly.

"Why is Diane their top suspect?" Cletus seemed to be working through a mental list of questions.

"Well, first, she won't talk."

Cletus's lip curled. "She won't talk at all?"

"According to Jackson, she talks through her lawyer. But you both know this, 'cause it's how y'all made your statements too. The police submit questions, she sends through a response. That's why they stopped bringing her in. No use. Jackson said it just makes her look really guilty, even though no one thinks she is."

Cletus didn't seem surprised by any of this. "What's the story she told the police?"

Ashley's forehead wrinkled. "Diane hasn't talked to you?"

Before I could answer, Cletus cut in, "Just tell us what Jackson said."

Cletus's sister inspected me for a moment before answering. "Well, okay then. According to the written statements submitted by y'all's lawyer, Ms. Donner says she got a text from Jenn to meet her in the parking lot, and then—"

"What?" I looked to Cletus. "I didn't send her a message. I was with you."

"Go on Ash." Cletus's tone was grim. "What else?"

"Diane says she didn't go to the parking lot but went instead to the honeymoon cabin, because that's where Jenn left her phone for the night, and she knew Jenn didn't have the phone with her at the party. Diane claims she wasn't feeling well, with all the upheaval at the party, so by the time she got to the honeymoon cabin, she had a migraine and had to lie down with a pillow over her head. She says she didn't hear the shots or anything else."

Cletus grimaced as he listened to Ashley, visibly distressed. "Are you serious? That story makes no sense. She got a text from Jenn, but instead of going to where the text told her to go, she went to the cabin? What?"

"Hey"—Ashely lifted up her hands—"I'm just telling you what Jackson told me."

"But the police searched the cabins that night. They searched the whole lodge," Cletus said matter-of-factly.

"Yes. Diane's statement says that around 8:00 PM, which would be after the shooting, after they noted all the cars in the lot—hers included —but before they searched the cabins, she drove home with her phone off, and went to bed."

"Again, are you serious?" Cletus seemed stunned.

"Yes," Ashley confirmed.

"That's her story?"

"Yep. And the thing is, it checks out—as far as they can tell. They didn't have enough man power that night to keep an eye on all the parking lots, *and* tape off the crime scene, *and* question everyone in the barn, *and* search all the rooms and cabins of the lodge, *and* maintain a police presence elsewhere in the county. Diane had closed the lodge to outside guests for the whole weekend, so why would they use resources to watch empty rooms?"

"Is that why they're outside her house now? Watching and listening?" Cletus tapped his fingers on the table lightly. "They don't believe her story?"

"Oh now, see, that's something Jackson wouldn't talk about." Ashley lifted her eyebrows, her eyes getting big. "Anything about the night of the murder and all the evidence and suspects, he was happy to answer all my questions. But when I asked where they were getting the money to keep Diane under that kind of watch—'cause you know the sheriff doesn't have that in his budget—Jackson clammed right up. But he did say it was, uh, he said something like, 'That's not my jurisdiction.'"

"And they're not making a secret about it either," I piped up. "They *wave* to me every time I drive past. It's like they just want to intimidate her or something. And none of them are from the sheriff's department. I don't know these people."

Cletus's gaze lingered on me, and I got the sense he didn't want me to volunteer what he'd learned from his friend Alex, that the bugs in my momma's house were FBI. He also looked like he was making a mental note of something.

"One thing at a time. Let's get back to Diane." His fingers ceased tapping and he lifted his chin toward Ashley. "Why else is she a suspect. She won't talk, they don't believe her story, but what else do they have?"

"They have a partial fingerprint on the car, where someone with bloody hands touched the door, and they think it's hers."

"Is that so?"

"Yep, but they can't be sure because she won't submit to being fingerprinted. And she won't leave her house, so they can't lift one off a discarded coffee cup, a grocery store cart, or something like that."

"My momma's fingerprints have to be all over the lodge. Why not take one from there?"

"The lodge is private property. Lots of people's fingerprints are all over the lodge. Unless they can prove a fingerprint is hers one hundred percent, then they can't link her to the partial print. Jackson seemed real frustrated about it. Also, Diane has the most obvious motive. Everyone knows their divorce was bitter and contentious, even though she was able to keep almost everything in the end except that vacation home, all that lawyering must've cost her buckets of money. Oh! And last year I guess Diane said she wanted to kill Kip? At least that's what Elena Wilkinson told the police." Ashley ticked each reason off on a separate finger.

"So Elena talked to the police?" Cletus seemed to find this surprising. "I thought she lawyered up that night too?"

"She did lawyer up at first. However, a day later, she went in and made a statement on her own."

He leaned back in his chair. "Do you know what Elena told them?"

"I think so, or I can tell you what Jackson told me. Elena said Kip had been drinking that night, real sore he wasn't invited. He got in the car and she was worried, 'cause he'd been drinking, right? So she got in the car and he drove them to the lodge. She said she tried to stop him from going in, but he was crazy, and she couldn't talk sense into him. Elena made it real clear that Kip had every right to be there, since his daughter was getting married."

I felt my heart harden with every word Ashley spoke. My father had no right to be there. He'd forfeited those rights the moment he'd lifted a hand to me. *He'd forfeited them way before that, you just forgave him too easily.*

Ashley stretched, grimacing. "Sorry, can one of y'all get me a soda water or a ginger ale or something? If I stand up, I get dizzy, and then sometimes I'll be barfing again."

"Yes, absolutely." Cletus shot out of his seat, crossing to the fridge with quick steps. "Jenn, do you want anything?"

"I'm fine, thanks."

"Oh, Jenn. This is important." Ashley turned to me. "Elena also said, and I thought y'all should know this, she felt the restraining order last year against her and Kip was served just for the purpose of screwing him over in the divorce settlement. She felt like they would've gotten more money—more than just the vacation house and boat in Key West—from Diane if Jenn had dropped the charges. She blames Jenn for losing Diane's money and the stake in the lodge."

"I—" I shook my head, horrified. They'd assaulted *me* and that was somehow my fault? "What a—"

"Raging bitch," Ashley filled in. "It's fine. You can say it. You're with family."

I chuckled, feeling tired all of a sudden. My emotions were giving me whiplash. One minute I'm having a hard time talking about my father's murder, now I'm having uncharitable thoughts about the man and his mistress. I didn't understand myself.

"Anyway." Ashley sighed. "We all know what happened next. Kip and Elena walk in, cause a fuss, blah blah blah. Jackson and the other deputy walked them back to the car. They leave. Then—"

"Wait." Cletus twisted the cap off a bottle of ginger ale and set it down in front of Ash. "Who was driving?"

"What?"

"Who was driving? When Elena and Kip left?"

"I don't know. Why?"

"Elena said Kip had been drinking, right? And he sounded like it at the party. I bet Elena was driving when they left. Jackson wouldn't have let a drunk man drive."

"That's true." I nodded. "I was thinking the same thing at the party, when my—when he was talking. He wasn't just buzzed, he was drunk."

"Do you want me to ask Jackson?" Ashley looked between Cletus and me. "I can call."

"Yes." Cletus reclaimed his seat and lifted the coffee cup. "But only if interacting with him won't agitate your stomach."

Ashley sent Cletus a glare. "Jackson is nice. Y'all need to stop treating him like an enemy. That stuff with us in high school is all in the past. And besides, I think it's pretty obvious he told me all this stuff 'cause he wanted me to tell you."

"Say again?" Cletus lowered his coffee cup, never taking a sip.

"Jackson can't be seen or heard talking to you. He knows someone has Diane under surveillance—hopefully you've already figured that out. Anyway, he probably figures he can't talk to you without someone listening in or it raising red flags. But, off the record, since we're old friends, he can talk to me. I'm not being watched. He gave me a picture of the *rope* for hootenanny's sake. What am I going to do with pictures of the rope?"

"Crabbing rope is expensive. Perhaps he thought to tempt you with a fishing trip." Cletus narrowed his eyes, but I could tell he was just teasing his sister.

"Come on, Cletus. Jackson said—and I quote"—Ashley dropped her voice to imitate Jackson's—"'Let me know if any new questions arise, or if *someone* has any good theories about where we should be looking' end quote."

"Hmm."

126

"I see you, stroking your beard. I see that glimmer in your eye." Ash lifted her soda bottle toward Cletus. "You like Jackson, admit it."

"I don't dislike him."

She took a swig of the soda, her mouth curving on one side. "Well, anyway. I don't have much longer before I gotta go, so let me finish."

"You'll find out who was driving, still an unknown, but we do know Elena and my father drove away."

Ash nodded at my statement. "That's right. According to Elena, they didn't make it home. They turned around because Kip said he wasn't ready to leave and wanted to get Diane alone, to see if they could come to some sort of understanding about walking Jenn down the aisle at the wedding."

"Pardon me?" Cletus's lip curled.

"Elena said Kip regretted causing a scene, and all he really wanted was to be recognized—or some such nonsense—and given his proper due as Jenn's father."

"Ugh." He pressed a hand to his stomach. "Now I think I may need to empty my stomach."

"Right?" Ash snorted, sending her brother a commiserating look. She glanced at me and her gaze turned immediately contrite. "Oh gosh, Jenn. I'm sorry. Listen to me, I'm awful. That wasn't very nice of me. And—oh, I'm so sorry. I'm not feeling my best. I should've been more sensitive. He was your daddy and—"

"No. It's fine. I know it's frowned upon to speak ill of the dead, but the thought of my father walking me down the aisle makes me want to barf too."

Ashley reached for my hand and squeezed. "If you don't mind me asking, who is walking you down the aisle?"

"I asked Billy."

Ashley's grin was immediate.

"You did?" Cletus's question drew my attention to him. The wrinkles lining his forehead, and the way his eyes had widened with what looked like wonder, struck me as incredibly cute.

"Yes. I know this might not make a lick of sense y'all, since I think I'm only about ten years younger than your brother, but he's been very . .

. paternal with me. You know? Or what I figured having an interested father would be like. Giving me good advice and always caring about what I'm thinking or feeling, checking in. He even remembered my birthday and told me he was proud of—of—what? What's wrong?"

Ashley, quite abruptly, had burst into tears. "I'm sorry," she rasped. "I'm so sorry, it's just—yes. I know what you mean. I know exactly what you mean." Withdrawing her hand from mine, she covered her face. "These stupid hormones."

Cletus's gentle smile told me he approved of my choice. He then abruptly frowned. "Wait. Can he walk you down the aisle and be my best man?"

"You haven't asked Billy to be your best man yet?" Ashley's tears dried up as quickly as they'd started. "What the heck is wrong with you? Have you asked anyone?"

"I was getting around to it." He sniffed, looking down his nose at his sister. "I have a list."

"Well a list is no good if you don't ask!" She banged a fist on the tabletop. "Jenn asked us ages ago."

I nibbled my bottom lip, wondering if I should pick someone else to walk me down the aisle. I hadn't meant to usurp Cletus's intentions for his brother.

"Don't fret, Jenn. Billy can do both, no rule against it. He's used to multitasking. But—you—ask him soon. And everyone else on your list." Ash narrowed her eyes on Cletus. "The wedding is a little over a month away. Time's a tickin'. There's tuxedo fittings, all sorts of things to schedule."

"What? A tuxedo? No." Cletus lifted the coffee cup again, and this time he did take a sip. He flinched, making a face like it was still too hot.

"You're not wearing a tux?" His sister looked truly dismayed. "You better be in a tux. This wedding is going to be beautiful."

"Nope. I want my groomsmen to wear coveralls. The real nice kind. Dickies."

I closed my eyes and pressed my lips together, knowing that Cletus was teasing his sister. He might not have asked his groomsmen yet, but he'd already bought the tux he'd be wearing months ago from Billy's bespoke suit tailor.

Ash leaned back in her chair, shaking her head. "And you want me to make you the godfather of my child."

Cletus, enjoying himself way too much, affixed a somber façade to his features. "Let's stay on topic, shall we? What happened—according to Elena—when they got back to the lodge?"

"Fine. Elena says they parked. After that she doesn't remember."

"What?" I asked, the levity from moments ago forgotten. "She said what?"

"She says they parked the car. The next thing she remembers is the sheriff waking her up in the woods."

"How is that possible?" I pressed, feeling my blood pressure spike.

"She was hit over the head." Ash said, like this explained Elena's loss of memory.

"In the car?" Cletus stroked his beard.

"She can't say. But I do know she was definitely hit over the head. When I was with her that night, she was disoriented and had a legitimate contusion, a blunt force head trauma."

Still stroking his beard, Cletus leaned forward. "Anything else?"

"Yes. Here's something interesting. That list I gave you? They tested everyone on it for gunpowder residue. That's what the marks next to the name are. Elena's results came back positive—"

"Then she did it!" I sat up straight, jabbing an excited finger into the air.

"No, listen," Ashley addressed me. "Her hands had gunpowder residue, but she explained this away by claiming she and Kip had gone shooting earlier in the day. Her story checked out, they had gone to a range. Plus, when they found Elena unconscious, she was wearing gloves, and the gloves had no residue on the outside."

"What about my mother?"

Ashley gave me an encouraging smile. "Her test came back completely negative. No residue."

"I have two more questions," Cletus announced, waiting until we were both looking at him before asking, "When did Elena ask for a lawyer?"

Ashley licked her bottom lip, then bit it, her gaze dropping to the table. "I don't know. Before I showed up, though. I can ask Jackson about that too."

"Do that. Okay, second question, what kind of gloves did she have on?"

Ashley blinked, then stared straight ahead. "I don't know. They were, uh, brown, I think? Sorry."

Cletus smiled. His gaze, sparkling with mischief, came to me. "I think we have what we need."

CHAPTER TWELVE

JENN

"All wars are civil wars because all men are brothers... Each one owes infinitely more to the human race than to the particular country in which he was born."

— FRANCOIS DE SALIGNAC DE LA MOTHE-
FENELON

We chatted for a bit longer, about the wedding mostly, as Ashley stood from the table very slowly and sipped on her ginger ale.

"I'm so excited, and I can't wait to see Duane and Jess." She smiled despite how the color seemed to drain from her cheeks the moment she straightened. "I've always wanted a big, splashy wedding."

"And so you shall have one. Take ours."

"Very funny, Cletus." Her nose wrinkled and her lips curled like his words smelled bad. But, in fairness, she'd been wearing a face of slight disgust since walking in the door. *Morning sickness.*

"When the time is right"—I cut in, sending Cletus a quelling look—"your wedding to Drew will be wonderful, and please let me help."

"Thanks, but I honestly don't know if we'll ever get married."

This seemed to frustrate Cletus because his eyelids drooped and his mouth mashed itself together, but he said nothing, just glared at his shoes.

"Can I ask why not?" I was curious. She'd done such a great job with our wedding and had really seemed to enjoy herself. Plus, she'd just admitted to always wanting a big, splashy wedding. "No pressure. If it's just not your thing—"

"No, no. It's fine. This might sound strange, but I imagined planning it with my mother. Now that's she's gone, I feel so stuck. On the one hand, I don't want to plan something without her. But on the other, I'm not willing to compromise on the dream." Ashley snorted lightly, like she found herself silly. "It's such a dumb dream. But it almost feels like, if I elope, it's like I'm admitting that my mother isn't here anymore, that she's gone, and some dreams will never be."

Oh my heart.

I'd never wanted a big wedding. Perhaps because of my youth. How I'd been thrust into pageants, beauty contests, and all nature of splashy events at my mother's insistence. That said, I didn't mind what our wedding had morphed into. I loved that Ashley and my mother had seemed to have the time of their lives planning it. I loved that my mother had been made happy and distracted over the last year.

But mostly, I loved that the wedding—just like the plans for the engagement party—had become a family affair, with all of Cletus's siblings and significant others pitching in. It was shaping up to be beautiful, yes, but also a demonstration of their love for Cletus, and me, and for each other. And I loved *that*.

"You know, I even have my grandmother Oliver's wedding dress? My momma had it restitched, certain I'd wear it for my wedding. I tried it on last October, on the anniversary of my momma's death, just to feel closer to her. And . . ." Ashley pressed her fingers to her lips and swallowed a few times before she could continue. "It fit like it had been made for me. And that made me so sad 'cause she'll never see me in it."

Cletus sniffed, lifting glassy eyes to his sister, but his silence persisted.

"I don't know what to do." Ashley laughed, wiping at her cheeks and giving her head a subtle shake. "But I do know I want to marry Drew. Maybe we should just . . . elope and be done with it."

"Don't do that," Cletus said, his voice low and rough as he stood and walked to grab her coat. "You deserve to live your dreams, Ash. Give it time. There's no rush."

Ashley turned big eyes to me, and now she laughed in earnest. "Oh? Really? Mr. *When-will-y'all-get-married-already*?"

"I've changed my mind."

His sister lifted an eyebrow at this statement.

"It does happen!" Holding out her jacket, he crossed to her. "Now put this on. You'll be late for work."

"I won't, I have another half hour before I have to be there. But I should go. I want to stop by the OB's office to pick up the sonogram pictures. Their printer was broken when I had it done."

"Can you snap a picture of the sonogram?" he asked. "With your phone?"

"Sure, but—Cletus—there's not much to see yet. Wait until week eighteen, when I'm out of the first trimester. I know I can't wait for this nausea to stop, I feel so gross all the time."

"Well, just the same." He pressed a kiss to his sister's cheek. "By the way, you're gorgeous, Ash. You're going to make a great mother."

"Thank you, Cletus—"

"And I'm going to make the best godfather."

She smacked him lightly on the shoulder, rolling her eyes. "We'll see."

"Who else is in contention?" he asked, making me wonder if he had plans to launch a smear campaign.

"I'm not telling." Ashley turned to me and pulled me in for another hug, speaking to her brother while she did, "And don't go trying to pump Drew for info either."

"Did I miss the party?" Jethro shuffled into the kitchen, an empty plate in his hand. He was showered and dressed but looked exhausted.

"Did you know Ash and Drew are pregnant?" Cletus squinted at his oldest brother.

"I did." Jethro placed his dish in the sink, and then turned, winking at his sister. "Why? Didn't you?"

Cletus made a sound like *harrumph* and crossed his arms. "Oh, by the way, you wanna be a groomsman?"

"Sure." Jet's smile widened and he looked a little more awake. "Do I need a new tux, or . . .?"

"We're wearing Dickies. Coveralls, " Cletus said flatly, sending Ash a grumpy look.

"Oh good Lord." She appealed to the ceiling.

"Cool." Jethro nodded, shrugged, and shuffled toward Ash, placing a kiss on her cheek, stopped in front of me and placed a kiss on my cheek, and then paused in front of Cletus. He hesitated for a second, then placed a kiss on Cletus's cheek, wrapping his arms around his brother. "Thanks for including me."

Cletus frowned, saying, "You're a dummy," but he returned his brother's hug.

I looked to Ashley and found her eyes watery again. "I need to get out of here before I start crying again. Jenn"—she gave me an unsteady but happy smile—"don't worry about the wedding shower. We'll have it here. Tell your momma I'm happy to take over the planning."

"Are you sure? I can—"

"No. I'm sure. I love to help." Ashley's smile spread. "Okay, see y'all later."

Meanwhile, Jethro had released Cletus and was now shuffling toward the kitchen doorway. "We got to go too. Shelly is upstairs with Ben. Ash, I'll walk you out."

Cletus came to stand next to me, reaching for and holding my hand as we watched his siblings go. When we heard the front door close, he turned to me. "What are your thoughts?"

"About what?" Goodness knows we'd covered a lot of ground with Ash.

"About your father's murder." His gaze moved over my face. "I hope you know I wasn't trying to be insensitive with my questions. But we needed information she had."

"I know. It was hard, especially when y'all were talking about the mode of . . . you know. But I agree. And now I feel like we should've done something sooner. Why do I feel like they're planning to arrest my momma any day now? And Cletus—" I stepped closer, lowering my voice even though he'd said no one was listening to the Winston house "—why are the FBI and DEA involved?"

"I'm still puzzling over the DEA and your house. I need to talk things over with Alex, see what he thinks. Speaking of which, let's go back to the carriage house. I need to message him." Cletus used his leverage on my hand to pull me to the kitchen table. He picked up the pictures of the rope and the list of suspects, tucking them in his back pocket. He then steered us to the back door.

"And the FBI?" I asked, following him outside.

"I suspect the FBI is invested in the case because of Repo."

"How so?"

"The Iron Wraiths have been on the FBI's radar for a long time. Repo knows where all the bodies are buried, but—more importantly—he's the money man. I suspect they got a tip that Repo and your momma are involved. If I had to guess, and this is pure conjecture, I'd say they're putting pressure on your mother to help them bring in Repo."

"Ugh."

"Like lining up dominoes. Diane is charged with Kip's murder, first degree. They negotiate a lower charge—manslaughter, maybe—and she brings in Repo. Repo turns state's evidence and brings down the Wraiths."

"That man." I ground my teeth, my temper spiking. "Why did he have to pick my mother?"

Cletus didn't respond, so I inspected his profile. "Please. Don't tell me you still think he loves her?"

"Then I won't tell you."

I pulled us to a stop. "Cletus. You can't be serious."

"I theorize the FBI thinks using your mother as leverage will make Repo turn state's evidence. If I'm right, then Repo cares about your mother a great deal, enough to turn against his club brothers, and that's no small thing."

"He's probably the one who shot my father in the first place. Maybe

Repo doesn't want my momma telling the FBI that. Maybe that's why she won't leave the house, because she's afraid of him."

"No." Cletus shook his head. "No. I don't think Repo shot your daddy."

"Then why was he there? To see my mother?"

Cletus opened his mouth as though to answer, his eyebrows pulling together, but we were interrupted by Billy exiting the carriage house.

He stopped short at the sight of us, waited for a beat, then said, "Hello."

"We're staying for a bit, in the carriage house." Cletus announced.

A little smile played over Billy's lips. "Miss my company, Cletus?"

"No. Also, you're walking Jenn down the aisle?"

My features twisted in an apologetic grimace, but Billy sent me a *don't worry about it* look as he responded to his brother. "Yes, I have that honor."

"You think you could also handle being my best man? If not, I'll find someone else. Jenn's request takes first priority." Cletus crossed his arms, his tone and expression grumpy, and that made no sense.

As I looked at how Cletus held himself, stiff and straight and bracing, I saw the hint of vulnerability there. Of course Cletus was acting grumpy. He hated being vulnerable.

Billy, who knew Cletus and his moods better than anyone, including me, seemed to understand this too.

"I guess I'll be doubly honored." His smile grew soft and his eyes, always thoughtful but usually a bit aloof, warmed until they shimmered. "Thank you."

"Well." Cletus nodded, and kept on nodding. "You are welcome."

"Does this mean I get to plan your bachelor party?"

"Never mind, I rescind the offer."

Billy chuckled, finally walking toward his car. "Too late. I have Jenn as a witness. What's done is done."

Cletus turned as Billy brushed past. "This shall not stand!"

"That shouldn't be a problem. I believe your stripper friend—George, right?—I believe he rappels from the ceiling, if memory serves. No standing involved."

The rest of the weekend passed too quickly. I did end up going into the bakery and making Ashley those lemon custards, which I dropped off to Drew at their place before she'd returned home. Cletus and I spent the night in the carriage house both Saturday and Sunday but didn't take that shower together. The second bedroom didn't have an en suite bathroom. Out of respect for Billy and the thin walls, restraint was the order of the day.

Now, you might be thinking, *This woman is nuts. Thinking about shower sex while her mother is being hustled by a criminal and being targeted by the FBI, her own home has been tapped by the DEA, and her father's murder was just weeks ago.* But, y'all, when shit is going down and there's no way to stop it, you need nice things to look forward to.

For me personally, during these trying times, being close to Cletus was the nicest, best part of my day.

However, yes, I also thought it was nuts how often my mind wandered to thoughts of Cletus, naked, wet, in the shower, soap gliding along his—

OKAY! See? This is what I had to deal with. And don't lie, now you're thinking about it too. I think we can all agree, the man is distracting. Moving on.

Cletus and I did a lot of talking, and that was nice. But not much of it centered on my father's unsolved murder until Sunday night. While getting ready for bed, Cletus had marched into the room and declared, "Elena did it."

I'd been putting moisturizer on my face and turned from the mirror. "What?"

"Elena. She's guilty."

He hadn't been forthcoming with any of his theories yet, saying he needed time to let it marinate, so this proclamation seemed significant. "You think Elena was the strangler?"

"Absolutely."

"I think so too." I set the moisturizer container down and finished rubbing it on my face as I rushed to say, "Let me tell you why."

"Perfect. Tell me. I'm ready to compare notes." Cletus sat on the mattress, giving me his full attention.

"A few things, actually. First, because of what you asked Ashley, about who was driving. You're right, Jackson wouldn't have let my daddy drive away drunk."

"Excellent." He gave me a single nod, looking proud.

"Elena must've been the one to drive, which means she turned them around and brought him back. My guess is she made sure he was good and drunk and helped him into the driver's seat. Then she got in the back and—well, you know."

"Exactly my thoughts." Cletus twisted his lips to the side, inspecting me. "Are you okay?" he asked, then winced. "Sorry, I promised myself I wasn't going to ask you that."

I thought his question over. "I'm . . . not okay. But right now my focus is on clearing my momma's name. And, on that note, the gloves are also weird."

"The gloves." Cletus's small smile returned, his eyes twinkled, and he looked at me like I was wonderful.

"She scratched your face at the party, no gloves. But in the forest when they found her, she's wearing gloves. Why did she have gloves on? Sure, it was chilly, sixty-five or so, but not glove weather right after sunset—"

"What about the rope?"

"Okay, yes. I don't know. Tell me about the rope. I don't know anything about rope."

"The knot. A farmer's knot instead of a traditional noose. Elena grew up in farm culture, we know that from last year and all those chickens. She'd know how to tie that knot, no problem. And you use that kind of knot as a sorta hook or a handle, it doesn't slip, much better than a real noose if the killer were someone small and needed all the leverage they could get."

"What did you mean in the kitchen yesterday with Ashley? When you said something about *sinking rope*?"

"Oh, yeah. I can't figure that out. The rope the killer picked is incredibly strong, heavy, and it sinks. It's usually used for fishing , crab traps and such. There's got to be a reason why she picked sinking rope. It's an unusual feature for rope, but not an unusual rope."

I thought for a minute about that. "Maybe she—she'd planned to throw it in the pond after? Let it sink to the bottom?"

"Maybe . . ."

We both simmered in our thoughts for a moment.

"Why do you think . . ."

"What? What is it?" he pressed.

"What is her motive?"

"That's a good question." Cletus nodded somberly, glancing up at the ceiling. "Maybe we'll find out tomorrow at the reading of the will."

"Oh. I forgot that's tomorrow. Shoot."

Cletus watched me for a moment before saying, "You don't have to go."

"No, no I want to go."

"You want to see if your brother shows up."

"Yes, actually. I'm sure my father's will reading itself will be a waste of time. My guess is he probably wrote a letter to tell me how disappointed he is in my choices." I wasn't looking forward to any of it except the possibility of seeing Isaac.

"Why do you think he asked for Billy to be there?"

"I guess we'll find out." I shrugged. "He always liked Billy, maybe he left him something?"

"Too bad your momma won't be there. It'd be helpful to get her side of the story."

"I wish I could get her to leave the house. She's . . . it's weird, Cletus. I think it's more than the shock of seeing my father dead, more than the police watching. It's like she's shut completely down. There's something else going on with her. She's scared, I think."

"Facing murder charges is scary business. Having the FBI breathing down your neck is difficult."

"But she didn't do it."

"No, I don't think she did. But she saw something. She was there right after. She put her hands on Kip, maybe to stop the flow of blood."

"I can see her doing that, just being totally in shock. Do you think she saw the shooter?"

He nodded sadly, free of any artifice. "I think she must have."

"Then why won't she just talk to the police? Why won't she talk to us? I brought her dinner tonight and she wouldn't even get out of bed. But what can I do? I can't say anything. The FBI is listening." I was so worried about her.

"I do not yet have the answers to those questions."

I sat down heavily on the mattress next to him. "We need to figure out who did it. If we clear her name, the FBI will have to back off."

"It could be anyone who wasn't in the barn when your daddy was shot, anyone on that list of suspects Jackson gave us. Like Posey Lamont and Roger Gangersworth, they hated your father, felt he stole money from them when their business venture failed. In some cases, like Danvish for instance, and Miller, they lost everything, their farms, their livelihoods. Everything."

"I just don't see any of them being a killer."

"What was Miller doing at the party? You were right. I double-checked and Miller wasn't on the guest list."

"You know he wants his cows back. He was probably hoping to get a minute with my mother."

"Jenn, none of them have a solid alibi, some of them have no alibi."

"According to the list, you and I don't have a good alibi either, but we didn't kill him."

Cletus huffed. "Heck, Old Man Blount could've done it. He wasn't invited, but he threatened to kill your daddy last year. Remember that? In the hospital when your momma was found next to his bee boxes?"

"He was raving, Cletus. He'd just lost all his honey producing bees. I think he's threatened to kill everyone in town at least once, or they've threatened to kill him. No. I think it must've been Repo."

Cletus didn't look convinced.

"Well, one thing is for sure." I stood, screwed the cap back on my moisturizer and returned it to my toiletry bag. "We need to get my mother out of her house and talking. The sooner the better."

CHAPTER THIRTEEN
JENN

"You have to do your own growing no matter how tall your grandfather was."

— ABRAHAM LINCOLN

"That woman is two drumsticks short of a picnic," Cletus muttered, his gaze trained on Elena Wilkinson. Or rather, the shrouded figure we assumed was Elena Wilkinson.

We'd pulled into the parking garage in Knoxville with a few minutes to spare. Cletus then texted Billy, letting him know we'd arrived. Not three seconds after he'd finished, my father's BMW pulled up and parked about three cars over from us.

A woman in a long black skirt, black shirt, and a black lace veil covering what looked like blonde hair stepped out. She locked the car with a keyless fob and strolled toward the elevator. It was my father's car, the one he'd been murdered in and, at this realization, my stomach rolled.

I followed her progress in the passenger side mirror, knowing I was making a face. "She kills him by strangulation and wears a black veil to the will reading. Unbelievable." A hollow sort of hardness sat in my stomach, pressing against the bottom side of my lungs. *Cynicism.*

That's what it was.

Cletus unclicked his belt, reaching over and squeezing my hand. "Are you ready?"

Gathering his hand between mine and turning it palm up, I traced the lines with my fingertips. I loved his hands. They were big and strong, scarred, rough with calluses, but so incredibly gentle whenever he reached for me, or held me, or touched me. I loved how much of Cletus could be understood by his hands.

Bracing myself for what was to come, I let the worry fall away. With Cletus here, by my side, I'd be in good hands. "I think—"

"Get away from me!" Elena's forceful screech interrupted our quiet moment, and we both turned.

I tried to peer out the back of the car, but Cletus had the better view. His side faced the elevators.

"Uh oh." He bolted out of the driver's side door.

I was a little slower to follow since I still had my seatbelt on. But as I opened my door, I heard more angry shouts.

"She's just as responsible as he was," a voice I recognized as belonging to Nancy Danvish hollered over the others. "And we're here to see that we get our land back, our money back, like shoulda happened last year."

Coming around the car, I stopped dead in my tracks, struggling to comprehend the scene. Everyone was there—not everyone who hated my father, but a lot of them—all the suspects on the list Jackson had given to Ashley, plus Richard Badcock and Old Man Blount. They blocked the elevator, barring Elena's entry, all enraged faces and unveiled aggression.

"You signed over that land. We bought it fair and square, *Nancy.*" Elena's typically timid tones had adopted an edge of hysteria, and she flinched away as Cletus stepped between her and the crowd. "Don't you touch me, or you'll be sorry."

Cletus held his hands up. "I have no wish to ever sully myself thus, Ms. Wilkinson." Then to the crowd he lifted his hands higher in the universal gesture for *settle down.* "Y'all shouldn't be here."

"We know y'all are meeting with the attorney, it's public record. We want assurances y'all are going to do the right thing and sign our farms back over to us. Where's Jennifer?" Vanessa Romero stepped forward, pointing an accusing finger at both Elena and Cletus.

"And I demand the restitution for my bees! Kip dragged his feet long enough to die, don't think I'm letting his estate off the hook for what's due me." Old Man Blount might as well have been holding up a pitchfork.

I clicked my tongue, my heart aching. I felt so sorry for these folks. Nancy Danvish, Nikki Becker, Vanessa Romero, and Kenneth Miller as the farm investors, but also Roger Gangersworth and Posey Lamont for the chunk of their savings they'd poured into the failed farm stay venture. They'd made the mistake of believing my father, and now they were paying too big a price.

Of course, Old Man Blount and Richard Badcock had their claims too. The civil cases against my father hadn't yet been settled, he owed them payment for damages, and he'd died before justice could be served.

"God love you, since He's the only one who can," spat Nikki, shaking her head. "You and Jenn need to do the right thing, Cletus, if you still know how."

"Nikki Becker. Jenn and I have nothing to do with it." Cletus sounded entirely reasonable. He glanced over his shoulder. I could tell he searched for me, likely to make sure I was safe.

Another vehicle pulled up just then, stopping between where I stood at a distance and the ruckus. Billy's truck idled as he jumped out. "What do you think you're doing? This isn't how to behave."

"You'll make sure they do what's right, won't you Billy?" Nancy appealed to Cletus's brother. "You'll make sure that woman does what's right?"

Elena, unmoved, crossed her arms, staring each of them down in turn—

Wait. No. Not all of them.

Yes, her eyes, fierce and hateful, had settled on each face with disgust until she'd reached the back row of the mob—Roger Gangersworth,

Kenneth Miller, and Old Man Blount—at which point her glare dropped and she seemed to recoil. Almost like . . .

Like she's afraid.

But which one? Which one had inspired the fear?

I studied each man in turn and, honestly, I had no idea. All three looked equally irate, ready to do the woman—and Cletus—harm, just like everyone else gathered. Yet Elena's reaction had been real and swift.

Why would she fear one of them but none of the others?

———

"I realize this here is an atypical request, but I sure do appreciate y'all making time." Luis Leeward, perched at the head of the conference table, turned a friendly—but also somehow condescending—smile to Isaac and me. "As you know, I was a good friend of your father's. I know you kids sometimes had a contentious relationship, but I hope you know he only wanted the best for you both."

We were all gathered in a conference room—Cletus, Billy, Elena, me, Isaac, and my father's lawyer—seven floors above street level with windows that might've had a view forty years ago, but which now just looked into a taller building.

After Billy arrived and dispelled the crowd through whatever magic he inherently possessed to persuade folks against their own worst impulses, Elena had taken the elevator with us and selected the chair directly across from mine. The woman was, as Cletus had said, two drumsticks short of a picnic.

Other than the dark wood table and matching chairs, a coffee station sat along the wall closest to the entrance. A few plastic-wrapped danishes rested on a tray lined with a paper doily that sat in the center of the table.

The carpet was dark blue, the walls were beige, the curtains bracketing the windows were red and gold damask, and the entire office smelled faintly of parmesan cheese and air freshener.

Isaac's eyes seemed to narrow by degrees with every word out of the lawyer's mouth until his clear blue irises were hidden behind slits. "My father's intentions for me and for my—for her, are irrelevant. He's dead."

Isaac picked a piece of lint off his pants. "We can dispense with any additional commentary, Mr. Leeward. Read the will."

My brother had arrived last and five minutes late. He hadn't looked my way since strolling into the room, and I tried not to notice he'd taken the chair farthest from mine. But I did notice, and I also noticed how Elena seemed to shrink as he'd entered, her gaze never straying in his direction.

She still didn't look at him now as she said, "This is what he had to deal with, from his own *children*. Such ingratitude, such disrespect." Elena lifted a hand and then let it fall to her thigh. "Unbelievable."

I'm not an angry person. I do not thrive on whatever part of the brain seemed to derive pleasure from rage. That was not me. But in this moment, listening to the woman who I suspected had killed my father reprimand *me* for my treatment of *him* made me want to—

"Don't do it." Cletus said under his breath, snagging my attention. His gaze held compassion but also recognition, like he could read the violence in mine. I gathered a deep breath and released it slowly, working to find the lid for my temper.

I shouldn't have come. Clearly, Isaac didn't care to speak to me, and Elena hoped to piss me off. This had been a mistake.

Leeward cleared his throat in what I suspected was a nervous habit. He'd cleared his throat when we'd arrived, he'd cleared his throat when Isaac entered, and he cleared his throat now. "This letter was written two months ago, when your father updated his will."

"He—Kip did what?" Elena's question was both breathless and sharp.

"He updated the will." Luis Leeward repeated, not quite making eye contact with Elena. "Now that we're all here and settled, let's get started. 'Elena, Billy, Diane, and my dear children. If Luis is reading this letter, it means I have departed this earth and am watching you from heaven.'"

I shut my eyes, lowered my chin, and pressed a palm to my forehead. Perspective, personal truth, relative reality, how strange the nature of the human experience. My father never saw his own faults. Indeed, to him, he had none. Everything he'd done, all the choices he'd made, had been justified by the lens through which he viewed this world. We all sit in judgment of each other, the bad decisions and evil deeds others make. Perhaps the most difficult of all truths is that no one can ever know, or understand, or share your own. What a lonely journey life was.

"'I have asked Luis to read this letter because I want you all to know that you and your well-being are the things that matter to me the most. Everything I've ever done, I'd done with each of you in mind.'"

Billy shifted in his seat, and I moved my eyes to him. He looked desperately uncomfortable. The absurdity of the situation made me want to laugh. Poor Billy. He'd never courted my father's fanatical favor. I had to wonder, did my father have a crush on Billy? Was that what had really been going on? Because, obviously even to the end, my daddy had been blind to Billy Winston's indifference for him.

"'We won't be reading the will itself as I have summarized my wishes here. All legal documents should've already been sent to probate and are a matter of public and court record by now. I asked Luis to keep this fact a secret from all of you in particular until you were all gathered, because it's important to me that you learn of my wishes from this letter, not from a will written with all that legal mumbo jumbo.'" Luis chuckled here, like he found the term *mumbo jumbo* to be charming.

When no one else laughed, he cleared his throat and continued, "'I need you to know, I forgive those of you who have slandered my good name. I promised my God I'd leave this world forgiving each of you who needed it. Hopefully, this act of charity and grace on my part will help you forgive yourselves.'"

If the words hadn't been so tragically ludicrous, I might've burst out laughing.

"'First, my dear Billy. The son I should've had. I hope you know that—'"

"You can just skip it," Billy interrupted and lifted his hand in a dismissive gesture.

Mr. Leeward peered at Billy over the rim of his glasses. "Are you sure? 'Cause he left you something."

"Donate it."

"Uh, pardon me?"

"Whatever it is, I do not want it. Donate it."

Mr. Leeward patted down his front suit pocket and fumbled for a moment, eventually pulling out one of those thick, fancy-looking fountain pens. "Okay then. Where shall I donate the car?"

"The car?" Elena placed her hand on the table, angling her body toward the lawyer.

"Yes. Kipling left Mr. Winston his BMW."

Billy shrugged. "How about you donate it to a women's shelter."

"What?" Elena's question cracked like a whip. "But what am I going to drive?"

"I have the name of one," Cletus spoke up, pulling out his cell phone. "It's the one Claire McClure used to volunteer at before she moved to Nashville. I'll email it to you both."

Billy considered his brother for a moment before glancing at his knees. "Sounds perfect."

"All right then. So noted." Mr. Leeward tucked his fancy pen back in his pocket and ignored Elena's loud huff of displeasure. Blinking a few times at the letter, he began again, "Let's see. Ah yes. 'Diane. I leave you nothing but the grace of my forgiveness, which is more than enough considering. Be grateful I haven't asked God to damn you to—uh—hell.'" Mr. Leeward fiddled with his glasses, the words obviously inspiring a tad bit of discomfort. "'As my wife, you were willful and—'"

"How long does this continue?" Cletus asked. "Can we vote to skip it? She's not even here."

"Moving on," Isaac said almost cheerfully, and I glanced at him. He wore a smirk, his attention affixed to Mr. Leeward's face.

"Yes. Of course. This section does go on for quite a long time. Ms. Donner isn't here, so we should skip it. I'll just make sure I make a copy for her." Leeward set down two pages of the letter, presumably filled with hateful rhetoric for my mother.

"Ah, yes. This is better. 'Elena, my love. Thank you for always being the better woman. You have my gratitude to sustain you in your life. I'll always be in your heart.'" Leeward sent Elena a small, encouraging smile, then turned his attention back to the letter. "'Isaac, you have been a disappointment—'"

"Hold on." Elena lurched forward. "What else?"

"Pardon?" Leeward inclined his head as though to hear her better.

"What else? That can't be all."

"No, no." The lawyer gestured to the letter in his hands. "There's more."

"Oh. Good." She reclined, looking relieved.

After clearing his throat, Luis Leeward added, "We still have Isaac and Jennifer."

All eyes turned to Elena. She grew very still. "No, Mr. Leeward. I mean, what else did he say about me?"

"Uh—" Another clearing of the throat. "Ms. Wilkinson . . ." Mr. Leeward paused, chuckling nervously, his sparse eyebrows darting upward. Looking pained, he sent an unmistakably pleading glance to Billy. "Mr. Winston, may I implore upon your, uh, leadership skills here."

"What is it you'd like me to do, Mr. Leeward?"

"Would you mind reading the rest of the letter?" His hands shook a little as he held it out to Billy, and I didn't know if it was because he was nervous, afraid, or just had a slight tremor. "My voice is failing me, I think. Seeing as how Kipling was such a good friend of mine, it's a hard thing for this old man to do."

"Certainly." Billy stood, his imposing height, stature, and presence shrinking the room. He took the letter from Leeward, scanned the page he held, and something quite interesting happened. He smiled.

Not a big smile. In fact, it was a small smile, real small. The kind Billy wore when he was trying not to smile.

Billy did not clear his throat. "Ms. Wilkinson, to your question, there doesn't appear to be any additional mention of you in this letter, unless it's on a later page. I will hand it over to you once I finish reciting it, should you wish."

"I—I . . ." Elena's mouth opened, closed, opened as the blood drained from her face. "I—are you sure?" Her brittle voice finally cracked.

Ignoring Elena's quiet breakdown, Billy rushed through the words, delivering them with stoic efficiency. "'Isaac, you have been a disappointment to me your whole life. Even as I contemplate death, I think you are my biggest regret' . . . etcetera." Billy lifted his attention to Isaac, his gaze mimicking his tone. "I'm not reading this to you, Isaac. Point is, your father has nothing kind to say, and he left you nothing."

"Thanks. Got it." Isaac, still smirking, nodded once. He didn't look the least bit upset. Amused, bemused, but not upset. However, my brother had always been a master at pretending not to feel anything. Growing up, I'd been the only person he confided in, the only person he trusted with any part of himself.

My heart pinged, aching terribly, and my eyes stung with a rush of feeling. I didn't miss my father. I didn't care about the letter or the will or any of it. Elena could swim in her vault of riches.

I missed my brother. He was the only reason I'd come. I'd wanted to see him. I missed him.

Abruptly, Isaac's eyes cut to mine, and held. Instinct had me looking away, a smarting of embarrassment heating my cheeks as my throat tightened with uncomfortable emotion. His gaze had been indifferent, cold. I doubted the same could be said about mine.

He didn't want to know me, fine. Fine. *Fine.* FINE.

But it still stung.

Billy discarded two more sheets of paper, presumably a list of all the ways my brother had been a letdown, and took a deep breath before continuing, "'Jennifer Anne, I leave you the remainder of my worldly possessions. I think with this—'"

"No!" Elena was up on her feet, the single word a lightning strike in the otherwise still room. "No, no. He didn't. He wouldn't!"

Billy cast her an irritated side-eye and soldiered on, "'I think with this unselfish gesture on my part you might feel sorry for how you treated me and misjudged me since coming of age. Though I do forgive you, I hope you do not forgive yourself as easily for your transgressions against your father, whom you did not honor according to your Godly duty. Your disobedience . . .'" Billy sighed, scanned the rest of the words on the page he held, glanced at the next page, and shook his head. "Jenn, do you want to hear any more?"

I gaped, my brain processing Billy's words—my father's words—in slow motion. "Wha—what did you say?"

"This isn't right," Elena shrieked. "You're lying!"

Billy leaned over the table and placed the page he'd been reading in front of her. "There you go, read it. It's handwritten."

Her gaze frantically searched the page and a strangled-sounding whimper launched from her lips. Frenzied, she grabbed for the rest of the pages, reading each quickly, and slamming them down on the table.

"I don't understand," I said dumbly, looking to Billy, then to Cletus. "Why would he do that? He—he couldn't stand me."

Meanwhile, Mr. Leeward attempted to continue business. "We should schedule a day to review the extent of your holdings, Jennifer. I took the liberty of gathering your father's account statements so you could review the liquid assets. The will was sent to probate, but his estate is held in trust."

"This isn't right!" Elena, having gone through each page at least three times, fell back in her chair, her hands balled into fists of frustration, her eyes on me filled with such loathing and hate. If she could've strangled me in that moment, I felt absolutely certain she would've.

Tearing my eyes from the evil intentions in hers, I shook my head to clear it. "I don't know why he did this. But I don't want it. I don't want anything from him. I'd like to follow Billy's lead. I'd like to donate—"

"Well now, hold on, little lady." Leeward lifted a hand as though to halt my words and picked up a sealed envelope, holding it out toward me. "You are the owner of quite a lot of property. The question of donation is not a simple one. Your father was a man of significant holdings."

Elena started to cry. Loudly. "She doesn't deserve it, any of it! I loved him, I stood by him. She didn't, I did!"

In the face of her despairing display, I felt nothing but jaded. All the pomp and circumstance, the black veil, the clothes, the tears, the wringing of hands, the gnashing of teeth. What a show. A year ago, I might've felt moved. But today, suspecting what I did, I decided to embrace misanthropic instincts and dismiss her completely.

But Cletus sent Elena an irritated glance, leaning forward and turning his body in front of mine as though to shield me from her hysterics. "You're referring to the farms, Mr. Leeward? The Romero, Becker, Danvish, and Miller parcels?"

My brain stuttered, and I placed a hand on Cletus's forearm. "Wait, wait. The . . . the Miller farm?" Immediately, my heart took off at a thundering gallop, and for the first time since walking into the office I felt awake to my surroundings.

The Miller farm. With its wildflower field, pond, acreage, grazing prairie, forest, and view. What a temptation.

"I believe, by 'Miller farm,' you're referring to the dairy property, correct?" Mr. Leeward glanced at Elena and squirmed in his seat. "Well, yes. But I believe that Ms. Wilkinson was in talks with its previous owner to transfer the deed back. She can speak better to that."

Instead of speaking, Elena buried her face in her hands and cried louder.

"Of course," Mr. Leeward lifted his voice to be heard over her wailing, "you are under no obligation to honor any agreement initiated by Ms. Wilkinson, or by your father prior to his—uh—death." The lawyer's features seemed confused on how to arrange themselves, caught somewhere between a grimace and a solicitous smile.

But I was only half listening to the man, my mind on overdrive. *I want that farm.* I'd wanted the Miller farm since the first time I'd seen it. I loved it. I loved the location, the topography, the versatility of potential uses. It was the most ideally situated spot for my hopes and dreams. The house could be demolished, but the land . . . *I want it!*

And yet, it wouldn't be right to keep it. I knew Mr. Miller was desperate for his land, land my father had basically stolen from him. Furthermore, I knew he was desperate to have his cows returned, willing to pay back the exorbitant price my mother had forked over at auction.

Ugh. I wished my father hadn't left it to me, any of it. I would've been happier without having to make the choice, even though I already knew which choice I'd make. *It's not mine to keep.*

"Pardon me, sir." Cletus leaned forward slowly. A peculiar something, a carefulness in his tone had me surfacing from my messy thoughts. He placed a hand on the conference table and narrowed his eyes on Elena as he spoke, "The Miller farm, the dairy, did Kipling wish to transfer ownership, or was that something Ms. Wilkinson initiated—as you say—after his death?"

"Don't answer that," Elena stood again, sniffling, swiping at her cheeks. "As my lawyer, I forbid you from answering any questions about me, or my personal business, asked by *these people*."

Cletus's lips parted, he blinked, and he exhaled a short puff of breath. I recognized this combo as a rare display of genuine surprise.

He said, "You—"

She stiffened.

"—and Miller."

Elena Wilkinson flinched. Her eyes rimmed with true terror, her chest rose and fell rapidly, her whole body shaking as she stared at Cletus and he stared back, and I struggled to catch up with the implications of what he'd just said.

Elena and Kenneth Miller?

She grabbed for the haphazardly stacked letter she'd just discarded, shoved it into her bag, and fled the room, leaving the rest of us staring after her.

Except Cletus. Cletus hadn't turned his head to watch her go. Likely because he knew where—and to whom—she was going. And why.

I have no idea how long my stupor lasted, only that, when what Cletus had said finally permeated my brain, I felt the weight of Isaac's concentrated attention on me.

"You had no idea," my brother said like he was realizing the words as he spoke them.

I looked at him, frowning. "No idea about what?"

"About the will. You didn't know he'd changed it." The way he inspected me, like I was someone he didn't know, felt like a punch in the stomach.

My chin wobbled, and I stood. "Of course I didn't know, *Twilight*. Do you think I'd be here if I knew? I don't want anything from him, I never did."

"Then why are you here?" He didn't stand, and his question sounded unpremeditated, like he really had no idea, like he really wanted to know why I was there.

"You . . . are a bastard," I said, the words barely above a whisper and

—to my shame—ripe with tears. "And I wish you well with your brotherhood of bastards. Goodbye, Isaac."

I turned away from him before he could see the tears fall. Not waiting for Cletus or Billy or anyone else, I strolled right out of the conference room and into the hallway, my chin held high. I might be sad, but I was also mad. Anger would see me through until I made it to the car. Once there, I'd have myself a good cry. When we made it home, there would be wine. But for now, I floated on a cloud of fury.

At least that had been my hastily constructed plan before I came face-to-face with Deputies Boone and Williams, standing next to the reception desk and the gaping receptionist. Behind them were other folks in uniform and a smattering of two or three others in suits.

"Jennifer Sylvester," Boone's remorseful gaze betrayed what his steady, deep tenor did not as he said, "You're under arrest for the murder of Kipling Sylvester."

CHAPTER FOURTEEN
CLETUS

"I loved Ophelia. Forty thousand brothers could not, with all their
quantity of love, make up my sum."

— WILLIAM SHAKESPEARE, *HAMLET*

"Why haven't they scheduled her arraignment yet?" I couldn't stop
pacing.

Pacing. Pacing. Pacing.

I'd been pacing nonstop for twenty-four hours. If I'd been in a
different frame of mind, the frame of mind that entertained worries for
anyone or anything else other than Jennifer, I might've been concerned
for my mental health.

As it was, I was not, and did not, and I couldn't stop pacing.

"The prosecutor gets three days to decide whether or not to press
charges, Cletus."

"I know, *Jethro*."

He held his hands up and watched me like he was concerned for my
mental health. "I'm not going to tell you to calm down, but wearing a
hole in the pavement outside the station isn't going to help. You need to
come home. Let the lawyers—"

154

"Don't." I sliced a hand through the air. "Don't say, 'Let the lawyers handle it.'"

Boone wouldn't let me ride with them in the elevator, so I'd taken the stairs. I'd followed their car all the way to the station. Beau and Shelly had gone out and rented an RV so we could spend the night in the parking lot. Jethro had arrived at 6:34 AM with coffee and breakfast. He'd even achieved the correct ratios of apple cider vinegar, coffee, and molasses. If I hadn't been so busy pacing and going out of my mind with worry, I would've been impressed.

Jethro leaned back against his car where Beau and Shelly were also leaning, watching me pace. Drew and Billy were inside the station, trying to strong-arm the sheriff into allowing me a visit. All attempts thus far yesterday and this morning had been denied, as I suspected they would be.

Flo had explained several times that, since I wasn't her husband, I had no rights to her. And she had none to me. Never before had I wished as fervently that we'd already eloped. But Billy, her congressman, had been allowed to see her. He'd said she was in good spirits. I wanted to strangle someone.

Sienna, currently at the homestead watching Benjamin, had called her legal teams from LA and New York. A swarm of lawyers would be converging on our present location any minute. Diane had sent her legal team, and they were inside already, but Sienna assured me that her people were the most ridiculously expensive, poised to argue lawyers she could find. God bless her.

My dear sister, trying a different approach, was right this minute bringing Jackson James a baked good of some sort. Never before had I been so thankful for her influence over blond law enforcement. Hopefully, it worked.

Since I could do nothing but think and pace, I decided I'd figure a way to break her out of jail, should the need arise. I knew I could count on Evans to help. Now I just needed to figure out a way to ensure he had transport duty to the courthouse—

"Your phone is ringing, Cletus." Shelly's flat as paper voice pulled me from my machinations.

"Pardon?"

"Your cell phone." The tall mechanic walked over to me, reached in my back pocket, and handed me my phone. "Answer."

"Thanks." Shaking myself into the present, I glanced at the number. When I recognized it, I cursed. "What do you think you're doing?"

"It's an emergency."

Fucking Burro.

I paced away from my family toward the RV. "Don't ever call me on this number."

"Cletus—"

"Today is not the day." I reached for the handle to the recreational vehicle, climbing the stairs, prepared to deliver a scathing censure. He knew better.

"Don't hang up! This is an emergency. Isaac is here. He needs to meet with you."

I curled my lip in disgust, shutting the door to the trailer behind me. "I don't care what Isaac needs."

"It's about Jenn."

"Tell him to fuck off."

"No, you're gonna want to hear what he has to say."

"I'm gonna want him to eat shit and die." I began to pace the short length of the vehicle.

"Trust me, stop being so ornery."

"You know I don't trust you."

"Okay, fine. Then I guess your fiancée is going to jail for the rest of her life. Is that what you want?"

I stopped pacing, deciding that Burro would be the person I strangled.

"What's the harm? Give him ten minutes. I promise—I swear—you will not regret it."

Growling, I spun in a circle, looking for a pen. "Fine. Give me the address."

"I'll text it to you."

"Whatever." I marched back to the door, pulling my car keys from my pocket.

"And bring Jethro."

"What? Why?"

"Just bring Jethro."

"Fine, whatever. Goodbye." Pushing open the door and slamming it behind me, I pointed at Jet.

"Who was that?" He straightened from his car.

"Jet, you're with me." I tossed him my keys. I was too discombobulated to drive. "And leave your phone here."

He caught them easily and withdrew his cell, handing it to Beau. "Where are we going?"

I stopped in front of Beau and Shelly, glancing at the address Burro had just sent, recognizing it as a convenience store up in Hill country, and gave Beau my phone as well. "You two, can you stay here?"

"Absolutely." Beau answered for them both. "Shop is closed, we're here for you."

"Good. Thanks." I turned to leave.

Beau called after me, "Don't worry. Jennifer will be fine."

I lifted my hands in the air and yelled, "You don't know that, don't say that. You don't know that. Don't make promises you can't keep," without turning around.

"I wasn't making a promise," Beau ground out. "I was—never mind. Just, we'll let you know if anything changes."

"You can't," I grumbled, sliding into the Geo's passenger seat. "You have our phones."

───

"What is this?" I snapped, glaring at the two men hovering just outside the door to what looked like an old fishing shack. A pile of wood had been stacked to the left of the door and the porch roof sagged, shingled with cedar. It looked like it might collapse should anyone slam the front door in a fit of temper.

Repo gestured for us to follow them inside. "Come on. We need your help."

"My help? Wait a minute. Burro said this was about you helping Jenn." I pointed a finger at Isaac once we were inside.

The first address Burro had texted was the convenience store in Hill country. Which is to say, it operated near the Hill family compound in the mountains. Once there, Jethro explained—following standard Iron Wraith modus operandi—we needed to go inside and ask for the keys to the bathroom. The old guy behind the counter wrote something down on the back of receipt paper.

A new address.

Jethro knew it. Before we left, Jet bought a stick of gum, left a twenty-dollar tip, and we were off.

"It's about Diane. Diane is being blackmailed." Repo rounded a small primitive table in the middle of the room, around which were set four chairs. "Here, sit down. We'll explain—"

"I'm not sitting down, and neither is Jet. Who is blackmailing Diane? Or do you know?" I crossed my arms.

Repo was the one to answer. "Kenneth Miller."

Jethro looked to me. "Farmer Miller? The one who sold Ms. Donner the cows?"

Inspecting the two men and the severity of their expressions, I decided to take a seat. "Okay, now you have my attention. But Jet isn't sitting. Continue." I'd put two and two together at the will reading and it equaled Farmer Miller being in league with Elena Wilkinson. The ex-dairy farmer blackmailing Diane offered further proof of what I already knew to be true: he'd been the shooter.

"Diane got a note, a handwritten note"—Repo sat across from me— "on white paper in black marker. It was a few days after the murder. It said something about knowing what she did and having her gun."

"Diane doesn't have a gun." I peered at Isaac. "Unless you bought her one."

Isaac said nothing. He glared. At me. Mute.

Meanwhile, Repo leaned his elbows on the table. "Right, but the note said they—the blackmailer—had the murder weapon and her fingerprints are all over it."

I felt like I already knew the answer to the question, but I asked anyway. "Are they?"

"No. She never touched it." Repo—expression open, honest, candid —looked how I felt. Desperate. "But the note said they'd send the gun to the police."

"I mean—let them." I shrugged, standing and turning for the door. "It's a bluff."

"Is it?" Finally, Isaac spoke.

Repo was on his feet again, his hand stretched out to me. "I don't know how much you know, Cletus, but Diane did run from the police that night. She shouldn't have, and that's my fault because I misunderstood what I was seeing, but she did run. She didn't kill Kip."

I sighed, rubbing my face with both hands. I didn't want to be here, but here I was.

Turning back to the two Iron Wraiths, I spread my arms wide. "Fine. Okay. Why don't you back up and tell me what happened that night, Repo? What do you know?"

"Diane didn't kill him," he said on a rush. "She opened that car door. She tried to stop the bleeding, and when I saw what she was doing, I thought . . ."

"You thought she'd shot him." Jethro filled in the blank.

Repo nodded, looking gutted. "I got her out of there. Took her to the bakery. I had to get the blood off her hands. Then we ran like hell. They chased us through the woods, but we got to my bike first. She didn't do it."

"So you keep saying." I let my hands drop to my thighs with a smack. "If she didn't shoot Kip, then why are y'all worried about her fingerprints being on a gun she didn't fire?"

"Her fingerprints *are* on the car. Bloody ones." Repo gripped his forehead, seeming earnestly grief-stricken.

I worked to assemble these missing puzzle pieces into the picture I'd already sketched. "But the police can't confirm the bloody print is hers because she won't leave her house. They have no way to lift her prints if she doesn't leave the house."

Repo glanced at Isaac, and they both nodded.

"Whose idea was that?" My attention bounced between them.

Isaac shifted his weight from one foot to the other. "My idea."

"Smart."

He nodded, accepting the compliment.

"But I still don't understand the blackmail. Why do you think Miller is the blackmailer?"

"Because of the cows." Repo jabbed his finger at the top of the table, his other hand on his waist. "The blackmail demands. All they want is the dairy cows from the lodge."

"Are you kidding me?" Jethro scoffed. "Is this a joke?"

"No," Repo said, looking like he wished it were.

"What do you need me for? Go get your fancy fraternity brothers to go beat the shit out of him." I glanced at my watch. We'd been gone too long.

"I can't." Repo shook his head. "The Wraiths can't know about Diane and me. It'll put her in danger."

I started to say something, I didn't know what, likely something flippant, when Isaac added, "And it would put Jennifer in danger too."

Gritting my teeth, I glanced at Jethro. He nodded subtly, confirming what they'd said was true.

"Well, then turn in the blackmail notes to the police. Call his bluff. What is wrong with you?"

"What if he did put her prints on the gun?" Repo's stare settled squarely on Jethro, like he was trying to communicate something of importance, or make a request. "Jet. Help me. We can't take that chance."

I looked at my watch. Another minute had passed. "He's probably lying."

"Cletus," Jethro stepped up next to me, his eyes on Repo. "Miller might be telling the truth, it could be he put her prints on that gun. We've, uh—" Jethro rubbed his forehead, looking agitated "—I've done it before."

"What?" I reared back from my brother. "You did what?"

"I've put false fingerprints on a weapon."

Now I fully faced Jethro, inspecting him. A long moment passed where we stared at each other until I said, inanely, "Is that so." But it was so. At one point in his past, my eldest brother's moral compass had been darker than mine.

Jethro looked like he might be sick, and his voice was rough with guilt as he said, "It was a long time ago."

"That's why you wanted me to bring Jet." I glared at Repo. "Because y'all did the same thing to someone else."

Repo looked to Jet, an apology clear as day written all over his face, and gave me a stiff nod. "Plus, he'd know how to get here, once you made it to the convenience store."

"Okay. Fine." I tossed my hands up. "What makes you think Miller knows how to do something so nefarious as put prints on a gun?"

"Fuck it, Cletus. You're missing the point." Repo surged forward, yelling at me with gusto.

"What is the point?" I ground out. We were talking in circles, and I was tired of dancing.

"The point is, it can be done. Miller might not be bluffing. Jenn isn't the one in danger here. If that gun is turned over and the fingerprints match the print on the car, it's only a matter of time. They're gonna come after Diane with a warrant. They're gonna arrest her for murder. The FBI is parked outside her house because they're sending me a message"—he jabbed a finger at his chest—"trying to get me to turn state. They've been trying to get me to turn state's evidence for years."

"And they're using Diane to get to you," Jethro said, but he was watching me for my reaction. They all were.

"It's not fair to her." Repo sounded tortured, looked tortured too. Like he hadn't slept in weeks. Like he was close to tears and his wit's end.

I'd been right. Repo was in love with Diane. Ass over ankles, destroyed, wrecked for her. *What a world.*

"Then why don't you just turn yourself in? Hmm?" I gripped the back of the wooden chair I'd been sitting in earlier, leaning forward. "Turn state's evidence now if you want them to back off?"

"Don't you think I've thought of that? If I turn myself in, I have no bargaining chip if Diane is arrested. I'd much rather her face a manslaughter conviction than a first-degree murder charge."

"Fine. Fine." I picked up the chair two inches and slammed it back to the ground, grinding my teeth. I couldn't think. "Don't turn yourself in. What I want to know is, why the hell are we here? You say Jenn isn't in any danger, but she's the one who's been arrested."

"Jenn isn't in danger," Isaac said with all the chill of a sea turtle. That's to say, very chill.

"How can you be sure?" I endeavored to mimic his chillness, desperately wanting what he said to be true.

"The plan to arrest Jenn has been in the works for weeks, a backup plan if they couldn't get the evidence needed to arrest my mother. They were always going to arrest Jenn right after the reading of the will, using her surprise inheritance as motive. That, plus the weak alibi, is more than enough to bring her in but not to charge her."

I ignored the comment about Jenn's weak alibi—as I was Jenn's alibi and she was mine—and asked, "How do you know this? And if inheritance is motive enough for Jenn, then why isn't hatred enough of a motive for Diane? Why not arrest Diane already? They'd get her fingerprints for sure."

He ignored my questions, instead answering one I didn't ask, "The police got their hands on my father's will the day after the murder, before it was sent to probate, way before the reading yesterday. My father changed his will one month before he died. That looked bad for my sister."

"Did you think Jenn did it?" I don't know why, but I needed to know.

Isaac breathed in and out several times, his expression infuriatingly inscrutable, and finally grumbled, "It is a possibility that didn't seem far-fetched."

I gripped the back of the seat again. How Jenn's brother answered this next question would determine whether he'd be walking out of here alive. "So you, what? Went to the police with your suspicions?"

"No. No way." Finally, some emotion. "I discovered the FBI's plan to arrest Jenn after it had been put into motion. Those devices in your house, listening, watching, those are mine. I needed to know what y'all were up to."

I couldn't believe my ears. "Wait, you—"

"Yes."

For the first time in my life, I couldn't keep up. "You thought your sister killed her own father, so you put cameras in her house?" How could he possibly think this?

"Like I said, I needed to know what y'all were up to."

"Why?"

"Because I'd kill him." Isaac was back to being chill as a sea turtle despite the violence of his words, but I could see he meant what he said.

I must've been looking at him with surprise, or what he interpreted as horror, because he continued, "You don't know what it was like in that house. Jenn made the best of it every day. And my mother, she—she was both a lifeline and a lead weight around my neck. But our father—"

Isaac glanced to the side, blinking once slowly as he inhaled through his nose. "I don't know how Jenn did it. She could always deal better than me."

"And you left her," Jethro said, his voice lacking any judgment. Maybe because he'd also left us. "You left your sister in that house, with him."

"I had to get out. If I hadn't, I would've killed him years ago." Isaac's glare shifted to me. "And Jenn had our momma to keep her safe."

"A lifeline and a lead weight." I shook my head at Isaac's shitty justification for shitty actions. He didn't deserve Jennifer in his life, and I made a pledge right then and there: Isaac Sylvester would never have contact with Jenn. He would never speak to her. He would never know her. He was out. Forever.

"I needed to know what you and Jenn were saying." Isaac glanced to the side again. "I wanted to know before anybody else."

I wiped a hand over my face once more, trying to focus. I had too many questions. "How'd you get your hands on DEA surveillance equipment?"

Isaac flinched with what looked like surprise, his eyes slicing to me. "How'd you know those were DEA?"

"Answer the question, Isaac."

The muscle in his temple ticked. "None of your concern."

"Really? None of my concern?" I wanted to laugh.

"That's need to know. How'd you know they were DEA?"

I threw his words right back at him. "That's need to know."

Something burned behind his eyes, but he put a leash on it, his voice even more tightly controlled, "Fine. You have your secrets, I have mine. But we both know for certain Jenn didn't do it."

"But you thought she was guilty."

"Before the will reading, I thought . . ." He looked to the side like he had twice before, his chest rising and falling. "It doesn't matter. She didn't do it. My mother didn't do it."

"And what would you have done if it had been Jenn?"

"I would've helped her."

"I find that hard to believe, *Twilight,*" I spat. "And I think she would too." Isaac winced, and then again, for a fourth time, looked to the side. *This is his tell.* I was certain of it. When Isaac Sylvester couldn't mask his thoughts, he looked to the side. I made a mental note.

I felt Jethro's eyes on me. I looked at him. Unmistakable concern had etched itself on his features. "You . . . you feeling okay?" he whispered bracingly.

Making a noncommittal head movement, I checked my watch again. I knew I wasn't acting like myself; being so free with my thoughts, dislike; being forthright with those I didn't trust. But with Jennifer arrested, my patience was threadbare.

I hadn't slept.

I'd paced.

If something happens to her . . . I winced at the thought, my chest on fire. God, I wanted to tear the world apart. *I shouldn't be here.*

"We're running out of time." Repo stepped forward. "What Isaac is trying to say is, they—the FBI, the police—they also think Jenn is innocent, but they're tired of waiting out Diane. They're trying to drive her out of the house, to the station where she'll either confess out of fear for Jenn or she'll slip up and leave a print they can lift."

"Again, like Cletus already asked, if they're so desperate for her prints, why not arrest her already? They have motive and a crap alibi." I had a feeling Jethro was speaking so I didn't have to.

"It's her lawyer. Genevieve Taylor is notorious, a shark," Isaac said, and though he remained chill, I got the sense he admired the woman.

"They know if they mess up Diane's arrest and her prints aren't a match, they're screwed. They don't care about messing up with Jenn, they have no plan to charge her. But no one wants to arrest Diane until the case is airtight. However, if they lift her prints—legally—they'll tie her to the bloody print on the car, and then that's it."

"Then Diane is arrested and charged, and Repo is turning state's evidence to knock her charge down to manslaughter," I filled in. *Just like dominoes.*

"So what do you want from Cletus?" Jethro crossed his arms again, his shoulder bumping mine, his voice hard.

Repo turned his pleading eyes to my brother. "We need to get Diane out of the house, out of Green Valley, and I want to use the wedding shower to do it."

"You want to go on the run?" My brother obviously found this diffi-cult to believe. "With Ms. Donner?"

"That's right," Repo confirmed.

"You think she'd go with you?" Jethro pressed. "Her life is here."

"I do. She's scared. The blackmail has her terrified. Even if I hadn't told her to stay put in the house, I don't think she'd leave anyway. At least with me, she wouldn't be alone, waiting for the other shoe to drop."

"But she'd be looking over her shoulder for the police, waiting *for the other shoe to drop.*" Jethro lifted his hands, his entire demeanor communicating, *what the hell are you thinking?*

"And you'd leave the Wraiths?" I asked, quieting my mind as best I could so I could read Repo's reaction to the question.

He didn't hesitate. "For Diane? In a heartbeat."

I believed him. I looked to Isaac and saw he believed him too. Which begged the question, *Where did Isaac's loyalties truly lie?* With his mother? Jenn? The Wraiths? Repo? Why had he inserted himself into these matters?

"I'd keep her safe." Repo pointed to his chest with both hands. "I know how to do it. I know how to disappear. And it wouldn't be forever. Just until y'all—you and Jenn—can clear her name. We need you to help."

"Repo"—I shook my head because part of what he'd just said was nonsense—"you leave the Wraiths, you can never return. Maybe we clear Diane's name, maybe she gets to come back. But you go with her, you're never coming back."

A moment stretched where the older man held my stare, his unwavering as though to communicate that these facts, as I'd spelled them out, did not bother him. "I know, Cletus. I know how it works. But I'm still going to do it. Diane is my priority."

"Aren't you worried?" Jethro examined the older man. "Leaving the Wraiths without a money man?"

"I have an apprentice."

"Who?" I asked.

Repo lifted his chin. "Someone you think is smart."

I didn't get a chance to ponder his response other than to assess the veracity of it before Jethro tapped my arm. "But the wedding shower? When is—"

"Yes." Repo cut in. "The shower. It's the perfect cover. There will be a ton of people, confusion. We can—"

"No. No." Now I cut in. "That won't work."

"Cletus, if she's going to leave, the wedding shower gives her the best chance," Repo beseeched. "I've given this a lot of thought."

"No." I shook my head adamantly. "They'll be listening, watching. They'll expect it. What would you have her do? Wear gloves? That won't look suspicious. And besides, even if they weren't expecting her to run, we need more time. We need days, not hours, before they figure it out."

"Then what do you suggest?" Isaac asked, sounding like he really wanted to know, like maybe this was the real reason they'd asked us to come, and that gave me pause.

They want me to plan the escape, not just help execute it.

A new, simmering discontent burned like acid in my stomach. It was almost as though someone had informed them of my gift for helping folks escape untenable situations.

Burro is gonna pay for this. Later.

I pointed to Jenn's brother. "Isaac."

"Yes?"

"Isaac, you need to start visiting your momma this week."

Repo narrowed his eyes on me. "Okay . . .?"

"He should come and go at odd times, always wearing his helmet until he's inside the house, always leaving with the helmet on. Mother and son will talk about nothing important. He'll become a regular but random visitor. After a time, they won't mark him coming and going."

"And how does that help us?" Isaac sounded interested, ready to put the plan into action.

"Because, after the wedding shower, Diane is still right where she's supposed to be, at home and depressed. After the police knock on her door for some bullshit reason and see she's home and that she didn't make a run for it, that night or the very next day, Isaac will visit. Wearing his helmet. Diane will leave, dressed like Isaac, wearing his helmet."

Repo and Isaac stared at me, then at each other.

Jethro chuckled. "That's awesome."

Isaac shook his head. "That's crazy."

"No, wait, this is a good idea." Repo pointed at me, clearly seeing the genius in the plan.

"Cletus, my mother is five foot three. I am over six feet. It'll never work."

"It will work," Jethro piped up, sounding cheerful, like maybe he missed his checkered past. Just a little.

"Jet is right, I'm right, it'll work." I sighed, tired, and checked my watch for what felt like the hundredth time. "They got cameras on the house from the road, not in the house."

"How do you know whether they have cameras in the house?" Isaac growled.

"Need. To. Know." It was just past noon. If they held Jenn for the full three days before releasing her, someone was going to pay dearly. I didn't know who yet, but someone. "The law won't notice how short or tall someone is with a camera that far away. We'll get matching outfits, buy her a replica of his leather jacket, his cut, boots, everything. Make sure it looks like it fits the same from a distance. We'll stuff it so she appears thick and muscled. All they'll see is someone dressed like Isaac, leaving the house with a helmet on, just like Isaac always does."

"But they are listening. They'll know it was her who left, not me.

They'll hear that she's gone. They got a wiretap, they're listening." Isaac shook his head, still trying to poke holes in my concrete fortress of a plan.

"That's easy to fix." I needed to wrap this up. "We record Diane now, in every room, her typical day, and we make sure she does the same thing at the same time—more or less—and when she leaves, we hit play. Again, in every room."

"You want to . . ." Isaac's attention turned inward, like he was trying to keep up. Good. It was his turn to be lost.

I went on, "We play two or three days on a loop. They pick up the sounds they expect to hear. That'll give her a three- or four-day head start."

"What about the bike? She doesn't know how to ride a motorcycle." Jet scratched his chin.

"Actually, she does." Repo's statement immediately drew our attention.

"She does?" Jet's hand dropped.

"Yep. She rides," the older man confirmed, looking proud. "She's been driving my bike for weeks. I mean, she was. Before."

"She rides." I nodded. "It's all set."

"How does Isaac get out of there?"

I scowled at my brother and his question. *Meet Jethro Winston, Mr. Monkey Wrench.*

"He waits 'til dark, slips out the back," I replied with the answer that should've been obvious.

Another Jethro question, "What if he gets caught?"

"I won't get caught," Isaac said, swinging his glare to me. "You're good at this, Cletus."

Uncertain whether this was meant as a compliment, I asked, "Thank you?"

"You're welcome."

"What about me?" Repo rubbed his hands together, which was definitely his tell. The man was excited, anxious, restless, his typical laissez-faire demeanor nowhere in sight. "Where do I go? Where do I meet her?"

"Repo, Diane will meet you at the Dragon. Your job will be to get her out of Green Valley while leaving Isaac's bike at the bar. Isaac will get himself over there, unseen, no one the wiser. Jenn and I will meet you at whatever safe house you pick."

"What?!" Jethro, Repo, and Isaac all asked in unison.

I glared at each of them in turn, letting my attention linger on Isaac last. "I want those listening and recording devices out of Jenn's house before she's released, and I want to know how you got in and out of the house without tripping the system or being caught on the security cameras."

"Fine, but—"

"And that dude in the white Ford? I want him to stop following me."

"He loses you half the time anyway." Isaac made like he was going to roll his eyes but seemed to catch himself just in time.

"He was one of yours?" I asked, inspecting him. I'd made the demand on a hunch without knowing for sure. But something I did know for sure: Isaac wasn't *just* an Iron Wraith. He worked undercover for some part of the government, that much was clear. I suspected DEA. FBI was also a possibility.

Isaac didn't answer, instead saying, "There's no way you and Jenn are going to that safe house. You'll be followed."

"Nope." I shook my head.

"How can you be so sure?" Repo asked, looking nervous.

"I have my ways of evading unwanted attention, and that's all either of you need to know."

"Trust him. He does," Jet said.

I sent my brother a small smile, hoping he'd take it as confirmation that he and I were still good. Jet may have been a sketchy asshole in his youth, but he was a changed man. He'd asked and I'd already forgiven him for everything, case closed. New details weren't going to alter anything between us.

"I don't know, Cletus." Repo looked from Isaac to me. "Is the risk—"

"That's my ask. That's the price for my help." I glared at Repo as I backed away. Their time was up. I needed to get back to Jenn. "If you want Diane safely out of town, away from the police and Farmer Miller's threats, Jenn gets to say goodbye to her mother. Nonnegotiable."

CHAPTER FIFTEEN
JENN

"… the sentimental person thinks things will last. The romantic person has a desperate confidence that they won't."

— F. SCOTT FITZGERALD, *THIS SIDE OF PARADISE*

When I'd asked Billy how Cletus was doing, he said, "Don't you worry about him."

So I'd said, "Billy. Tell the truth."

He'd said, "He wouldn't want you to worry about him."

Which I took to mean that Cletus was doing just about as well as I expected given he'd had to watch me be arrested and they hadn't yet allowed him a visit. The truth was, other than worrying about him, I was probably doing much better than he was.

If I were going to be arrested and held in lockup, the sheriff's station wasn't bad. I knew all the deputies as I'd baked them birthday cakes every year and often brought in goodies for holidays. They gave me my own room, or cell. Evans played cards with me during his breaks. Monroe brought me a few books to pass the time. Boone checked in every hour or so during his administrative shift. He looked worried, asked if I needed anything, and apologized "for everything."

My arrest wasn't Boone's fault, I felt sure of that, but he sure seemed to feel responsible. He'd taken the cuffs off as soon as we reached the police car and had walked beside me when we entered the station, remarking on the nice weather. I asked about his momma's rose garden. We'd chatted more throughout the check-in process about his momma—or the "processing" process?—and I'd been offered coffee, tea, or water to drink as I'd waited for my lawyer. He insisted on taking my mug shot twice 'cause he said the first one was bad.

I liked Boone.

Genevieve, my momma's lawyer, had arrived within the hour and argued with anyone she could find, objecting to my arrest, objecting to my treatment—even though I told her I'd been treated well—objecting to the lack of an arraignment date, objecting to the fact that I'd been sitting in one of the questioning rooms but hadn't been questioned.

When they asked if she wanted me to be questioned, she rose hell. I liked her. She was good at arguing.

I felt desperate for contact with Cletus. This was the longest we'd gone without each other's company in over a year. Everyone was being so nice, but I *ached* for him. I longed to know he was safe. It might've been a strange thought, but with Elena out there, I felt safer in here.

Maybe I should've been afraid, locked up in a prison cell—or a holding cell, I guess—but I wasn't. I got the sense everyone was waiting. The deputies, the sheriff, the men and women in suits who would inspect me as they walked by seemed to be biding time. I didn't recognize the suit-clad folks, but they seemed to know me. Yes, they were all waiting for something to happen, and I felt certain it didn't really have anything to do with me.

And then there's Miller.

I wished Cletus and I had been given a moment to discuss Farmer Miller and Elena, and what conclusions Cletus had drawn after Mr. Leeward's offhanded statement. I could guess, but I wanted to hear his theories, discuss possibilities, listen to him talk, watch him think, kiss his face, touch his body, have him touch my—

Okay, sex fiend. Settle. Think about football, or wounds, or paint drying, or something else unsexy. Here I sat trapped, incarcerated for my father's murder, and I'd spent most of the time daydreaming about being alone and naked with Cletus and what I wanted him to do to me when we saw each other next. It's true. I needed to accept it. I was a sex fiend. *Oh well.* Being a sex fiend for Cletus was better than being a murderer.

On Wednesday, I'd talked Evans into passing Cletus a note. Evans promised me he would. Therefore, I was especially anxious Thursday morning, for Evans to start his shift, hoping Cletus would respond, but also since my time in holding was drawing to an end, one way or the other. My lawyer—and the pack of legal experts Sienna had sent—informed me I couldn't be held for longer than seventy-two hours without charges being filed. With time winding down, they either needed to move forward with arraignment or let me go.

Speaking of Sienna's legal experts, as far as I knew they were still in town and had vowed to remain, putting pressure on the sheriff's office. I don't think they frightened the sheriff any, but Evans had said they'd terrified the heck out of Florence McClure. She'd had to go home early on both Tuesday and Wednesday afternoons with a headache.

Thursday morning, Evans slipped a response from Cletus inside a to-go container from Daisy's.

"Daisy says hi and hang in there," the deputy had said with a wink, giving me a thumbs-up before leaving me to my breakfast and correspondence.

I chuckled at his encouragement. Really, these guys were too cute sometimes.

As soon as he left, I opened the box. Despite the mouthwatering aroma of sausage and biscuits with preserves and a big old Boston cream doughnut, I picked out the folded piece of paper first, setting the food to the side and hungrily opening Cletus's note.

I was not disappointed.

Dear Jenn,

I'm lost without you. But don't fret. Beau rented an RV and I've been in the parking lot all day and every night. We've been close this whole time, just a few feet apart. Could you feel me? I confess, I could not feel you and my whole being mourned the loss. My bones feel brittle, like they can't hold my weight. And I'm so tired.

I'll rest and there you are, smiling, the brilliance of your soul shining through your exquisite eyes, your soft skin beneath my hands, your sweet taste—

I had to lower the letter for a moment to catch my breath. *Goodness.* How easily he could twist me up with just words. Vaguely, I wondered if the RV had a bed.

Y'all don't need a bed.

I fanned myself with the letter, wondering if—when this was all over—we might be able to rent an RV and travel a little. Continuous close quarters with Cletus sounded lovely right about now.

Before I could finish reading, the sound of approaching footsteps had me folding the letter quickly and stuffing it in my bra. Hurriedly, I reached for my breakfast, shoving half a biscuit into my mouth just as Genevieve rounded the corner, dressed in a black business suit and wearing a perturbed expression.

"They're releasing you," she announced, her eyes sliding to the side, to somewhere I couldn't see. "The cute deputy is handling the paper-work. Ms. Diaz can send her pack of lawyers back to New York and Los Angeles."

I stood, bringing my breakfast with me and talking around the biscuit, "Which cute deputy?"

Genevieve sorta smirked. "The one who looks like a young Derek Luke."

"Oh." I nodded, finally able to swallow. "Boone."

"How are you holding up?" She looked between me and the impres-sive breakfast. "Any complaints?"

"Other than wishing I were out of here, living my life? Uh, no. Not a single one."

"Yes." Her intelligent gaze swept over me. "I can see why. Your own cell, separate from everyone else in lockup. A real mattress"—she lifted her chin to the bed behind me—"with sheets, blankets, and pillows."

"I think this is the cell the deputies usually use for naps," I explained. "That's what Evans said."

Genevieve's perturbed expression returned, like she resented my treatment had given her nothing to argue about. "I'm glad they're being kind, you shouldn't have been arrested in the first place. I'll be filing a complaint against the arresting officer."

"Don't do that. It's almost over, and Boone was only following orders. And, like you said, he's cute."

"Him being cute doesn't excuse a superfluous arrest." She seemed to grow an inch taller, a swirling and crackling of scheming and strategy behind her eyes. "I'll make him sorry."

"What if he said sorry instead and took you out to dinner?" I picked up one of the breakfast sausages and took a nibble.

Genevieve's razor-sharp gaze cut to my face and she inspected me, saying, "I don't date law enforcement. Conflict of interest."

"That's too bad. Boone is not just cute, he's a great investigator, super smart, and a solid human. Maybe you should make an exception."

As I spoke, her eyebrows slowly pulled together, like the phrase *making an exception* was not in her vocabulary. "I do not subscribe to bending rules, Ms. Sylvester," she said finally. And yet she sounded just a wee bit uncertain, like my suggestion had tempted and confused her.

I shrugged, trying my best not to smile at her consternation. "Well now, that really is too bad. I wouldn't have this nice meal here if someone hadn't seen fit to bend a few rules. Sometimes, when it doesn't hurt anyone, a little rule bending can be fun. By the way"—I lifted the breakfast box to her—"do you want a doughnut?"

To my surprise, Jethro was the one to pick me up from the station and drive me back to the homestead.

"Cletus would be here if he could," the oldest Winston brother assured me. But I wasn't assured until, once we were out of the station, he added quietly, "It's something to help your momma, time-sensitive, and real important. Kind of a *now or never* sorta thing."

Feeling a little better, but still anxious, I almost missed the big RV sitting in the lot, parked closest to the wing of the building where the main lockup was housed. I grinned, my heart flooding with warmth.

Cletus hadn't been facetious in his letter; he really had stayed in an RV the whole time.

I can't wait to see him!

We made it to the homestead three years later. No, it didn't take three years, but it sure did feel like it. During the drive I decided, after setting eyes on Cletus and kissing his face off, I would need to go see my momma. She was probably worried sick. Truth be told, I'd been surprised she didn't come to the station. I thought for sure my being arrested would've snapped her out of her daze.

"Oh, look. He's already here. He made record time." Jethro pointed to Cletus's Geo as he cleared the trees of the Winston's winding drive-way. "I expect him to be in the carriage house. Billy is at—"

"Thanks, Jethro!" I had the door open before he'd come to a full stop and darted from the car, taking off at top speed and doing the mental calculations in my head.

It was now just past 1:00 PM on a Thursday. If Roscoe were coming home for the weekend, he'd be here past 9:00 or 10:00 PM. Billy didn't come home from the office until 7:00 PM at the earliest, unless the family gathered for a special occasion. *Does me being released from jail count as a special occasion?*

Lord, I hoped not. I needed *at least* three hours alone with Cletus's body. *Yes! I said his body! We've already established my sex fiend status. Accept it.*

Pushing through the front door to the carriage house, I stopped, scanned the family room and the small kitchen just beyond, working to catch my breath.

"Jenn?"

I spun around to face the door I'd just run through, finding Cletus jogging up the path. The heavy weight of anxiety and worry and all sorts of other unpleasant emotions completely evaporated, my chest expanding with air and relief. I felt like I could finally breathe.

And, my goodness, he was handsome. Just so damn handsome. His messy brown hair streaked haphazardly with stubborn blond and red highlights, his beard framing his gorgeous mouth and full lips, his bright, brilliant eyes that looked at me like I might be the most wonderful person, place, and thing in the entire universe.

My heart swelled, my eyes stinging, and I attacked him as soon as he crossed the threshold, jumping in his arms and likely suffocating him with kisses.

"I missed you. I missed you so much," he said, kicking the door shut behind us and carrying me to the bedroom. He kicked that door shut too. His hands were everywhere, searching, grabbing, making me feel a little better about my own reaction and need.

"Take your belt off," was all I could manage, tugging at the hem of his white long-sleeve T-shirt. *Priorities people*. I could handily remove all his clothes in less than a minute *if* he wasn't wearing a belt.

Disobediently, he worked to divest me of my clothes instead, removing my skirt, panties, shirt, and bra. The letter—his letter—I'd tucked away between my breasts went flying, but I'd think about that later. His mouth felt frantic, he placed urgent kisses along every inch of my neck, shoulder, collar bone. I moaned, breathless at the wonderful, ticklish sensation of his beard, lips, and teeth, waking each nerve ending, goose bumps rising over the surface of my now bare skin.

"Take off this belt," I demanded, gripping the leather roughly. "Or I swear I'll destroy all your belts. I'll burn them."

A breathy chuckle rumbled from his chest, a deep, purely masculine, taunting sound. And he did not obey, instead toeing off his shoes and sliding his hand down the front of my body possessively, capturing my breast, weighting it, rubbing his thumb over the center. "I want to—"

I pushed him away, separating our bodies, undeterred by whatever plans he'd been scheming. Not this time. I wanted what I wanted and, for once, he was going to capitulate.

"Cletus," my voice shook as I held myself away, capturing his eyes. "Take it off. Now."

The look he gave me was a dark one, his left eyebrow lifted a scant millimeter above his right. "My sweet Jennifer, I missed you," he said, reaching for me, *not removing his belt*.

Straightening my back, irrationally angry with this man I loved and lusted, I stepped away, lifting my own eyebrow and giving him my own dark look. He wanted to push? He wanted to play? Fine.

Game on.

Turning, I walked to the bed and climbed on top of it, positioning myself in front of the floor-length mirror leaning against the other wall. On my hands and knees, giving him a full view of my bottom and the apex of my spread thighs.

I saw his frown in the mirror. "What are you doing?"

"What does it look like I'm doing?" I locked eyes with him and saw his dark look dissipate, replaced by wonder. He appeared stunned.

"Cletus!"

His hands moved to his belt, unfastening it lightning fast. "You want me to take you from—"

"Yes! Like before." I arched my back, restless. "Do I need to draw a diagram?"

"That will not be necessary." His gaze dropped to my spread legs, growing instantly hazy. Free of belt and pants in record time, he gripped his impressive length, and my mouth watered at the sight. I felt the mattress depress as he placed a knee between my legs, his other palm coming to my backside, sliding to my hip, and squeezing.

I tensed in anticipation, deepening the curve of my arched back. He cursed, and then he was inside me. A second later his eyes met mine in the mirror, and I lost my breath. Him. Behind me. Mounting me. Us. Naked. His lips. His chest. His arms. The ridges of his stomach flexing and contracting as he moved.

Like the one time before when he'd taken me this way, Cletus used quick, punishing thrusts, his thighs slap, slap, slapping mine. He was deep, so deep inside. His gaze murky, shamelessly watching wherever he liked. He looked almost callous, gritting his teeth, his jaw a severe line.

And I panted with need, unable to catch my breath. This was what I'd wanted, what I'd wished for over the last few weeks but had been reluctant to ask. I could cry with how great it felt, how great he felt inside me, the sting every time he entered, pushing me forward. The twisting and pooling in my belly as I instantly hovered on the precipice of climax, knowing I wouldn't reach it until he deigned to stroke a skillful finger between my folds. The anticipation, the longing—God, *the longing*.

"Jenn. Look at me."

Not realizing I'd closed my eyes, I opened them, and ours immediately caught in the mirror.

"Watch us . . " he said, the command just above a whisper.

I moaned helplessly, my body clenching around him, because, once again, it was the word he hadn't said.

Watch us *fuck*.

He held my gaze for just another second before his broke away to blaze over my body. I trembled, doing as he commanded, watching him look at me; watching him move his hands from my bottom to my hips, my sides, and pull me upward, exposing my front to the mirror. He didn't enter me as deeply this way, but he held me entranced as he nuzzled my neck. One of his hands splayed over my stomach, the other fingering my breast with movements meant to tease rather than satisfy.

Everything about what he was doing at present felt like one giant tease. With me upright, he rolled his hips in a way that maintained the shallowest of penetration; my clitoris swollen, aching, and neglected; the barely there, taunting brush of his fingertips against my nipple; his mouth kissing my neck so sweetly it felt cruel, with the barest hint of suction.

I whimpered. "Please." Restless. Tortured. Elated.

"How long have you been thinking about us like this?" Maybe to anyone else he would've sounded calm. But I, intimately familiar with this particular edge in his tone, recognized his control slipping away. I shivered.

I wanted to touch him—all of him—so badly. Inexplicably, I loved that I could only hold on to his muscled thighs, that I had no choice but to take whatever he gave me, rely on him for balance. And simply feel and watch.

Our eyes again locked. Held. The unveiled lust in his stare made me dizzy. What madness was this?

And why did I find the hunger, the possessiveness, and—yes—the callousness in his features so damn sexy? He looked at me like I was his plaything, an object, something to use for pleasure. He looked at me like he had plans for my body that I may or may not find objectionable, but that he didn't care.

As I watched myself in the mirror, my knees spread wide open, my breasts jumping each time he entered me—but never deeply enough—I realized I was looking at him the same way. I had plans for his body, and superficially, I didn't care if he liked them or not. I wanted what I wanted. Namely, him, taking me from behind, torturing me, prolonging the anticipation, just as he was now.

He seemed to like my plans just fine. Which, in the midst of all my mindlessness, longing, bare skin, and trembling limbs made me wonder what would've happened if he'd said no. Would I have thrown a fit? Tried to force him?

The answer instantaneously resounded between my ears: *No. I would never.*

The fact that he clearly enjoyed the view and his level of control—or lack thereof—in this position only enhanced my gratification. The fact that he couldn't seem to get enough of me, that his appetite for me matched my appetite for him, it all thrilled and excited me to no end.

I didn't want him reluctant or yielding. I didn't want to have to talk him into anything. I wanted him enthusiastic and, excuse my crassness, *fucking my brains out.*

I watched our reflection as his big hand lifted to my throat and tipped my chin back, turning my head to capture my lips in a kiss, his tongue a gentle slide, a cherishing exploration as he pumped into me with renewed vigor. The revering kiss so dichotomous to the ferocity of his greedy, forceful invasions at my center. He seduced me, coaxed and lulled with his tongue while conquering my body elsewhere, making my insides heat and hum.

Drunk on his kiss, I barely noticed as he captured one of my hands where I gripped his thigh and positioned it between my legs. Then I jolted, separating our mouths, whipping my head around to face his steady stare in the mirror. His gaze shadowy and intent, he guided our fingers—together—around my slippery apex and my breaths came fast and ragged, every nerve in my body attuned and focused on the inch ignored until now.

And in the next moment, my head flung back, and I cried out. I was possessed, transfixed by the unearthly rapture coursing through every vein, every cell, every atom.

Pushing me forward to my hands and knees, he quickened his pace, stroking and tapping me between my legs as I struggled for balance, to get my hands back under myself. But I couldn't. I don't know what I did other than writhe on the bed in absolute ecstasy, my hips bucking instinctively, searchingly to some primal rhythm. His arm trapped between me and the mattress, his chest and stomach pressed fully to my bottom and back, Cletus drove into my spasming channel with a ruthlessness that felt unequivocally essential, hitting that deep, sweet spot with every single forward motion.

It was, he was, I was, life was perfection. For those endless moments, perfection. My body felt so beautiful and powerful. Everything in balance. Pleasure and pain, longing and satisfaction, hope and fear. Like before, in the bakery kitchen, it just went on and on. Every time I thought my orgasm was at an end, a new peak built, and I was lifted again into the stratosphere.

In the end, my heart beating manically in my chest, I could barely breathe, and—to my surprise—I was crying.

He turned me from the bed, gripping my shoulders. "Honey . . . Jenn are you—"

I sniffled, seeking to bury my face against his chest and hold him tight. I needed the weight of his body on me now, his solid frame, the spicy, warm scent of him.

But he held himself away, his eyes wide as they darted over my face. "Did I—Oh God, Jenn. Did I hurt you?" His voice broke and he sounded horrified.

"No," I said between sobs, still crying, reaching for him again.

He evaded me, and I could feel more than see his terror in how his body grew stiff and he sought to distance himself, give me space I didn't want.

"No! Cletus, no! You are so—I—everything is so—I needed—and you—and I—"

I couldn't complete a thought in my brain let alone speak a full sentence, so I kissed him instead, pushing him onto his back and climbing on top, pouring all of my happiness and love and joy into this connection, holding his head down to the mattress by wrapping my fingers in his hair. I needed him to know how badly I'd needed exactly what we'd just done.

How badly, wonderfully, terribly, wholly, entirely, and completely I needed *him*.

CHAPTER SIXTEEN
JENN

"After such a nocturnal reconnoitre it is hard to get back to earth, and to believe that the consciousness of such majestic speeding is derived from a tiny human frame."

— THOMAS HARDY, *FAR FROM THE MADDING CROWD*

Once he'd realized that my tears were the good kind, we laid together for a long time. Cletus didn't seem capable or inclined to talk, instead wishing to simply touch me, caress and pet my body, while I did the same to him. It was so nice. Peace for my soul in a storm of dread.

Eventually, he found his voice and burst my bubble of avoidance. "I have to tell you what happened."

I stiffened. "What? What happened?"

His arms squeezed. "Nothing unmanageable. Nothing we can't think through and solve."

"Okay . . ." I lifted my head and rested my chin on his chest so I could see his eyes. "Tell me."

Our legs tangled, he bent his knee slightly, his calf rubbing along mine. "While you were being held on Tuesday, one of my contacts with the Wraiths reached out on behalf of your brother—"

"My brother?"

"—and Repo."

I blinked, initially surprised my brother and Mr. Repo would want to talk to Cletus. As I considered the matter, I saw more clearly why it would make sense for the two of them to be in cahoots. Mr. Repo and Isaac were "brothers" in the Wraiths. Mr. Repo was, after all, secretly dating my mother. It never occurred to me that Isaac might know about their relationship—probably because my mother hadn't told me—but I supposed it wouldn't be inconceivable for Isaac to have known.

"What did you do?" I asked, pressing my cheek to his chest again and tracing the line of his shoulder with my fingertips.

"I met with them, at an undisclosed location, and learned details of which you should be aware." Cletus then explained what had occurred while I'd been trapped in the police station: his conversation with Mr. Repo and my brother, that my mother was being blackmailed and they suspected Miller, the plan to help her get out of Green Valley, how the law had tried to force her hand by arresting me. All of it.

When he finished his tale, I gave myself a few minutes to review and consider each of the newly revealed details—many of them truly bizarre, like the nature of the blackmail demands—before speaking. "So let me see if I have this right. On the night of our engagement party, Mr. Repo found my mother in the parking lot at the bakery, trying to stop the bleeding? Or trying to wake my father up?"

"I believe both."

"And so Mr. Repo, what? Thought she'd done it?"

"Repo saw her hands covered in blood, panicked, and thought maybe she'd done it. His priority seemed to be getting her out of there, first and foremost."

"Well, he should've just asked her what happened and promptly called the police."

"Hindsight is twenty-twenty. To a man like Repo, calling the police is always going to be the last option. Often, it's never an option."

That made sense. However, it was also stupid.

"Okay, so. He takes her to the bakery, she washes her hands—that's when you see them from the pantry—Jackson bangs on the back door. They run out the front, into the woods from the north, down the slope to his bike. Then he . . . Wait, what happens next?"

"He took her to a safe house for a few minutes. I guess she told him that she didn't kill Kip, and he realized his mistake."

"Quite a mistake," I grumbled, feeling salty. Why hadn't he just called the police instead of jumping to conclusions?

"They came up with a plan, a cover story. He then took her back to the lodge and she picked up her belongings. She drove home, changed, and the police came by in the early morning to bring her in."

I nodded, irritated with Mr. Repo for sure, but also relieved to finally have a version of events from my mother's perspective. I'd known in my heart that she didn't kill my father. Except—

"So I really don't understand this next part. According to Mr. Repo, Mr. Miller then started sending her blackmail notes, wanting his cows in return for not turning over the murder weapon with her prints?"

Cletus sighed and then explained that no one—not Repo, not Isaac, not Diane—had any idea what Miller was thinking. Did Miller have the gun used in the shooting? No idea. If he had the gun, how'd he get it? No idea. If he had the gun, did he actually have my momma's fingerprints on it? Possible, but no idea.

"So why didn't Isaac spy on Miller? Why'd Isaac decide to spy on us?" I asked, aggravated with my brother for many reasons.

"I do not know why Isaac didn't put Miller under surveillance when it became clear that the man was attempting to blackmail Diane. That's a question I didn't ask, and it's a good one. But, as I said, Twilight—Isaac—claimed he thought perhaps you'd killed your father."

I snorted, rolling onto my back as I rolled my eyes. "That's preposterous. I don't believe that. I do not believe Isaac thought I was the murderer for a single second. That's a lie." Not unless everything I thought I knew about my brother, and our past, and our relationship had been a lie.

Cletus turned on his side, propping his head in his hand and his elbow on the mattress. I met his eyes when I felt them inspect my profile. "Then what's your theory? Why would Isaac record us?"

I shrugged, moving my attention to the ceiling. "I don't know, but it wasn't because he thought I did it, unless I really don't know him at all."

Cletus seemed to weigh my words. "Interesting . . ."

"Anyway," I said on a huff. "Someone—we're assuming Miller, and I do think it's him—claims they have the gun with my mother's prints, and he wants the Guernsey cows in exchange for the evidence. But we don't know if it's a bluff or what."

"Correct. But your momma left a partial bloody print. Wait, back up. Why do you think Miller is the one blackmailing your mother, other than the obvious *Give me the cows or else* nature of the blackmail notes?"

"You remember at the will reading? Before I was arrested?"

"Yes. I remember you being arrested." His tone sounded carefully detached, like watching me be arrested wasn't a memory he'd like to keep.

I gave him a small smile, scratching my nails through his beard. "Cletus, it honestly wasn't that bad. Everyone was real nice. Evans played cards with me, and Boone—"

"Let's talk about your incarceration later, if you don't mind." He didn't meet my eyes, and his had grown distant. Clearly, my being arrested had been more traumatic for him than it had been for me.

"Fine. But you should know, it felt more like a vacation than anything else. Anyway—" I stretched, enjoying the friction of our naked bodies sliding against each other as I did so "—before the will reading, Miller was one of the people blocking the elevator. You remember?"

"Yes."

"I don't know if you picked up on this, but when Elena looked at the back row of folks gathered—Roger, Kenneth Miller, and Old Man Blount—she seemed terrified by one of them. I couldn't be sure at the time which one, but now I do think it was Miller."

"She looked terrified?" He stroked his beard. "Interesting."

"There's also what you said—or started to say—when Leeward brought up the Miller farm."

"Ah, yes. We haven't discussed this yet. It appears Elena initiated the process of signing Miller's land back over to him, before she knew you'd inherited everything."

"Why would she do that?" I asked, but the pooling of dread in my stomach told me the pressing suspicion I hadn't fully acknowledged—that Miller and Elena were in cahoots—was also shared by Cletus. For better or worse, I still held out hope Mr. Miller wasn't the villain in any of this.

"I suspect Elena and Miller were, perhaps are, working together."

Damn. "I guess I do too, since she was going to give him back his land, and it looks like he's the one blackmailing my mother. Only why did she look afraid of him before the will reading? If they're working together, why did he show up at Leeward's office with the others?"

"Unknown. But all good questions."

"I'm just so disappointed in Farmer Miller if this is the case. Sending my momma blackmail notes, working with Elena Wilkinson. I expected better of him."

Something flickered behind Cletus's eyes, telling me he had his own thoughts on the matter, but instead of sharing them he cleared his throat and wiped his expression clean. "Back to Isaac and Repo and the plan. Do you have any other questions?"

I lifted my fingers to my forehead and rubbed, thinking back to Cletus's retelling of his meeting. "So my momma left the handprints on the car, and that's why she won't leave the house. Mr. Repo told her not to, just in case the police can lift her prints while she's out."

"Correct, except Isaac told her not to. He's the one who cautioned her against leaving the house."

"And now y'all have come up with a plan to help my mother evade the FBI's watchful eye, sneak her out using my brother as a decoy, while setting up some sort of sound system in her house to make it seem like she's still there after she leaves."

"Also correct. That's where I was earlier today instead of picking you up. Sorry about that." He snagged my hand rubbing my forehead and kissed the back of it, his gaze apologetic. "The task was time-sensitive."

"But the wedding shower isn't for a few weeks."

"Yes. However, we need three or four solid days of recording we can use for playback after your mother leaves. Not every day will be usable. Alex sent me the equipment yesterday. He told me a month's worth of recording would be best."

A giant weight had settled on my chest, growing heavier and heavier the longer we discussed my father's murder, Mr. Repo, the blackmail and Miller and Elena, Isaac and his weird decision to record Cletus and me, and my mother going on the run. I just realized I'd been twisting the sheet next to me into a tight spiral with my fingers, so I flattened my hand on the mattress.

"What are you feeling?" Cletus asked, his tone quiet, gentle. "I know it would come as a shock to both of us, but please let me know if I made an error in judgment."

I turned my head to look at him, inspecting his handsome features. "What do you mean?"

"Helping Isaac and Repo, going along with their plan, improving it. I'm not going to assume anymore. So I'm asking."

"No. I—you did the right thing. My mother is—she's—well, she's fading away in that house. Even if she doesn't go on the run, we need to get her out of there, give her a breather, a chance to tell someone, ideally us, her version of events freely without the pressure of the FBI listening."

He nodded, his attention and palm dropping to my breast, weighing it, massaging. I fought a squirm of delight, worked to keep my mind focused on the issue at hand, even though all I wanted to do was say, *Whatever. I give up. You decide. Let's have sex.*

Surrendering to bliss, ignoring my worries, and instead having sex with Cletus was always the temptation. *Let Cletus decide.* I trusted him to decide. So why not just let him do it? I could pretend everything would work out just fine while he also kept me well stocked in breast massages and orgasms.

But that wasn't right. A thorny, blossoming of guilt made breathing momentarily difficult. Listening to Cletus talk about all the ways he'd been running around town, meeting with folks to help me, help my mother plan her escape, thwart Elena Wilkinson and Kenneth Miller, while also fretting about my well-being made me realize how much time and energy he'd already forfeited.

Meanwhile, how had I spent my time? Hanging out in a jail cell eating biscuits, refusing to sort through my feelings about the unanticipated bequeathing of funds and property by my father, and having sex fantasies. That's what I'd been doing.

I needed to pitch in! I needed to help. Not just use him for his big head. . . *either of them.*

Focus, Jennifer. What else?

I rubbed my eye, giving myself a little shake. "So, like I said, Isaac is lying about why he recorded us. I'm sure of that. But where did he get the DEA equipment?"

"Unknown," came Cletus's distracted response, communicating that he didn't wish to discuss his theories regarding Isaac's ability to get his hands on DEA equipment, assuming Cletus had any theories.

Of course he had theories. He always had theories.

I decided to let the matter drop, for now. "Okay. Then why do you think he's helping Mr. Repo? Helping my mother escape? Why do you think he cares? Do you think it's Mr. Repo? Isaac has been in town for years and, except for that one altercation in the Piggly Wiggly, he's ignored me and my mother."

His big hand continued its ministrations on my body and mumbled, "Perhaps loyalty to Repo. Or perhaps it's to assuage his well-deserved guilt about being a terrible son and brother."

My eyebrows ticked high on my forehead. Basically, in Cletus speak, this response meant he wished to change the subject away from Isaac as he had nothing kind to say on the matter and didn't want to upset me.

"Any more questions?" he asked, his thumb circling my nipple, making it increasingly difficult to focus.

I shook my head, covering his hand on my body with my own so I could form words. "I—I don't think so. It's . . . a lot. I need to think."

He nodded, leaning forward to kiss me. What I thought would be a light peck turned out to be a seductive drag of his lips against mine.

"I want you," he whispered, nuzzling my nose, the rasp in his voice making my toes immediately curl.

I fought to swallow, tracking his eyes as he leaned back an inch. His gaze had already darkened, his hand gliding south, and I became increasingly aware of the hard length pressing against my thigh.

And just like that, despite my best intentions, my brain scattered.

The weight on my chest dissipated.

The swelling, thorny guilt dissolved.

And I succumbed to blissful surrender. To temptation. To Cletus.

"I feel like I'm using him."

"Who?" Shelly sat in one of the big Adirondack chairs Jethro had made for the porch.

"Cletus."

"What are you using him for?"

"For, you know." I blushed. I felt the heat scale up my neck as the necessary word refused to leave my mouth.

"His sausage?" Sienna guessed from her chair, sharing a perplexed glance with Shelly.

"Yes," I admitted finally, not sitting. I was too on edge. "More specifically, s-sex." There. It was done. The word was out. *I am ridiculous.*

Sienna narrowed her eyes and mashed her lips together, obviously fighting a smile.

Meanwhile, Shelly frowned as though my statement was an unfinished riddle. "And?"

I turned away from their expectant expressions, leaning against the porch railing and gazing out at the chairs, streamers, and leftover plates of food from my wedding shower. The event had just wrapped up. I should have been out there helping Drew, Ash, and everyone else clean up the yard, not boring my friends with nonsensical thoughts.

But they'd dragged me over here, insisting they required my help. Then they'd cornered me, demanding to know why I'd been in such an odd mood since being released, why I'd been melancholy, distracted, and withdrawn. Sienna had asked if I was truly okay with my mother not being there for the party. Shelly had asked if I needed to speak to a therapist about all the upheaval in my life.

My difficulties and worries stemmed from all of it: my mother's absence, the upheaval in my life, and my unhealthy fixation with Cletus's . . . sausage.

But my present distraction and melancholy was more about me being confused than anything else. I didn't know how to feel about myself, how to think about myself. I'd tried to make it a joke—*I'm a sex fiend!*— but that didn't feel right either. My confession probably didn't make a lick of sense to anyone. It didn't even make much sense to me. I couldn't understand myself, so how could I explain my worries to Sienna and Shelly?

I twisted my fingers and faced Sienna and Shelly again, a lump in my stomach. "No. Listen. It's bad. I can't seem to get enough of him. I think about doing it—with him—all the time. The poor man has me waking him up in the middle of the night."

Even now, even after the swelling guilt, even after promising myself to be less of a sex fiend, what had I been doing leading up to our wedding shower while Cletus persisted in his diligence to help my mother?

I ignored everything of pressing importance and filled my time with Cletus.

I ignored Mr. Leeward's calls about my "inheritance," overwhelmed by it all. I ignored and pretended not to notice the way folks in town stared and whispered after my arrest, despite the fact that I hadn't actually been charged with anything. I ignored and avoided all wedding planning activities, suggesting to both my mother and Ashley that we just call the whole thing off. Neither would hear of it and, despite not attending, my momma helped with the last-minute details for the wedding shower. She also finalized the remainder of the wedding week plans, tasking her assistant to be present, just in case she was "busy elsewhere," to ensure the events progressed flawlessly.

At least she was finally out of bed, doing something.

What I did: I went to work; I took my momma dinner and gave her hugs, cheered by the slight improvement in her mood but concerned by this plan for her to go on the run; I daydreamed about taking advantage of my sweet man. And when I wasn't ignoring or doing any of the above, I was literally taking advantage of my sweet man.

My relationship with Cletus felt like the only thing in my life going right—so very, very right—and I worried. Giving our shared moments so much of my focus and attention didn't seem proper for me or fair to him.

Shelly and Sienna spent a few seconds sharing a look, but it was Shelly who said, her tone flat as a board, "Yes, poor man."

"Stop. I'm being serious." I half leaned, half sat on the porch rail. "Shelly, you said something earlier today about him showing up tired to work?"

"Yes. He's been tired and sloppy. I sent him upstairs for a nap last week."

"Well, I'm afraid I'm the reason." I clutched my forehead, ready for a reprimand. It was not okay for me to be tiring him out so much when his schedule was so full.

"I feel so sorry for him," Sienna said, not sounding sorry for anyone.

Ignoring her comment, I continued, "I'm being selfish, I know I am. But he keeps going along with it. I'm worried." Now that I was actually talking about things out loud, I realized the extent to which selfishness had cast a shadow over my self-image. I was not this person. I was not. *I will be better . . . after tonight.*

"Jennifer, you are mixed up." Sienna sighed. I felt her examination of me. "But you shouldn't be worried. If Cletus wanted you to stop or pause or give him a breather, he'd ask."

"I don't know that he would. He loves me, I know he does, and sometimes I think he'd never say no, even if he wanted to."

"Jenn, is that really what you think?"

I twisted my lips, peeking at Shelly. "Maybe?"

"No, Jenn. No." Sienna shook her head adamantly. "Cletus is one of the most self-actualized people I know. If he didn't want to have sex with you—or even if he did in general but needed a break—he would tell you. He's the sort of person who is always going to prioritize telling you the truth over worrying about your feelings. I know this because he and I have this in common."

"You care more about being honest with Jethro than hurting his feelings? Really?"

"Telling the truth will always hurt less than a lie."

I sighed, feeling a little better, but . . . not really.

"Agreed." Shelly lifted her water glass toward Sienna. "Given Cletus's inability to spare yours—or anyone else's—feelings, I don't understand why you're worried."

"Because it doesn't change the fact that I'm lusting after him like a harlot instead of focusing on things that matter. What does that say about me?"

"That you are a harlot?" Shelly guessed.

"Exactly."

Shelly's confusion was obvious. "And?"

I glared at her. "Shelly."

"I'm with Shelly on this." Sienna tilted her wineglass toward Shelly. "Harlots have orgasms. Given the choice between harlotry and chastity with the man I love—for me personally—I'm going to choose harlotry ten times out of ten."

"No, y'all. I'm being disrespectful. I'm thinking of him like some sort of sex toy."

"As you should." Shelly nodded, like this was only right and just.

"Oh my God, Shelly." I covered my face and peeked through my fingers. They didn't understand. How could they? "Listen, I've been raised to approach sex like any good, Christian Southern woman should approach everything else in life."

Sienna and Shelly once more swapped looks.

"Go on. How does any good, Christian Southern woman approach life?" Sienna egged me on.

"Carefully. With restraint, hospitality, and politeness. But also, without embarrassing my family."

"Or enjoying yourself too much?" Shelly said.

I squirmed.

"No, Jennifer. Shelly is right." Sienna stood from her seat, and I heard her steps cross to me before she peeled my hands away. "Listen to yourself. You are talking about a man you sincerely, deeply, soulfully love. And who loves you just the same. I may have been raised in a Catholic family, but my parents spared me the shame when they taught us about sex. In fact, I probably could've benefitted from a little bit of shame."

I huffed, not understanding. "What does—"

"Here." Shelly set down her water glass and skootched to the end of her seat. "You're the one who brought up God, Jenn. So let's talk about God. Do you think, honestly, God would give us these bodies that are capable of doing and feeling these glorious sensations if he wanted us to feel shame about it?"

I said nothing, but I had the thought, *She sounds like Cletus.*

"But that doesn't mean we turn it—sex or anything else—into the center of our universe." Sienna used her grip on my hand to thread our fingers together, looking at me like I was cute and wonderful, but also maybe like she felt a little sorry for me. "Take tomatoes as an example."

"Tomatoes?"

"If all you ever did was think about tomatoes, all you did was eat tomatoes and buy tomatoes and live your life with the singular goal of surrounding yourself with as many tomatoes as possible in order to achieve peak tomato lifestyle while ignoring other relationships and responsibilities, that would be a waste of a life and ultimately bring nothing but unhappiness. And you'd eventually die of cancer from eating so many tomatoes."

"I . . . uh—" I laughed, not following.

"It's the same thing with sex. Or money. Or fame. Or fortune. Or anything else that might feed a very specific part of your psyche, maybe even speak to a piece of your soul. But no one 'thing' on earth is ever going to satisfy you completely, forever." She released my hand and used her fingertips to push a strand of hair from my temple, gifting me a patient, gorgeous smile.

I was so mesmerized by the sparkly charisma of Sienna's stellar smile, I muttered, "You haven't had sex with Cletus," without thinking.

Shelly barked a laugh. It was so sudden and unexpected, especially since she rarely smiled, let alone laughed, it startled me out of my Sienna-smile haze. Heat crawled up my cheeks.

"Oh my goodness." Shelly wiped at her eyes, a big old grin on her exquisite features.

Sienna, also laughing, shook her head and stepped back, crossing her arms as she considered me. "Well, I could say, 'You've never had sex with Jethro,' but that's the thing. I don't love Cletus like you do. You don't love Jethro like I do. Neither of us love Beau like Shelly does."

"But that's also part of the problem." I appealed to both of them equally. "What we're doing, it doesn't feel like 'making love' sometimes."

A hint of concern dampened Shelly's lingering grin. "What does 'making love' feel like?"

I thought about it for a moment, having trouble finding just the right words, so I settled for the first that came to mind. "Warm, cozy, sweet, sincere. I guess, in my teenage fantasies, what I always thought it would be like."

"And what you're doing with Cletus now . . .?" Shelly lifted an eyebrow, her concern persisting.

"It feels—" Heat rose anew to my cheeks, my ears, up my neck, but I ignored it and forced the words out. "Sometimes rough, hot, hard, painful, but in a really good way, you know? It makes me feel lost but awake. I don't know how to describe it, I guess."

Sienna blinked a few times, like my description had caught her off guard, but she said, "That's a pretty good start."

I wasn't finished. "It feels animalistic, primitive. While making love feels more civilized, enlightened, refined—"

"Polite," Shelly supplied, crisp and succinct. "You think making love is polite and the other—let's call it 'humping like rabbits'—is rude?"

I cringed at the phrase she used, but I supposed it was a fair description. "Maybe. Does that make sense?"

"It does." Sienna cut in. "But what I don't think you understand is that part of the benefit—the joy—of being in a fully consensual relationship with someone is that you get to do whatever it is you want to do with that person—as long as they consent."

"Consent is key." Shelly leaned back in her chair again, folding her hands over her stomach. "Whatever you're doing, it's between you and Cletus, and no one else. You and Cletus."

I frowned, processing this statement, *It's between you and Cletus, and no one else.*

"Plus, you love each other. If you both want to hump like rabbits, then hump like rabbits. If you want to make love, make love. If you want to dress up and role-play something completely scandalous, do it." Sienna laughed, sounding joyful. "You get to share your kink, whatever that is, with someone who is amazing, and who adores you. So let him share it."

"My kink . . ." What even was my kink? Did I know? Did everyone have a kink? What if I didn't have a kink?

"And when he wants to share his kink with you, be open to it," Shelly added.

Sienna nodded, like this point was extremely important. "Yes, be open to kink."

Goodness! Did Cletus have kinks?! *He's never mentioned any.* Just the thought of Cletus sharing his kinks made me want to find him right now, demand a list, and start . . . doing it, whatever it was.

"But, if you hate his kink, tell him." Shelly's voice turned stern. "No one should be forcing another person into nonconsensual kinkery."

"Yes! That." Sienna pointed at Shelly but continued to address me gently, "If you don't like one of his kinks, or he doesn't like yours, talk about it. Find new kinks together. The sex part of a successful relationship is all about finding someone who has compatible kinks, and then indulging them. Together."

CHAPTER SEVENTEEN
JENN

"Man is now only more active - not more happy - nor more wise, than he was 6000 years ago."

— EDGAR ALLAN POE

I took three things away from my conversation with Sienna and Shelly:

1. Lusting after Cletus didn't make me fundamentally weird or wrong.

2. What happened between me and Cletus was no one's business but ours. If he was happy, I shouldn't fret unless he spoke up and expressed concern.

3. I couldn't let my desire for Cletus become the center of my universe. Whether I liked it or not, there were other things needed doing, other situations I'd let linger in favor of indulging my Cletus fantasies. It was time to confront those things and situations. Once done, I could get back to the Cletus fantasies, *in moderation.*

Which was why I'd decided to stop by my mother's house after the wedding shower instead of heading home with my man. There'd be plenty of time for us to be wrapped in each other. Neglecting present pressing issues and worries would only make those issues and worries worse in the long run.

In the spirit of confrontation, I knocked on my momma's door, waited a tick, then entered. "Momma? I'm here, and I brought you food from the shower. Are you feeling better?"

I understood why my momma couldn't come to the wedding shower. Cletus had suggested she wear gloves all day to avoid leaving fingerprints, but we both knew this was a silly idea. She couldn't wear gloves on a sunny spring day without raising eyebrows and suspicions, even more suspicions than her absence from society.

Most folks had just assumed she'd been torn up about my father's death, seeing as how they'd been married for so long and had two children together. In the end, we'd decided to perpetuate this story by having her feign a lingering illness instead of attending the shower at the Winston homestead. Of course, the unmarked van along the street outside her house raised a few eyebrows, and folks were starting to whisper more and more about the possibility of her being a suspect.

They didn't whisper these thoughts to me, obviously. Especially since I'd been the one arrested.

Regardless, I did feel badly about continuing to keep Ashley in the dark and hoped I'd get a chance to make things right in the future. *I'll throw her wedding shower! Maybe I'll ask Drew to jump out of the cake.* It was an idea I tucked away for later.

"I'm in the back office, dearest. I felt a little better, so I decided to finalize the seating plan for the reception." Her wan voice traveled down the hall, and I knew some of the words were for the benefit of the FBI, still watching the house from the road and listening in daily.

I carried the covered plate of food to the office and stopped just inside the doorway. She'd been telling the truth; my mother sat in the office chair working on the seat assignments, a pile of RSVP cards on one side of the keyboard, a printed-out spreadsheet on the other, and a seating diagram on the computer screen.

"You do look sick still," I said, even though she looked great. Turning to face me and wearing a small smile, I noted that she'd showered, put on makeup, did her hair, and had dressed in a cream-colored pantsuit, the jacket hanging on the back of her chair. My heart did a sad flip-flop because it was the outfit she'd planned to wear to the wedding shower today.

My momma waved me forward, opening the notebook we used to write messages back and forth when I visited. This had been my idea and started up right after I'd been released at my arrest. It was so nice to "talk" to her again. Understanding the extent to which she was being watched by the law had been a relief. Now we could circumvent their systems.

Placing the loaded plate on top of her desk, I said, "I have just a few simple things, since I knew you weren't feeling well," while unwrapping a giant plate covered in a sampling of the yummiest dishes: spinach dip and homemade pumpernickel bread, veggies and smoked salmon dip, fancy cheeses and artisan sea salt crackers, sausage pie, coleslaw, fried chicken, macaroni and cheese, green beans with bacon and onions, and collard greens (also with bacon).

"I suppose I should eat something." Her eyes twinkled but her voice sounded pitiful.

I worked to keep my laugh at bay as she pointed to what she'd just written in the notebook while also digging into the food with gusto.

"Please do eat, at least the crackers," I said as I read her short note,

Do you have pictures of the shower? How are you? You look wonderful! How was it? Did y'all play the games I sent Ashley? Did you apologize to her for my absence? She's done so much!

"I'll try to eat. Do you mind if we just sit quietly for a while and put something on the radio? I'm so tired." My momma, picking up her plate, darted out of the office and tipped her head toward the kitchen, her way of asking me to follow.

"Sounds good. I'll put on a record." I picked up the notebook and pen, writing my response to her questions as I walked to the living room. Once there, I paused my writing to select a classical bluegrass recording and set it on her record player. Cletus had related Alex's advice regarding records. They were more difficult to filter out using computer programs than digital recordings, which was why we'd started using them over the past few weeks.

I finished my handwritten responses and joined her at the kitchen table, pulling the camera Shelly had used to take photos of the afternoon's event. My mother poured us both a glass of wine and embraced me with a tight hug before we both took a seat. She then proceeded to eat all the food as we corresponded via her notebook.

I do have pictures, here's the camera. I'm good, but I'm worried about you. More later re: that. Thank you! Sienna helped me pick out my outfit. She's so good at that kind of stuff. It was fun. You were missed, we played all the games, and Beau was sure to take video so you could see the fun. Ashley was gracious as always and didn't seem to mind. She and Drew were very cute and won most of the games, was great.

I want to discuss the plan for your "escape" before things get too much farther along. Are you sure you want to do this? Do you really want to run away with this man? I feel like it might be unnecessary. Maybe you could go in and amend your story? Tell the truth?

I turned the book to face her, studying her expression. She'd never spelled out what had happened from her perspective that night. If Mr. Repo had left anything out during his one meeting with Cletus weeks ago, then we were still in the dark. I couldn't wait to get her out of the house so she could actually speak.

My mother read my note, smiling, frowning, nodding thoughtfully, and sighing when she got to the end. Lifting her gaze, which looked equal parts torn and determined, she picked up the pen and wrote,

Glad the shower went well and can't wait to see the photos and videos. Baby, I feel so—

She paused here, rubbed her forehead and nibbled on her lip before continuing,

—I do not want to leave you or the lodge or Green Valley. I am so proud of you, who you are and who you've become. I don't want to miss out on a single minute of your life. Yet I don't know what else to do. I didn't kill your father, but that doesn't seem to matter to anyone. I WON'T let anyone use me against Jason. I won't let your father take over this part of my life, this precious, wonderful, surprising adventure I've just started, like he took so much else from me while he was alive.

She underlined the words *I WON'T* three times. When she'd finished writing, she sent me a searching look. By "Jason" I knew she meant Mr. Repo. Apparently, Jason was Mr. Repo's real name, but no one used their real name with the Wraiths. Cletus's father, Darrell, was known as "Romeo," and Isaac went by the moniker "Twilight."

Torn, I frowned at her words. I understood where she was coming from with respect to my father. I didn't resent her relationship with Mr. Repo, aside from not knowing or liking the man much. Likewise, I'd be lying if I claimed to 100 percent support her relationship with the guy. He—Mr. Repo, Jason, whatever his name—was a criminal. He'd been arrested, charged, and served prison time more than once.

Plus, my momma had kept their relationship a secret from me and from everyone, and now she wanted to run off with him? Go on the run from the police? What would their life be like? And what happened if she didn't love him next year but we still hadn't cleared her name? What if he mistreated her? What would she do then? As someone who'd spent their first two decades of life feeling trapped by circumstances, I didn't want the same thing to happen to my mother.

Seeing my expression, she quickly added,

I love him. I love Jason. I won't let him go to jail because of me. I won't. At least out there with Jason, I might be on the run, but the truth is I'll be freer than I have been in over twenty years. I feel imprisoned already, here, with those people watching all the time.

When she lifted her eyes this time, they were glassy, looked sad instead of undecided, but the determination remained.

Twisting my lips, I nodded even though I still hadn't resigned myself to the plan Cletus, Mr. Repo, and my brother had concocted. Writing notes back and forth on paper wasn't an effective method for arguing someone out of a crazy plan. There had to be another way for her to be free, for us to clear her name.

In my heart, I held out hope we'd find another way.

A sudden knock on the front door followed by an impatient double ring of the doorbell drove a spike of alarm down my spine. Startled, my mother and I stared at each other. Cletus had said the FBI or the sheriff's office would definitely come by today or tomorrow to check on my mother, make sure she was still in the house even if she didn't attend the wedding shower.

Another series of knocks and a triple doorbell ring pushed me from my stunned stillness and into action.

I pointed to her bedroom and then her face and clothes. If the visitor was FBI, verifying we hadn't smuggled her out somehow, then she couldn't be seen looking as well and pulled together as she was presently.

If it were anyone else, her assistant for instance, she'd need to look under the weather since we'd told everyone at the wedding shower she'd been ill.

Nodding, she stood and tiptoed to her bedroom while I placed my hand over my heart, waiting until her door had closed before strolling unhurriedly to the foyer. I had no reason to rush. I had no reason to be afraid. I peered out the peep hole, telling myself I would be calm, cool, collected—

What the—? I jumped back, my heart sprinting.

"Ms. Donner, Jennifer, I know y'all are in there." Mr. Miller stood right up against the peep hole, trying to peep inside.

Fingers shaking, I pulled out my phone and texted Cletus,

Jenn: Mr. Miller is at the front door. He wants to talk to my mother!!!!!!

His knock sounded again. "I see your car out here, Jennifer. I'm not wanting to cause trouble or make a ruckus. It's just, Ms. Donner, look. I've come to talk to you about my cows and my farm."

I grimaced. *He means blackmail,* I thought grimly. It seemed Miller had grown desperate. Instead of mailing her threatening letters like he'd been doing since my engagement party, he'd obviously decided to deliver a message in person. Today.

A multitude of questions remained regarding Miller and his involvement in my father's death. If he and Elena were in cahoots, why? Why would she want to be in cahoots with him? What were they cahooting about? And why was she afraid of him now? Had Miller tried to blackmail her too? Cletus and I suspected—strongly suspected—Elena had been the one to strangle my father with the fishing rope. Had he seen it?

Seen her? Did he really have the gun in his possession or was that a bluff? And if he had the gun, did that make him the shooter?

Staring at the trailing three dots on my phone screen—an indication of Cletus's imminent response—I willed him to type faster. Finally, his message came through,

Cletus: Keep him outside on the front porch. DO NOT open the door. Someone will be there in less than three minutes. I'm ten away.

"Jennifer, Ms. Donner, be reasonable. Open the door so we can talk."

Still holding my phone, I stepped right up to the door. "Mr. Miller, it's Jennifer. I—we—you know, my momma has been real sick, and I don't think she can see visitors today. Maybe next week?"

"Jennifer, I can barely hear you. Open the door so we can talk face-to-face."

"I—I can't—"

"Now, don't turn me away until you see my offer."

"Farmer Miller. Please understand—" I glanced at my phone screen, less than a minute had passed "—I just had my wedding shower this afternoon, did you know that? I think your niece was there, such a lovely—"

"Jenn, I always liked you. You're a nice girl. And I'm sorry it's come to this, but I need those cows back, and I need my land, and so—I suppose—this offer is for both of you. *Both. Of. You.* And I don't think it's something you'd appreciate if'n I made the offer out loud. I know it's something you're going to want to *see.*"

Oh goodness. Well.

I glanced at the phone again. Two minutes left.

"Be smart. Open the door. Let me show you what I mean." He lowered his voice from a shout, deepened it to a threatening baritone.

Gulping in air, I placed my hand on the doorknob. "Mr. Miller, I will open the door. But you have to give me a solemn oath that you will stay on the front porch."

"If you want me to stay on the front porch—out in the open—after seeing my offer, then I will do so. But if you invite me in to discuss terms, then I will. Now open the door because I am ten seconds away from making my offer out loud."

Cletus had told me not to open the door, but I didn't have a choice, I didn't have ten seconds.

Miller had to know the house was being watched—*of course he knows, everybody knows! It's not like the FBI van is making an effort to be clandestine seeing as how they wave at me every time I drive past*—which meant he'd deduced they were also listening. I placed my hand on the lock, ready to flip it.

Working to hide my fear, I slowly unlocked the door, counted to three, and slowly opened it just wide enough to slip outside and close it behind me. Miller had to back up as I did so, but he still stood close, hovering, maybe giving me just two feet of room.

Other than the hovering, the first thing I noticed was the crazy quality in his eyes. "Glad to see you're open to being reasonable. That's good," he said.

I set sweaty hands on my hips and poked out my chin, working real hard to keep my voice firm. "Now, sir. If you would—"

The words died on my lips. Instead of a check or a contract or whatever I thought maybe he wanted me to see, he held up a white piece of paper with words written in black marker that read, "I know what you did, both of you. I know what you're covering up. And if you don't want the police to find out your secrets, you'll do as I say. Right now."

I read the note three or four times, my heart slowing to a sluggish pace by the time I lifted my attention to his scornful features. My ears rang. My throat felt full and dry. Anger, thick and hot, pumped through my veins.

I was tempted—so very tempted—to call his bluff out loud, to read the paper he showed me and ask him what the hell it was about. I had nothing to hide. He didn't know *poo* about me. And if he thought I'd give him his farm back now, well, he was mistaken. That field? Mine. That pond? Mine. That prairie and mountain view? Mine and mine.

"I am not interested in this offer," I said deliberately, much calmer than I'd expected the words to arrive.

The sneer fell from his face, and he blinked, visibly shocked.

"And frankly, I'm insulted," I continued, not needing to dig very deep for fury. "How. Dare. You."

Farmer Miller—*nay, Mr. Miller!*—stumbled back a step, his blinking now on overdrive.

But I was not yet finished. "You conspired to cheat my mother out of a good deal of money last year, but she paid full price for those cows. You've been more than fairly compensated for them. You may have signed over your land while under false assumptions, believing the string of lies my father told you, but you are an adult. You are responsible for your bad business decisions, no one else."

He gulped, staring at me, and stumbled on the porch step, needing to grip the banister to keep from falling. He was still a foot taller than me; but clearly, he was the smaller person in every way that mattered.

"I can't believe I ever looked up to you. I can't believe I made excuses for you, to my mother, to Cletus. I stood up for you last year. Even after what my father put me through and all your scheming with him, I asked my mother to consider selling you back those cows over the summer. Did you know that? And when I found out my father had left me your farm, I was planning to sign it back over because I believed it was the right and good thing to do. But not anymore."

Mr. Miller lowered his gaze to the porch, but his features were still within my view. He also lowered his hand holding the paper. The man swallowed thickly, his brain obviously working, a hint of remorse taming some of the crazy in his eyes.

"I thought the best of you. And what did you do? You betrayed me. You betrayed everyone who ever thought of you as a good and decent person. You betrayed yourself. Shame, Mr. Miller. Shame on you."

As I finished, the sound of car tires on gravel pulled my attention to the driveway just as Shelly's brown car barreled into view. She and Beau jumped out of the car, not even cutting the engine, and ran over to the porch.

Mr. Miller didn't look up as they ran past him, Beau stepping in front of me while Shelly flanked my side and rushed to ask, "Are you okay?"

I nodded, but said nothing, so darn angry I couldn't see straight.

"Mr. Miller." Beau leaned a hand against the porch rail, forcing Miller down the three remaining steps until he stood at ground level with the three of us above. "It's time to go," the redhead said, sounding sterner than I'd ever heard him.

Miller glanced between us—first Beau, then Shelly, then me—and heaved a weary sigh. "Fine. I'm going. I'll leave. But, Jennifer, I can't let this go. I am real sorry, but I won't. Those Guernseys, that land, they're my life." His tone held more desperation than threat, an appeal for understanding. He seemed close to tears, his words roughened with emotion. "You have to understand, it's nothing personal, but I'll do what I have to do to get back what's mine. Tell your momma, time is running out. She has a week, no more. I'm sorry."

With that, he turned, shoulders slumped, and walked back to his car.

CHAPTER EIGHTEEN
JENN

"The more one judges, the less one loves."

— HONORÉ DE BALZAC, *PHYSIOLOGIE DU MARIAGE*

Thankfully, deputies Boone and Jackson came by that night after Cletus had arrived and Beau and Shelly had departed. The two men interrupted our dinner of soup and salad, looking relieved when my mother came to the door. They both sent me and Cletus—where we stood behind her in the foyer—unmistakable silent apologies with their eyes.

The purpose of their visit was supposedly to ask follow-up questions about my mother's version of events on the night of the engagement party. Neither of them seemed at all surprised when she told them to speak to her lawyer. They nodded, told us to have a good night, and my mother closed the door.

I couldn't decide if I felt relieved or panicked. On the one hand, after Miller's threatening ultimatum this afternoon, giving us just one more week, I was grateful Boone and Jackson had checked in so that we could move forward with the plan. On the other hand, moving forward with the plan meant my mother might be leaving for good.

Before I could sort out my feelings, we returned to the dinner table and ate silently for fifteen more minutes. Cletus then said, "Looks like we should be going," and pulled out a cell phone I didn't recognize, one of those old flip type phones. He tapped out a message and showed us both the screen before sending,

Cletus: We're heading out.

I knew the seemingly innocuous message was for Isaac because that was the first part of the plan. Cletus would text, *We're heading out* to Isaac. Isaac would then let Mr. Repo know.

Next, Isaac would take his bike to my mother's, wearing his helmet until he walked inside, just as he'd done for the last several weeks.

After an hour, as soon as my mother left on Isaac's motorcycle, dressed like my brother, he would turn on the playback system Cletus had wired weeks ago that made it sound like my mother was moving around, still at home. He would also message Mr. Repo again, letting the man know my mother was inbound for the Dragon Biker Bar.

Isaac would wait a few hours, keeping an eye on the front and ensuring the playback system was working. He'd then leave through the back after midnight.

Meanwhile, my momma would ride to the Dragon Biker Bar, meet Mr. Repo, and leave for the safe house. Cletus and I should, hopefully, be there already by the time they arrived. I would say my goodbye in the short time allotted, and then . . . that'd be it. Theoretically, she'd be gone for who knows how long, until Cletus and I cleared her name by building a case against the real killers, one of which we felt certain was Elena Wilkinson.

I'm not saying I agreed with the plan, but that was the plan.

Presently, as we pushed back from the kitchen table, my mother nodded upon reading Cletus's outgoing message. She stood straight and stiff, stubborn steel behind her gaze, the strength my father had never fully succeeded in badgering out of her. I'd concluded over the past year he'd wanted her bent, not broken. If she'd been broken, she might've been less effective at making the money he used for his big boats, vacation house, and fishing trips in the Florida Keys.

I hugged my mother goodbye, hoping and praying I'd be seeing her again in a few hours at the safe house. *One thing at a time.*

Cletus and I had gone around and around about the plan, with me always asking if—once we had her alone and speaking freely—she'd finally tell us her version of events from the night of my father's murder. Then maybe we could clear her name *now* and she wouldn't have to leave with Mr. Repo at all.

Cletus had never responded with anything but, "We'll see," leaving me frustrated because I could tell he didn't think this was a possibility.

Nerves twisting my stomach into knots, Cletus and I drove to my house in silence. Alex had confirmed my house was free of cameras and listening devices the day after Cletus's meeting with Isaac and Mr. Repo and the day before my release from the station. Nevertheless, Cletus had requested Alex fly his magical drone over the structure every so often, just to be sure. Even when all the sweeps and scans came back clean, neither of us seemed moved to talk much when inside the house.

Alex had my full confidence, but our trust of privacy in the home had been shattered. We would have to move at some point, I knew and accepted that.

As soon as we arrived at my house, Cletus and I changed out of our regular clothes and wordlessly slipped on black tactical gear, another gift from Alex. Then we were off, navigating the woods on foot for three miles until we made it to the Green Valley community center. Neither of us spoke, but he'd grabbed my hand a few times, giving me a searching look and a squeeze. I'd answered the searching looks with a small smile and the hand squeeze with one in return.

Unsurprisingly, the parking lot was full of cars for Saturday bingo, but also equally empty of people. Cletus walked right up to a black truck, pulled out a set of keys and unlocked the passenger side door first. As we'd walked around the back, I saw it had Tennessee plates. An older Chevy, it was one of the smaller models they used to make in the 1970s and 1980s.

"Should I ask whose truck this is?" I whispered the question even though there didn't seem to be anyone around.

"It's Carter McClure's, but he only uses it for hauling, which is why you didn't recognize it. I believe my brother Jethro arranged to borrow black beauty tonight and tomorrow to load mulch for flower beds," he responded, helping me up into the seat. "Note the illegal tint to the windows. So you can't see inside? It's just like the kind I have on the Buicks and the Geo. We did this for Carter last year, but since the vehicle is over thirty years old, he gets to pretend like it was always that way. That plus the black paint job makes it near invisible at night, a real safety hazard with the lights off."

Hmm. Invisible. Now I didn't need to ask why we were using this particular truck.

"How did you arrange for Jethro to borrow the truck so fast? We didn't know until an hour and a half ago that tonight would be *the night* for my momma's escape."

"I didn't arrange it. Jethro really does need to use it for moving mulch. I offered to drive it over from the community center tonight. Carter and Mrs. McClure are here for bingo, they took two cars. They'll drive home together. This just saved Carter and Jethro a trip."

"Are you serious? We just got lucky? When did you get the keys?"

Cletus shrugged, shutting my door, and I recognized the shrug for what it was: a nonanswer. I followed his progress around the hood, then I leaned over the driver's side seat, planning to unlock the door for him. But I found it was already unlocked. Furthermore, a set of car keys rested in the seat.

"What the heck?" I picked them up, lifting them toward the scant light provided by the parking lot streetlamps, and scowled. "Cletus, here are the car keys."

He shrugged again, nodding. "You can put them in the glove box, I already have a set."

"How did you get a set of keys to this truck?"

Cletus turned the engine, put on his seatbelt, and faced me. "If you want me to answer the question truthfully, I will. If you don't, I won't."

Inhaling deeply, staring at him and his patient expression, I shook my head while reaching for my seatbelt. "You have a copy. That's why. You have a copy of Fire Chief McClure's truck keys. And, no, I will not ask why, so please don't tell me."

I had too much on my mind. I couldn't currently ponder the shade of Cletus's gray morals at present, especially since I was relying on them to help my mother.

He took off, heading toward the Foothills Parkway. We passed it and kept going. I bit my lip, chewed on it. Then I chewed on my thumbnail, watching the silhouettes of dark trees speed by against a starry sky. I wasn't in the mood to talk, and it seemed like he wasn't either.

I don't know how long we drove, it felt like hours, but I knew it couldn't have been longer than thirty minutes. At one point, Cletus pulled into a convenience store attached to a gas station, said he'd be right back, and walked into the shop.

Five minutes later he returned, holding a piece of paper. "These are the directions. You read them and tell me where to go."

The directions looked like chicken scratch on receipt paper but, miraculously, they worked. Off one of the switchbacks, we pulled up to a fence with a keypad requiring a code. I read Cletus the five numbers at the bottom of the receipt paper and a motorized gate swung open, revealing a ranch house built into the slope side of a mountain. No porch to speak of off the front, but a nice circular driveway for plenty of cars. Or motorcycles.

"Do we . . . wait here? Or go inside?" I asked once Cletus had cut the truck's engine, positioning it at the end of the circle.

He made a small sound, it sounded frustrated. "I don't like this. I don't like the gate, and I don't like that if someone decides to park in front of me, I'd have to drive over them in order to leave. I don't like it."

"What do you want to do?"

"We have a little while. Let's drive up the road and see if we can park somewhere else. Then we can walk back, check out the fence, the perimeter, assess points of exit and entry besides the gate."

"You don't trust Mr. Repo?" I studied him. Even in profile, I could see he'd twisted his lips as though in deep thought.

"I don't trust anyone. Except you." He started up the engine again and we did as he'd described, parked a little ways up the road, able to mostly hide the car at a scenic pull-off.

But as we walked back, something about his last statement nagged at me. Walking along the road in our tactical gear, I asked, "If you don't trust Mr. Repo, should we allow my momma to go with him? I mean, if it comes to that?"

Cletus hemmed and hawed—as much as Cletus Winston was capable of hemming and hawing—and kept his eyes forward as he answered, "It's not up to me whether your momma goes with Repo or not. It's up to your momma."

"Yes, but if you know something about him, about his past that might change the way my mother feels about him, you should tell her. She shouldn't be running off with someone she doesn't really know."

"I am not aware of the extent to which Repo has shared his past with Diane. On that, I haven't been briefed."

"Maybe you could make a list of what you do know about him?"

He slid me a side-eye. "Jenn."

We'd made it to the corner of the fence and instead of continuing on the road side of it, Cletus walked into the woods and along the perpendicular side. "Cletus, this is my mother. I don't want her going on the run with someone who will mistreat her. If you know something about him that might impact her willingness to leave with him, you have to say so."

Cletus halted at the end of the fencing. It didn't terminate at the slope, but instead at several tens of feet before it, allowing us to walk directly onto the property without using the gate. "I don't know anything about Repo that will lessen your mother's opinion of him, unless she doesn't already know he's an Iron Wraith."

He thought he was so clever in his choice of words, but I could read between the lines he drew. "Does that mean you know something about Mr. Repo that will improve my mother's opinion of him? You know something good?"

"I know a few things. It's up to each person to decide if they're good or not."

"But you think they're good?"

"I think they make him an unusual person."

"In a good way?"

He turned to me as soon as we reached the boundary of the circular driveway, bringing us to a stop. "I know he's the money man for the Iron

Wraiths and has been for over twenty years. I know he keeps the organization out of human trafficking, and he's the only reason why they haven't dabbled in it as of yet. I know he doesn't allow underage persons in the Dragon, and if a member is caught with a girl under eighteen, they're branded. If they're caught with a girl under the age of sixteen, they're—uh—hurt badly and kicked out."

I clutched my throat. "Branded?"

"Yes. Branded. But between you and me, I still think they get off easy."

"Branded with what?"

"With a branding iron he picked up in Texas during his time there."

"W-what is the brand?"

"It's a huge 'I,' or a Roman numeral '1,' about six inches in length and one inch wide. Each time they're caught, they get a brand on their lower back. After three times, he brands their—" Cletus made a face, gesturing to his front pants area "—equipment."

"Oh my goodness."

"Yep. I've been told equipment doesn't work right after being branded." If I wasn't mistaken, Cletus grimaced as he said this.

"That's . . ." I didn't know what that was.

"Point is, no one breaks the rules. Repo is a man who keeps his word. In the last twenty years, he's made the Wraiths rich and powerful. He's not afraid to fight and he's tough as a badger, he's smart and wily, he's loyal. But he's also a bad man who encourages other men to do bad things for profit."

"And we're trusting him with my mother."

Cletus took my hand again, guiding me behind an overgrown Lynwood Gold Forsythia, hiding us from view should anyone enter through the gate. "We are not trusting Repo. We are trusting your mother to have good judgment about her own future."

"How is that different than trusting him? Maybe he's misleading her."

Cletus inspected me, long and hard, before saying quietly, "For what it's worth, I do not think he is."

"Why? What makes you say so?"

"Repo is leaving the Wraiths for her."

"So?"

"So, for a man with no family, no home, a man who has spent twenty years with the same club, gone to jail for his brothers, fought for them, devoted his life to them, that's a lot."

I chewed on that, staring at Cletus and the sobriety of his features. I then searched within myself. Obviously, I would never join a motorcycle club. For one thing, they didn't accept females as members typically. For another, the life itself—as described by others—disgusted me on many levels. I then thought about my brother and the choices he'd made. He'd chosen them to be his family, over me, over my mother. He'd chosen *them.*

"Mr. Repo has no family?" I brought Cletus back into focus. I could see him well enough under the full moon and bright stars.

"He has . . ." Cletus sighed, then looked away. "He has no family that he can claim."

More messages between the lines. "So he's like Isaac? He has parents and siblings, but choses to ignore them?"

"No. Repo was an orphan. He came out of the system in Texas. He has no parents or siblings."

That made me narrow my eyes. "Then what did you mean? He has no family that he can claim?"

Cletus avoided my gaze.

"I can spot your double-talk a mile away. What does that mean? He has family, but he can't claim them?"

The side of his mouth tugged upward, like he reluctantly enjoyed my ability to see through his truthful deceptions. "Fine, smarty-britches. Repo has kin, but it's a secret. None of his MC brothers know or suspect."

"But you do?"

"I deduced, based on anomalies observed over time."

"Meaning, you were paying attention when others weren't."

"Indeed." He shifted his weight from foot to foot, peeking around the overgrown shrubbery toward the gate.

I considered this new information, then asked, "Is it a bad secret? Or a good one? What I mean is, is it—his kin, the circumstances—something that damages his character? Should my mother know?"

"I suppose, whether or not this secret improves Repo's character, given that he's a man who has dedicated his life to criminal activities and pursuits, depends on a person's perspective."

I crossed my arms. "That is not an answer."

Unexpectedly, Cletus bent forward and placed a light kiss on my nose, saying, "I know, but it is the truth."

The whirring of the gate, finally opening, almost had me jumping out of my skin. Cletus and I watched from behind the bush, tracking the two leather-clad forms as they pulled into the circular driveway, the gate swinging shut behind them. The smaller of the two figures looked left and right, as though searching.

I tried to feel relieved that the plan had worked thus far, but I didn't. Yes, she was out of the house. But so what? This wasn't the end, this was just the start. *The start of her life on the run.*

"Where's Jenn?" My mother asked, pulling off her helmet as soon as the larger figure had cut the engine. "They were supposed to be here already, right?"

The man also pulled off his helmet, revealing Mr. Repo as he drawled, "They're here. If I know Cletus Winston, he parked elsewhere."

"What? Why?"

"Trust issues." Mr. Repo paired this with what looked like an unconcerned shrug as he reached for my mother to help her off the bike. "Hey, come here."

Cletus, crouching next to me, chuckled quietly, and glanced down at the dirt.

I tilted my head toward them. "Should we . . .?" I wasn't yet convinced she'd be leaving tonight. But on the small chance she was, I was anxious to spend as much time with her—the real her, not the shadow she'd been since my father's death, stuck at home, unable to speak freely—as possible.

Cletus placed his hand on my forearm, keeping me in place. "Wait a minute."

Scrutinizing him, I could tell he wasn't anxious or worried. Yet he also didn't seem to be in a hurry to greet them or let them know we were close by, watching. Biting the inside of my lip, I settled on my haunches and turned my attention back to my mother and . . . *him*.

Mr. Repo took her helmet, hanging it on the handlebar. He hung his on the other. He then gathered her in his arms, and I braced myself for a sloppy and demanding kiss, or roaming hands, or something similarly off-putting and aggressive.

Instead, and to my surprise, he held her. He just held her.

Entranced, I stared. Her arms didn't encircle him; she had her hands tucked under her chin, her ear pressed to his chest and her eyes closed. She looked relaxed, like she'd given him much of her weight and didn't doubt he'd support it.

But it was his face that caught my attention and held me captivated. The big man looked . . . gosh, there's no word for it except comparing his expression to something else. I guess he looked like how I felt sometimes at the end of a long day, the moment I lay down in bed and snuggled under the covers, when my burdens were behind me and only peace lay ahead.

Relieved was part of it. Content. Happy. And gratitude. A fair share of gratitude.

"Huh." I tilted my head to the side, studying them as Mr. Repo's head also tilted. Now he rested his cheek on top of her hair as he swayed gently, as though to sooth her. His arms were wrapped tight, like she was precious, and his hands didn't move, didn't roam. Nothing about how he held her looked at all aggressive.

"What's going through your mind, Jenn?" Cletus whispered.

"I guess—I don't know." I felt myself frown, likely because my chest quite suddenly ached.

"Try. What are you thinking?" He leaned closer to me as we both continued to watch my mother and Mr. Repo.

Cletus had held me like that, and sometimes I did the same to him. His brothers and their significant others, Ashley and Drew, I'd seen them all do the same. Often.

"It's just, I don't think my mother and my father ever—" I couldn't continue, my throat felt too tight. Forcing a swallow, I tried again, "Did your father ever hold your mother like that?"

I felt something in Cletus shift, a stillness followed by a sadness, and I looked at my beloved. "No," he said. "No. He never held her like that. But Bethany held him like that. She held all of us"—he lifted his chin, his voice raw—"just like that."

CHAPTER NINETEEN
JENN

"This is my last message to you: in sorrow, seek happiness."

— FYODOR DOSTOYEVSKY, *THE BROTHERS KARAMAZOV*

"What happened, Diane?" Cletus positioned himself next to me and leaned against the kitchen island, his arms crossed.

My mother looked to Mr. Repo where he sat next to her at the table, her eyes wide. "Didn't Jason already tell you everything?" I got the impression she wasn't looking for Mr. Repo's approval or permission. More like she sought his support.

How strange it was to see them together, the easy way they were with each other. It . . . bothered me.

"Repo gave me a summary, from his perspective, but Jenn and I would like to hear your version of events."

Cletus and I had eventually interrupted them outside where they embraced by the motorcycle. My mother had immediately come to me, holding me for a long stretch while I considered Mr. Repo over her shoulder. He'd met my scrutiny with calm indifference, giving away nothing of his thoughts.

Or maybe he'd met my probing glare with just calm and not indifference. I couldn't tell.

Anyway, he and Cletus had watched us, allowing us to have a moment, then we'd all gone inside. Mr. Repo offered to make tea. I didn't want any. Cletus also passed. The older man proceeded to make my mother a cup, exactly how she liked it, without having to ask.

Had my father known how Momma took her tea? Did he ever make tea for her?

I pushed the questions away because they unsettled me. But I continued openly scrutinizing this man, watching his every move as he took the seat next to her at the kitchen table and offered his hand, palm up, an unobtrusive request.

She'd grinned at him, thanked him for the tea, and fit her palm in his. Their fingers entwined. They smiled at each other. His looked a little shy. My brain kept tripping over how they glowed when their eyes met, how they never seemed to want to look anywhere else but at each other. Considering the danger and uncertainty facing them both, their united front of happiness struck an off chord.

Had I ever seen my mother happy before?

I knew the answer before I'd finished asking myself the question. She'd been more carefree this last year, especially once the divorce papers had been signed. She'd been happy sometimes.

However, for the period between this past Christmas and the day of my father's death, she'd been happy all the time. I thought the culprit for her mood shift had been the planning of my wedding. Clearly, I'd been wrong. And maybe this was the real reason why I felt such discord in the face of her—their—contentment.

She'd kept him a secret.

Presently, the man paired a gentle, encouraging smile with a small head nod, and I scowled for reasons I didn't fully understand.

Cletus and I were standing next to each other, facing Mr. Repo and my mother where they sat at the table a few feet away. Cletus must've been looking at me because he caught my expression and nudged me with his elbow. "You got something on your face," he whispered.

I blinked, working to clear my features. My mother had been through enough already; despite how she looked at Mr. Repo, beneath the surface she seemed exhausted. Cletus was right, she didn't need me scowling at her.

Masking my thoughts just in time, my mother's gaze swung our way. She gathered a deep breath. "You mean on the night of the engagement party?"

"Yes," Cletus answered, his tone academic and conversational. "You haven't been able to speak freely until now. Specifically, we're most interested in what you can tell us about the shooter. If it helps, you can start from the beginning. "

"Yes, I think I will start from the beginning." She nodded, her eyes lowering to her teacup. "Y'all were there for the tussle. So I guess I can skip over that. Let's see—um—after Kip and—uh—Elena Wilkinson left, after the deputies escorted them away, I went back to the party. Then, after a while of trying to make nice and being asked about where y'all went, I sent Cletus a text. Just a few minutes later, I got a text from Jenn telling me to meet her in the bakery parking lot."

"That wasn't me. I didn't have my phone," I said, noting that so far her story matched the one she'd told the police.

"I know that now. But at the time you and Cletus were missing, weren't you?" My mother lifted a sardonic eyebrow and sent us both a chiding look, an expression I hadn't seen on her face in ages.

Usually this look flustered me—less now than when I'd been younger—but presently all I could do was smile, feeling relief in the face of her judgmental spirit and reprimand.

"Indeed," Cletus conceded, sounding almost cheerful. "Then what happened?"

"Like I said, I got a text from Jenn's phone—I don't know who sent the text, just that it came from her phone—telling me to meet her in the bakery lot. You can read the message if you want, I still have it saved."

"Maybe later." Cletus dismissed her offer. "You left the party?"

"I did."

"Did anyone see you?" I asked.

"I have no idea. I left thinking I was coming to meet you, I wasn't worried about who might be watching. So I walked to the lot and—" her gaze dropped, she swallowed like the action was reflexive "—and I saw a man running through the parking lot, running like he was in a hurry. He stopped at a car and walked up to the driver's side. My mind was working because I was thinking, 'Wait, is that Kip's BMW?' I got mad all over again, thinking he'd come back to stir up more trouble."

"Did you see the man? Did you get a good look at him?"

"No, not—not really."

"What can you tell us?" Cletus looked to me and then back to my momma. "Was he tall or short? Big or small of stature? Fat or thin or neither?"

"He was tall, wore dark clothes. His back was to me most of the time, but he had big shoulders. A big frame. It could've been anybody."

I twisted my lips, thinking back over the list of suspects Jackson had given Ashley. *Tall, big shoulders.* Kenneth Miller, Old Man Blount, Jedidiah Hill—and even Cletus—they all fit this description. Kenneth Miller was heavier set than the others, Jedidiah Hill wasn't as tall.

"It could've been anyone. I was too far away and busy thinking about being mad at Kip for returning. But I did see it happen." My momma covered her face, her voice breaking, and Cletus backed off, seeming to sense that she needed a minute. After breathing in and out several times, she sniffed and dropped her hands. "I was marching over there, and the man banged something against the rear window, banged it hard. He yelled something I couldn't make out. Then, all of a sudden, there was a gun, and the man was pointing it at the driver's side window. I stopped, not sure what I was seeing, or not believing my eyes. He . . . he shot into the car." My mother's stare seemed unfocused and entranced, like she was rewatching the events unfold.

"What was he wearing? The man with the gun." Cletus asked, his voice just above a whisper, like he didn't want to break her out of a trance.

"He—the man was—a—a suit, I think."

"What color was it?"

"I don't know, it was dark. Dark clothes. Maybe it wasn't a suit. He had a jacket. Everything was dark. I just saw him lift his hand and shoot into a car. I was so startled, I didn't even scream. I just fell to my knees in the grass."

"What happened next?"

"He said something. He spoke to Kip. He said something like, 'Time to come out' or 'Get out of the car.'"

"The man in the suit talked to Kip? After he shot him?" Cletus maintained his serene tone.

"I know it doesn't make any sense, it didn't make sense to me at the time, but he did."

A thought occurred to me. "What about his voice? Did you recognize the man's voice?"

Despite my attempt to mimic Cletus's gentle cadence, she flinched, her gaze cutting to mine. "No," she said, her voice firm.

I did my best to keep my features clear of expression because, in that moment, I got a nagging sense that this statement was a lie. I pressed, "But you heard the words?"

"I was too far away, *Jennifer*. Too distressed." Renewed anxiety entered her voice and she seemed to be talking to herself now. "Even if I thought I recognized the voice, there's no way I can be certain. It could have been anyone."

"I'm not asking you to be certain, just—Momma, who did it sound like?"

Her attention flicked to Mr. Repo, and she gathered a deep breath that sounded unsteady. "I don't know. I honestly couldn't say. All I know is the man with the gun told Kip to get out of the car, or that's what I thought at first. But then someone else opened the back door of the car, the passenger side, and started running away."

Cletus brushed the back of his hand against mine before I could question her again about the man's voice, cutting in, "Who ran away?"

"I have no idea. I was too busy watching the man with the gun, afraid to move."

"Momma, could you tell if the person who ran was big or small? Was it a woman or a man?"

"Small, I think. Small, but real fast. She—she, maybe a woman? She ran like the devil was chasing her."

Cletus and I shared a look, and he asked, "What happened after that?"

"Um, I—uh, the—the man ran after her. The man with the gun ran after the person who'd jumped out of the back seat, shooting at her. He shot into the bakery, up high, and I heard glass break."

"Which direction?" Cletus pushed away from the kitchen island. "Which direction did they run?"

"Uh. Away. North, I think. Wait, yes. Of course it was north, past the bakery and into the woods."

"Okay. North." Cletus scratched his cheek, his gaze unfocused. "Then what did you do?"

"I waited for, I don't know, a second, a minute, then I ran to the car and I saw—I saw—" She sucked in a breath, her lashes fluttering. "I opened the door, and I didn't know what to do, so I pressed my hands to where the blood was, trying to stop it. I thought maybe he was going to be okay, just passed out. But God, Cletus, I knew. I looked at his face and his eyes were wide open, and he was already gone. He was gone and still I tried waking him up, but he wasn't asleep—"

Mr. Repo reached for her under the table, and his touch seemed to end her babbling. Her head fell forward and she covered her forehead with her palm, whispering, "He was dead."

"You touched his cheek." This was a confirmation of an earlier suspicion and I spoke it out loud, my heart twisting. "You were trying to wake him up."

Even after everything he'd done to her, all the ways he'd terrorized her and us growing up, she'd tried.

"Yes. I shook him, I grabbed his face. I just thought if I could wake him up . . ." My mother heaved a sigh that sounded like it originated from her soul, her shoulders slumping forward.

"That's where I found her."

Mr. Repo's quiet words had Cletus and I looking at him.

He leaned forward, his eyes on me. "She was kneeling outside his car, her hands covered in blood, trying to get him to wake up."

Each gravelly word out of his stupid criminal mouth sounded like a butter knife scraping along a plate. It wasn't like me to dislike a person I didn't know. I couldn't accurately pinpoint why he irritated me so much other than the obvious: Mr. Repo was a criminal, and if he'd minded his own damn business my mother wouldn't be in this mess.

Crossing my arms, I returned his open gaze with a glare. "Speaking of which, why were you there?"

If my hostility bothered Mr. Repo, he didn't show it. His eyes moved to my mother, and he seemed to be considering her. After several seconds, I got the sense he wasn't considering her so much as considering his words.

Stalling.

Eventually, his attention shifted to Cletus, his stare now hard. "I reckon you know why."

"Because you wanted to see Momma?" I asked, inserting myself into their exchange. I'd been the one to ask the question. If Cletus suspected a different motivation, he hadn't shared it with me.

"Before we go down that road paved with land mines"—Cletus placed his hand on my back and rubbed a big circle between my shoulder blades—"let's get back to the events of March second. Repo found you outside Kip's car, Diane. Covered in blood. What happened after that?"

"No, just her hands," Mr. Repo corrected, sounding tired. "I pulled her away. She was in shock."

"I was in shock. I couldn't believe it," my mother echoed, staring at her palms like they were still covered in blood. "Jason said we had to wash off my hands before anyone saw me. I thought maybe the bakery door was still unlocked—the desserts for the engagement party were in the freezer—so we went there."

"And you washed your hands while Re—uh—Jason looked for a towel?" Cletus quit rubbing my back and crossed his arms once more.

"That's right. But then Jackson was at the back door all of a sudden and"—my mother balled her hands into fists—"I panicked."

"We panicked." Mr. Repo covered her hand again. "It was my mistake, I misunderstood what I saw in the parking lot. But, yeah, we panicked, and I pulled her out of the bakery. We made a run for it."

"Which way did you run?" Something about the way Cletus asked the question had me looking at him.

"I guess it was north."

"You went north." Cletus kept his eyes forward, his features schooled. I knew him, and in that moment, I knew he had a suspicion he wasn't yet ready to share. "Why would you go north? Isn't that the direction the man with the gun ran?"

Mr. Repo seemed confused by this question. "I didn't know that. I'd parked my bike down the slope, and so that's where we ran."

"You didn't see the gunman or the woman on your way to the lot from the slope?" Cletus pushed, his tone light but his eyes narrowing.

"No. I didn't see the gunman or the woman. I'd parked my bike hours before and was coming back from the direction of the barn."

"You were at the barn? Why were you at the barn? I don't remember seeing you on the guest list." I didn't keep my tone light, not caring if I sounded antagonistic.

"Jenn, wait a minute. Before we get to that, let me finish this," Cletus said, giving me a quick, tight smile. "Let me make sure I have this right: you parked your bike earlier in the evening, walked up the slope unseen, went to the barn—for reasons we shall address later—then left the barn. Why'd you leave the barn?"

"I realized Diane wasn't there, she'd left. It was time for me to go so I thought I'd find her, say goodbye, and get on my way. Then I heard the shots."

"And you ran toward them," Cletus guessed.

"Not at first. I got low, found cover. When they stopped, I ran toward the sound. Like I said, Diane was missing, I worried. I wanted to lay eyes on her, make sure she was safe."

My mother sent Mr. Repo a cherishing look, a small smile on her lips. The sight unsettled me, and I gave myself a mental kick.

If she's happy with this tattooed, muscly reprobate, let her be happy.

I'd let her be happy if she were truly happy. But I could not comprehend my mother being happy in a relationship she'd kept secret from her own daughter.

Jennifer Anne Sylvester, stop being sore she didn't tell you.

I wasn't.

I'm not.

Cletus was speaking and—since I'd been busy arguing with myself—I only caught the tail end of his recap. ". . .came from the barn. You heard the shots, you took cover briefly. You didn't see the man with the gun or the woman run into the north woods. You were looking for Diane. You then ran toward the shots. You found Diane at the car with Kip, y'all went to the bakery, washed her hands. Jackson pounds on the door, you take off into the north woods for the bike, having no idea that's where the gunman and the woman went."

"And I wasn't thinking about it, honestly." My mother appealed to the both of us. "I didn't think about it. I was so out of it. I just went where Jason told me to go."

"That's understandable," I said, giving my momma a sympathetic smile.

Cletus stroked his beard, a habit he'd picked up recently that made him look very mad-scientist-like. "When did the police come get you, Diane? When did they come to the house?"

"Early in the morning. Then they asked that I come with them to the police station."

"And so you did," Cletus said unnecessarily, but it seemed like maybe he was talking to himself.

"Yes, I did. And I called my lawyer as soon as I made it to the station. Jason said not to talk until she was present. Genevieve told me to keep quiet and not answer any questions at all, so I didn't."

"You pretended to be overwhelmed?" Cletus said, his tone leading and a little sneaky, like he was trying to catch her in a lie.

"No." She shook her head, her expression open. "That wasn't me pretending. Even if I'd wanted to, I wouldn't have been able to speak that morning. I was so . . ."

"She was still in shock. She was in shock for days." Mr. Repo's hand came to her shoulder, squeezed.

"How do you know?" I snapped.

"Because I snuck in to check on her," he answered evenly, like my tone had been congenial instead of surly. "I'd come in through her window at the back. And I'm glad I did because that surveillance van showed up two days after the murder."

"They didn't believe me, it seems. I didn't kill him, but I guess I did lie." My momma smiled like she thought this was funny, like we were talking about someone else who'd made a mistake and was now possibly going to go away for a murder she didn't commit.

Cletus's gaze fell on me, sympathetic yet firm, even though his words were for my mother. "Forgive my candor, but the story you told the police makes no sense. They know you're lying. Your alibi is nonexistent. You have motive. They can't confirm the prints on the door—the partial bloody handprint—is yours, but as soon as they do, they'll issue a warrant."

She covered her face with her hands again, breathing out.

He wasn't finished. "No judge in his right mind is going to give her bail, not with the resources she has available and all the friends she has in this town. Breaking someone out of jail is so much harder than keeping them from it in the first place. Believe me, I know."

Maybe Cletus thought I needed to hear the words in order to understand how truly trapped she was. To understand only one path remained to her unless we could prove, without a shadow of a doubt, someone else had killed my father.

She had to leave. Now. Before they arrested her and matched her print to the one on the car. We stood there in contemplative silence as the grim and certain burden of my mother's situation pressed down on us.

Or maybe it only pressed down on me. A weight of frustration and helplessness and dumb, stupid acceptance.

This isn't fair.

Whether or not my momma's secret relationship with Mr. Repo had contributed, she'd seemed truly happy these last few months. Happy and content and busy. She hadn't brought up my father in months. The wedding planning with Ashley, our shared mother-daughter time, the success of the Donner Dairy, the planned renovations at the lodge—my mother had been thriving.

And then my father shows up and ruins it all.

Where remorse at the uncharitable thought might have twisted in my stomach before, before these last weeks of worry and resentment, all I felt now was a stark gratitude that he was dead. My father had shown up that night intent on ruining the evening, but I'm certain he'd never planned to die.

And yet that's what he's always done. He shows up and ruins things, even in death.

I ground my teeth, irritated because I felt guilty for not feeling guilty, the constant emotional spin cycle where my father was concerned. I couldn't seem to break free of it. When would I let go of him? Let go of the expectations he'd never lived up to and the regret I carried that I could've done more to help him be a better person.

"We have no choice," Mr. Repo said, pulling me from my thoughts. He locked eyes with my momma. "We have to go. Tonight. It's the only way."

Cletus's eyes were still on me, like he was waiting for me to say something, to agree. I didn't meet his gaze, I couldn't look at my momma. If I did, I'd cry. I didn't want to cry.

So I looked at Mr. Repo and said around the rocks in my throat, "This sucks."

His attention lifted to me. Despite all the attitude I'd thrown at the man up to now, he gave me a small smile. "It does. But I know how to run. I promise, I'll keep her safe."

Finally, Cletus did speak. "If anyone can avoid police detection, it's him." The words low, quiet, imploring, like they were meant only for my ears, a reassurance. But Cletus didn't touch me. Maybe he knew doing so might make me lose it.

I glared at Mr. Repo even though this wasn't really his fault. He didn't say anything, didn't try to defend himself or my mother, didn't give words of consolation or defend this impossible decision. The man had made his promise to keep her safe and, apparently, that was all he offered me. Features open yet resigned, he returned my glare with a patient stare.

"Jennifer."

My name spoken from my mother's lips automatically pulled my attention to her. She'd stood at some point and now faced me. Her eyes wide and rimmed with red, her lips trembling, her hands shaking, she looked terrified.

Abruptly, my nose and eyes stung with the tears I'd avoided until now, and I choked out, "Momma."

She opened her arms. "Come here."

So I did. She gathered me in a hug just as my face crumpled. *Dammit.* I'd been fooling myself, thinking we'd find another way, convincing myself that as soon as she spoke freely and we heard her side of the story, we'd be able to clear her name. *I hate this.*

"I don't want to go to jail, baby." Her throat sounded like it was full of rocks too. She cleared it, but her voice continued to shake. "But if you asked me to stay, I would. I would do anything for you and—and your brother. *Anything.* I'd go to jail if it meant keeping y'all safe, if you needed me to stay." I felt the tremors in her body as she spoke.

I petted her hair to soothe her even as my tears flowed freely. "I hate this."

"I do too."

"You have to go, I know you do. But I don't want you doing anything that you'll regret," I said around a sob. "I don't want you to feel trapped."

We held each other, swaying. I felt her tears on my neck, so I held her tighter and swallowed down the bitterness.

We'd come so far. This last year and a half, our relationship had altered so much. It had been difficult, but we'd done it. My mother was so different now from the domineering and demanding maternal presence of my past.

She'd listened to me. She'd gone to therapy. She'd worked on herself. She'd changed *for me.* She'd wanted to be better *for me.* She loved me. Now she was leaving me.

And I had to love her enough to let her go.

After a long while, she sniffled and pulled back, wiping at her eyes with one hand while keeping the other on my shoulder.

"We'll be fine," she said unconvincingly, a half-hearted smile on her wobbly lips. "Let me just go freshen up for a minute, splash some water on my face. Then I'll—I'll make more tea, okay? Anyone want some tea?"

"I'll have some more," Mr. Repo said with infinite gentleness. I wondered at his request since he hadn't consumed any of his tea. The full tea cup from earlier sat untouched in front of him.

Mr. Repo then cut Cletus a hard glare, which prompted my fiancé to say, "Yes, please. Tea sounds really great."

"I'll have a cup too," I muttered, feeling the absurdity of the words as they came out. I felt like I was drifting, floating on a current I couldn't escape.

What was happening? How had we arrived here? And what could I do to make things right?

Ever since that night of the party, things had been spiraling out of control. I'd tried to ignore it. I'd tried to confront it. Nothing helped.

"Jennifer."

I looked up at the sound of my name, surprised to see my mother was no longer in the room with us. I heard water run from a faucet.

"Jennifer," Mr. Repo repeated my name, and I gave him my eyes if not the entirety of my attention. I couldn't.

I felt . . . lost. *So lost.*

He'd also stood at some point, and the man hooked his thumbs in his pockets as he spoke, "You don't know me, but I keep my promises. I will take care of your mother. She will want for nothing, she'll be safe."

"Except her family," came my dull reply. "She'll want for nothing except her family."

His chest rose and fell with a silent, deep breath, the muscle at his temple jumped as he flexed his jaw. I stared at this man who was right about one thing: I didn't know him. I mean, yes, I'd seen him around town my entire life. I recognized him as a citizen of this part of the world and a member of the Iron Wraiths. But beyond that, I had no idea who he was.

"I still don't understand why you were there that night," I said, my tone tired instead of hostile. "Why were you there, Mr. Repo? You never answered. Were you there for my mother? To see her?"

"That was part of the reason, yes," he answered solemnly, and by all accounts sincerely.

And yet I didn't know him. *How do I know if he's being sincere?*

"So why else? What other reason did you have? Hmm?" I crossed my arms, angling my chin. "Did you plan this?"

"No." The word was quiet, contrite, like he was doing his best not to upset me further.

It pissed me off. "Then why were you there?" I whispered harshly, not wanting my mother to hear.

Mr. Repo licked his bottom lip, his gaze jumping to someplace behind me—maybe Cletus—then falling to the floor before lifting to mine once more. He didn't look belligerent, but something about the angle of his jaw and the grit in his eyes told me that Mr. Repo was never going to answer my question.

"He hoped Jessica James would be there," Cletus said all of a sudden, matter-of-fact, like wanting to see Jessica James would explain Mr. Repo's appearance the night of our engagement party.

I scrunched my face, not trying to hide my confusion or temper. "That makes absolutely no sense. Why on God's green earth would Mr. Repo care if Jessica James was—was . . ." I didn't finish the question because a memory—or rather, a series of memories—flashed in my mind's eye like a slideshow.

I was and always had been a people-watcher. I'd recognized Mr. Repo, his a familiar face, living in the same town. Additionally, he'd been one of the Iron Wraiths I saw most often with my brother, always from afar.

But I also recognized him because he'd been places where an Iron Wraith had no business being.

Outside of church on several Sunday mornings after the early service, which the James family always attended because the sheriff didn't want to miss football games.

Buying hot dogs at a baseball game between Green Valley and Lawrence middle schools when Jessica happened to be the pitcher. Yep, Jessica James had been the pitcher for the middle school baseball team. Isaac had also been on the team, which was why my family had been there. We'd been homeschooled, but he'd been allowed to join the local public school's sports teams. Of note, I had not been allowed. Girls didn't play sports according to my daddy.

But Jessica had, and she'd been stellar. I remembered being envious, watching her after the game with her family. Jessica's daddy, the sheriff, had been so proud.

Jessica's daddy.

"Are you Jessica's father?" I blurted and, even in my state of surprise at the eruption of words, I didn't miss how Mr. Repo's eyes dropped to the floor again, like the weight of my stare, of the question, was too much to bear. He also seemed to have trouble swallowing.

Once more we stood in silence. The only sound being the water from the faucet in the bathroom where my momma freshened up. It ran and ran and ran.

But eventually Mr. Repo did swallow, and he did answer, "Not in any way that matters," his voice imbued with immeasurable sadness and regret. The words nearly knocked the wind from my lungs.

Had this man just admitted to being Jessica James's biological father?

Last year, Jessica had told me of her recent discovery that her maternal aunt had actually been her biological mother. Her biological father, she'd said, remained a mystery. No one seemed to know who he was, and her aunt had died before Jessica could ask.

Which meant Jessica had no idea.

He'd been here, the whole time, watching her grow up. And he'd definitely watched her, I felt certain of that. If Jessica and I had been friends growing up, if I'd been privy to more of her life than just Sunday service and baseball games, then I knew without a doubt I would've spotted Mr. Repo in the background, hovering, watching, but not speaking up. Not claiming.

"Why didn't you—"

"Tell her?" He chuckled, but there was no humor in it. "Why would I do that? Why would I ruin her happy life?"

"But—but you're her—"

"I'm not." His eyes were flinty. "The sheriff, that's her daddy. Janet, that's her momma. Jackson is her brother. They're her family, not me.

Jessica has always been where she belonged. How much of a selfish asshole would I have to be to take her away from people who were better equipped to love and care for her than I've ever been?"

"What about her mother?"

Mr. Repo laughed again, this time it sounded bitter. "That woman didn't know how to love. She knew how to have fun, how to . . . make money. How to be brilliant. How to be cold. But loving came about as naturally to her as walking with two legs comes to a snake." After the words were out, he closed his eyes, shook his head, looking tired. "No. Jess . . . Jessica James isn't mine."

"Then why show up at our engagement party?" For some reason, I needed to know.

Maybe it was because my father had also shown up uninvited. He'd shown up my whole life and, mostly, I'd wished he hadn't. He'd shown up that night and wanted to ruin everything, make everything about him and what he was due. He didn't care about me, about hurting me.

But here was this other man who'd shown up. He'd shown up at baseball games and said nothing, just quietly rooted for his daughter and asked for nothing. Clearly, her happiness mattered to him. He wanted to see her, to see she was happy, but didn't feel like he had to be the center of it or the cause. Here was a man who had a claim and never staked it because doing so might cause harm.

And suddenly, I knew why.

I understood.

"You love her," I whispered. Tears again pricked my eyes. "That's why." I pressed my lips together to still my wobbly chin, but it was too late. Cletus must've perceived the unsteadiness of my voice because he was next to me in a flash, his hand on my back, quiet support. "You love her. And that's why you want what's best for her, even now. That's why you stayed close but never intervened. You love her, and that's why her happiness matters more to you than what you could've gained as her father if you'd made it known." I shrugged at the futility of his situation, and at the futility of my own. "You love your daughter, Jason."

He stared at me, eyes glassy. I stared at him, tears spilling down my cheeks. But I didn't care, because at least now I knew for sure. I could stop feeling guilty for not feeling guilty. I could stop trying to mourn for a man who only ever saw me as something to be used, controlled, exploited.

Jason had shown up to the engagement party because he loved his daughter. My father showed up to my engagement party because he never loved me.

And now I could let him go.

CHAPTER TWENTY
CLETUS

"Nothing travels faster than the speed of light with the possible exception of bad news, which obeys its own special laws."

— DOUGLAS ADAMS, *MOSTLY HARMLESS*

I still hadn't pieced together all the details. But at some point I was going to have to inform Jenn of my suspicions. Namely, I suspected her brother, Isaac Sylvester, was a horrible, soulless, evil dumpster fire of a human.

"Are you excited?"

My brother Jethro's cheerful interruption of my careful internal deliberations had me blinking up at him. Presently, I was on the ground of the auto shop, staring unseeingly at the underside fender of Belle Cooper's Cadillac, most of my body obscured beneath the car.

"Pardon?" I frowned, disliking that he'd caught me unawares while debating weighty matters.

Prior to Diane's departure, I hadn't informed Jenn of my suspicions about Isaac because, though the possibility had always been there, I'd felt no degree of certainty until Diane relayed her version of events.

Then, like flooding after a hurricane, the possibility of Isaac's involvement could no longer be ignored.

Unfortunately, keeping this suspicion to myself had put me in a perpetually perturbed mood. I wanted to talk it over with her, think through it, but how could I broach the topic?

These pancakes are delicious, and I know you're going through a lot at present, but have you considered the possibility that the reason your momma was so adamant about not recognizing the shooter's voice is because the man with the gun that night was your brother? Also, more bacon while you're up, please.

Jethro stopped rubbing his hands together and peered at me with a measure of caution. "Uh—"

"What do you want?" I snapped, rolling myself out all the way. "I'm backed up here, so unless this is a blueberry emergency, make it quick."

"We're not backed up, Jethro." My brother Beau, smarmy ginger and contradictor extraordinaire, poked his head out of the hood he'd been tucked behind, adding, "So unless he's talking about constipation, he's lying."

I wasn't technically lying about being backed up. My preoccupied state over the last few weeks meant my output had been lower than normal. Beau and Shelly had pitched in the last few days, and we were now all caught up.

But I had 100 percent been lying—through omission—to Jenn.

I hadn't told Jenn yesterday, or the day before that, or the day prior to that about her brother because my lady's soft heart had been suffering since Diane's exodus three weeks ago. Despite valiant attempts and meticulous consistency, no amount of foot rubs, back rubs, or—*ahem*—other rubs had vanquished my love's melancholic mood. She slouched. She sighed. She stared at nothing. Her smiles never quite reached her eyes. It was the difference between a sunny sky and an overcast one; the sky remained in the same familiar position, but nothing about felt it the same.

"She doesn't always need to be sunny," Sienna had said yesterday during our early morning yoga. "You're worried about her, we all are.

But she's sad, and she has every reason to be. She just lost her father and now her mother. Give her time."

She just lost her father and now her mother.

That was the truth and the crux of the issue. How could I tell Jenn about my suspicions when doing so might mean losing her brother too? The blond muscly menace had returned to his previous modus operandi, functioning as an Iron Wraith, in town, always at a distance. He never saw his sister purposefully, never reached out to her.

But he was still here. Present. And yet, if I spelled out the facts as I knew them to be, it wouldn't matter if his body existed in Green Valley, his soul—and therefore him—might already be gone. Lost to her.

Yes, I'd promised I wouldn't keep information to myself, lie, or obfuscate facts anymore. But this . . . this wasn't information. This was a nuclear warhead covered in murder hornets and the plague.

Sometimes, rarely, and by rarely I mean just this one time, I really hate knowing things.

Jethro, appearing uncertain, glanced over his shoulder at Beau and then back to me. He then set his hands on his hips as I got to my feet. "Are you sick? Does this mean you're not coming to dinner?"

"My bowels are none of your concern." I tossed a wrench into the nearby toolbox and stuffed the rag in my grip into my back pocket. He inspected me with a worry that had me regretting my words. So I lied. "But, yes, I have been having some tummy trouble. If Sienna wouldn't mind making me one of her coconut smoothies, I'd be much obliged."

His brow unknit itself, and he nodded. "Sure. No problem. I just came from the store, and I'll text her on the way home. But, just to be clear, y'all are still coming for dinner tonight, right?"

"Correct. And to your earlier question, we are excited. Have Duane and Jess recovered from their jet lag?"

My surly younger brother and the love of his life had flown into town just yesterday. They planned to stick around long enough to attend the wedding next week and visit loved ones, which of course included the James family: Deputy Jackson James, Janet James, and Sheriff Jeffery James. They planned to be in attendance at dinner tonight, which I suspected would likely reek of conversation missteps and awkwardness, seeing as how Jenn had been arrested two months ago.

I'd only seen the sheriff a handful of times since the discovery of Diane's clandestine departure. The man hadn't seemed at all surprised by her inexplicable absence. In fact, Sheriff James seemed relieved. After interviewing Jenn and I—and always in the presence of lawyer Genevieve Taylor—the FBI also packed up and absconded Green Valley. Our stories had been synchronized, unimpeachable, and Jennifer's distraught tears had been very, very real.

In fact, so distracted was she by her momma's flight from the law, Jenn didn't seem to notice the whispers. She didn't seem to notice folks had drawn their own conclusions about Diane's abdication of her Green Valley business mogul throne. Mind, these were the same folks who couldn't draw a straight line along a ruler's edge or tip over a bucket if the instructions were written on the bottom, but they felt right at home drawing conclusions.

The general topics discussed by gossip mongers revolved mainly around: Diane Donner being a vulpine murderess; poor, simple Jennifer being greatly used by both her parents; how the heck would Jennifer manage the lodge and the inheritance left by her deceased father; whether or not our wedding should be canceled due to all the scandal.

I couldn't shield Jennifer from the constant onslaught of pitying glances wherever we went. As such, we rarely went anywhere. But the wedding—whether or not to move forward as planned—was not up for discussion.

Jennifer didn't wish to cancel the wedding. She'd been adamant we move forward as planned. In private, I suspected Ashley's hard work thus far was part of the reason for Jenn's stubborn determination. The other part likely had to do with Jenn's father. She didn't wish to sacrifice any more of her life due to his actions, or inactions, or death.

And so, I'd been supportive.

But I fretted.

And then there's still the matters of Kenneth Miller and Elena Wilkinson to deal with. I'd have to address their nefarious behavior eventually.

Elena hadn't shot Kip, but she'd strangled him. She'd fled into the woods with the shooter in pursuit. Obviously, the police not being privy to Diane's version of events meant they could persist in their ignorant assumption that Kip had been strangled and shot by the same person.

And Miller. Did he have the gun? If so, how'd he get it? *And where in tarnation was he?* Questioning Elena and Miller was on the back burner, mostly because I couldn't find either of them, not since Diane and Repo had left town.

"Oh no, I wasn't asking if you're excited about dinner." Jethro flashed me a big old grin, pulling me once more from my reverie. It was the cheekiness of the grin that had me bracing my bowels. "I was asking if you're excited about tomorrow."

I glanced to the left, then to the right. "What's tomorrow?"

"Your bachelor party," he said, his grin faltering. "Did you forget?"

"No. No. I didn't forget." I shook my head, reaching in my front pocket for my rag. When I didn't find it there, I glanced around the floor of the garage, searching for it.

Jethro watched me for a bit, his eyebrows pulling together again. "It's in your back pocket."

"Hmm? What's that?"

"Your rag. Is that what you're looking for?"

I reached around and, sure enough, the rag was there. "Ah. Yes. Thank you."

His eyes narrowed as they inspected me. "Well, clean up. Dinner is in an hour."

Using a clean portion of the rag to rub at the grease on my fingertips, I grumbled, "What does it look like I'm doing?"

"You know what I mean. Go change."

Now I scowled. "And you know I don't like changing. I got zero changes left today."

"You're not going to change for bed?"

"'No. Not that it's any of your business."

Jethro crossed his arms, giving me a flat look. "So you're telling me that you wear greasy coveralls to bed?"

"'Course not. I have clean pants and a clean shirt beneath these clothes, which I shall wear to the family dinner. After which, I shall remove all my clothes and take a shower before bed. Would you like to know what I'll wear to bed tonight? I'll give you a hint, it doesn't require me to change after the shower."

"You know what, never mind." He started to roll his eyes but caught himself just in time. "I'm not arguing with you about whether removing clothes or putting on clothes counts as changing. Whatever. Sienna is making her special roast. Jenn is supposed to be bringing the dessert. What time can we expect y'all?"

"Uh—" I glanced at the wall clock "—you said one hour, right? We'll be there in an hour."

"Good. Are you picking her up or is she meeting you there?"

"Why so many questions?" I rubbed harder at a stubborn patch of grease.

"Because you've been distracted lately, and late."

"He's picking her up from the bakery after work," Shelly—somewhere unseen—supplied the answer. And then I heard a baby giggle and my foul mood was eclipsed by this new data point.

"Wait. You brought Ben?" I craned my neck, looking for him.

"Yep. Shelly has him. Her hands were clean."

My frown deepened. Benjamin was in the building. Jethro had brought Benjamin, and here I was not holding my nephew. See? This is what fretting got me: A) telling lies about gastrointestinal distress, and B) lack of baby awareness.

"Are you okay, Cletus?" Jethro stepped closer, his eyes moving over me.

"I'm perfectly adequate. And also, to answer your earlier question, I am looking forward to George's act with the breathless anticipation that only a senior citizen former Navy SEAL turned stripper can inspire."

His gaze flickered over me again. "You sure? 'Cause you don't look excited."

I scratched my neck, wondering if he wanted me to be upset. If he wanted me to feign discomfort, I could do that. "When is it again?"

"Tomorrow." He shuffled a half step closer. "You remember we decided to have the party this week instead of next? So it wouldn't interfere with the rehearsal dinner."

"I remember, thank you."

He continued peering at me searchingly. "Are you nervous about the wedding?"

"No."

"But you're upset the groomsmen aren't wearing Dickies?"

That drew a small, unbidden smile on my face. "Actually, no. I've made my peace with it." Drew had innocently informed Ashley that not only had I asked Roscoe, Drew, Beau, and Duane to be groomsmen via text message, but I'd also arranged for them to be measured for Dickies coveralls. I'd originally meant it as a joke, but the more I'd considered the matter, the more I'd warmed to it. Wearing coveralls meant I could ask them to do messy deeds. What good were groomsmen if they couldn't do messy deeds?

Ash had uniformly—pun intended—put her foot down and scheduled tux fittings for any of my brothers who required updates to the suits they'd worn for Jethro's nuptials. Billy, of course, didn't need a new suit. He already owned eleventy thousand. *The dandy coxcomb.*

What Ash didn't know, however, was that the Dickies coveralls had arrived, all custom cut and tailored, tucked safely in the back of my Ford. Perhaps the groomsmen would wear them to the service, perhaps not. But they'd definitely wear them to the reception. Otherwise, the dirty deeds I had planned would undoubtedly besmirch their formal attire.

But I digress.

"Then what's the problem? Something has you feeling low." His voice hushed, he dipped his chin to catch my eye. "Whatever it is, you can talk to me."

I stared at my brother. I stared and stared and debated and an idea formed. "Come with me."

Turning, I crossed to the stairs leading up to the second floor office. I walked up the stairs. I opened the door, leaving it ajar just long enough for him to enter. I closed it behind him and said, "Remember when you were a horrible, soulless, evil dumpster fire of a human? Or, at least, when you acted like one?"

Jethro's eyes widened, then narrowed. "Yes, Cletus. I remember."

"And then you weren't?"

"Yes," he said through clenched teeth.

"What made you change your ways?" I stroked my beard, inspecting him. "What inspired you to become a better person?

Jethro inhaled slowly, his jaw relaxing, and his eyes moving up and to the left. "Well. . . Honestly, it was Ben's death. Or rather all the stuff that happened after Ben died."

"Really? Tell me more." Maybe if I could gain some insight as to what prompted Jethro to change his ways, I could work toward a similar aim with Isaac. Jenn believed people could change for the better. Jethro was a living example, proof that her belief was possible.

"I got news that Ben died, and . . ." he sighed, his eyes still up and to the left. "As you know, he was somebody who always believed in me. Even though I would do stupid, selfish, horrible things, he was always that one person who told me it wasn't too late to be better. That deep down, I was a good person." His eyes came back to me. "And don't take this as an insult or anything other than a reflection of my own insanity and selfishness at the time, but it was like everybody else had already written me off. Expected me to live down to their expectations." He chuckled, looking away again and mumbling, "Billy in particular."

I nodded, swallowing around some thickness I wasn't in the mood to contemplate. "And Ben's belief in you made all the difference?"

"No. Not at all. I never believed him, truth be told. I thought of myself as irredeemable. Ben dying made the difference. It felt like, you know, that was it. Everyone else—even me—thought I was an asshole and got what I deserved. If I went to prison, if I died, well then, I'd asked for it. Oh well, good riddance."

Swallowing became even more difficult. "Jet—"

"No, just listen. You asked, so I'm telling you." He lifted a scolding finger. "But this isn't about feeling sorry for me. I don't feel sorry for me, so you shouldn't either. My point is, the day he died, I felt like the last person on earth who loved me died."

I nodded, absorbing this but not contradicting him. We loved him then. But we were so tired of being disappointed. Our love was tough love, not the accepting—and in my opinion, enabling—love of Ben McClure.

"And you know what happened next." Jethro gave me a half smile, rolling his eyes at himself.

"You tried to steal Drew's motorcycle." I tried not to laugh, and failed. "I remember. He beat the shit out of you."

"Yes." Jethro also laughed, his eyes unfocused with memory. "He wouldn't press charges, and neither would I. But he drove me to the hospital so I could get checked out. I was so mad." Jet shook his head, a smile lingering on his lips. "Here was this guy who'd been accepted into my family, like he belonged there, whereas I was always left out in the cold. I hated him. And you know what he said to me? Before I got discharged? After staying with me all night and meeting with the doctor, asking questions about my recovery and medication, you know what he said?"

"No, what?"

Jethro held my gaze for two beats of my heart before saying, "'Don't you want something better for yourself?'"

I felt my brows pull together, and I thought about Drew's words, picking them apart, putting them back together.

Don't you want something better for yourself?

"I reckon I can't explain why that—that struck some kind of chord, a note I hadn't heard in—" Jethro's bottom lip pushed out, and he shrugged "—maybe ever? He didn't tell me I could change, that I should think of my mother, my family, all the trouble and pain I had caused. He didn't say he loved me, that he believed in me, that I was still good. Hell, he probably thought I was a little shit, dirt on the bottom of his shoe. What he was really saying was, 'Love yourself, man. 'Cause no one else is going to take the wheel and make it happen. Don't you want better for *you*?'"

Jethro—my dumbass, sweet, considerate, repentant brother—dropped his eyes to the floor and grinned. "With those words in mind, I asked myself that night what I needed, what I really wanted."

"What did you want?"

"That particular night? Comfort," he said plainly, his gaze stark. "So I went to Claire's and spent the night with her, holding her, letting her cry. And I cried too. And you know what, it felt right. It felt so right. Doing what was right for me was ultimately my path back to y'all."

"Meaning?"

"I wanted my family. That's what I really wanted, and had wanted, for years. I decided I'd do whatever it took to be a better man, to be the brother you, Ash, Duane, Beau, Roscoe, and—yeah—even Billy's stubborn ass, be the brother y'all deserved. Be the son Momma deserved. Make amends. That's what *I* wanted for *me*."

I wrinkled my nose and squinted at him, my voice a tad higher than my typical baritone. "So you became a park ranger and took up knitting?"

He laughed at that, and so did I, dispelling much of the solemnity that hung heavy in the air. "I suppose, when I thought about it, I didn't know anyone who was better people than Ben and Drew. So, yeah. Being a ranger was always Ben's dream. And Drew, well, I wanted to work with him. He had y'all's respect, and that's what I wanted. So that's what I did."

"And the knitting?"

"I knew Ash knit. I'd always had trouble connecting with her, so I figured. . ." He shoved his hands in his pockets and shrugged again, giving me a lopsided grin. "Plus, what else was I going to do? I never left the house in those days. Momma and I sat and talked, watched TV, but I didn't like being idle."

Jethro and I studied each other for a good long minute. These outstanding questions about Jethro and his motivations, ones I hadn't realized bothered me, had just resolved themselves in a satisfactory manner. Jethro was my brother. I'd always loved him, but I hadn't always respected him, not when he couldn't be bothered to respect himself. But now he did, and now I did, and here we were.

I was proud of him. And satisfactory resolutions always put me in a better mood.

Naturally, my mind turned to Drew, the quiet mountain of a man, and all the ways he'd changed our lives for the better. Helping us open the auto shop, helping our momma with Darrell, helping Jethro, helping Ash —and all of us—through our mother's death, and I wished, just once, I could do something for him in return.

Note to self: force Drew to accept some ostentatious offering of gratitude. Ensure it is grandiose in magnitude and cannot be returned nor exchanged.

"Why are you asking me about this?" Jethro tilted his head an inch to one side, as though to inspect me from a new angle.

"What do you think of Isaac Sylvester?" I posed the question before I could give myself an opportunity to think better of it because, dammit, I needed input.

Jenn needed—deserved—to know about my suspicions. But I needed to break them to her in such a way that wouldn't leave her broken if they turned out to be true.

Jethro wouldn't go to the police, he'd done shady shit in his past, he knew the Wraiths, the hold they had on their members. Furthermore, he'd abandoned his mother and siblings once upon a time. Who better to consult than Jethro?

"Isaac Sylvester?" he asked, looking confused by my apparent subject change.

"That's right. Jenn's brother."

"I don't know that I ever think of Isaac Sylvester."

"But remember when you and I met with him and Repo, while Jenn was in custody? What did you think about him then? What was your impression?"

Jethro scratched his jaw. "Well, he—uh—I guess he seemed reserved. Careful."

"Reserved and careful? Expand on that."

"He said very little, even when he did speak. Almost like he'd originally planned to just listen and let Repo do all the talking. And he hesitated each time he had to talk, like when you asked if he thought Jennifer had killed Kip. It took him forever to answer. And when he did, it wasn't really an answer."

"What do you mean?"

"Well, you asked him, point blank, something like, 'Do you think Jenn killed Kip?' And what did he say? Some double-talk, right?"

"He said yes, didn't he?" I searched my memory, trying to recall Isaac's exact words. I thought for sure he'd said yes.

"No. He said something like, 'It is a possibility I'd considered,' or 'I'd considered it because it seemed likely' or something like that. He never just out and said, 'Yes.' He kinda skirted the question. You would ask questions and he would answer a different one."

Now I was back to frowning, staring at nothing, and realizing—belatedly—that Jethro was absolutely correct. And, *dammit all to hell*, I'd been so distracted by Jenn being in custody, agitated and desperate, I hadn't been thinking clearly during the meeting.

Furthermore, the worst part was, Isaac hadn't lied. Everything he'd said was the truth.

Jenn isn't in danger.

They were always going to arrest Jenn right after the reading of the will, using her surprise inheritance as motive.

Those devices in your house, listening, watching, those are mine. I needed to know what y'all were up to.

I needed to know what you and Jenn were saying. I wanted to know before anybody else.

"Fuck," I said on a breath, my fingers pushing into my hair as my suspicions matured into an undeniable fact. "Fucking fuck fuck."

Burro had told me Isaac had been there, at the lodge, at the slope north of the woods, but I'd dismissed it as irrelevant, a son driving to the scene of his father's demise. But no. Isaac had been there the whole time.

And then Burro arranged the meeting with Isaac, Repo, me, and Jethro. Isaac wanted to know what I knew because *he'd* shot Kip.

Isaac was the shooter.

"Cletus?"

I waved away Jethro, still thinking, still arranging the puzzle pieces I'd had all along.

If I'd been paying attention during the meeting with Isaac and Repo, I would've seen it then instead of a month later when Diane told her side of the story. If I'd been able to focus, take my time, if I hadn't been frantic, maybe Diane wouldn't have had to leave Green Valley. Maybe Jenn would still have her mother.

But Isaac had taken advantage of my disheveled mind. He'd taken what he wanted. And I'd played right into his hands.

He'd even admitted it. He'd told me, he'd told us! He'd said the words and I wasn't listening,

Because I'd kill him.

I had to get out. If I hadn't, I would've killed him years ago.

"How could I be so stupid?"

"What?" I heard Jethro's shoes shuffling on the linoleum floor, moving him a little closer, real alarm in his voice. "What's wrong?"

"I am what's wrong." I shook my head, laughing bitterly.

I didn't think it was possible for me to despise Isaac any more than I already did. I'd been wrong. The details of precisely how were still fuzzy, but Isaac's motives were all so clear now.

Aren't you worried? Leaving the Wraiths without a money man?

I have an apprentice.

Who?

Someone you think is smart.

At that point in the conversation I'd just called Isaac smart, hadn't I? I'd just praised him for suggesting his mother not leave her house so as to thwart the police taking her prints.

Isaac was the *smart* apprentice.

He'd killed his father, set up his mother, threatened his sister, all to get Repo out of the way.

And now there wasn't a damn thing I could do about it.

"Cletus."

"Not now, Jet." I waved my brother off again, gritting my teeth. Repo couldn't ever come back, and of course Diane would never let her son take the fall—

"Your phone is ringing," Jethro said, reaching into my side pocket, withdrawing it, and smacking it against my chest. "Looks like it's the bakery."

I swallowed though my mouth was dry and accepted the call, my mind not actually engaged with the action. "Hello?"

"Cletus? It's Blythe. Hey, so, listen. We called the police, but—"

"What's wrong?" Unsurprisingly, the words *called* and *the* and *police* shoved me out of my epic brain implosion. "Where's Jenn?"

"That's the thing . . ." Her voice wavered. "Cletus, someone took her."

CHAPTER TWENTY-ONE
JENN

"When a strong woman recklessly throws away her strength she is worse than a weak woman who has never any strength to throw away.

— THOMAS HARDY, *FAR FROM THE MADDING CROWD*

It was my fault. I had no one to blame but myself for getting in Cletus's Geo.

I should've known better. *I should've known!*

Cletus rarely picked me up in the Geo. It was too small, he'd always said, and he liked the bench seat in the Buick. He liked me cuddled up next to him. He liked holding my hand. He liked placing kisses on my head or on my mouth when we stopped at a light or stop sign.

Maybe if I'd been feeling less sorry for myself, or maybe if I'd been feeling less frustrated and cheated by life, or maybe if the banana cake I'd baked for Mrs. Lavery's tea luncheon tomorrow hadn't fallen like a skydiver with no parachute, I would've taken notice. The illegally dark tint to the windows meant, no matter what, I wouldn't have observed the lack of a person in the driver's seat as I approached.

But, if I'd been thinking, I would've paused upon opening the door. I would've glanced inside before getting in.

Instead, I'd opened the passenger side door, slid in, closed the door, and had been promptly chloroformed from behind. Granted, I couldn't be sure the big towel they'd smashed against my nose and mouth contained chloroform specifically, but the end result had been the same. I'd lost consciousness.

When I awoke sometime later, my hands were tightly bound at 3 and 9 o'clock to the Geo's steering wheel. I sat in the driver's seat, and I felt like I'd been lying in the bed of a dump truck while garbage had been piled on top of me.

"Wake up, precious," a woman's voice said moments before I felt a rough slap against my cheek. "Rise and shine, my wittle banana cake quween."

I tried to swallow but my head hurt too much. I realize the two actions should be unrelated to each other, but those were the facts.

"It's time for us to go on a wittle drive," the woman sing-songed sweetly, too sweetly, like she'd seasoned the words with sugar, honey, maple syrup, and agave nectar.

When I continued to blink slowly, struggling to focus, I felt some-thing cold and hard press against my temple. "Wake the fuck up, princess. Or I'll paint the window with your brains."

Click.

I stiffened, my eyes flying open, and quite suddenly I was awake. In pain, but awake.

"That's better." She removed the gun.

I exhaled a shaky breath, glancing over as my heart pinged around my chest, and a bolt of something both freezing and scorching jolted up my spine, neck, and into the back of my brain as I realized who sat in the seat next to me, holding the gun pointed at my face.

"Elena."

"That's right." She smiled sweetly. But her eyes were terrifying and her voice again shifted to something different, almost child-like. "I'll turn the engine, and you drive. Mm-kay? Think you can handle that, pumpkin?"

Gripping the wheel, I nodded, trying to catch up. *What is going on?* "Where am I?"

Think, Jenn. Think! Make a list. What do you see? What do you know?

I could see Elena had been crying. She wasn't crying anymore. It was dark outside. The car's headlights were off, but the interior lights were on. I couldn't see past the hood. I smelled . . . something bad. Real bad. Like dead animal bad. And it was close, pressing, like I was on top of the smell. I gagged.

"Throw up if you need to, I don't care." Keeping the gun trained on me, she reached forward and turned the key. The engine came to life. She then put the car into drive. It started to move even before I'd put my foot on the gas. At that point I realized she'd backed us into a scenic pull-off I didn't recognize—or couldn't recognize due to the lack of exterior visibility.

"I—I need the headlights," I croaked, my tongue like a lead weight.

"Press the gas," she whispered.

"And—can you turn the lights off in here? I can't see."

"Shut up and press the gas," another whisper, like she was egging me on.

I had the presence of mind to not press the gas, but it didn't matter, the car glided forward anyway, my visibility zero. Breathing in through my mouth, I ground my teeth and pressed on the brakes. I wasn't going anywhere until I could see. I wasn't—

Wait.

What the—

Nothing happened.

I pumped the brakes again. Again, nothing happened. "The brakes—"

"What brakes?" she asked sweetly, and giggled. "There are no brakes, there are no lights, there are no seatbelts, there is just forward. Forward and the end."

Unthinkingly, I glanced down at myself even as we glided forward. *Oh shit oh shit oh shit.* I didn't have a seatbelt on. I looked at her, ready to yell, and I saw she didn't have one on either.

"Oh my God." I steered. I was blind, but I steered, careful not to press the gas. It didn't matter, we were on a decline. We were picking up speed. It didn't matter what I did, we were going to crash.

Think. Think. Think.

"Turn on the lights! I can't see. You're going to die too."

"I know. I'm ready." She sighed, like this was no matter. "And Kenneth is already dead, so don't worry about him." Elena tossed a thumb over her shoulder, and on reflex I looked in the back seat and—

"Oh my God." My words were more breath than sound. I swallowed the rising bile, blinked away the tears in my eyes. Mr. Miller's corpse lay in the back seat. From the look—not to mention the smell—he'd been dead for a while.

What do I do?

"That's what Kenneth gets for trying to blackmail me, trying to force me to give him back the farm. But, surprise! It wasn't mine to give. It was yours."

"He—what?" This was happening too fast. Too fast.

What do I do?

"Your brother is responsible. Everything had been going swimmingly until he showed up with his big gun and shot Kip. Why did he do that? Kip was already dead. I know because I killed him with the fishing rope from his STUPID FUCKING BOAT!"

I winced at the volume and level of insanity in her voice, my shoulders curling forward. "You—you—"

"Yes. I strangled him. I killed him. I hated him."

"I thought—"

"That I loved him? Oh, I did. But he let my sister go to jail, and that, I can't forgive him for that. And I hate fishing. I hate it. I hate Florida. I hate the Keys. I hate Kip. And I *really* hate you." She didn't seem to be talking to me, and I couldn't really make sense of what she was saying anyway.

I was too focused on trying not to die.

"Shit!" I jerked the wheel as we almost careened over the side of a cliff, the switchback coming upon me suddenly. My whole body shook.

What do I do?

Meanwhile, Elena giggled with glee. "That was a close one!"

What do I do?

Images, faces of people I loved—the Winstons, my mother, my brother, the children I would never have, *Cletus*—flashed through my mind. Regret. Agony. Fear. Pain. A tsunami rising, choking me, pulling me under, blinding me further.

I can't think about any of that.

I pushed it away, all of it.

THINK!

"Your brother should also be in the back seat. It's my one regret, not killing him too. He tried to frame me, did you know that?"

"Frame you?" *What the hell?* "I thought you said—"

"He shot your already dead father." Elena started laughing again, like she couldn't control it, like this was the biggest joke ever. "He shot him and then—and then he chased me." Her laughter ended abruptly, her voice growing faint, reflective. "He got me. He took off my glove. He put my hand on the gun. And then the bastard knocked me out, left me there to take the blame. But I had Miller. He didn't know I had Miller."

What do I do?

I opened my mouth to say something but jerked the wheel away from another cliff just in time, the wheels skidding off the side of the road for a breathless three seconds before I regained control.

"Miller shouldn't have betrayed me. He should've rescued me." She sounded sad, so sad. "I told him I'd take care of it. Why didn't he rescue me? Our plan would've worked. Except . . . then you took it all."

"You were working with Miller?" I turned the wheel to keep us from crashing into a wall of trees at the other side of the switchback, my throat on fire because I knew the next turn would lead over the edge of a cliff again. I needed to be ready for it, but we were going faster with every inch of road.

What do I do?

"Of course. Of course. Don't you see? He came first, we came second. I needed the room cleared of the pesky police so everyone could see and watch your mother lose her fucking mind." She giggled again. "They all love to watch. Miller did his part, he even got your mother to the lot, and it was all so perfect—" She pressed her fists into her eyes for a short second and then tore them away. "No, no. I want to see. I want to see you die."

By the skin of my teeth, I turned the wheel just in time to avoid the cliff.

DAMMIT! *WHAT DO I DO?*

"It's only a matter of time, sweet, stupid Jennifer." In my peripheral vision, I saw she'd pushed out and turned down her bottom lip, her eyes on me. "You're going off the side of the mountain and you'll die. Or you're going to crash into the mountain, fly out the window, and you'll die. Those are your options. Pick one."

Think. Think. Thi—

"Wait," I said. "Wait!"

And I knew.

I knew what I had to do. We were only going to go faster. If we went off the side of the cliff, I would die. But if I could crash into the trees—

Lifting my feet from the floor, I braced them directly on either side of the wheel against the dashboard and pointed the car at the wall of trees on the inside of the road. The car was too old to have airbags. Without a seatbelt, my legs would be the only things keeping me from flying out the windshield. I felt her eyes on me, her confusion, and I stiffened my arms, tensed my legs.

Now or never.

The last thing I heard was Elena saying, "What are you doing?" followed by the sound of broken glass, snapping, crunching metal. We collided, head-on, and pain—so much pain—shot up my legs.

And then all was black.

CHAPTER TWENTY-TWO
CLETUS

"Men outlive their love, but they don't outlive the consequences of their recklessness."

— GEORGE ELIOT, *MIDDLEMARCH*

I couldn't kill Elena for kidnapping Jennifer because the woman was already dead. Or so I'd been told by Jackson when he called me with the news, suggesting I meet Jennifer's ambulance at the hospital because she was unconscious. She'd been in a car crash. And both her legs were broken.

Dear God.

Lowering the phone, I tucked it in my back pocket and closed my eyes, working to reseal the lid on my temper and panic.

Earlier in the evening, when Blythe had called and told me someone had kidnapped Jennifer using my two door Geo, I'd taken great care to gather each and every unwieldy emotion, stuff it down, seal it up. Far, far down. I would not be caught unprepared, distracted, or agitated. Not like Jenn's arrest.

She'd watched dumbfounded from the bakery window as a woman squeezed out of the back using the front passenger door, which when open revealed Jenn unconscious in the front. The lady then ran around the hood, got in the driver's seat, and took off.

This time, I would be chill. Like a fucking sea turtle.

Speaking of sea turtles...

I eyeballed this piece of excrement tied to the chair across from me. Finding Isaac hadn't been difficult, though I hadn't told Burro why I required Isaac's—sorry, Twilight's—precise location. Billy had been my next call. We'd converged on Twilight at the Pink Pony with nary a sound, causing no scene nor any objection from the strippers or the owner.

My older brother—who I could always count on whenever I required retaliatory action against the Wraiths, no matter how violent—had been standing patiently by during the last half hour as I'd questioned Twilight.

I'd learned nothing substantive so far, unsurprisingly, as the man was a sea turtle of chill.

I'd asked why he'd shot Kip. No reaction.

I'd asked where the murder weapon was. No reaction.

I'd asked whether his momma knew he'd done it. No reaction.

I'd asked whether Repo knew he'd done it. No reaction.

The only reaction we got—at all—was to my very first questions: "What did you do with her? Where is she?"

He'd seemed genuinely confused. "Who? Jenn? What happened to Jenn?" he'd asked, an edge of concern in his tone and behind his eyes.

"You know who. Where is she?" I'd repeated.

He glared at me, confusion and concern still lingering, but that could've been an act.

Twilight was lucky Jackson had called when he did. Billy, growing less patient with each passing minute, had taken off his suit jacket. He'd taken off his suit shirt leaving him in just a T-shirt and suit pants. He'd cracked his neck. He'd been looking at the back of Twilight's head like it was a cantaloupe he couldn't wait to crack open. Billy didn't eat cantaloupe usually, more of a watermelon man, but that didn't matter.

My brother Billy never needed a reason to fuck up a Wraith. Didn't matter which Wraith, any Wraith would do. If he could, he'd hand out beatings to Wraiths like Oprah handed out her favorite things to audience members—*you get a beating and you get a beating!*

Point was, beating Wraiths within an inch of their lives seemed to be one of only two things he loved more than his family. The other "thing" was a person. So, not a thing, but still a noun.

I digress.

"So, I might not have been forthcoming earlier," I said while unrolling the sleeves of my shirt. I'd rolled them up earlier to keep blood splatters off the fabric, when or if the necessity had arisen. I didn't want blood on my shirt, I would've had to change my clothes.

Isaac merely stared at me, but his jaw ticked. A small tell. He was interested in what I would say next. Therefore—ignoring the urgency working to steal my breath and shove me out of this room so I could get to the hospital ASAP—I waited for Twilight to ask me.

Eventually, after looking down and to the side, grinding he teeth, flashing his eyes, he did. "Who was that? Is this about Jennifer? Is she okay? Where is she?" The questions burst forth and he tried to lean forward, toward me, as though forgetting Billy had taken great pleasure in tying him up.

"That was Jackson," I said lightly, smiling a little. "Now it's your turn."

He frowned. "What? What the fuck does that mean?"

"I answer a question, you answer a question." I inspected my nails. Specifically, I inspected the black grease that never went away, no matter how much time I spent scrubbing. No biggie. Getting my hands dirty never bothered me.

"Fuck. You."

"I don't believe I asked a question which would warrant that answer." I glanced over Twilight's head to Billy. "Did I?"

My brother smirked, shook his head. "I don't recall any."

"Hmm . . ." I tapped my chin. "What to do."

Billy walked up behind Twilight, stopped just behind him, and eyeballed the back of his head. "I have an idea."

Twilight sucked in a breath, no longer looking chill. "You dumb motherfuckers. You think I won't be missed?"

"By whom?" I asked, honestly curious. "Jennifer? Nooo." I shook my head. "She knows what you are. People don't miss trash."

"By the Wraiths?" Billy seemed to mull this over. "I doubt it."

"I know!" I lifted a finger into the air. "By the DEA, right?"

Twilight blinked twice, real fast. Meanwhile, I ignored the look Billy was giving me. I could guess what it looked like since I'd neglected to mention that Twilight was likely, in fact, undercover DEA. But what I didn't know was whether Twilight's tapping of Jenn's house had been sanctioned by the DEA or if he'd gone rogue. I couldn't imagine Kip being murdered had been sanctioned . . .

"No, son. The DEA doesn't give a shit about you." I said, giving my head a somber shake. "You shot your daddy, so he's gone. You framed your mother for it, so I doubt she's going to—"

"I didn't frame her. I framed Elena!" In a fit of unveiled rage, Twilight attempted to surge to his feet. I didn't flinch because Billy placed a hand on the blond man's shoulder, forcing him back down like he was swatting a fly.

Twilight was big, strong. Billy was bigger, stronger.

"You framed Elena. Okay. That sorta answers a question." A surge of urgency, shouting that I wrap this up and get a move on, repeated loudly and insistently inside my brain. *Hurry!* the urgency pleaded. *Hurry up hurry up hurry the fuck up!*

I ignored it.

I would be chill. Nothing would distract me ever again because I would never be caught unawares ever again. Jennifer's future safety depended on it. *If she has a future . . .*

Swallowing against a rough thickness, I shoved that thought away. I couldn't think about that. I wouldn't think about that.

Instead, I pressed onward. "Jackson called to tell me Elena—the woman you supposedly framed for your father's death—kidnapped Jenn. Your turn."

I could feel the weight of Billy's gaze on me, searching, worried.

I ignored him.

"You don't want to—I don't know—get going, then?" Twilight asked, sounding angry and looking at me like I was insane.

257

I shook my head. "Your turn. How did you frame Elena? Actually, no." I shook my head faster. "I want you to tell me the whole damn story. We'll see what I choose to answer next."

Twilight glared at me but surprised me by responding almost immediately. "Fine. Elena reached out to me before your engagement party. Weeks before. She wanted my help killing my—killing Kip. I met with her and she told me her plan. She'd brought this fishing rope—you know the kind used for crabbing?—back from their last trip to the Florida Keys, took it off the boat. She really wanted to kill him with it."

"She took it off his boat?" I had an *ah ha!* moment and subsequently felt like an idiot. Of course. I should've realized Kip's big boat in the Keys had been the source of the rope.

"Yes. Said she hated the boat, hated Florida, hated him. She'd already somehow swiped one of the Donner Lodge's credit cards, ordered a roll of it to be sent to the lodge. She then planted it in my mother's office and cut off a length matching the one she had from Kip's boat."

"So what were you supposed to do?" Billy asked, sounding curious.

"She wanted me to go to the party, draw the police away, and then she and Kip would make a scene. Then they'd leave. She said she'd talk Kip into coming back to the lodge somehow and then she'd kill him in the car, strangling him with the rope. She'd toss it into the pond after and then leave a tip with the cops to drag the pond, putting the gloves in my mother's office to be found with the roll of leaded Polysteel."

"That's all she wanted you to do? Cause a distraction with the police?" Billy looked at me, and I could see he had a hard time believing the only thing Elena wanted was Isaac to show up and draw the police away. I agreed.

"She wanted to be the one to kill him, she was adamant. But no. That's not all she wanted me to do. She wanted me to serve as lookout, make sure no one saw her in the car strangling Kip or tossing the rope in the pond. Make sure she could get in and out of my mother's office unseen to plant the gloves. She also wanted me to get my hands on Jennifer's phone, text my mother, ask her to meet me—as Jennifer—in the parking lot. Then she wanted me to anonymously call the cops that Kip was dead in his car, or that I'd seen something bad, etcetera. Once that was done, she wanted me to drive her to their home on my motorcycle, her alibi being that she'd stayed at home while Kip turned around and came back to the party on his own."

"That's an insane plan." Billy made a face.

Isaac half-turned his head but didn't look up at Billy. "Well, she's insane."

"Why didn't you turn her in?"

Isaac glanced down and to the side, his jaw working, surprising me again with his answer. "I wanted him dead. I reckon y'all know what that's like."

Billy and I shared a look, but too much pain resided there, too many scarring memories. Our gazes cut away almost instantly.

I cleared my throat against the emotion I refused to entertain and asked, "So, what? What did you do?"

"I told her I wouldn't do it, and I told her I wouldn't stop her. I waited at the edge of the parking lot where I knew she'd planned to kill him. But I—" Isaac blinked real fast again, sucking in a breath "—I changed my mind. When it came right down to it, I didn't want him to die. So as soon as I spotted the car, I ran over and banged my gun against the back window, hoping I wasn't too late."

"But you were," Billy guessed, lowering to his haunches to untie Jennifer's brother.

"I was. She'd already killed him, with the rope." He slid his jaw to one side, then the other, his stare hooded. "Anyway, seeing it was done and that she might get away with it—"

"Wait. Why didn't you just keep her there? Call the cops?"

"Because, fuckface, I'm an undercover agent, as you well know. Do you think babysitting my father's murderer until the cops show up to arrest her, giving them a statement, *cooperating* would look good to the Wraiths? No. It would blow my cover. And I've worked too goddamn hard and put up with too goddamn much for my father's death—that worthless piece of shit—to mess it up."

Billy and I shared another look, but Billy was the one to say what we both were thinking, "Fair enough."

Now that Isaac was untied, I tossed my keys to Billy and tilted my

head toward the door. "Let's go. You drive. You"—I pointed at Isaac—
"come with us. I want the rest of this story before we get to the hospital."

Isaac grabbed my wrist before we could move. "Wait, wait a second.
Tell me what happened to Jenn. I'll go, but what happened?"

"Elena kidnapped her using my Geo. Somehow, Jenn ended up
driving the car into some trees going over sixty. Neither of them had
seatbelts on. Jenn broke—" I had to stop, suck in a breath, fist my hand
to stop the tremor "—both of Jenn's legs are broken, she's unconscious,
the ambulance took her to the hospital. Elena is dead. Miller, in the back
seat, is also dead. That's all I know."

Isaac nodded, all color draining from his face, his next breath just as
shaky as mine had been. "Fuck," he said on an exhale. "Let's go."

With that, the three of us ran to the car, leaving Billy's suit jacket and
shirt behind in the little room at the back of the Pink Pony. Isaac and I sat
in the back of the Buick while Billy took the front.

As soon as we were on the road, I said, "Go on. What happened? Tell
us the rest."

Isaac's gaze cut to me. It looked confused, like he wasn't sure what I
was talking about.

"Elena and Kip," Billy supplied. "What happened?"

"Oh." Appearing out of sorts, Jenn's brother rubbed his temple,
shaking his head as though to clear it. "Yes. I got there, and he was dead.
She'd—already—with the rope. So I shot into the car, planning to pull
her out of it, force her to take the gun, and then leave her behind to face
the consequences. I'd already removed the roll of fishing rope from my
mother's office, so that wasn't an issue . . ." Isaac's voice tapered off.

I met Billy's stare in the rearview mirror. Billy didn't know yet
because I hadn't told him, but I knew what happened next.

Elena had run from the car, disinclined to go peacefully. Isaac had
chased her, shooting into the bakery, unaware Jenn and I were inside.
He'd chased Elena into the woods. Once there, he must've knocked her
out, left her.

Probably with the gun?

What about Miller? . . . *Miller.*

"Did you knock out Elena? In the woods? What did you do with the gun?"

"I—uh," Isaac glanced down, breathed out. "I knocked her out, took off her glove, wrapped her hand around the gun and left her there for the police to find. But Miller—I found out later he'd agreed to be her accomplice—he must've found her and taken the gun, put the glove back on."

"Where does Repo come in?" I asked. "When did you two team up?"

"I saw him leave with my mother. We'd parked on the same slope. His bike was already there when I arrived, so I hid my bike when I parked. The day after, when I realized that my mother and Jenn were under suspicion, I pulled him aside and asked him what he knew. He spilled his guts, seemed grateful I'd asked, and then asked me for help. He wanted to run with Diane right away, but I told him to wait. Burro likes me, told me that you could help—and I knew Burro was your contact—so when the FBI began solidifying their plan against my mother and Repo, I asked Burro to reach out to you, bring you in so we could plan my mother's escape in such a way that wouldn't get them caught."

"Why not just let Repo take the fall?" Billy asked as though this had been the obvious course of action.

Isaac shook his head. "No. My mother is in love with him. She never would've let that happen. Believe me, I tried to talk her into it on more than one occasion. She's . . . stubborn."

"So we helped your momma and Repo leave," I said and thought, stewing in this new reality. "And you helping Repo had nothing to do with taking over as the money man for the Wraiths?"

Isaac looked at me like I was nuts. "They would never trust me in that role. No. That's Catfish's job now. He's next in line for any senior level post."

"Catfish? You mean Curtis?" Billy's glare zeroed in on Isaac, and he sounded sore about this information. "Are you sure?"

"Yeah. He's always wanted the responsibility, wants it real bad. He'll do anything to get ahead. If he has things his way, he'll take over for Razor when the time comes."

Billy's eyes cut back to the road, but I could feel waves of rage roll off him as he took a turn too sharply, forcing me to hold on to the ceiling and brace a hand on the back seat.

"And you're not at all worried? You think the DEA is going to be fine with all this? Helping Repo and Diane escape, shooting your father, knocking out Elena?" I asked, just to see what Isaac would say.

"Who is going to tell them?" Even in the dim light of the car I could see Isaac's gaze was cool and flinty. "You?"

"I don't have any reason to communicate with the DEA, as long as they don't bug Jenn's house again," I said, making sure he understood the implied threat.

"They didn't know about the bugs, either. I'm not working for them right now anyway . . ." he trailed off, scowling. "The gun should've been *with* Elena. Her glove should've been off," Isaac ranted suddenly. "Miller must've taken the gun as insurance, as a way to blackmail Elena to get his farm before everyone knew Jennifer had inherited. And blackmail my mother in order to get the cows. He tried to play them both."

"We need to find it," I said to no one in particular. "If Miller had the gun and it has Elena's prints, that's it. Your mother can come home."

"But Repo can't," Billy announced, his eyes still on the road. "There's no going back to the Wraiths. Even if you clear Diane's name, he's stuck on the run from them."

"But at least Diane would have a choice, if things go south with Jason," I argued, thinking through our options. We had to find that gun. If I could find a way to give Jenn back her mother's freedom, I'd grab on with both hands.

"I have a question," Billy said from the front. "At the will reading, why'd you seem so sure Jennifer knew she was getting everything?"

"She didn't go to the funeral. I'd expected to see her there, and when she wasn't . . . But she went to the will reading—"

"She didn't know, by the way," I chimed in, rubbing my face, fighting back the dread threatening to blind me. "Jennifer had no idea he'd left her anything. She didn't think you'd be at the funeral, and the only reason she went to the will reading was to see you."

I felt Isaac grab my shoulder roughly, forcing my attention to him. "Is she going to be okay?" He sounded raw, his eyes panicked and glassy.

"What did Jackson say *exactly*? Her legs are broken, but how badly? Anything else? Is her back okay?" His voice cracked with the last question.

I hesitated, and then covered his hand to remove it from where he gripped my shirt, unable to believe I was about to do what I was about to do. "Jenn is strong," I soothed, not knowing where I found the strength to comfort anyone. "She's the strongest person I know. She'll make it."

"You are responsible for Jennifer. You are responsible for keeping her safe." His throat worked as he stared at me, his eyes wild. "If she dies, you die," he threatened, fatally serious.

"Yes, I know." My lips tugged to the side and I nodded, my chest heavy and too tight, each breath excruciating as I contemplated the unthinkable. "If she dies, I will die."

I'll have no choice.

CHAPTER TWENTY-THREE
CLETUS

"Crying is all right in its way while it lasts. But you have to stop sooner
or later, and then you still have to decide what to do."

— C.S. LEWIS, *THE SILVER CHAIR*

Isaac was Jennifer's next of kin, and she had no durable medical power of attorney. As such, he'd been the one they consulted on her treatment. He'd been the one asked to make decisions. He'd been the one to whom they gave the official report.

Meanwhile, I stood, seething in a hidden corner while Jackson James filled me in. Since he'd been the officer on the scene, he'd also been privy to the official report. And I, being nothing but an unmarried fiancé of the woman in question, apparently ranked in the zero-eth spot.

"She's okay." Those were the first words out of Jackson's mouth upon tugging me over to the corner. "The first set of X-rays look real good. She broke both legs, but—miraculously—no other broken bones. Her back looks fine, no fractures, no swelling except at her neck. She's got whiplash and must've hit her forehead on the wheel. She'll be in a wheelchair for a while, have to wear a neck brace, need physical therapy, but after a while, she'll be just fine."

I covered my face with both hands, unable to look at anything as those unwieldy emotions I'd held at bay for the last several hours finally reached up out of the abyss and kicked the shit out of me.

Even though I heard his words and understood them, I needed a minute. Actually, several minutes. Maybe hours. I leaned my back against the corner and slid to the floor, setting my elbows on my knees. And I cried.

I wasn't ashamed. Men need to cry. Life can be shitty and overwhelming and if a man doesn't cry when he can't do anything else, then he turns bitter, resentful, and deranged. I was none of those things because I cried.

Maybe Jackson didn't know what to do with me crying, maybe he was shocked, maybe he never cried. But I sobbed quietly for a long time before I felt a hand on my shoulder.

"My sweet Cletus."

It was Ashley.

I reached for my sister and would've likely tackled her if I didn't have the last-minute presence of mind to remember she was pregnant, and under no circumstances should she be tackled. Even so, she caught me, held me tight, and let me cry on her shoulder while she ran a hand up and down my back. I let it all out. When I'd released all the pent-up fear, misery, worry, and self-recrimination, I cried my relief, my joy, my hopes, and my gratitude that we'd been given another chance.

Jenn will be okay.

Others came. Others held me. Billy, Duane, Jess, Sienna, Jethro, Beau, Shelly, Drew. I cried on them too. Roscoe eventually showed up and he was already crying and—thank God for that little rascal—he gave me the opportunity to console someone else, and that's when I was finally able to stop.

We all sat together, waiting in the room that had been aptly named and best reflected its purpose, more than any other room that existed (i.e. the waiting room). Jess brought over coffee no one drank but we were happy to hold as it gave us something to do with our hands. Jackson served as the go-between, ferrying information from the hospital staff to me, not seeming to care he wasn't supposed to share patient details with nonfamily members. All signs, he'd said, were looking better by the hour.

At one point, in between updates, Drew turned to Ash and said, "We have to get married," just like that.

She nodded, as though she'd been thinking the same thing. "Agree. We'll get married." She swiped at her eye. "We'll go down to the justice of the peace next week."

Drew nodded, looking grim. He glanced at me. I thought maybe I could read what he was thinking. He never wanted to be where I was, a life partner with no rights.

"You can get a medical power of attorney," Beau piped up, threading his fingers with Shelly's. "That's what we have. It's even better than being married, for this kind of stuff. Sometimes, even if you're married, other folks can try to interfere if they don't agree with decisions being made. But a medical power of attorney is difficult to contest."

Shelly nodded her agreement. "It is what I recommend. Even if you get married, get the medical power of attorney too."

"Then we will," Drew said, like the matter was settled, putting his arm around Ashley.

"But you should also get married." Roscoe, staring at the black circle of his full coffee cup, spoke with a sandpapery note to his voice. "I probably don't get a vote, but I'd love to see Ash in Grandma Oliver's dress."

"Agree," Jethro said, giving our sister a small smile.

She returned his smile, hers just as warm and affectionate.

But then she chuckled, it sounded sad. "I'm not wearing that dress to the justice of the peace. You can forget it."

"You should wear the dress," I said and thought at the same time, sounding belligerent even though that hadn't been my intention. I worked to gentle my voice as I added, "You should wear it and have the wedding you want. Life is so damn short, Ash. Wear it. Have that big splashy wedding. It won't be perfect, but absolutely nothing is. And that's why life is so great." I made a fist on my knee, staring at my sister, hard.

Her eyes filled with tears and she nodded, her chin wobbling. "Okay," came her raspy response. "But it'll have to wait until after the baby, because—"

"No!" I stood, giving my head a firm shake, my coffee sloshing over the side of the cup. I paid it no mind, I was possessed with a thought and I could not think beyond it until the idea had been released. I pointed at my sister. "This is what's going to happen. You and Drew are getting married next week. There's still time for a license. The wedding you wanted, it's all ready. Take it. You know we don't want it. You know Jenn never did."

Maybe the words were a tad rude, but Jenn had almost died. I'd almost lost *everything* tonight. I would not wait to marry her until next week. I was many things, but unmarried would no longer be one of them.

"What—" Ashley glanced at our brothers, at Drew, at Sienna, at Jess, at Shelly. Unsurprisingly, they were all giving her little, hopeful smiles. Finally, after many attempts to spit out the words, she said, "You can't be serious!"

"Cletus has all the good ideas," Sienna said, winking at me.

"And don't worry about your bridesmaids," Shelly took over, her eyes sparkling with excitement. "I'll call Janie. She'll organize the Chicago contingent. They'll be here."

"And I'll call Paul." Sienna, referring to the head honcho of her personal stylist and famous people team—or whatever those folks are called—nodded excitedly. She pointed at Shelly first, then Ashley. "He will get the dresses sorted, the makeup, the hair—no problem."

Ashley sent a wide-eyed stare to Sienna, Shelly, and each of us in turn. "This is madness. I can't take their wedding!"

"It's your wedding, and you know it," I said firmly, my mind made up. "I'm not getting married next week. If it's up to me, if you don't want it, it's canceled. Don't let all the deposits and your hard work go to waste."

"But Cletus—"

"I don't have time for your wordy protestations. I need to call George." In fact, I was already pulling out my phone.

"The stripper?" Jethro cocked an eyebrow at me, his voice hitching. "What are you calling George for?"

"George can also do weddings. I mean, officiate them. I already have the marriage license. Hey, Duane"—I snapped at the surlier of the twins

—"run over to Jenn's place and grab the license. I know you miss driving American cars. Take Jess. The license is in the top drawer of the table as you walk in." I turned back to the phone, mumbling to myself, "I'll get him over here now. As soon as Jenn wakes, we're getting married."

I was tired of being left out of decisions about Jenn, first at the police station when she was arrested, and now here at the hospital after she'd almost died. And what if something happened to me? I didn't want to think about how my family would go about trying to decide on my treatment. I wanted Jenn to take the lead. I wanted it to be *her*. Enough was enough.

"This is madness, Cletus. What do we tell people?" Ashley was still protesting, but I also saw she'd begun to seriously consider taking over the wedding she'd planned. The wheels were turning in her head and, based on that look in her eye, they were headed in the right direction.

She just needed a little push.

"Tell them nothing." I shrugged. "Besides, they're all the same people you would've invited anyway." I turned from my family and selected George's number from my contacts. "Here's an idea: ask Drew. See what he says. You're not marrying yourself."

As far as I was concerned, the matter was settled. I lifted the phone to my ear and listened to it ring, waiting for George to pick up.

But I did turn over my shoulder just in time to watch Ashley face Drew, a giant hopeful grin on her face, and ask, "What do you think? Will you marry me?"

The big guy gave her a whisper of a smile with his mouth, but in his eyes were all the stars in the sky as he said, "I thought you'd never ask."

Jennifer and I were married a little past midnight.

She'd woken up around 10:00 PM and had asked for me repeatedly before I'd been allowed back to see her. I'd arrived with George in tow, claiming he was her minister. Ash and Billy snuck in a few minutes later to serve as our witnesses and best peoples—Ashley as the maid of honor, Billy as the best man.

Jennifer, not at all dazed, seemed eager to get married, especially after it was explained that Ashley and Drew would take over the wedding next week. Furthermore, she appeared quite pleased at the idea of being married by a former Navy SEAL AND stripper.

She held perfectly still, resting in the bed with a small, expectant smile on her face, holding my hand as we recited our perfunctory vows. It was all over in five minutes, but Ashley was a blubbering mess by the end of it. I loved that she cried so freely, allowing her emotions to ebb and flow as needed, reckoning it was good for her soul and the one she carried.

We signed the license, asked the nurse to make a few copies, and I made a mental note to get the original filed first thing in the morning.

Jennifer, my wife, was understandably weary. Thus, after our nuptials, George, Ash, and Billy snuck out and I pulled a chair over to her bed. But I didn't sit. Jenn couldn't move her neck and I'd be out of her field of vision if I used the chair. Reaching for her hand, I reminded myself not to hold it too tightly.

"There's no rush to talk about what happened," I said, ensuring my fingertips remained gentle as a feather in her hair. "But I want you to know, you're safe."

She didn't nod, but she did blink, like the memory of what had happened to her overwhelmed her vision. I did not squeeze her hand.

Many seconds passed before she finally managed to speak. "It was terrifying."

I absorbed her words, digested them, and said what I'd always wished someone had told me when I'd been through the most traumatic event of my life 'til now, "It will haunt you."

I held her eyes fast, letting her see I knew what it was to be terrified, and continued, "I will be with you every step of the way, holding your hand, following where you lead. I think therapy is part of the answer, but I'm not going to push you in that direction unless I reckon you need it."

She sniffled, trying to smile. "I think therapy is probably a good idea."

"Excellent. I'll talk to Shelly tomorrow. We'll get you the best." I did squeeze her hand then, just a little. "But Jenn, *it is over*. You never have to go back there. You have a future, and it will be beautiful. Having a beautiful future doesn't lessen what you've lived through, it doesn't mean you're not grieving hard enough or that you're ignoring weighty matters. It means you honor everything you've been through, all the hellish obstacles, and you recognize that you're worthy of happiness, of beauty, of peace."

Tears had started leaking out of her eyes while I spoke. Her face didn't crumple, but her chin gave a few shakes. I kept mine steady. She didn't need me sobbing all over her. She needed comfort, that was my job now. Just like it had been my family's job to give me comfort.

"Don't say anything. I'm right about this." I gave her a somber nod, and it made her lips curve. "Also, you would do well to remember one of the main reasons you love me so much is because I'm always right."

A sad little laugh erupted from her and she immediately winced. I winced automatically in response and kissed the back of her hand. I was sorry I'd made her laugh. But also, I wasn't sorry, because she'd just proven to herself she still could.

Jennifer sighed, her eyes staring forward, but turning inward. I used the ensuing silence to take a survey of her bruises, the big one on her forehead in particular, and all the scrapes and cuts, cataloguing each one, grateful that she was so strong and smart and brave.

"Cletus," she said my name on a sigh, interrupting my inspection. "I love you so much."

"I love you," I said, renewed emotion clogging my throat now that the ceremony was over and I had nothing to do but stay close and hold her hand. "But you knew that already."

"But you know I love hearing it."

"Are you in pain?" I asked, needing to know.

"They gave me some stuff that seems to be doing the trick. Nothing major, 'cause they're still worried about the concussion." Her mouth moved like it was going to yawn. She suppressed it. I got the sense yawning would hurt. "I can't wait to be able move my neck. That probably hurts worst of all."

"I'm going to become a massage therapist," I said and decided as soon as the words left my mouth. "Also, Jethro and I are going to build you a workstation at the bakery, a special one you can use while you're in the wheelchair." Another something I'd just said and decided.

At this news, she gave me a gentle smile, her gaze turning dreamy as it moved over my face. "You know what? I'm glad you're here, husband."

My heart tossed itself against my rib cage, a reminder that it belonged to her, wholly and completely. "I wouldn't want to be anywhere else, wife."

CHAPTER TWENTY-FOUR

CLETUS

"Words are easy, like the wind; Faithful friends are hard to find."

— WILLIAM SHAKESPEARE, *THE PASSIONATE
PILGRIM*

They sent Freddie Boone and Jackson James to question Jenn two days later.

Just to be an ass, I'd wanted to ask, *Where's the FBI? Don't they tell y'all what to do and who is guilty of what crime?* but I didn't. The last several months of failed police investigation hadn't been Freddie and Jackson's fault.

Even so, as I watched them over the rim of my morning coffee, gently questioning Jenn, my tongue tasted of bitterness and resentment. I had no love loss for Elena, nor Mr. Miller. They were dead, fine. And the sheriff's office was just now—three days after it happened—getting around to documenting all the details? Fine.

But the difference between the resources made available to Sheriff James's office during the days after Kip's murder versus Jenn's abduction? That rankled. My feathers were officially ruffled. *Riled* even.

The only reason the FBI had shown up and donated resources to

Sheriff James after Kip's death—parking that damn van outside Diane's house, tapping her, watching her—was because of Repo's relationship with Diane. In retrospect, it felt like the only reason Diane had been the prime suspect was because some federal employee had wanted it that way. They wanted Repo to turn state's evidence against the Wraiths, they figured they could use Diane to get to Repo, and so Diane—they'd decided—killed Kip.

Never mind the fact that Elena's alibi and version of events from that night had more holes than a colander. And who had paid the price for the police ignoring Elena as a suspect? Jenn.

Jennifer had paid the price.

"Cletus." Jackson glanced down at his notepad, scratching behind his ear. "You can stop plotting our murders with your eyeballs any time now."

"But I haven't finished," came my very calm reply.

Boone, crossing his arms, glared at me. "You blame us? For what happened to Jenn?"

Jennifer closed her eyes and sighed. "Can we just finish with the questions before y'all start with that? The person to blame is Elena Wilkinson."

"Who would've been in jail if y'all had done your job"—I lifted my cup toward the pair—"which means you're to blame. Case closed."

Boone chuckled, though he did not look at all amused. "Well, if it matters, Elena was our prime suspect and has been for weeks. So . . ." He shrugged, looking intensely frustrated.

I frowned. It was severe. "Is that so? Then what the hell—"

"Wait, wait a minute." Jenn lifted both hands. "Does this mean my mother isn't a suspect anymore?"

Jackson and Boone shared a look before the blond deputy shook his head, his mouth in a regretful looking line. "I'm sorry, Jenn. Your momma is still very much a suspect. There's an APB out for her arrest."

"Since when?" I started to cross my arms and stopped when I remembered I still held a full coffee cup. I hadn't been aware of any APB.

"Since yesterday, when we found out the lodge ordered the same kind of rope used to strangle your father," Boone answered shortly, flipping through his notepad.

"Was there an APB for Elena? Ever?" I knew I sounded salty and I was fine with sounding salty.

Neither of them responded. Both avoided my eyes.

"Well, that's just great. There's an APB out for Diane since yesterday. Meanwhile, Elena abducts Jenn. And while we're on the subject, how'd Elena kill Miller without y'all knowing?"

"Come on, Cletus," Jackson near growled, looking as irritated as I felt. "You know we don't have the resources to follow Elena Wilkinson around."

"But you have the resources to park a van outside of Diane's house and watch her for weeks?" I countered calmly, as though I were merely curious.

A flash of what looked like anger burned brightly behind Boone's glare. "They had their investigation—which we had no control over— and we had ours. If you want me to deny that Diane Donner was and is a suspect, I can't. But they didn't give us any resources to help solve Kip Sylvester's death unless it suited their goals. We are doing our best with what we have. Regardless, finding *the real* killer has always been our goal, not harassing folks."

"Oh? Like arresting the daughter of the deceased at the reading of her father's will?" I stroked my beard, infusing my tone with more calm curiosity. "You mean like that?"

"Off the record—" Jackson sighed tiredly, swinging his apologetic stare between me and Jenn "—if we'd had a choice, that never would've happened. And I don't know if it makes any difference to y'all, but Boone and Williams volunteered. It was going to happen no matter what, we couldn't stop it, and Boone and Williams wanted to make sure you were treated kindly."

Absorbing this insight, I narrowed my eyes on the deputies and looked at them. Really, sincerely looked at them. Boone looked like he'd lost weight, his hair and beard needed a trim, his eyes were puffy and fatigued. And Jackson . . . well, about the same as Boone.

"And we didn't even know Miller was missing." Jackson rubbed a hand over his weary features. "The man has been homeless for months, living out of his car. No one reported Miller missing, his kids had no idea and his ex-wife doesn't keep in touch."

"I didn't know Miller was homeless," I said because they'd caught me off guard.

This explained why I hadn't been able to find a forwarding address for Miller and why all attempts to track him down had been fruitless. It also explained why Isaac hadn't tried—*or maybe he hadn't been able to?* —bug Miller like he'd bugged Jenn's house.

If I'd known I wasn't looking for a house or apartment, maybe I could've found Miller and questioned the man before Elena—

Well. No use thinking about that.

"Why did Elena kill Miller?" Boone, seemingly done with defending himself—or taking a short break from it—addressed his questions to Jenn. "Did Elena say why she killed him?"

"She was ranting, rambling. I wasn't thinking about her words, I was really just trying to keep the car from going off a cliff." Jenn twisted the blanket over her lap with her fingers. She was doing much better today, her color was better and her eyes were brighter. They had her sitting up, but she still wore the neck brace and both her legs were in casts.

Jennifer had already relayed the details of her story twice to Jackson and Boone but they hadn't yet gone over what Elena had said to Jennifer. It wasn't a long story—basically consisting of being drugged, waking up with her hands tied to the steering wheel at night with no headlights and no brakes as Elena forced her to try to keep the car from driving off a cliff with Miller's dead body in the back seat—but my blood pressure had threatened to kick the lid off my temper each time.

This never should've happened to her. Elena should have been in prison.

If only Diane had ignored Jenn's text message and stayed in the barn that night.

If only Repo hadn't misunderstood what he'd seen and hadn't whisked Diane away that night.

If only Isaac hadn't shot Kip, but instead held Elena at the murder scene and called the police that night.

If only Isaac had killed Elena when she ran away from the car into the woods instead of firing warning shots over her head into the bakery that night.

If only Miller had left the gun where Isaac had dropped it that night, next to Elena, instead of taking it, putting Elena's glove back on, and using the gun to blackmail both Elena and Diane.

If only . . .

"I can understand that your focus was on staying alive, but if you can remember anything Elena said, anything at all, it would be very helpful, especially about Miller." Boone gave Jenn a soft look heavily seasoned with guilt.

"Okay . . ." She gathered a deep breath, stared over their heads at the wall. "Elena said Miller was trying to force her to give him back the farm."

"But you inherited the farm, right?" Boone scribbled something on his notepad. "You inherited everything."

"Yes." Jenn started to nod. She stopped herself, wincing. "Everything but my father's car. But it was obvious to us during the will reading that Elena thought she was going to inherit everything. She was very surprised." Jenn glanced to me.

"This is exceptionally true," I confirmed. "If you need someone else to corroborate, you could ask Billy or Mr. Leeward. They'll both attest to the fact that Elena had no idea Kip had changed his will."

Boone nodded, still scribbling. "Do you know why your father changed his will?"

"Don't answer that," I cut in, plotting Boone's murder in my head all over again. "Deputy Boone, you know that's a question Lawyer Genevieve Taylor has instructed Jennifer not to answer unless Lawyer Genevieve Taylor is present." Then to Boone I said, "Please keep your questions focused on the car crash."

"Fine," he grounded out, sighed, then asked, "Jenn, do you remember anything else Elena said about Miller?"

"Um, yes. She talked about how Miller had betrayed her, tried to blackmail her." Jennifer's words were halting, and her eyebrows pulled together as though finding this information within her brain took effort.

"She said she'd strangled—she'd killed my father with rope she'd taken off his boat."

"So you're saying Elena confessed to your father's murder?" Jackson perked up at this.

"She said she'd used the rope from his fishing boat in the Keys and strangled him, more or less. She said she hated the boat and the house down in the Keys, and she hated me, and him." Jenn seemed to squirm, her gaze anxious. "Do you think this might help my mother? Do you think you have enough to determine Elena killed my father?"

"I don't know, Jenn." Boone gave his head a little shake, still scribbling. "Why did Elena hate him? Did she say?"

"Uh . . ." Jenn closed her eyes. "Because of her sister? She really hated the boat. But my father, I think she said something about blaming him for her sister going to prison last year. At least that's the impression I got. Sorry."

I resisted the urge to touch her, to tell Boone and Jackson that their time was up. It was important she get these details out. Not just for the current investigation into her abduction, and not just for the murder investigation of Kip Sylvester, but also for Jenn's peace of mind. Understanding why something terrible happens—or what the perpetrator was thinking at the time—can sometimes help a victim process what happened.

For example, I knew why my father had done what he had to me, to Billy, to our mother, to our family. I didn't think his reasons were good ones, but that was also helpful. He did what he did because he was—is—evil. And so, since he was—is—evil, I never had to think about him or pay him any mind other than plotting his murder.

If that's still on the agenda . . .

I didn't have the mental resources at my disposal at present to give the matter the deliberation it required. But suffice it to say, watching Jenn over the last several months, and then listening to Isaac's side of the story earlier in the week, had given me pause. Maybe, instead of exacting revenge on my father, it would be better to simply push Darrell Winston completely from my mind.

Maybe the right answer was to downgrade him to zero bandwidth and just move on, once and for all, and enjoy every second of my beautiful future with Jenn, without the stain of Darrell Winston's blood on my hands.

Worth consideration.

"Anything else, Jenn?" Boone looked up from his notepad. "Anything else you can remember that might help?"

"I'm sorry, I don't think so. She taunted me, she giggled a lot, she talked about how much she hated fishing, but I don't think any of that's helpful." Jennifer, seeming to realize she'd been twisting the blanket, flattened it out and smoothed it with her hands.

"Okay. Well, if you think of anything." Boone, giving her a tight smile, closed his notepad and gave her a short nod. "I'm glad to see you're . . ." His eyes moved over her, and he seemed to struggle for a moment. "I'm glad your injuries, though serious, weren't worse."

Jackson huffed a laugh. "You know Boone, you should write greeting cards. 'Get better, if you want to, but no pressure.'"

"'I'm glad you didn't die in that car crash, that would've sucked,'" Jenn also teased, laughing. I noticed she did so without wincing, and I took heart in her smile.

"Yeah, yeah." Boone rolled his eyes, but he also smiled. "Feel better, Jenn." Then he squinted at me and said as he left the room, "Cletus. See you around."

I lifted my chin toward Freddie Boone, returning his squint. But truth be told, I wasn't as sore at the man as I had been. He was a good detective, a good person, and it was obvious now that he'd been working hard to do the right thing.

"Hey, Cletus. Do you have a second?" Jackson titled his head toward the doorway.

I scowled, but nodded. "Fine. I'll be right there."

Turning to Jenn, and careful to keep my coffee cup from spilling on her cast, I placed a featherlight kiss on her temple. "I'll be right back. This shouldn't take long, wife."

"See that it doesn't, husband." She nodded, her eyes full of sparkles and glitter at my use of the word *wife*.

I'd discovered over the last few days that nothing made her happier than when I called her wife. Likewise, she adored calling me husband. I took this as proof that we should've gotten married months ago, as I'd wished.

See? More proof I'm always right.

Feeling her happy gaze at my back, I walked to the door, mildly surprised to see Jackson still hovering inside the room, as though he'd been watching us.

"Hello, Jackson," I said, walking past. "Are we . . .?"

"Yeah, of course." He waited until I was out the door to give Jenn a wave. "I'll be by later with my momma and Jess, if you're up for more visitors. But don't feel like you need to if you're tired."

"That sounds really nice! I'm looking forward to it. Bye, Jackson." Jenn sounded cheerful but a tad fatigued.

The deputy gave her a nod. He turned toward the hall, gesturing to me that we should walk down toward the waiting room.

I followed, checking my watch, tempted to start a timer for three minutes.

"Hey, so—" he stopped at a corner of the waiting room, his eyes looking distracted "—who is getting married on Saturday? Not you and Jenn?"

"No. Ashley and Drew have taken over the wedding, which is appropriate since my sister planned the whole thing and it's more representative of her tastes than ours."

A genuine smile suffused his whole face and person, driving the exhaustion from his eyes and replacing it with happiness. "Well, that's so great!"

I blinked, my back straightening, because his reaction to this news confounded me. Jackson's unrequited feelings toward my sister had never been a secret, so why did he look excited for her to marry someone else? Uncertain what I wished to ask or convey, I simply settled for, "What?"

"It's great, don't you think?"

"Of course I think it's great, but—" I gave him a once-over, my eyes moving down and then up. *Was this someone else in a Jackson James costume?* "Why are you so happy?"

"I'm happy for Ash, for Drew." He stared at me for a beat, the grin on his features turning to confusion. Finally, dawning comprehension lit behind his eyes. "Oh, come on, Cletus. I'm not still hung up on Ash. That was all over a long time ago."

"Really?" I wouldn't have been able to cover my astonishment had I tried. "Then—" I started, stopped, shook my head, and started again, "Are you sure?"

"Yeah. I mean, I love Ashley, I always will. She's awesome. And so, absolutely, yes. I'm thrilled for her and Drew. The way they look at each other, it's like, they should've gotten married ages ago, right?"

"How do they look at each other?" I was officially confuzzled, and I do not use that word lightly.

"Like how Jenn looks at you," he said, lifting his chin toward the hall we'd just walked through. He turned his attention to me, his expression thoughtful. "I want somebody to look at me like Jenn looks at you, how Ash looks at Drew."

"And how does Jenn look at me?"

"She adores you. It's obvious to everybody. She thinks the sun rises and sets with you. You are so lucky." He tapped me on the shoulder, and I didn't even mind.

Once more I really, truly looked at Jackson James, but not to inspect him for signs of fatigue or to gauge his level of dedication to his job. Unfortunately—or, fortunately, depending on one's perspective—it appeared that Jackson was one of those rare souls with hidden depths. And, man, that irritated me. At first.

I suppose I'm not always right. Just 99.9 percent of the time.

"You want someone to look at you like how Jenn looks at me," I repeated, considering the words and all the information I had on Jackson James. He wasn't a philanderer, but he was an indiscriminate baker.

"Of course."

"Jackson, you do realize that in order for somebody to look at you that way, you have to be with the same woman more than once?"

He chuckled. It sounded self-deprecating. "I know that Cletus, and I'm working toward it. But there are so many beautiful women." He grinned, and I knew if I'd been almost anything but a heterosexual man, his grin would've been both charming and alluring.

"And you have to sample them all?" I asked, a little charmed despite myself. *What is happening? I need more sleep.*

"Well, no, I guess I don't *have* to."

I shook my head, smiling ruefully, because I was fairly certain Jackson and I had just officially become friends. "So, Jackson. I'm going to fill you in on a little secret. I don't know if anybody's told you this yet, and you clearly haven't figured it out for yourself, but if you sleep with one beautiful woman, you've slept with them all."

His smile dropped, and he looked almost offended. "I don't know if that's necessarily true."

"Oh no, it's true. I'm right." I let my certainty show. "Because once you sleep with *the* beautiful woman, you'll never want to be with anybody else again."

His frown deepened, pinching his eyebrows together, like he didn't follow.

I spelled it out for him. "See, the difference between *a* beautiful woman and *the* beautiful woman is that God put her on this earth just for you. And when you meet her, you'll never want to be with *a* beautiful woman ever again."

He blinked, rearing back a bit on his heels, and something akin to sad realization turned his features hard, like I'd related something he didn't like even though it resonated.

Studying him for a long moment, I endeavored to work through what I'd said that might've distressed my new friend so much, and decided to add, "I'm not saying there's only one 'the beautiful person' for each person out there, I'm not saying that. In fact, I reckon there's likely multiples of 'the beautiful person' for each person. So it's not like you get just one chance. But you do need to give someone the opportunity to become 'the beautiful person' instead of—"

"You know what?" He cut me off, seeming even more agitated than before. Jackson cleared his throat, glancing over my shoulder. He shook his head as though to clear it. "Never mind. I gotta go. See you later."

And with that, Jackson James left me standing in the corner of the hospital waiting room, staring after him, feeling like I'd just shoved my whole foot in my mouth—for reasons unbeknownst to me—with seventeen seconds still left on our conversation timer.

Walking back to Jenn's room, I replayed the conversation a few times in my head, unable to figure out where I'd failed to effectively impart my glorious wisdom.

"There are multiples of 'the beautiful person,'" I mumbled as I walked into Jenn's room.

"What's that?" She peered over the screen of the tablet I'd set up for her. It had a holder with an arm attachment hooked up to the side of the hospital bed, so she could place and move it wherever it suited her neck.

"Oh, nothing." I sipped my coffee. It was no longer hot. "What are you watching?"

"Nothing really, just looking through my options." She pushed the arm down, lowering the screen. "Tell me, how was Jackson? What did he want to talk about?"

"He wanted to know what was happening with the wedding, if you and I were going to go through with it or not. I explained that Ashley and Drew were stepping in and stepping up, that the wedding would be theirs." I stood at the foot of the bed. It seemed to be the best place to stand with deference to her neck brace.

"Oh. Good."

"Do you regret it?" Though the coffee was now tepid, I took a sip while refocusing the entirety of my attention on my wife and her well-being. I'd have to marinate on the Jackson situation later.

"What?"

"Not regret, precisely. But does it bother you that we got married in the hospital on a rush?"

"Oh, that." Her eyes were sparkly again as they moved over me. "No. Not at all. When I woke up and Isaac was in my room, I was so confused. He didn't stay, didn't seem to want to be with me if I was awake. Then, after asking for you a hundred times, you showed up with the officiant, with George. It was like you'd read my mind."

Good.

"Did you and Isaac get a chance to talk?"

"No." Much of the sparkly happiness drained from her features.

As soon as Jenn and I were married and his opinion on her care was no longer requested, he'd disappeared.

I'd already filled Jenn in on the story Isaac had told Billy and I, doing my best to relate the conversation word for word. She'd seemed very relieved when I clarified that Isaac had only shot Kip after Elena had killed him first, a situation where thirty seconds made all the difference, I supposed.

She didn't seem at all surprised by her brother's involvement in Kip's murder—that he'd been the shooter—which made me wonder if she'd already come to the same (or similar) conclusions I had prior to her car accident. But she did seem surprised to learn he was an undercover agent, planted in the Wraiths by some government agency. This, more than anything, seemed to upset her.

"Do we want to tell Boone about Isaac's involvement?" I asked carefully.

"I don't know. I can't think."

"It would clear your mother's name."

"But at what cost? I think my mother knew the shooter was him, know it was Isaac. I think she's been trying to protect him. If my brother goes to jail for this, she would never forgive me."

"What if Isaac—"

"I don't want to talk about Isaac," she said suddenly. "He's . . . living his life. And that doesn't include me or us." She affixed one of those smiles to her face that didn't reach her eyes. "How about you? Do you regret how we got married?"

I twisted my lips as I glanced at the blanket on her lap. "No. And yes."

"Really?" She seemed surprised, and maybe a little disappointed.

"Jenn. Your instincts were sound." I'd given the matter a good deal of thought while Jenn rested.

"What instincts?"

"You wanted a wedding that involved our families. And I don't regret marrying you, obviously. But I think maybe we should do a do-over—"

"A do-over?"

"—yearly."

Her eyes widened and her eyebrows jumped high on her forehead. "Excuse me? What does that mean?"

"Just what I said." I braced my feet apart, preparing to pontificate. "Our love, our wedding, it can't be contained by a single day of celebration."

"That's why folks have an engagement party, wedding shower, rehearsal dinner, *and* a wedding day. And anniversaries, Cletus."

I waved away her statements as they were irrelevant to us. That typical course did not suit me. "No. No, that won't do. We need yearly wedding days. Yearly vows. Yearly ceremonies and receptions. You convinced me."

"*I* convinced *you*?"

"Do you think my family's joy for our marriage can be contained to a single day? It might be the singular most important day in their lives, especially if we serve my sausage! And we want to limit it to just one day? That's not fair to anyone. That's selfish. Don't you see? We should spread it out. Spread the love so it doesn't overpower people."

Jenn crossed her arms, her lips pressed together like she was working hard not to laugh. "You want never-ending weddings. That's what you want?"

I nodded. "To you? Yes."

"Says the man who wanted no wedding."

"Ah, but you see—" I wagged a finger, crossing to where she rested, setting my coffee down on the table. Bending at the waist, I cupped her cheek and carefully brushed a kiss against her lips. "I'm saying, you were right." I leaned back a few inches.

"I was right." Her eyes, now warm, moved between mine. "About the wedding?"

"About the wedding, and so many other things." With care, I pushed strands of her soft, unwashed hair away from her temple. The doctors said I'd have to help her wash it. I couldn't wait. "But in this case, about the wedding, yes. You were right. And furthermore, if I had my way, every day would be our wedding day."

Jenn smiled, her gaze sweet and dreamy. "Every day?" she asked, like the thought delighted her.

"Yes. Every day we'd wake up, George would come to the house, and he'd marry us in the morning. Every day, I want you to know that I would marry you, that I love and adore you no less but always more than the day before."

She covered my hand on her cheek, her eyes filling with emotion. "Oh, Cletus. That's so . . ." She never finished the thought. Instead, her attention dropped to my lips and her chin lifted by the barest fraction of an inch.

She wanted a kiss. I gave it to her and immediately wrestled restlessness, wanting to give her so much more. More kisses and presents and sausage and vacations and laughter and joy. I wanted to give her the best part of me, the best part of the world, the best of our future, right now, this very minute.

And again, as I often had to do when faced with this restlessness, I reminded myself that we had time.

But whatever it was, whenever and whatever she needed or wanted or craved, I would always and forever make sure it was hers. Just as I would be hers, always and forever.

EPILOGUE
JENN

Doubt thou the stars are fire;
>Doubt that the sun doth move;
>Doubt truth to be a liar;
>But never doubt I love."

— WILLIAM SHAKESPEARE, *HAMLET*

Three months after I'd been discharged from physical therapy, six months after all my casts and braces had been removed, twelve months after the accident, and over two years after I'd shown up on the Winston's doorstep, threatening a bearded, frightfully clever, sinister man with blackmail if he didn't help me find a husband, I married Cletus for a second time.

"Are you nervous?" Ashley fiddled with my veil, locking eyes with me in the mirror.

"I little," I admitted, looking at myself. It was the dress I'd chosen while shopping with my momma. I'd lost some inches and gained some muscle since we'd picked it out, so the seams had been taken in by a seamstress, but I still loved how I looked in it just the same.

My gown resembled the dress Grace Kelly had worn to her wedding in the 1950s. The lacy, long-sleeve portion could be removed, revealing a strapless bodice beneath. I loved everything about it from the big puffy skirt to the dainty lace details to the row of silk buttons.

"You look like a princess," Ashley whispered, somehow both giddy and reverent. She'd agreed to be my matron of honor (again), and I was so grateful. "I'm so glad y'all decided to do this."

As I studied myself in the mirror—the veil, the tiara, the little silk gloves ending at the wrist—I agreed, but maybe not for the reasons Ashley thought.

George wouldn't be officiating. He was already booked for an event in Nashville and didn't want to fly all the way to Washington State for a short, ten-minute ceremony. But the Winstons had come. Billy, Jethro, Benjamin, and a pregnant Sienna; Drew, Ashley, and baby Bethany; Beau and Shelly; Duane and Jess; and, of course, Roscoe.

They made the time to fly up and meet us in Seattle. We all cruised to a big old Victorian on low-bank waterfront, facing westward, on one of the San Juan Islands. We then spent a week fishing, clamming, visiting, and going for walks on the pebble beach.

That was why I agreed with Ashley. Here we were, surrounded by folks who loved us (and no folks who didn't), having a splendid time. After the ceremony, we'd have a clam bake and sausage roast on the beach. I'd made my vanilla cookies and lemon custard cakes for dessert. We would all dance beneath lanterns and stars, tell family stories, and drink champagne.

I couldn't have imagined a more perfect wedding day.

A knock sounded on the door. A moment later, Billy poked his head in, his eyes closed. "Is everyone decent?"

Ashley answered for both of us, "Of course. And we're dressed too."

He chuckled, opening his eyes and blinking the room into focus. When his gaze came to me, it widened, and he blinked some more, like I was a sight to behold.

"Jennifer, you look stunning." He slipped inside the room, reaching out a hand, which I accepted.

"She really, really does." Ashley fussed with the back of my dress. "I had no doubts. No doubts at all."

That was a lie. She'd had doubts.

When Cletus and I had picked them up in Seattle, she'd taken one look at us and said what her entire family had been thinking, "What the hell happened to you two? Are you . . . did you get shipwrecked?"

The boat we used to ferry everyone over to the San Juan's was actually my boat, one I'd bought for myself. Over a month before the second wedding, we took a honeymoon trip. Cletus and I launched from New Orleans and navigated to the waters of Washington on our own.

As it turned out, I loved to fish. And when we'd picked up with Winstons, we probably smelled like fish.

I'd sold my father's old boat, his house in the Keys, and a bunch of random investment properties, none of which I'd known existed until Leeward had detailed the extent of my late father's holdings. After some investigation—because I couldn't figure out where all the wealth had come from—we discovered my father had been siphoning money from my mother's business during the entire length of their marriage.

One of the first things I did after reviewing the holdings with Mr. Leeward was sign back the farms my father had swindled. I also redistributed the monies folks like Roger Gangersworth and Posey Lamont had invested in my father's farm stay scheme.

Of course, I couldn't return the Miller place to Farmer Miller. Ultimately, I decided to send each of his three children a one-third portion of the fair market value and keep the place for myself. The house was in disrepair, but that was no matter. Cletus and Jethro were making plans to knock it down and build something new. But there was no rush. Maybe in another year or two. After I was finished fishing.

Presently, Billy rolled his lips between his teeth to hide his smile and looked at the carpet. "Uh, Ashley, you're needed at the beach. I've been sent to collect Jenn. It's time."

"Oh!" She stepped back from me, her eyes studying my back before moving to my reflection in the mirror. "You are exquisite perfection. I am —" she glanced down at herself, at the blue dress and white shawl she'd chosen to wear "—also fine. Billy always looks great. Okay!" Clapping her hands together, Ashley gave me one last smile and darted from the room. "See y'all soon."

Billy stood still, perfectly so, until he heard the door snick shut, then he released my hand and turned for the closet. "Just give me a minute." Once there, he pulled out a navy blue bundle, shook it out, and unzipped a zipper at the front of it.

When I realized what it was, I gasped, and then I laughed. "That's—are you putting on coveralls?"

He nodded. "Everyone else already has theirs on. Cletus waited until Ashley was in here with you. I just need to . . ." he trailed off, removing his stunning jacket and tie, laying both on the bed carefully. He toed off his shoes and stepped into the Dickies coveralls.

"He is—" I shook my head and laughed some more. "I love him so much."

"Thank God for that," Billy mumbled. He finished pulling on the coveralls, zipped it up, and now shoved his feet into rubber boots that had been stored under the bed. "If I'm being honest, I'm actually grateful to Cletus. I didn't want to wear any part of that suit on the beach, or the shoes. These pants are old, I didn't figure Ashley would notice."

If my momma had been here, she would've had a conniption fit, and that thought made me want to both laugh and cry.

My mother was still a wanted woman. Even after everything that happened with Elena, she was still the prime suspect in my father's murder. Cletus and I had failed to find the gun we were now sure Miller had hidden somewhere. If we did—no, *when we did*—I felt certain it would have Elena's prints on it. Perhaps then my mother could come home.

Of course, that's assuming she'd be willing to leave Jason.

I'd kept her house, but we'd put it up for rent. Also, about ten months ago, I'd officially handed over the day-to-day business of the lodge to my mother's trusted second-in-command, Monsieur Auclair. He supervised the lodge's renovations, I resumed running the bakery once I felt up to it, and we met over coffee and madeleines once a week to review accounts, status reports, and staffing decisions.

Cletus continued managing the dairy. He sometimes joined our weekly meetings, but usually only piped up when asked about the status of the cows. I suspect he just really enjoyed the madeleines, coffee, and listening to me give directions and be bossy.

The latter portion of this suspicion was confirmed when Cletus, dressed in a tailored suit, suggested we role-play one evening and gestured to a business outfit in my size he'd placed on the bed.

"You're the boss, and I'm the subordinate," he'd said with entirely too much twinkle in his eye.

This whole "subordinate" business lasted about three minutes before he took over and . . . yeah. I'm sure y'all can guess how that ended up.

Currently, I nodded, because what else could I do about the groomsmen wearing Dickies? Besides, I didn't care. I thought it was funny.

I crossed to the bed and picked up my bouquet. "Well, shall we?"

"Just—just a minute." Billy reached into one of the zippered pockets of his coveralls and pulled out a velvet box. He then walked over to me, his eyes looking proud as they conducted another sweep. "When my grandmother got married to my grandfather Oliver, she had no family there. She was an orphan, or so the story goes, and brought nothing to the marriage but herself. So, my great grandfather gave her a necklace."

He paused, opening the velvet box and revealing a white gold or platinum necklace, the chain comprised of delicate but wide filigree sections with diamonds set in star shapes at each of the links.

The necklace was so beautiful, I gasped.

I mean, I gasped like no one had ever gasped before.

I then coughed because I'd gasped so hard.

"I—I'm—sorry—sorry." As I coughed I was careful to keep my neck perfectly still. It still gave me trouble.

Even after being discharged from physical therapy, I still saw an acupuncturist, massage therapist, and chiropractor for my back. My neck hurt sometimes. My legs ached right before a big rainstorm at night, but not during the day. We kept the special cabinets and countertop Cletus and Jethro had built in the bakery which allowed for wheelchair access, and sometimes Cletus would borrow my old crutches "for reasons." I never asked why, not sure I wanted to know.

But I did always ask Cletus how his day was, because I always wanted to know.

Billy watched me as I choked and sputtered, his eyes full of concern, giving my back a tiny pat and rub. He walked over to the dresser to pour me a glass of water. "Are you okay? I didn't mean to injure you moments before you walk down the aisle."

"I'm okay," I rasped, accepting the glass gratefully. Once I'd caught my breath and trusted myself to speak, I shook my head. "Billy, I can't— I can't accept this."

"I don't care if you accept it or not, Jenn. It's yours." He moved to step behind me, and in the edge of my vision I saw him take the necklace out of the box before he disappeared. The next thing I knew, I felt him drape it around my neck.

"Kind of like," he continued, his voice quiet and distracted as he concentrated on the clasp, "it doesn't matter if you accept us or not. We're yours. All of us. I hope you know, you now have six brothers and four sisters."

I breathed in through my nose, working to keep my mind from correcting him, because he was right. I didn't have seven brothers, I had six. Drew, Billy, Jethro, Duane, Beau, and Roscoe. *Not Isaac.*

I'd rarely seen Isaac since the accident. Sometimes I'd catch a glimpse of him around town, but it was unusual. I couldn't quite work out why, but discovering his undercover status had seriously fried my gizzards. He'd been in town all that time, not actually an Iron Wraith, and had chosen to have no relationship with me or my mother, deceiving us.

Perhaps he was "one of the good guys," but I no longer thought of him as "a good guy."

However, maybe because I have a soft heart and maybe because I really am a little soft in the head, I portioned out some of my father's money and planned to combine it with a percentage of the yearly profit from the lodge. I put it all in a trust for my brot—I mean, for *Isaac*—to inherit upon his thirty-fifth birthday. I also kept it a secret from him.

If he could keep secrets, well then so could I.

When Billy finished fastening the necklace, he came back around to face me, his attention where the precious metal and diamonds lay against the lace of my dress. "There now. I know you're not an orphan, but I couldn't shake the feeling that this belongs to you." He grinned, looking pleased until he lifted his eyes to mine. "Are those tears because you were choking? Or did I just make you cry?"

My chin wobbled, so I had to firm it and look away before I could respond, "You just made me cry."

"Aw." He chuckled, his gaze impossibly fond as he placed a hand on my shoulder and squeezed. "Please don't cry. Ashley will kill me if you ruin all that stuff painted around your eyes."

That made me laugh, and he laughed, and the tears stopped, and we both sighed.

He reached for the water glass, which I relinquished, and set it back on the dresser. He then moved into position at my side and offered his arm. "You ready?"

Instead of responding, I said, "Thank you, Billy."

He glanced down at me, a question in his eyes.

I answered before he asked. "Thank you for walking me down the aisle. Thank you for being Cletus's best man—twice. Thank you for this necklace. Thank you for welcoming me into your family, from the very start. Thank you for never thinking I was ridiculous, for always treating me like—" I had to stop, because if I didn't, I'd start crying all over again.

Billy's eyes turned liquid, and he covered my hand where it rested on his elbow. "Thank you, Jenn."

I sniffled, a burst of laughter—at myself for succumbing to water-works on my *second* wedding day—coming from my lips. "What for?"

"For loving Cletus," he said, his tone serious, solemn, like maybe he'd worried for his brother once upon a time. Like maybe he'd spent sleepless nights hoping and praying Cletus found someone with whom to share his life, like it was a possibility that Cletus would end up alone while the others paired off, and that I'd been an answer to that prayer.

"Don't thank me for that." I laughed, wrinkling my nose and shrugging. "You know I can't help myself."

"That's how I know you're worthy of him. He feels the same." He pressed my hand tighter to his arm, walking us to the door as he added, "And that's how I know he's worthy of you."

I did cry again. But this time, I hadn't been able to stop myself. Ashley didn't kill me for ruining the paint around my eyes, probably because she also cried. In fact, most everybody wiped away a few tears when I spotted my mother standing in the matron of honor spot instead of Ash.

Yeah. I lost it. And poor Billy had to deal with me gasping again. I didn't cough, but I did rush down the aisle to hug my mother.

"I wouldn't have missed it for anything, baby. Shh. Don't cry," she choked out, holding me tight. "You look so beautiful. I missed you so much. Stop crying," she sobbed.

And I laughed, because it was such a *my mother* thing for her to do: tell me not to cry while she was crying.

Eventually, we separated, and we smiled at each other, and I felt the loss of her over the last year acutely, in every moment we'd been apart. But I also felt the joy in our reunion, and that almost—almost—made up for it.

"Your husband is responsible," she said, pulling a hankie from her sleeve and dabbing at my eyes. "Now, come on. No more tears. This is about you and Cletus."

On cloud nine, I turned and looked at Cletus whose eyes were also bright as they met mine. He wore navy blue Dickies coveralls with a light blue tie; his hair was a curly mess, tousled by the breeze; his beard was still bushy despite being trimmed; and his smile was huge.

He looked absolutely, breathtakingly gorgeous.

"Are you surprised?" he whispered, bending his head toward mine and taking my hand.

Not trusting myself to speak, I nodded. Tangentially, I was aware of Billy taking his place next to Cletus, and the celebrant—a boat captain we'd befriended during our travels—giving us both a happy grin, ready to get started.

But I couldn't see past this wonderful, sneaky, clever, sinister, handsome man, who still wanted to marry me every single day.

Not caring that it wasn't time yet, I wrapped my arms around his neck, and I kissed him.

Our love story might've been a little mixed up. Some folks might even call it weird. I'd threatened *and* blackmailed him. We'd become friends. We'd fallen in love. We'd made love. We'd become engaged, sorta. We'd become engaged for real. I'd almost died, a few times. We'd married, waited a year, took a honeymoon, and now we were getting married again.

But that was us. This story was ours. We were weird.

I was so glad I'd stayed away from the normals, because I wouldn't have traded being weird with Cletus for being normal with absolutely anyone else.

-THE END-

Subscribe to Penny's awesome newsletter for exclusive stories, sneak peeks, and pictures of cats knitting hats. Subscribe here: http://pennyreid.ninja/newsletter/

ABOUT THE AUTHOR

Penny Reid is the *New York Times*, *Wall Street Journal*, and *USA Today* Bestselling Author of the Winston Brothers, Knitting in the City, Rugby, Dear Professor, and Hypothesis series. She used to spend her days writing federal grant proposals as a biomedical researcher, but now she just writes books. She's also a full time mom to three diminutive adults, wife, daughter, knitter, crocheter, sewer, general crafter, and thought ninja.

Come find me -
Mailing List: http://pennyreid.ninja/newsletter/
Goodreads: http://www.goodreads.com/ReidRomance
Facebook: www.facebook.com/pennyreidwriter
Instagram: www.instagram.com/reidromance
Twitter: www.twitter.com/reidromance
Patreon: https://www.patreon.com/smartypantsromance
Email: pennreid@gmail.com …hey, you! Email me ;-)

OTHER BOOKS BY PENNY REID

Knitting in the City Series

(Interconnected Standalones, Adult Contemporary Romantic Comedy)

Neanderthal Seeks Human: A Smart Romance (#1)

Neanderthal Marries Human: A Smarter Romance (#1.5)

Friends without Benefits: An Unrequited Romance (#2)

Love Hacked: A Reluctant Romance (#3)

Beauty and the Mustache: A Philosophical Romance (#4)

Ninja at First Sight (#4.75)

Happily Ever Ninja: A Married Romance (#5)

Dating-ish: A Humanoid Romance (#6)

Marriage of Inconvenience: (#7)

Neanderthal Seeks Extra Yarns (#8)

Knitting in the City Coloring Book (#9)

Winston Brothers Series

(Interconnected Standalones, Adult Contemporary Romantic Comedy, spinoff of Beauty and the Mustache)

Beauty and the Mustache (#0.5)

Truth or Beard (#1)

Grin and Beard It (#2)

Beard Science (#3)

Beard in Mind (#4)

Dr. Strange Beard (#5)

Beard with Me (#6)

Beard Necessities (#7)

Winston Brothers Paper Doll Book (#8)

Hypothesis Series

(New Adult Romantic Comedy Trilogies)

Elements of Chemistry: ATTRACTION, HEAT, and CAPTURE (#1)

Laws of Physics: MOTION, SPACE, and TIME (#2)

Irish Players (Rugby) Series – by L.H. Cosway and Penny Reid

(Interconnected Standalones, Adult Contemporary Sports Romance)

The Hooker and the Hermit (#1)

The Pixie and the Player (#2)

The Cad and the Co-ed (#3)

The Varlet and the Voyeur (#4)

Dear Professor Series

(New Adult Romantic Comedy)

Kissing Tolstoy (#1)

Kissing Galileo (#2)

Ideal Man Series

(Interconnected Standalones, Adult Contemporary Romance Series of Jane Austen Reimaginings)

Pride and Dad Jokes (#1, coming 2022)

Man Buns and Sensibility (#2, TBD)

Sense and Manscaping (#3, TBD)

Persuasion and Man Hands (#4, TBD)

Mantuary Abbey (#5, TBD)

Mancave Park (#6, TBD)

Emmanuel (#7, TBD)

Handcrafted Mysteries Series

(A Romantic Cozy Mystery Series, spinoff of *The Winston Brothers Series*)

Engagement and Espionage (#1)

Marriage and Murder (#2)

Home and Heist (#3, coming 2022)

Baby and Ballistics (#4, coming 2023)

Pie Crimes and Misdemeanors (TBD)

Good Folks Series

((Interconnected Standalones, Adult Contemporary Romantic Comedy, spinoff of *The Winston Brothers Series*)

Totally Folked (#1, coming 2021)

Give a Folk (#2, coming 2022)

Three Kings Series

(Interconnected Standalones, Holiday-themed Adult Contemporary Romantic Comedies)

Homecoming King (#1, coming Christmas 2021)

Drama King (#2, coming Christmas 2022)

Prom King (#3, coming Christmas 2023)